New York T . small town in
the Sierras : to the quirky
character: Look for Jill's
bestsellin; ances are sold.

Visit her w :e book list and
daily blog detailing her city-girl-living-in-the-mountains adventures.
For other news, find her on Facebook /JillShalvis, or follow her on
Twitter @JillShalvis and Instagram /jillshalvis.

Jill Shalvis. Delightfully addictive:

'Packed with the trademark Shalvis humor and intense intimacy, it is definitely a must-read . . . If love, laughter and passion are the keys to any great romance, then this novel hits every note' *Romantic Times*

'Heart-warming and sexy . . . an abundance of chemistry, smoldering romance, and hilarious antics' *Publishers Weekly*

'[Shalvis] has quickly become one of my go-to authors of contemporary romance. Her writing is smart, fun, and sexy, and her books never fail to leave a smile on my face long after I've closed the last page . . . Jill Shalvis is an author not to be missed!' *The Romance Dish*

'Jill Shalvis is such a talented author that she brings to life characters who make you laugh, cry, and are a joy to read' *Romance Reviews Today*

'What I love about Jill Shalvis's books is that she writes sexy, adorable heroes . . . the sexual tension is out of this world. And of course, in true Shalvis fashion, she expertly mixes in humor that has you laughing out loud' *Heroes and Heartbreakers*

'I always enjoy reading a Jill Shalvis book. She's a consistently elegant, bold, clever writer . . . Very witty – I laughed out loud countless times and these scenes are sizzling' *All About Romance*

'If you have not read a Jill Shalvis novel yet, then you really have not read a real romance yet either!' *Book Cove Reviews*

'Engaging writing, characters that walk straight into your heart, touching, hilarious' *Library Journal*

By Jill Shalvis

Wildstone Series
Lost And Found Sisters
The Good Luck Sister (e-novella)
Rainy Day Friends

Lucky Harbor Series
Simply Irresistible
The Sweetest Thing
Head Over Heels
Lucky In Love
At Last
Forever And A Day
It Had To Be You
Always On My Mind
Once In A Lifetime
It's In His Kiss
He's So Fine
One In A Million
Merry Christmas, Baby and Under
The Mistletoe Omnibus (e-novella)

Heartbreaker Bay Series
Sweet Little Lies
The Trouble With Mistletoe
One Snowy Night (e-novella)
Accidentally On Purpose
Chasing Christmas Eve
Holiday Wishes (e-novella)
About That Kiss

Cedar Ridge Series
Second Chance Summer
My Kind Of Wonderful
Nobody But You

Animal Magnetism Series
Animal Magnetism
Animal Attraction
Rescue My Heart
Rumour Has It
Then Came You
Still The One
All I Want

JILL SHALVIS

rainy day friends

HEADLINE
ETERNAL

Published by arrangement with William Morrow, an imprint of HarperCollins Publishers

First published in Great Britain in 2018
by HEADLINE ETERNAL
An imprint of HEADLINE PUBLISHING GROUP

1

Cataloguing in Publication Data is available from the British Library

ISBN 978 1 4722 4488 8

Offset in 12/14.5 pt American Garamond BT by Jouve (UK), Milton Keynes

Printed and bound in Great Britain by CPI Group (UK) Ltd, Croydon, CR0 4YY

FSC www.fsc.org MIX Paper from responsible sources FSC® C104740

Headline's policy is to use papers that are natural, renewable and recyclable products and made from wood grown in well-managed forests and other controlled sources. The logging and manufacturing processes are expected to conform to the environmental regulations of the country of origin.

HEADLINE PUBLISHING GROUP
An Hachette UK Company
Carmelite House
50 Victoria Embankment
London EC4Y 0DZ

www.headlineeternal.com
www.headline.co.uk
www.hachette.co.uk

JILL SHALVIS

rainy day friends

HEADLINE
ETERNAL

Published by arrangement with William Morrow, an imprint of HarperCollins Publishers

First published in Great Britain in 2018
by HEADLINE ETERNAL
An imprint of HEADLINE PUBLISHING GROUP

1

Cataloguing in Publication Data is available from the British Library

ISBN 978 1 4722 4488 8

Offset in 12/14.5 pt American Garamond BT by Jouve (UK), Milton Keynes

Printed and bound in Great Britain by CPI Group (UK) Ltd, Croydon, CR0 4YY

FSC www.fsc.org MIX Paper from responsible sources FSC® C104740

Headline's policy is to use papers that are natural, renewable and recyclable products and made from wood grown in well-managed forests and other controlled sources. The logging and manufacturing processes are expected to conform to the environmental regulations of the country of origin.

HEADLINE PUBLISHING GROUP
An Hachette UK Company
Carmelite House
50 Victoria Embankment
London EC4Y 0DZ

www.headlineeternal.com
www.headline.co.uk
www.hachette.co.uk

To the cities of San Luis Obispo, Avila Beach, and Paso Robles, all of which I used heavily as my inspiration for Wildstone. Years ago they started out as the places where my dad lived and an annoying six-hour drive to visit him, but quickly became my favorite area of California. I lost my dad this year, which negates me having to make the trip . . . and yet I still do. Old habits die hard, and because of that, I can still sometimes be found on the beach at Avila, walking downtown at San Luis Obispo, or hitting the wineries in the hills of Paso Robles. Thank you to the entire region and to my dad, who is no doubt sitting on a cloud somewhere in a comfy recliner, yelling at the newscast.

rainy day friends

Chapter 1

Anxiety Girl, able to jump to the worst conclusion in a single bound!

Most of the time karma was a bitch, but every once in a while she could be surprisingly nice, even kind. Lanie Jacobs, way past overdue for both of those things, told herself this was her time. Seize the day and all that. She drew a deep breath as she exited the highway at Wildstone.

The old Wild West California town was nestled in the rolling hills between the Pacific Coast and wine and ranching country. She'd actually grown up not too far from here, though it felt like a lifetime ago. The road was narrow and curvy, and since it'd rained earlier, she added tricky and slick to her growing list of its issues. She was already white-knuckling a sharp turn when a kamikaze squirrel darted into her lane, causing her to nearly swerve into oncoming traffic before remembering the rules of country driving.

Never leave your lane; not for weather, animals, or even God himself.

Luckily the squirrel reversed its direction, but before Lanie could relax a trio of deer bounded out right in front of her. "Run, Bambi, run," she cried, hitting the brakes, and by the skin of all of their collective teeth, they missed one another.

Sweating, nerves sizzling like live wires, she finally turned onto Capriotti Lane and parked as she'd been instructed.

And went completely still as her world darkened. Not physically, but internally, as her entire body braced for all hell to break loose. Recognizing sign número uno of an impending anxiety attack barreling down on her like a freight train, she gripped the steering wheel. "You're okay," she told herself firmly.

This, of course, didn't stop said freight train. But though she'd been plagued with overactive fight-or-flight preceptors, all of which were yelling at her to run, she couldn't.

Wouldn't.

Not this time. Which didn't stop the dizziness or sudden nausea, or make her lungs work properly. And that was the hardest thing about these attacks that were new to her this year, because it was always the same fears. What if it never stopped? What if someone saw her losing it and realized she was broken? And the worst part . . . what if it wasn't an anxiety attack? Maybe this time it was a seizure or a brain aneurism.

Or a stroke. Hadn't her great-aunt Agnes died of a stroke?

Okay, stop, she ordered herself, damp with sweat now and doing that annoying trembling thing where she shook like a leaf. *Breathe in for four, breathe out for four, and hold for four.*

Repeat.

Repeat again, all while listing the meals she'd had yesterday in her head. Peanut butter toast for breakfast. Tuna salad for lunch. She'd skipped dinner and had wine and popcorn instead.

Slowly but surely, her pulse slowed. *It's all good,* she told herself, but because she wasn't buying what she was selling, she had to force herself out of the car like she was a five-year-old starting kindergarten instead of being thirty and simply facing a brand-new job. Given all she'd been through, this should be easy, even fun. But sometimes adulthood felt like the vet's office and she was the dog excited for the car ride—only to find out the destination.

Shaking her head, she strode across the parking lot. It was April, which meant the rolling hills to the east were green and lush and the Pacific Ocean to the west looked like a surfer's dream, all of it so gorgeous it could've been a postcard. A beautiful smoke screen over her not-so-beautiful past. The air was scented like a really expensive sea-and-earth candle, though all Lanie could smell was her forgotten hopes and dreams. With wood chips crunching under her shoes, she headed through the entrance, above which was a huge wooden sign that read:

CAPRIOTTI WINERY, FROM OUR FIELDS TO YOUR TABLE . . .

Her heart sped up. Nerves, of course, the bane of her existence. But after a very crappy few years, she was changing her path. For once in her godforsaken life, something was going to work out for her. *This* was going to work out for her.

She was grimly determined.

The land was lined with split-rail wooden fencing, protecting grapevines as far as the eye could see. The large open area in front of her was home to several barns and other structures, all meticulously maintained and landscaped with stacks of barrels, colorful flower beds, and clever glass bottle displays.

Lanie walked into the first "barn," which housed the reception area and offices for the winery. She was greeted by an empty reception counter, beyond which was a huge, open-beamed room containing a bar on the far side, comfy couches and low tables scattered through the main area, and walls of windows that showed off the gorgeous countryside.

It was warm and inviting and . . . empty. Well, except for the huge mountain of white and gray fur sleeping on a dog bed in a corner. It was either a Wookie or a massive English sheepdog, complete with scraggly fur hanging in its eyes. If it was a dog, it was the hugest one she'd ever seen, and she stilled as the thing snorted, lifted its head, and opened a bleary eye.

At the sight of her, it leapt to its four paws and gave a happy *wuff.* At least she was hoping it was a happy *wuff* because it came running at her. Never having owned a dog in her life, she froze. "Uh, hi," she said, and did her best to hold her ground. But the closer the thing got, the more she lost her nerve. She whirled to run.

And then she heard a crash.

She turned back in time to see that the dog's forward momentum had been too much. Its hind end had come out from beneath it and it'd flipped onto its back, skidding to a stop in front of her.

She—because she was definitely a she, Lanie could now see—flopped around like a fish for a few seconds as she tried to right herself, to no success. With a loud *woof,* the dog gave up and stayed on her back, tail wagging like crazy, tongue lolling out of the side of her mouth.

"You're vicious, I see," Lanie said, and unable to resist, she squatted down to rub the dog's belly.

The dog snorted her pleasure, licked her hand, and then lumbered up and back over to her bed.

Lanie looked around. Still alone. Eleven forty-five. She was fifteen minutes early, which was a statement on her entire life.

You'll be the only human to ever be early for her own funeral, her mom liked to say, along with her favorite—*you expect way too much out of people.*

This from the woman who'd been a physicist and who'd regularly forgotten to pick up her own daughter after school.

Lanie eyed the sign on the reception desk and realized the problem. The winery was closed on Mondays and Tuesdays, and today was Monday. "Hello?" she called out, feeling a little panicky. Had she somehow screwed up the dates? She'd interviewed for a two-month graphic artist job here twice, both times via Skype from her Santa Barbara apartment. Her new boss, Cora Capriotti, the winery office manager, wanted her to create new labels, menus, a website, everything, and she wanted her to do so on-site. Cora had explained that they prided themselves on being old-fashioned. It was part of their charm, she'd said.

Lanie didn't mind the temporary relocation from Santa Barbara, two hours south of here. She'd actually quit her permanent graphic design job after her husband's death. Needing a big change and a kick in her own ass to get over herself and all the self-pity, she'd been freelancing ever since. It'd been good for her. She'd accepted this job specifically because it was in Wildstone. Far enough away from Santa Barbara to give her a sense of a new start . . . and an excuse to go back to her roots. She'd grown up only fifteen minutes from here and she'd secretly hoped that maybe she and her mom might spend some time together in the same room. In any case, two months away from her life was exactly what the doctor had ordered.

Literally.

She pulled out her cell phone, scrolled for her new boss's number, and called.

"We're out back!" Cora answered. "Let yourself in and join us for lunch!"

"Oh, but I don't want to interrupt—" Lanie blinked and stared at her phone.

Cora had disconnected.

With another deep breath that was long on nerves and short on actual air, she walked through the open great room and out the back French double doors. She stepped onto a patio beautifully decorated with strings of white lights and green foliage lining the picnic-style tables. But that wasn't what had her frozen like a deer facing down the headlights of a speeding Mack Truck.

No, that honor went to the people crowded around two of the large tables, which had been pushed close together. Everyone turned to look at her in unison, all ages and sizes, and then started talking at once.

Lanie recognized that they were smiling and waving, which meant they were probably a friendly crowd, but parties weren't her friends. Her favorite party trick was *not* going to parties.

A woman in her early fifties broke away. She had dark brunette hair liberally streaked with gray, striking dark brown eyes, and a kind smile. She was holding a glass of red wine in one hand and a delicious-looking hunk of bread in the other, and she waved both in Lanie's direction.

"Lanie, right? I'm Cora, come on in."

Lanie didn't move. "I've caught you in the middle of something. A wedding or a party. I can come back—"

"Oh, no, it's nothing like that." Cora looked back at the wild pack of people still watching. "It's just lunch. We do this every day." She gestured at all of them. "Meet your fellow employees. I'm related to everyone one way or another, so they'll behave.

Or else." She smiled, taking away the heat of the threat. "In any case, welcome. Come join us. Let me get you a plate—"

"Oh, that's okay, I brought a salad." Lanie patted her bag. "I can just go sit in my car until you're finished—"

"No need for that, honey. I have lunch catered every day."

"Every day?" She didn't realize she'd spoken out loud until Cora laughed.

"It's our social time," Cora said.

At Lanie's last job, people had raced out of the building at lunch to escape one another. "That's . . . very generous of you."

"Nothing generous about it," Cora said with a laugh. "It keeps everyone on-site, ensures no one's late getting back to the job, and I get to keep my nosy nose in everyone's business." She set aside her bread, freeing up a hand to grab Lanie's, clearly recognizing a flight risk when she saw one. "Everyone," she called out. "This is Lanie Jacobs, our new graphic artist." She smiled reassuringly at Lanie and gestured to the group of people. "Lanie, this is everyone; from the winemaker to the front-desk receptionist, we're all here. We're a rather informal bunch."

They all burst into applause, and Lanie wished for a big black hole to sink into and vanish. "Hi," she managed, and gave a little wave. She must have pulled off the correct level of civility because they all went back to eating and drinking wine, talking among themselves.

"Are you really related to all of them?" she asked Cora, watching two little girls, possibly twins, given their matching toothless smiles, happily eating chocolate cupcakes, half of which were all over their faces.

Cora laughed. "Just about. I've got a big family. You?"

"No."

"Single?"

"Yes." Lanie's current relationship status: *sleeping diagonally across her bed.*

Cora smiled. "Well, I'll be happy to share my people—there's certainly enough of us to go around. Hey," she yelled, cupping a hand around her mouth. "Someone take the girls in to wash up, and no more cupcakes or they'll be bouncing off the walls."

So the cupcakes were a problem, but wine at lunch wasn't. Good to know.

Cora smiled at Lanie's expression, clearly reading her thoughts. "We're Californians," she said. "We're serious about our wine, but laid-back about everything else. In fact, maybe that should be our tagline. Now come, have a seat." She drew Lanie over to the tables. "We'll get to work soon enough."

There was an impressive amount of food, all of it Italian, all of it fragrant and delicious-looking. Lanie's heart said *definitely* to both the wine and the lasagna, but her pants said *holy shit, woman, find a salad instead.*

Cora gave a nudge to the woman at the end of the table, who looked to be around Lanie's age and had silky dark hair and matching eyes. "Scoot," Cora said.

The woman scooted. So did everyone else, allowing a space on the end for Lanie.

"Sit," Cora told Lanie. "Eat. Make merry."

"But—"

"Oh, and be careful of that one," Cora said, pointing to the woman directly across from Lanie, this one in her early twenties with the same gorgeous dark hair and eyes as the other. "Her bad attitude can be contagious."

"Gee, thanks, Mom," she said with an impressive eye-roll.

Cora blew her daughter a kiss and fluttered away, grabbing a bottle of wine from the middle of one of the tables and refilling glasses as she went.

"One of these days I'm gonna roll my eyes so hard I'm going to go blind," her daughter muttered.

The twins ran through, still giggling, and still looking like they'd bathed in chocolate, which caused a bit of commotion. Trying to remain inconspicuous, Lanie pulled her lunch out of her bag—a homemade salad in a container, sans dressing.

"Are you kidding me?" Cora's daughter asked. "Do you *want* her to come back here and yell at us for not feeding you properly? Put that away." She stood up, reached for a stack of plates in the middle of the table, and handed Lanie one. "Here. Now fill it up and eat, and for God's sake, look happy while you're at it or she'll have my ass."

Lanie eyeballed the casserole dishes lining the center of the tables. Spaghetti, lasagna . . .

"Don't worry, it all tastes as good as it looks," an old man said from the middle of the table. There was no hair on his head, but he did have a large patch of gray steel fuzz on his chest, which was sticking out from the top of his polo shirt. His olive complexion had seen at least seven decades of sun, but his smile was pure little-boy mischief. "And don't worry about your cholesterol either," he added. "I'm seventy-five and I've eaten like this every single day of my life." He leaned across the table and shook her hand. "Leonardo Antony Capriotti. And this is my sweetheart of fifty-four years, Adelina Capriotti. I'd use her middle name, but she refuses to sleep with me when I do that."

The older woman next to him was teeny-tiny, her white hair in a tight bun on her head, her spectacles low on her nose, her smile mischievous. "Gotta keep him in line, you know. Nice to meet you."

Lanie knew from her research on the company that it'd been Leonardo and Adelina who had started this winery back in the seventies, though they'd since handed over the day-to-day reins to their daughter, who Lanie now realized was her boss, Cora. "Nice to meet you both," she said.

"Likewise. You're going to give us a new updated look and make me look good," he said. "Right?"

"Right," she said and hoped that was actually true. No pressure or anything . . .

He smiled. "I like you. Now eat."

If she ate any of this stuff, she'd need a nap by midafternoon. But not wanting to insult anyone, she scooped as little as she felt she could get away with onto her plate and pushed it around with her fork, trying to resist temptation.

"Uh-oh," Cora's daughter said. "We have a dieter."

"Stop it," the woman next to Lanie said. "You'll scare her away and end up right back on Mom's shit list."

The other one, whose shirt read: LIVE, LAUGH, AND LEAVE ME THE HELL ALONE, snorted. "We both know that I never get *off* the shit list. I just move up and down on it. Mom's impossible to please."

"Don't listen to her," the other woman said to Lanie. "I'm Alyssa, by the way. And Grumpy-Ass over there is my baby sister, Mia."

Mia waved and reached for the breadbasket. "I'm giving up on getting a bikini body, so pass the butter, please. Grandma says the good Lord put alcohol and carbs on this planet for a reason and I'll be damned if I'm going to let Him down."

Her grandma toasted her.

"Mia and I work here at the winery," Alyssa said and gently patted the cloth-wrapped little bundle swaddled to her chest. "This is Elsa, my youngest."

"Elsa, like the princess?" Lanie asked.

"More like the queen," Alyssa said with a smile, rubbing her infant's tush. "She's going to rule this roost someday."

"Who are you kidding?" Mia asked. "Mom's going to hold the reins until she's three hundred years old. That's how long witches live, you know."

Lanie wasn't sure how to react. After all, that witch was now her boss.

"You're scaring her off again," Alyssa said and looked at Lanie. "We love Mom madly, I promise. Mia's just bitchy because she got dumped last night, was late for work this morning, and got read the riot act. She thinks life sucks."

"Yeah, well, life *does* suck," Mia said. "It sucks donkey balls. And this whole waking-up-every-morning thing is getting a bit excessive. But Alyssa's right. Don't listen to me. Sarcasm. It's how I hug."

Alyssa reached across the table and squeezed her sister's hand in her own, her eyes soft. "Are you going to tell me what happened? I thought you liked this one."

Mia shrugged. "I was texting him and he was only responding occasionally with 'K.' I mean, I have no idea what 'K' even means. Am I to assume he intended to type 'OK,' but was stabbed and couldn't expend the energy to type an extra whole letter?"

Alyssa sucked her lips into her mouth in a clear attempt not to laugh. "Tell me you didn't ask him that and then get broken up with by text."

"Well, dear know-it-all sister, that's exactly what happened.

And now I've got a new motto: *Don't waste your good boob years on a guy that doesn't deserve them.* Oh, and sidenote: no man does. Men suck."

Lanie let out a completely inadvertent snort of agreement and both women looked over at her.

"Well, they do," she said. "Suck."

"See, I *knew* I was going to like you." Mia reached for a bottle of red and gestured with it in Lanie's direction.

She shook her head. "Water's good, thanks."

Mia nodded. "I like water too. It solves a lot of problems. Wanna lose weight? Drink water. Tired of your man? Drown him." She paused and cocked her head in thought. "In hindsight, I should've gone *that* route . . ."

A man came out onto the patio, searched the tables, and focused in on Alyssa. He came up behind her, cupped her face, and tilted it up for his kiss. And he wasn't shy about it either, smiling intimately into her eyes first. Running his hands down her arms to cup them around the baby, he pulled back an inch. "How are my girls?" he murmured.

"Jeez, careful or she'll suffocate," Mia said.

"Hmm." The man kissed Alyssa again, longer this time before finally lifting his head. "What a way to go." He turned to Lanie and smiled. "Welcome. I'm Owen Booker, the winemaker."

Alyssa, looking a little dazed, licked her lips. "And husband," she added to his résumé. "He's my husband." She beamed. "I somehow managed to land the best winemaker in the country."

Owen laughed softly and borrowed her fork to take a bite of her pasta. "I'll see you at the afternoon meeting," he said, then he bent and brushed a kiss on Elsa's little head and walked off.

Alyssa watched him go. Specifically watched his ass, letting out a theatrical sigh.

"Good God, give it a rest," Mia griped. "And you're drooling. Get yourself together, woman. Yesterday you wanted to kill him, remember?"

"Well, he *is* still a man," Alyssa said. "If I didn't want to kill him at least once a day, he's not doing his job right."

"Please, God, tell me you're almost done with the baby hormonal mood swings," Mia said.

"Hey, I'm hardly having any baby-hormone-related mood swings anymore."

Mia snorted and looked at Lanie. "FYI, whenever we're in a situation where I happen to be the voice of reason, it's probably an apocalypse sort of thing and you should save yourself."

"Whatever," Alyssa said. "He's hot and he's mine, all mine."

"Yes," Mia said. "We know. And he's been yours since the second grade and you get to sleep with him later, so . . ."

Alyssa laughed. "I know. Isn't it great? All you need is love."

"I'm pretty sure we also need water, food, shelter, vodka, and Netflix."

"Well, excuse me for being happy." Alyssa looked at Lanie. "Are you married, Lanie?"

"Not anymore." She took a bite of the most amazing fettuccine Alfredo she'd ever had and decided that maybe calories on Mondays didn't count.

"Was he an asshole?" Mia asked, her eyes curious but warmly so.

"Actually, he's dead."

Alyssa gasped. "I'm so sorry. I shouldn't have asked—"

"No," Lanie said, kicking herself for spilling the beans like that. "It's okay. It's been six months." Six months, one week, and two days but hey, who was counting? She bypassed her water and reached for the wine after all. When in Rome . . .

"That's really not very long," Alyssa said.

"I'm really okay." There was a reason for the quick recovery. Several, actually. They'd dated for six months and he'd been charming and charismatic, and new to love, she'd fallen fast. They'd gotten married and gone five years, the first half great, the second half not so much because she'd discovered they just weren't right for each other. She'd not been able to put her finger on what had been wrong exactly, but it'd been undeniable that whatever they'd once shared had faded. But after Kyle had passed away, some things had come to light. Such as the fact that he'd hidden an addiction from her.

A wife addiction.

It'd gone a long way toward getting her over the hump of the grieving process. So had the fact that several other women had come out of the woodwork claiming to also be married to Kyle. Not that she intended to share that humiliation. Not now or ever.

You're my moon and my stars, he'd always told her.

Yeah. Just one lie in a string of many, as it'd turned out . . .

Cora came back around and Lanie nearly leapt up in relief. Work! Work was going to save her.

"I see you've met some of my big, nosy, interfering, boisterous, loving family and survived to tell the tale," Cora said, slipping an arm around Mia and gently squeezing.

"Yes, and I'm all ready to get to it," Lanie said.

"Oh, not yet." Cora gestured for her to stay seated. "No rush, there's still fifteen minutes left of lunch." And then she once again made her way around the tables, chatting with everyone she passed. "Girls," she called out to the cupcake twins, who were now chasing each other around the other table. "Slow down, please!"

At Lanie's table, everyone had gotten deeply involved in a discussion on barrels. She was listening with half an ear to the differences in using American oak versus French oak when a man in a deputy sheriff's uniform came in unnoticed through the French double doors. He was tall, built, and fully armed. His eyes were covered by dark aviator sunglasses, leaving his expression unreadable. And intimidating as hell.

He strode directly toward her.

"Scoot," he said to the table, and since no one else scooted—in fact, no one else even looked over at him—Lanie scooted.

"Thanks." He sat, reaching past her to accept the plate that Mia handed to him without pausing her conversation with Alyssa. The plate was filled up to shockingly towering heights that surely no one human could consume.

He caught Lanie staring.

"That's a lot of food," she said inanely.

"Hungry." He grabbed a fork. "You're the new hire."

"Lanie," she said and watched in awe as he began to shovel in food like he hadn't eaten in a week.

"Mark," he said after swallowing a bite, something she appreciated because Kyle used to talk with his mouth full and it had driven her to want to kill him. Which, as it turned out, hadn't been necessary. A heart attack had done that for her.

Apparently cheating on a bunch of wives had been highly stressful. Go figure.

"You must be a very brave woman," Mark said.

And for a horrifying minute, she was afraid she'd spoken of Kyle out loud, and she stared at him.

"Taking on this job, this family," he said. "They're insane, you know. Every last one of them."

Because he had a disarming smile and was speaking with absolutely no malice, she knew he had to be kidding. But she still thought it rude considering they'd served him food. "They can't be all that bad," she said. "They're feeding you, which you seem to be enjoying."

"Who wouldn't enjoy it? It's the best food in the land."

This was actually true. She watched him go at everything on his plate like it was a food-eating contest and he was in danger of coming in second place for the world championship. She shook her head in awe. "You're going to get heartburn eating that fast."

"Better than not eating at all," he said, glancing at his watch. "I've got ten minutes to be back on the road chasing the bad guys, and a lot of long, hungry hours ahead of me."

"One of those days, huh?"

"One of those years," he said. "But at least I'm not stuck here at the winery day in and day out."

She went brows up. "Are you making fun of my job at all?"

"Making fun? No," he said. "Offering sympathy, yes. You clearly have no idea what you've gotten yourself into. You could still make a break for it, you know."

That she herself had been thinking the very same thing only five minutes ago didn't help. Suddenly feeling defensive for this job she hadn't even started yet, she looked around her. The winery itself was clearly lovingly and beautifully taken care of. The yard in which they sat was lush and colorful and welcoming. Sure, the sheer number of people employed here was intimidating, as was the fact that they gathered every day to eat lunch and socialize. But she'd get used to it.

Maybe.

"I love my job," she said.

Mark grinned. "You're on day one. And you haven't started yet or you'd have finished your wine. Trust me, it's going to be a rough ride, Lanie Jacobs."

Huh. So he definitely knew more about her than she knew about him. No big deal since she wasn't all that interested in knowing more about him. "Surely given what you do for a living, you realize there's nothing 'rough' about my job at all."

"I know I'd rather face down thugs and gangbangers daily than work in this looney bin."

She knew he was kidding, that he was in fact actually pretty funny, but she refused to be charmed. Fact was, she couldn't have been charmed by any penis-carrying human being at the moment. "Right," she said, "because clearly you're here against your will, being held hostage and force-fed all this amazing food. How awful for you."

"Yeah, life's a bitch." He eyeballed the piece of cheese bread on her plate that she hadn't touched. It was the last one.

She nodded for him to take it and then watched in amazement as he put that away too. "I have to ask," she said. "How in the world do you stay so . . ." She gestured with a hand toward his clearly well-taken-care-of body and struggled with a word to describe him. She supposed *hot* worked—if one was into big, annoying, perfectly fit alphas—not that she intended to say so, since she was pretty sure he knew exactly how good he looked.

"How do I stay so . . . what?" he asked.

"Didn't anyone ever tell you that fishing for compliments is unattractive?"

He surprised her by laughing, clearly completely unconcerned with what she thought of him. "My days tend to burn up a lot of calories," he said.

"Uh-huh."

He pushed his dark sunglasses to the top of his head, and she was leveled with dark eyes dancing with mischievousness. "Such cynicism in one so young."

A plate of cupcakes was passed down the table and Lanie eyed them, feeling her mouth water. She had only so much self-control and apparently she was at her limit because she took one, and then, with barely a pause, she grabbed a second as well. Realizing the deputy sheriff was watching her and looking amused while he was at it, she shrugged. "Sometimes I reward myself before I accomplish something. It's called pre-award motivation."

"Does it work?"

"Absolutely one hundred percent not," she admitted and took a bite of one of the cupcakes, letting out a low moan before she could stop herself. "Oh. My. God."

His eyes darkened to black. "You sound like that cupcake is giving you quite the experience."

She held up a finger for silence, possibly having her first-ever public orgasm.

He leaned in a little bit and since their thighs were already plastered together, he didn't have to go far to speak directly into her ear. "Do you make those same sexy sounds when you—"

She pointed at him again because she still couldn't talk, and he just grinned. "Yeah," he said. "I bet you do. And now I know what I'm going to be thinking about for the rest of the day."

"You'll be too busy catching the bad guys, remember?"

"I'm real good at multitasking," he said.

She let out a laugh, though it was rusty as hell. It'd been

a while since she'd found something funny. Not that this changed her idea of him. He was still too sure of himself, too cocky, and she'd had enough of that to last a lifetime. But she also was good at multitasking and could both not like him and appreciate his sense of humor at the same time.

What she couldn't appreciate was when his smile turned warm and inviting, because for a minute something passed between them, something she couldn't—or didn't—intend to recognize.

"Maybe I could call you sometime," he said.

Before she could turn him down politely, the little cupcake twins came running, leaping at him, one of them yelling, "*Daddy, Daddy, Daddy!* Look what we got!"

Catching them both with impressive ease, Mark stood, managing to somehow confiscate the cupcakes and set them aside before getting covered in chocolate. "Why is it," he asked Lanie over their twin dark heads, "that when a child wants to show you something, they try to place it directly in your cornea?"

Still completely floored, Lanie could only shake her head.

Mark adjusted the girls so that they hung upside down off his back. This had them erupting in squeals of delight as he turned back to face Lanie again, two little ankles in each of his big hands. "I know what you're thinking," he said into her undoubtedly shocked face. "I think it every day."

Actually, even she had no idea what she was thinking except . . . he was a Capriotti? How had she not seen that coming?

"Yeah," he said. "I'm one of them, which is why I get to bitch about them. And let me guess . . . you just decided you're not going to answer my call?"

Most definitely not, but before she could say so out loud

Cora was back, going up on tiptoes to kiss Mark on the cheek. "Hey, baby. Heard you had a real tough night."

He shrugged.

"You get enough to eat?" she asked. "Yes?" She eyed his empty plate and then, with a nod of satisfaction, reached up and ruffled his hair. "Good. But don't for a single minute think, Marcus Antony Edward Capriotti, that I don't know who sneaked your grandpa the cigars he was caught smoking last night."

From his seat at the table, "Grandpa," aka Leonardo Antony Capriotti, lifted his hands as if to say, *Who, me?*

Cora shook her head at both of them, helped the girls down from Mark's broad shoulders, took them by the hand, and walked away.

No, Lanie would most definitely *not* be taking the man's call. And not for the reasons he'd assume either. She didn't mind that he had kids. What she minded was that here was a guy who appeared to have it all: close family, wonderful children, a killer smile, a hot body . . . without a single clue about just how damn lucky he was. It made her mad, actually.

He took in her expression. "Okay, so you're most definitely not going to take my call."

"It's nothing personal," she said. "I just don't date . . ."

"Dads?"

Actually, as a direct result of no longer trusting love, not even one little teeny, tiny bit, she didn't date *anyone* anymore, but that was none of his business.

He looked at her for another beat and whatever lingering amusement he'd retained left him, and he simply nodded as he slid his sunglasses back over his eyes. "Good luck today," he said. "You really are going to need it."

And then he was gone.

He thought she'd judged him. She hated that he thought that, but it was best to let him think it. Certainly better than the truth, which was that the problem was her, all her. She inhaled a deep, shaky breath and turned, surprised to find not just Cora watching, but Mark's sisters, grandpa, and several others she could only guess were also related.

Note to self: *Capriottis multiply when left unattended.*

Chapter 2

Anxiety: Look out.
Me: For what?
Anxiety: Just look out.

That night Lanie got into bed at eight o'clock with a book and a glass of wine. The book was because she liked the idea of reading and also because it made her feel like the wine was justified and not a necessity.

Even if it was a necessity.

The habit had started six months ago on the night of Kyle's funeral, which was when Kyle's boss had to tell her that another wife had popped up.

Lanie had promptly moved out of the condo they'd lived in and rented a small town house in a different neighborhood. She hadn't yet made it her own, so she didn't have any plants or pets to worry about while she was gone, and any friends she'd had were work friends or had been Kyle's friends as well, and everyone had seemed to fade away.

Or maybe that had been her.

With a sigh and a big gulp of wine, she sat back against the pillow. Usually when she was to-the-bone tired like this, she couldn't think too much. But tonight she sighed and . . .

Proceeded to think too much.

This wasn't a big surprise given all the recent changes. She was still on Capriotti property, for one thing. Room and board had been part of her two-month deal, and she'd been promised her own cottage.

She'd jumped on it.

Ten acres of land had been cordoned off on the far west side of the winery property, just north of a small, hidden lake. There the Capriottis had built several houses, all belonging to family members, and a small series of cottages lined up like a motel, dedicated to employee housing.

There was both good and bad to this. Good because it was free. Bad because it was very interactive and there was little to no privacy.

Even as she thought it, there was a knock on her door. She froze for a beat and then got out of bed and put her eye to the peephole. A guy stood there looking back at her. He was lanky but solid, wearing jeans, boots, T-shirt, a military buzz cut, and an impassive expression. She'd met him earlier when Cora had introduced him. Holden worked as a horse wrangler and extra ranch hand whenever he was on leave from the army. Though he was in his early twenties, apparently he'd lived here at the winery for a long time. He stood there holding—be still, her heart—a plate of cookies.

Lanie opened the door a crack.

"From Cora," he said with a slight, slow southern drawl, and thrust the plate at her.

"Oh, but I couldn't—"

"I'm not supposed to take no for an answer," he said.

And then he was gone.

Okay, then. She went back to bed with her plate of cookies

and ate far too many of them because they were little bites of heaven. At this rate, by the time she left here in two months, she'd have gained a hundred pounds. But surprisingly, it was actually hard to feel any kind of anxiety at the moment, even though she'd given it a good ol' college try. The fact was, she was away from the city and she was in a gorgeous place with a fun job, and she was going to take her first deep breath in months and find herself again.

No matter what.

Her plan was to leave here a changed woman, one who remembered how wonderful it was to be on her own, empowered and . . . not anxious or stressed. Finding confidence would be a bonus. Being happy would be a pipe dream.

I don't care what you grow up to be, as long as you're self-sufficient and no longer need us for anything, her mother had said when Lanie had gone off to college.

She squeezed her eyes shut, shoved that very unwelcome memory far away, and tried to think of something else, anything else.

Am I hard to love, Kyle?

Maybe a little when you're overworked. Or tired. Or hungry . . .

Yeah, so that had been hard to hear from the man who as a beverage sales rep to all of Southern California had only been home two days a week, but she'd come to understand something. It wasn't about being unlovable. It was that she couldn't trust someone to love her. It'd started with her parents. Both physicists, they'd expected her to follow in their footsteps. Only problem was she'd hated math and science, instead preferring the arts.

Being the square peg had made her an enigma to them, and not in a good way. It wasn't that they'd been on her to change.

It'd been worse than that. Once they'd realized how different she was, they'd given up on her completely.

And apparently, so had Kyle. She'd really thought she'd known everything about him and their relationship, and yet he'd betrayed her. So she no longer believed in her own judgment and other people. "Gah," she told the dark cottage and flopped over, redirecting her thoughts to the only thing she could do something about.

The present.

DAY TWO OF Lanie's job went much like the day before. She had a nice big space they'd created for her to do her thing. It was an open floor plan, meaning everyone working had their own corner but they were all together.

Peaceful and quiet, it wasn't.

It turned out that Alyssa handled sales and hospitality, and spent most of her time on the phone charming the socks off people. Which had been fascinating to watch because Lanie herself hadn't gotten the charming-the-socks-off gene.

Mia was the tasting room manager, and in spite of not having the sunniest of dispositions, she was also head of tours. Mostly because no one else wanted to be, she'd told Lanie as she'd flitted in and out of the office a hundred times an hour, sprinkling sarcasm and cynicism every time she came and went.

"When life knocks you down," she said to Lanie after getting yelled at by a very rude customer, "calmly get back up, smile, and very politely say 'You hit like a bitch, bitch.'"

Lanie was pretty sure that wasn't Cora-approved.

"I hope my future husband looks at me in the mornings like I'm looking at this leftover pizza," Mia said after raiding the employee fridge. "Like, yeah, maybe it's looked better, but it still makes my heart happy."

There were others around too, many others, and everyone knew everything about everyone. And whether Lanie liked it or not, she knew things too now because she couldn't not hear them. Like about Cora's brother, who ran the company's social media platform. Uncle Jack had Crohn's disease and was supposedly on a strict diet, but he constantly cheated and then locked himself in the employee bathroom for hours at a time, during which, if you had a Twitter account, you could read his ongoing thoughts. Such as: *Inhaled four Cinnabons. #TacticalError #RookieMistake.* And then the one that had Cora finally changing the password so he couldn't sign in:

Dear people who type in all lowercase, we're the difference between helping your Uncle Jack off a horse & helping your uncle jack off a horse. Capital Letters.

In essence, Capriotti Winery was a small town all on its own where there were no secrets and the gossip mill was alive and well.

Not that anyone was going to learn *Lanie's* secrets. *You're just playing a part,* she reminded herself. *Just like you did with being a daughter. A wife . . . There's no need to let anyone know just how unsuccessful in love you've been.*

That night she got into bed and was nearly asleep when there came a quiet knock.

Cookies, she thought, and leapt out of bed. Her cottage was all one room—a kitchenette in one corner, bed in another, small couch and coffee table near the front door. She peeked out and found . . . no one. Then she nearly jumped out of her own skin when the knock came again, accompanied by a giggle. Actually, make that two soft giggles, and she relaxed as she opened the door and yep, found the cute little cupcake twins.

They wore matching Wonder Woman PJs, matching bare feet, and matching contagious grins. They had dark unruly hair and dark chocolate eyes like their dad's, and sweet, innocent smiles—*un*like their dad. "Uh, hi," she said and peeked out past them to see who was in charge.

But there was no one with them. "You guys okay?"

They gave matching bobblehead nods. The one on the right had her hair in a bun on top of her head. Her twin's hair was loose and in a complete riot around her face.

"So," Lanie said and paused, waiting for them to fill in some gaps.

Didn't happen.

"Is there something I can do for you?" she asked.

"We were wondering something," the one on the left said. Wild Hair. She looked at her twin. "Right?"

Her twin, missing her front teeth, nodded.

Lanie was at a loss. She knew nothing about kids. Less than nothing. She was an only child, and actually she couldn't remember ever even *being* a child, at least a carefree one with cute PJs and crazy hair and a silly, adorable smile. "Are you out here by yourselves?"

Twin nods.

Lanie had no idea who their mom was. She'd met a lot of people over the past two days, but not one of them had been introduced as Mark's wife. And since he'd joked about asking Lanie out, she was kind of assuming there was no wife.

Which didn't solve the mystery of their mom. "Maybe I should call your grandma—"

"Oh, but you can't!" Wild Hair said and slipped past Lanie into her cottage, tugging her sister along with her.

"Well, sure, come on in."

They giggled and Lanie resisted thunking her head to the door before turning to face her late-night intruders. "And why can't I call your grandma?"

"'Cuz we'll get in trouble," Wild Hair said. "We're supposed to be asleep."

Toothless nodded.

"Okay," Lanie said. "And you're not asleep because . . ."

Wild Hair bit her lower lip. "Can you keep a secret?"

"No," she said, not willing to be an accomplice.

The twins exchanged disappointed looks with those huge expressive eyes that nearly had her caving. She crossed her arms. "Listen, I might not know the first thing about little kids, but I do know when my leg's being pulled. You two are up to something. Spill."

"We, um . . . sorta took something from your purse earlier," Wild Hair said.

"You stole something from me?"

"No," Wild Hair said. "That's what bad people do. We . . . um . . . *borrowed*."

"What did you 'borrow'?"

"When you were working earlier, your purse fell over under your desk and stuff spilled out all by itself."

"All by itself, huh?"

"Yeah," Wild Hair said.

Toothless added a bobblehead nod.

"And we couldn't help but see you had a pretty smelly roller thingie," Wild Hair said.

Lanie did in fact have a roller perfume. It was her favorite scent and it was ridiculously expensive, but when she'd gotten this job, she'd treated herself to it.

Toothless pulled something from her pajama pocket.

The perfume roller.

Empty.

Lanie took it back. "Wow."

"We're sorry," Wild Hair whispered, and Toothless nodded again, and Lanie was reluctantly moved by their collective adorableness.

"Are you a-hundred-and-fifty-dollars sorry?"

They both gasped. "That's a lot!" Wild Hair said. "You shouldn't spend so much money."

And just like that, it got a whole lot easier to not be moved. "You girls owe me."

"But we only get five dollars a week," Wild Hair said, horrified. "And we only get that if we do our chores. Which we keep forgetting."

"Well, I'd start remembering," Lanie said. "And maybe pick up some extra chores too."

The girls looked at each other, again had some silent exchange, and then nodded solemnly.

"We will," Wild Hair said, very seriously now. Grin gone. "Don't be mad at us."

Feeling like a jerk, Lanie sighed. "It's not about being mad, or even about the money. It's more about breaking trust. You disregarded my privacy when you went through my things. And then you took something that wasn't yours and used it. Neither of those things are okay and they might make it so a person could decide not to like or trust you in the future. Do you understand?"

The twins nodded vigorously.

"But *I* like *you*," Wild Hair said to Lanie. "A lot. So I'd be really sad if you didn't like me back. Especially 'cuz I'm really, *really* sorry."

"Sorry for what you did, or that you have to pay me back?"

"Both?" Wild Hair asked with such sweetness that damn, Lanie had to work at biting back a smile.

"We really do like you," Wild Hair said, and Toothless nodded vigorously.

"I see you two at lunchtime," Lanie said. "You like everyone."

"No, we don't. We don't like Great-Uncle Jack's grandkids and we don't like Alyssa's boys, and we especially don't like the customers. They bend over to speak to us and use baby talk like we're short *and* stupid. And they treat us like we're five!"

"Aren't you five?" Lanie asked.

"We're six," the kid said proudly.

Lanie nodded with a reluctant smile. "Okay, good to know. What are your names?"

"I'm Samantha," Wild Hair said. "I go by Sam. And she's Sierra. Sometimes Daddy calls her Sea."

Toothless, aka Sierra, aka Sea, just stared at her with those guileless, fathomless, sweet eyes.

"She doesn't talk," Samantha said.

"Ever?" Lanie asked.

Sierra looked down to stare at her feet.

"Not anymore," Sam said. "But it's okay 'cuz I talk for her."

Lanie studied Sierra's bowed head and realized she wasn't looking at her own feet, but at Lanie's, which were also bare. She'd given herself a pedicure the night before, so she was sporting pretty purple toenails, which Sierra seemed fascinated by. "I'm sure someone's worried about you by now," Lanie said. "It's late."

"It's Grandma's turn to watch us," Sam said. "And she fell asleep watching her shows. Who's your favorite superhero?"

"Wonder Woman," Lanie said.

"Us too! Who's your second favorite?"

"Um . . . Thor."

"I like Thor too," Sam said. "Who's your third favorite?"

"Gee, I'd have to think about that one," Lanie said. "So about bedtime—"

"Do you have ice cream?"

Lanie felt her heart squeeze. Their dad should be with them at night at least, especially since by his own admission he worked long hours. These girls were so young, they needed their parents, something she of all people understood. "I'm sorry. I don't have ice cream," she said, although now she wished she did. "Actually, since I haven't been to the store, I don't have anything." Well, except the emergency Snickers in her purse. It was her favorite candy bar and also her PMS med of choice.

The girls seemed devastated at this. But then Sam eyeballed the couch, where some of Lanie's things sat. "You do have lipstick."

"Lip gloss," Lanie started to say, but the girls were gone, beelining for the couch. "I really think I need to get you back—"

"Ooh," Samantha breathed, lifting the lip gloss. "Pretty!"

Sierra did the same to the small bottle of purple nail polish that matched Lanie's toes and clutched it to her chest like it was a found treasure.

Lanie let out a breath and peeked out her front door and down the walk, hoping someone had sent out a search party.

No one, but then again, her hopes and dreams never came true, so why should they start now . . . "I'll tell you what," she said. "If you let me take you back to your beds, you can use my nail polish."

Sierra clasped the purple nail polish to her chest in glee.

"Now?" Sam asked excitedly.

"Tomorrow after work," Lanie said and gave herself an inner kick. What was she doing? The objective was to survive the next two months and move on with her life. The objective was *not* to get attached to anyone, especially these two crazy cuties.

The twins looked at each other and some silent communication went on. Then Sam met Lanie's eyes. "Can we use the lip gloss now?"

A young negotiator. Lanie was impressed. "Fine. Lip gloss now. Nail polish later."

"Tomorrow after work," Sam said. "Right?"

"Right," Lanie said. "Why do I get the feeling you're going to be a lawyer someday?"

"I'm gonna be a sheriff," she said proudly. "Like my daddy. Sierra's going to be the lawyer."

Sierra nodded.

Lanie held up her compact mirror for each girl in turn as they carefully applied the lip gloss. And then she pulled on a pair of sweats over her PJs and walked the girls to the big house. They went in the back door and tripped over a sleeping Gracie.

The English sheepdog was sprawled on her back, her four legs spread-eagled out at her sides, snoring—and drooling—away. "Love her killer instinct," Lanie said, and the girls giggled.

"Gracie would show a burglar where Great-Grandma keeps the silver," Sam said. "That's what Grandma always says. But at least she doesn't threaten to sell her to the glue factory anymore."

When Lanie looked at her, the little girl smiled. "Gracie was a very naughty puppy. She's one now, so she mostly knows better than to chew our shoes, but she still forgets sometimes."

Note number two to self: do not leave shoes out anywhere for Gracie to eat.

They all tiptoed past Gracie and then past a still-sleeping Cora on the couch. The TV was tuned to *The Bachelor* in the middle of a rose ceremony, where a group of women was having anxiety over whether or not they were going to get a rose. Everyone had their problems, Lanie supposed. She didn't want a rose. She wanted to go to bed.

Alone.

The house was huge. The girls led her upstairs, where there were three separate wings.

"We share a bedroom," Samantha said, walking into a pretty purple-and-white bedroom. "We've got two beds, but we like mine best."

And with that, they both hopped onto one of the two fluffy beds and dove under the covers.

"Sleep tight," Lanie said. "And *stay* in bed."

"Don't forget!" came Sam's voice. "Tomorrow we get pretty sparkly purple toes!"

Lanie laughed and turned from the room, gently shutting the door as she went, and . . . plowed into a tall, leanly muscled shadow, who grabbed her and kept her from falling on her ass.

Mark.

Lanie, heart pounding in her ears, took an automatic step back, crossing her arms over herself. "You scared me."

He didn't say anything. The hallway was lit only from the

glow of the TV on the floor below. He seemed bigger than she remembered. And in the dark hall, incredibly intimidating.

Uncomfortably aware of the fact that she was inside the family home, uninvited, she said, "I was in bed when the girls knocked on my door. I didn't want to send them out into the night alone, so I walked them back here."

Whatever he thought of that, he kept to himself. Leaning past her, he opened the bedroom door. There'd been bed-rustling sounds, but now the room went instantly silent.

Mark strode into the room. "If you think I can't recognize pretend sleeping, you can both think again."

If he'd spoken to Lanie in that scary baritone when she'd been the girls' age, she'd have peed her pants. But his girls squealed and tossed back their covers, and then two bundles flew at him with the now-familiar *"Daddy, Daddy, Daddy!"* coming from Sam.

Lanie held her breath, but he caught them both with ease, snuggled them in close, kissed each of them, and then . . . tossed them back onto the bed.

More squeals and peals of laughter, and Mark covered them both with the blanket.

"Daddy, Sierra has an owie!" Sam said. "She was playing a game in bed and the iPad fell and hit her in the head."

Mark took in the half-inch scratch on Sierra's forehead. "I can fix that."

"You can?" Sam asked while Sierra's eyes went hopeful.

Mark walked to the whiteboard on one wall, grabbed a pink marker, and came back to Sierra. He turned the scratch into a lightning bolt.

Sam shrieked in delight. "Now you're Harry Potter!" she told Sierra, who jumped up to look in the mirror on the closet door.

Beaming, happy, they both crawled back into bed.

Mark sat on the edge of the bed. "Do I even want to know why you left this house alone at night, when the both of you know better?"

"Daddy, she's got lip gloss and pretty purple nail polish that sparkles and everything!"

"She?"

"The new lady. Lanie."

Mark craned his neck toward the door.

Lanie leapt back out of sight, feeling her face heat. Why was she even still standing there? Horrified and embarrassed, she hurried down the stairs, her chest tight, her pulse in her ears. She'd gotten all the way to the kitchen when Gracie barked.

"Seriously?" Lanie whispered. "You're going to be a guard dog now?"

Gracie jumped up, put her paws on Lanie's shoulders, and licked her chin.

"Okay, okay," Lanie whispered. "We're friends now, right? Good." And with that she slid outside. She'd just shut the back door when it opened again.

She didn't look. Instead, she picked up her pace but for the second time that night she nearly leapt out of her own skin when a hand settled on her arm and pulled her around.

Mark.

"Sorry," she said, maybe gasped, because she was out of breath from holding her breath. "I wasn't eavesdropping." Much.

"Actually," he said. "The sorry is on me. They're insatiably curious."

"It's okay. I like them. No one else has asked me who my

third favorite superhero is. They're . . . cute." And she was surprised to find that was actually true.

"They're something, all right." Mark gestured her toward the trail, a hand at the small of her back. Not a flirtatious gesture. More like an impatient one.

"You don't have to walk me," she said.

"You got the two people who mean more to me than anything else on this planet home safe and sound," he said. "I'm going to return the favor."

"I can handle myself."

"Of that, I have no doubt," he said. "But I'm still going to walk you home."

"But—"

"Look," he said, exasperated. "I'm exhausted. How about we just get this over with." And then without waiting for an answer, he once again nudged her in the right direction. "Let's move."

"I don't take orders very well," she warned. "In fact, I barely take suggestions."

She got an almost smile at that and they walked through the night. In silence. At her door, he waited until she opened it to speak.

"Again," he said. "Thanks."

She met his gaze. "Is it really 'again' if it's the first time you said it?"

He let out a low laugh and scrubbed a hand over his stubbled jaw. "I'm not very good at this. So you're . . . okay?"

It was an odd question. She couldn't remember the last time someone, anyone, had asked her such a thing. "Why wouldn't I be?"

This got her an actual smile. "Are you always so prickly? Or is it something you save for just me?"

"It might be just you," she admitted.

Small smile still on his lips, he nodded. "Good to know. I've got to get back. I promised they could tell me a bedtime story."

"Isn't it supposed to be the other way around?"

"We take turns." He shook his head. "You know what takes longer than a kid telling a story?"

She had no idea, so she shook her head.

"Nothing," he said and startled a quick laugh out of her. And then before she could recover, he was gone, vanished into the night.

Fine by her. She crawled back into her bed and this time fell right asleep, although she maybe had a few crazy dreams involving a tall, dark stranger with a bad 'tude and a really great laugh and incredible hands. She had no idea if the incredible hands part was true, but in her dream it definitely was.

Chapter 3

Me: What can possibly go wrong, though . . . ?
Anxiety: I'm glad you asked . . .

The end of her first week found Lanie at her desk, working on her new designs. Ostensibly. Because what she was really doing was staring out the window at Mark and Holden.

Their shirts were off, and they were headfirst inside the engine compartment of a tractor, working on . . . something. It didn't matter what. What mattered was that they were a little hot and sweaty, jeans pulled taut across two incredibly nice asses, and it was an even better view than the lush countryside behind them.

She was very busy looking at said asses while on the phone with a silk and embroidery screener because Cora wanted the winery to open an apparel shop, and this fell into Lanie's territory. She was talking about the design she hoped to use and still staring outside—specifically at Mark's ass—when she realized he'd straightened and was looking right at her.

Watching her watch him. Brow raised.

Oh, crap. She ducked low, grimaced, and then peeked out the window. He'd been interrupted by three women. Winery guests, who were all dressed up in pretty sundresses, hats, and heels, looking like a million bucks as they sipped wine and flirted. That they were flirting with the same men Lanie herself had been ogling didn't ease her annoyance one bit.

Neither did the fact that Mark laughed at something they said, spoke a few words that made them laugh in return, and that's when Lanie remembered—she didn't like him much.

She was reminding herself of just that when her phone vibrated. It was a frantic text from Mia to come to the employee bathroom.

Good. Something to do. So she rushed down the hall where she found Mia in the bathroom on her knees praying to the porcelain god.

"Hangover," Mia moaned and curled up on the floor. "Drank too much last night. In other news, if you know a guy looking for a slightly alcoholic, psychopath girlfriend who swears too much, eats too much, and will probably try to fight him while drunk, I'm the girl."

"Good to know," Lanie said. "But I'm off men at the moment so I don't have any guys to recommend you to—in spite of those attractive attributes."

Mia laughed and then groaned, holding her head. "Do you have future plans?"

"Yeah. I'm hoping to see Australia sometime."

"No," Mia said. "Beyond that."

"Oh. Lunch?"

Mia snorted. "I really do like you. I need you to cover for me and take the tour I'm supposed to give in half an hour to a group of fifteen."

"Oh no. No, no, no," Lanie said, horrified at the thought. "I couldn't possibly give a tour."

"Why not? Are you bitchy with people too?"

"Of course not, I'm a delight."

Mia grinned and pointed at her. "You're doing this."

"Okay, first," Lanie said, pointing back, "I don't like people enough for that, and second, I don't know the first thing about giving a winery tour."

"Go to my desk. Ignore the planners, highlighters, ballpoint pens, to-do lists, and anything else that gives the illusion that I've got my shit together. Grab my iPad. There's a file marked 'Tours' on it with everything you need to know. Take it with you. Password is ihateeveryone247, all lowercase."

"Oh my God," Lanie said. "I was going to laugh, but I'm not sure you're kidding."

"I'm not. Are you afraid of public speaking?"

Only slightly less than, say, facing down a psycho madman. At her last job, she'd been in the middle of a presentation when Kyle's third wife had shown up.

"Yeah, I have a question," the woman had yelled from the back of the full conference room that had also held her boss and her boss's boss. "What kind of a bitch keeps all her dead husband's assets to herself when she wasn't the only wife?"

Lanie closed her eyes. "I'm not afraid of public speaking," she said to Mia. "I just don't do it anymore."

"Okay, but this is different," Mia said reasonably. "You're at a family winery and it's just chitchat. You can even make stuff up if you want. I do it all the time. Just don't tell Mom."

Lanie's heart was threatening secession from her rib cage. *Just say no. It's okay to set boundaries.* "Listen, you look much better now, not nearly as green, so—"

Mia leaned over the toilet and threw up some more, and then rested her head on the toilet seat.

Lanie sighed. "Maybe I should help you to bed—"

"No, I need you to help yourself to my iPad and do this tour. Please, Lanie."

"What happens if I don't?"

"I'll tell Uncle Jack you like older men and want to date him."

"Wow," Lanie said, and dammit, she went to the door.

"Wait—you're going to do the tour, though, right?" Mia called. "And not tell anyone why?"

So much for not getting personally involved. And now she was keeping secrets, which was like the *ultimate* involvement. "You're going to owe me," Lanie said.

"Anything. What?"

"A favor," Lanie said. "An unspecified favor to be chosen at a later date."

"Damn," Mia said. "I'm impressed. But yeah. Okay. A favor."

Lanie went to Mia's desk and easily found the iPad because Mia's desk was neat and organized—not a mess at all. There was apparently far more to Mia than sarcastic, caustic party girl, but for some reason Mia hid behind the image. But hey, Lanie was hiding too. Maybe everyone was.

The "Tour" file was extensive and she sat down right there at Mia's desk and began to read. The history of the winery turned out to be fascinating. Grandma and Grandpa Capriotti had come over from Italy, getting married on the boat—not for love but for family's sake—though it turned out to be a really incredible love story after all.

Half an hour later Lanie, heart pounding in her ears, stood in front of the tour group and . . . choked. She tried reading directly from the iPad but her voice was too quiet and quavery and everyone kept yelling at her to speak up. She was working on that when her cell rang. "Excuse me," she said and grabbed at the phone like it was a lifeline, hoping that someone, anyone, was calling to say they could take over the tour for her. "*Hello?*"

"Is this Lanie Jacobs, formerly Lanie Blackwell, married to Kyle Blackwell?"

She pulled the phone away to look at the number. She didn't recognize it. "Who is this?"

"Kyle's *other* wife, apparently. I understand you were the first, and as such the only legit wife, meaning you got the insurance policy."

Wow, that made wife number four. Impressive, really. She turned away from the tour group. "How did you get this number?"

"I paid a private detective to find you. Kyle and I got married the year after you did, on the very same day. Apparently Kyle didn't want to have to remember dates. I deserve half of that life-insurance policy payout. I earned it being married to that cheater!"

Lanie, incredibly aware of her audience, pasted a smile on her face. While she agreed that she wasn't any more worthy of the insurance money than any of the other women in Kyle's life, she hadn't yet figured out a way to make it right for everyone. In the meantime, she was over being painted as the bad guy. "You'll have to get in line," she said. "If you'll excuse me—"

"Don't you hang up on me! I can find you, you know."

On that lovely thought, Lanie turned off her phone. She took a deep breath and shoved the phone away. "Okay, so where were we?" she asked, turning back around.

Someone new had joined the tour.

Deputy Sheriff Mark. While she stood there and stared at him in surprise, the corners of his mouth tipped up slightly.

"I think it's time for some wine, am I right?"

In the tasting room, she let everyone mill around and talk while she ran to the bathroom, tore out a few paper towels, and shoved them inside her top and beneath her pits to stanch the flow of flop sweat.

"The first time is the hardest," Mark said quietly behind her.

She squeaked and pivoted. "I was doing fine before you showed up," she said, yanking the paper towels out from her shirt and tossing them into the trash. "You give me stage fright!"

Again, that slight curve of his mouth. "Okay, it's all my fault. So let me help you." Taking her by the hand, he dragged her out of the bathroom and back to the tasting room. He caught Owen's eye and the winemaker gestured them over. "Give us a minute, folks," Mark called out to the tour group, all friendly-like, adding a flirtatious wink.

Owen's desk looked like something right out of a science lab, covered with beakers and equations written on every surface. He'd been working on a sample and Mark offered Lanie a taste.

"What is it?" she asked suspiciously.

Owen started to answer, but Mark held up a hand to stop him. "Does it matter? Just drink."

She took a little sip.

Mark shook his head. "More."

So she took another. Whatever it was, it was actually quite delicious and . . . once it hit her system, she relaxed a little bit.

He flashed her a smile. "Now go get 'em, tiger."

She started over with the whole Capriotti love story and the strangest thing happened. The people were totally into it. They *wanted* her to be good at this, she realized. They *wanted* her to succeed, and it was a huge confidence booster. She loved their reactions to the story and in truth, she fell a little bit in love with the winery herself.

After the tour, Cora came into the offices and stopped short, tossing up her hands. "I remember every lyric to every eighties song, but hell if I can remember why I just walked into this room." She turned and walked out again.

And then suddenly she was back, carrying a bottle of wine. She set it down on Lanie's desk. "I remember! You're amazing. Mia caught the flu and you stepped up in a huge way today, doing a job that wasn't yours without complaint."

Lanie opened her mouth to admit she'd done *plenty* of complaining to Mia beforehand, but everyone around clapped and toasted her. Including Mark, who'd come in without her noticing, although she was pretty sure his expression was more amused than congratulatory.

"Anytime," she murmured, feeling like a fraud. They clearly wanted her to feel like one of them, but she knew nothing about being part of a big family. Plus, she didn't know their endgame. Or how they could really be so close and happy. She needed to learn to keep her distance better around them.

Especially Mark, because the man was one of those quiet troublemakers, she could tell—the kind that sneaked in under a woman's guard and made himself at home. And then decimated her heart and soul . . .

"You okay?" Cora asked quietly.

"I don't know." Lanie shook her head and spoke the utter truth. "It still feels a little bit like you're all too good to be true."

Cora didn't get insulted. In fact, she tilted her head back and laughed. "Oh, honey. Believe me, we're not all that good.

I mean, our hearts are in the right place, but trust me, we're human."

Just then, Uncle Jack walked by. He looked at Alyssa's artfully torn jeans that probably cost her a hundred bucks and said, "Hey, did you know there're holes in your jeans?"

Alyssa rolled her eyes and Jack farted audibly. "Jet power!" he yelled and kept walking.

Cora waved the air with her hand. "See? Proof we're a little insane. Now let's all get to work. Alyssa, open a damn window and someone get that man some Tums, pronto. Back to work, people!"

And back to work they all went.

Lanie settled in. Two months wasn't really a lot of time given what she'd been hired to do—which was basically a redo of the entire Capriotti brand. She was working on everything from design and execution of simple business cards to their wine club brochures to their complex catalogs. And then there was the website that needed to be completely redesigned and overhauled as well, not to mention label designs that would hopefully sit up and beg people to pull Capriotti bottles off busy crowded store shelves and into their shopping carts. Almost two-thirds of all purchase decisions were still made in-store, and a great wine label design could be what closed the deal. On top of that, she needed to properly execute and manage the packaging, ads, and logos that would end up on menus, table tents, shelf-talkers, bottleneckers, posters, banners, window clings, case cards . . . *everything*.

She was completely lost in the work when Samantha and Sierra appeared with hopeful faces.

"Purple toes!" Samantha yelled cheerfully.

Right. She'd promised earlier in the week, but the girls had been busy after school ever since. Tonight was the night, even though what Lanie *really* wanted was a hot shower, a marathon session of a really bad reality show, and a pot of mac and cheese all to herself. "Now? Don't you have more homework or another dance class or something?" she asked hopefully.

"Nope," Sam said.

Lanie looked at Sierra. "How about you?"

Sierra shook her head.

"I'm sorry," Lanie said, curling her hand around her ear. "I didn't hear you."

"She said no," Sam said.

Lanie slid her a look. "Maybe I was trying to get her to talk."

Sierra grinned.

So did Sam. "Everyone tries that trick. It never works."

Okay, then. They followed her to her cottage, where she began the pedis. She was painting Sierra's big toe when Sam asked, "Are you my daddy's girlfriend?"

Lanie jerked and painted Sierra's entire toe, making both girls laugh. She wiped off the polish and slid them both a look. "Of course I'm not. Whoever said such a thing?"

"We watched you out the window when Daddy walked you home the other night."

Lanie kept a careful gaze on painting toenails and most definitely didn't give away any of her private thoughts. "Which was a very nice thing for him to do. But it doesn't mean I'm his girlfriend."

"You stood close to each other and everything," Sam said. "We asked Grandma and Auntie Alyssa about it, and they got pretty excited."

Dear God.

"And you smiled," Sam said. "And so did he. He doesn't do that very much."

"Why?" Lanie asked before she could help herself.

"He has a sad," Sam said. "If you were his girlfriend, maybe you would take that sad away."

Lanie set the toenail polish down and bent low to blow on the wet paint, making Sierra giggle. Then she met Sam's gaze. "It doesn't work like that," she said gently. "Having a girlfriend or a boyfriend doesn't make you happy."

"Then what does?"

Yeah, genius, what does makes one happy? She put a hand over Sam's heart. And then Sierra's. "The happy comes from inside yourself."

At least she was pretty sure.

"Are you happy inside yourself?" Sam asked.

Ha. "I'm . . . working on it."

Sam cocked her head and then, with all the innocence and earnestness of a six-year-old, said, "Try cupcakes. My grandma's cupcakes can make anyone happy."

She felt her heart squeeze. Dammit, she was falling for them. It was a problem, a big one, because it made her instinctively want to curl into a ball and close herself off. And she could do it too. She'd managed just fine with the rest of the Capriottis, but with these two, resistance seemed futile.

So maybe it's okay to like them, a little voice inside her said.

But no one else.

"I'll keep that in mind," she said.

When she'd finished their pedicures, she returned them to the big house, doing her best not to run into anyone this time. But her luck wasn't that good. As they got close, Gracie barked happily from inside and then Alyssa opened the front door, releasing the beast.

The hundred-pound dog took a flying leap at Lanie and licked her chin.

"Okay," Lanie said, patting the biggest puppy on the planet. "Okay, then."

Alyssa hustled the girls inside with a quick hug. "The baby's waiting for you," she told them.

The twins went racing up the stairs in excitement, deserting Lanie without a backward glance. Alyssa gave her a smile that Lanie was instantly suspicious of.

"Hey," Alyssa said.

Be cool, Lanie told herself. *Just be cool . . .* "The twins are wrong," she burst out.

"Really? About what?"

Lanie grimaced and Alyssa smiled. "Do tell."

"Whatever the girls think they saw earlier in the week, they didn't. Mark was just walking me back to my cottage."

"Interesting."

Lanie sighed. "No, really—" She broke off as some yelling came from within the house. "What's going on?"

Alyssa rolled her eyes. "Family dinner. And by this time of day, my patience with everyone is literally at one percent."

"Don't you guys get enough of one another during the day?"

Alyssa laughed like Lanie had just told a very funny joke. "It's Uncle Jack's birthday. He's drunk and he asked his daughter Cecilia—the one who is supposedly our receptionist but hasn't been to work one day this week because she's spoiled—when she was going to get married and give him grandbabies. She reminded him that she's not all that into men. And then he reminded her that he didn't care if she was bisexual, asexual, pansexual, or metrosexual, he still expected additional grandkids."

"Oh boy," Lanie said.

"No kidding. Most of my wrinkles are from laughter, except for these right between my eyebrows." She pointed at them. "These are my 'WTF' lines and those suckers are deep, all given to me by our family dinners."

Lanie laughed.

"You think I'm kidding. We'll see how deep *your* WTF lines are at the end of your two months in this place. Anyway, so while the rest of us were looking up pansexual on our phones, Cecilia locked herself in the bathroom. And that isn't the worst of it. Mia had a Tinder meet-up." Alyssa put *meet-up* in air quotes. "She brought him by here first, probably for shock value. They're in the *other* bathroom doing God knows what. Meantime, Grandpa's going back and forth between the two bathrooms banging on the doors saying he needs in pronto, so you should run for the hills. Do it now before Mom sees you standing here and makes you come inside to join us."

"Your brother warned me to run too."

Alyssa smiled. "Mark's a lot of things, smart being one of them."

Lanie turned to walk away, but good manners had her hesitating. "Uh, you could come back to my cottage to escape if you want."

"Thanks, but I can't abandon ship. Family and all that, you understand."

She didn't, not really. But she nodded and left. She thought about running away, but that wouldn't solve any of her problems. So instead she got into her favorite PJs and crawled into bed with her laptop to marathon something good.

Family and all that . . .

Alyssa's comment played on repeat in her head. Every family had their faults, but some more than others. She knew all too well. Her own family was fractured and always had been. But the Capriottis fascinated her. They didn't judge. They stuck together no matter what—something she had zero experience with. She picked up her phone and stared at it for a long moment before starting a text.

Lanie: Hi, Mom.
Mom: What's wrong?
Lanie: Nothing. Just wanted to check in.
Mom: Why?
Lanie: I'm actually in town. Thought I could come by. See you and Dad.
Mom: . . .
Lanie: You there?
Mom: Your dad's in Europe for work for a month. And us Jacobses don't do casual visits.
Lanie: There's always a first time.
Mom: You need something? Are you in trouble?

Lanie sighed and set her phone aside. She told herself it was fine, that she was here to simply hit reset on her life and *not* get involved emotionally or otherwise. So she loaded Netflix and lost herself in a *Friends* marathon, season one, when everyone was at least as screwed up as she was.

Chapter 4

Me: It's not even that serious.
Inner me: Have a breakdown anyway.

River Green sat in her 1998 Camry in the Capriotti Winery parking lot peering through her dusty windshield. The place was pretty, real pretty. And upscale.

Way above her pay grade.

But since she didn't currently have a pay grade, that wasn't saying much. People were sitting on the patio at two huge white tables, smiling, laughing, talking, and eating from what looked like a huge feast of food.

Her belly rumbled and she rubbed it. "I know," she whispered. "I'm hungry too."

So hungry.

She didn't belong at those tables. Hell, she didn't belong anywhere, but that was a problem for another day. Today she was here doing recon. Trying to figure out how to go about her life goal.

Which was to get back what was hers.

Because her legs were cramping, she got out of the car and stretched her aching back. Twenty-one years old last week and yet she felt like an old woman. Driven by more than a little desperation, she walked up the path and peeked into the winery. The big, open, barn-like room had a reception area and yes, thank you, sweet baby Jesus, a drinking fountain with small paper cups available.

She made her way to it and drank. And drank. She needed to go back for her water bottle and fill that up too because this water was fresh and cool and helped her jumbled thoughts come together.

But more than that, she needed to get back to the car before anyone saw her. She went outside again, staggering a little bit because moving too fast had spots dancing across her vision.

"Not now," she murmured and did her best to shake it off. She got to the Camry and opened the driver's side door, but then put out a hand to lean heavily against it and give herself a minute.

"Hello," someone said.

River turned her head. A woman, maybe fifty years old. Dark brunette hair streaked with gray, dark eyes, and a welcoming smile. "Can I help you?" she asked River.

Shit. Crap. Damn . . . River shook her head. "No, thank you. I . . ."

The woman came around the car and took in River's body and smiled. "Ah. How far along are you?"

"Six months," River said softly and put a hand on her swollen belly.

"Six months is a wonderful time. You can feel the baby move around. Gives a purpose to your suffering," the woman said with a gentle smile. "Sit, honey. You look dead on your feet."

And before River knew what was happening, she was sitting on the wooden bench against the split-rail fencing, beyond which seemed like miles and miles of thriving grapevines on rolling hill after rolling hill.

The woman next to her smiled reassuringly and took in River's opened car, and the suitcase in it.

All her worldly possessions.

"You know what?" the woman said, standing, pulling River up with her. "It's way too warm out here in the sun for me. I need to get inside. You'll help me, won't you?"

"Of course," River said, but the truth was the woman was helping her, keeping a good grip on River's arm. Her vision got cobwebby and the next thing she knew, she was sitting in a comfy, cushy chair inside the cool reception area, her feet up on a low coffee table strewn with brochures on the winery and the surrounding areas, sipping water from a real glass with ice cubes.

"Better?" the woman asked worriedly.

River blinked. She'd nearly passed out. Oh, this was bad. Very, very bad. She needed to be able to take care of herself and her baby. "Much better," she said and mustered a smile past her panic and pounding heart. She started to get up, but the woman stopped her.

"Not yet," she said quietly. "Wait right here."

And then she vanished out the set of French double doors at the other end of the building.

River allowed herself a second to lean her head back and close her eyes as she ran a hand over her swollen belly. "We're okay," she whispered, as she'd been doing ever since the shocking day she'd learned she was pregnant.

With no time for a pity party, she straightened and started to hoist herself out of the chair, but was stopped short by the sight of the woman coming back into the room carrying a plate of food that smelled nothing short of amazing.

"I thought you might be hungry. I'm Cora, by the way," the woman said, handing River the plate filled with meat and cheese lasagna, baked bread, and a salad, all of it making her mouth water so that she lost her thoughts again and couldn't speak. It was a good thing there was a fork on the plate or she'd have dived in with her fingers.

She was halfway through the food before she realized that she was literally hunched over it like a wild, rabid dog, inhaling like she hadn't eaten in days. But it hadn't been that long.

Had it?

Cora's smile was nonjudgmental and easy. "What's your name, child?"

"River." She bit her lip. She shouldn't have said that. "I . . . thank you." She started to set the plate down on the coffee table but Cora shook her head.

"Finish," she said.

River had just stuffed in another bite when the next question came.

"Are you here about the temp job?"

River stopped chewing and met Cora's gaze. *Job?* "Uh . . . maybe . . . ?"

Cora smiled. "That would be lovely. It's for the receptionist position, which as you can see is empty. My niece Cecilia was working the desk, but she's taking some college courses and is feeling overwhelmed." She pointed to the HELP WANTED sign in the window.

River looked at it and her heart started pounding again.

"Once Cecilia figures out how to handle both classes and the job, she'll most likely come back," Cora said. "But that could be months and we need someone now. Do you have any experience?"

"Um . . ." River's mind raced but she didn't have to lie to answer this question. "I waitressed at the busiest truck stop in the country, the one on Highway 15 in Barstow."

"Wow," Cora said. "So you're good at serving assholes."

River blinked at the swear word coming out of sweet Cora's mouth. "Yes, ma'am. Very good," she said, tasting the irony.

"Oh, the only ma'am around here is my mom. You can call me by my given name. Any other experience?"

"Well . . . I was going to Barstow's community college at night to become an LVN, a licensed vocational nurse," River admitted shyly. Barstow wasn't the greatest little town in the world but for a while there, it'd been good to her. Until her world had caved in.

"Was?"

River put a hand on her belly. "I finished my first semester a few months ago but had to skip semester two." For lack of funds. A severe lack. Not to mention she'd been sick and so tired.

And devastated . . .

Cora was looking thoughtful and sympathetic, a powerful combination for River because it made her feel things when she'd been trying so hard not to feel anything at all. She had no idea what she thought she was doing here. She'd only intended to get a look at the place and figure out how to get back what was rightfully hers, but she'd been sucked right in.

"This job would be a piece of cake compared to waitressing and taking classes at the same time," Cora said. "The responsibilities are answering the phone and making people feel warm and welcome when they come in the front door. If they're here for a tour, you'll seat them, make small talk if they're interested, and keep them happy and comfortable until their tour guide comes for them."

"That sounds easy enough," River heard herself say.

Cora smiled. "It's a fun job. I had it myself when I was your age."

"And now you're the receptionist's boss?"

Cora laughed, a musical sound. "Baby, I'm everyone's boss. I run the place."

"Wow," River whispered in awe. "You must be really smart."

"Mostly I'm just a quick learner. And I bet you are too. The job isn't quite full-time hours, but it pays decently."

River wasn't sincerely considering this, was she? She wasn't here for this. Besides, she had bigger problems, and no matter how "decently" the job paid, she knew it still wouldn't be enough to make it so that she could afford a place to live.

Cora was quiet a moment, her head turned, her gaze pensive as she looked out the window. Possibly looking at River's car, although River hoped not.

She'd been on her own since age fifteen and it was a point of pride that she hadn't starved to death in the six years since. But while that much was true, she wasn't exactly proud of the fact that she was currently homeless.

Which brought her to her current mission, a mission she was forgetting about because Cora kept sweetening the pot.

"We're not super close to town. To make up for that, we also provide room and board."

River stilled. "Room and board, meaning . . ."

"We've got a series of small cottages for our employees if they so choose, and there's a community lunch every day. You'd be on your own for the other two meals, but there's always containers of food in the employee fridge, if you don't mind leftovers."

River actually reached down and pinched her thigh to make sure she hadn't passed out and was dreaming all of this. Decent pay *and* room and board? To not have to live in her car? It felt like Christmas.

"What do you think, honey?" Cora asked. "Are you interested?"

"Yes," River heard herself say. "Very."

"Great!" Cora looked pleased with herself. "When can you start?"

She'd clearly lost her mind. She'd come to case out the place and steal back what was hers, and now she worked here? "Right this very minute," she said.

Cora stood and took the empty plate in one hand and River's hand in another and helped her up.

Ridiculously grateful—getting up out of a chair was starting to be as difficult as . . . well, checking to make sure she had her shoes on—she followed when Cora pulled her along.

Her mom had told her to never be a follower, to make her own way along her own path, but River had been fifteen back then. On top of her world. She and her mom had been a team, a good one. She'd never known her dad, but she hadn't missed his presence. Granted, life hadn't been easy. They'd lived in a rough neighborhood and her mom had worked a lot, but together they'd been invincible. At the time, the thought of making her own path had seemed exciting, and easy.

It'd turned out to be anything but.

But even if she'd managed to resist Cora, River had a feeling that God himself would follow the woman's soft, sweet demands.

They ended up in the next building over, which was set up with open-room-style offices. Cora stopped at a desk in front of a woman who had to be her own age. She wasn't sitting, but instead stood behind her desk glaring at it.

"Mia," Cora said. "Meet River, our new temporary receptionist."

"Can't talk right now," Mia said. "A spider just landed on my desk. Oh, and in other news, it turns out when I'm startled, I can jump five feet in the air with just the power of my butt cheeks."

"As long as you didn't kill it," Cora said. "Spiders are our friends."

"Mom, are you kidding me? I murdered the shit out of that spider. Right now I'm just waiting to make sure he didn't call out the cavalry before I took him down."

Cora didn't so much as blink at this. She just shook her head, a small, indulgent smile on her lips. She clearly loved her daughter very much, and suddenly River knew why she was so drawn to Cora.

She reminded River of her own beloved mom. But because that was a slippery slope, she shut it down and smiled at everyone Cora introduced her to, until they came to a big L-shaped desk in the back corner, holding two impressive-looking printers, a big-screen computer, and a bunch of other equipment.

"River," Cora said, "this is Lanie. She's our resident graphic artist."

River froze, but Lanie stood up and reached out a hand for River to shake. "Nice to meet you."

River still couldn't move, and then Cora's smile started to

fade, so she galvanized herself into recovery. With a forced smile, she took Lanie's hand. "Sorry," she murmured. "Pregnancy brain."

Lanie nodded but didn't smile. Not as friendly as Cora, not even close, River realized.

Cora's cell rang on her hip and she looked at it with a frown. "I'm sorry, I have to take this. Lanie, River has offered to start right now. Can you take her back to the front desk at reception and wait with her until I send someone down with the forms she needs to fill out for employment? River, honey, after you fill out the forms and give them to Lanie, I'll have someone get your things into your cottage."

"Oh, no," River said quickly. "I can do that myself—"

"I'm sure you could, but what kind of a human being would I be if I let a pregnant woman do such a thing?" She smiled. "Besides, I have a misbehaving employee I want to torture. Don't make things too easy on him, you hear me?"

River had no choice but to nod. Still, there was no way she was going to let that happen. She didn't want anyone to know her humiliating truth, that not only was she alone and pregnant, but that she'd also screwed things up so much that she was living out of her car.

On the walk to the reception area, Lanie remained reserved but pointed out the staff room and where to put her things.

"So you're new too?" River asked.

Lanie looked at her. "Yes, how did you know?"

Shit. *You're an idiot.* "Uh . . . Cora mentioned it just now."

"No, she didn't," Lanie said and looked like she might've said something else, but two little girls came running down the hall and threw themselves at Lanie.

"Lanie!" one of them cried happily. "Look, we've got our own lip gloss now!" In unison, they pulled lip glosses from the pockets of their matching jeans. "Just like yours, only they're clear because Daddy said we can't wear color until we're forty or until he's too old to chase us, whichever comes first."

Lanie softened and smiled. "Nice. So where are you two really supposed to be right now?"

One of them grinned a toothless, guileless grin.

The other bit her lower lip. "Um . . ."

Lanie turned to a huge whiteboard schedule and ran her finger down the "twins" column. "Looks like you're supposedly with Grandma." She pulled her cell phone from a pocket. "Cora, did your phone call have to do with missing product? Say, a pair of three-feet-high missing product? Yep . . . uh-huh. Okay, I'll tell them . . . Sure thing." Lanie disconnected and crouched down to face both the little girls. "Your grandma says you have three minutes to get your 'cute little tushies' back into her office before she reports you missing to the sheriff, and the word is that the sheriff's *this close* to reducing your bedtime for bad behavior."

This caused twin squeaks of alarm, and then the two girls vanished hand in hand down the hall.

Lanie shook her head, but she was also still smiling a little bit, looking suddenly very human as she led River to the front desk without another word.

"You don't have to wait with me," River said when Lanie just stood by, looking at her watch.

"You don't know this yet," Lanie said, "but Cora's the sweetest, kindest tyrant you'll ever meet. She asked me to wait with you. I'm going to wait with you."

River nodded.

Lanie gestured to the chair. "You really should sit. Do you want some water or anything?"

"No, thank you," River said, feeling guilt settle onto her chest just as sure as her baby was tap-dancing on her bladder. Guilt and . . . confusion. Because for months now, Lanie had been the devil incarnate in River's eyes. But now she was wavering on that belief. Lanie was quiet and reserved and . . . human. And so much more accomplished at life than River could ever hope to be.

"So how did you know I was new?" Lanie asked.

And smart, River added with an inner wince. "You just seemed new."

Lanie studied her and then thankfully let it go without another word.

And not a minute later, someone came by with the forms and Lanie vanished.

The next three hours were a whirlwind.

River filled out the forms, answered the phone when it rang, and met more Capriottis. At some point, she went to the bathroom and came back to find a pregnancy book on her desk with a little bow wrapped around it. She hugged the book close and silently thanked her anonymous benefactor.

At five on the dot, a guy showed up. Twentysomething, he was dressed in jeans, a T-shirt, boots, and a backward baseball cap. He pulled off his dark sunglasses and gave her a nod, his face unreadable. "Ready?"

Her heart stopped. Had she done something wrong and he was escorting her out? "For . . . ?"

"Cora said to move you into cottage number five."

When she let out a whoosh of relieved air, he gave her an odd look that she ignored. "Thanks," she said. "But I've got it."

"Boss lady says otherwise. And as she's still pissed at me, she also said after I was done doing that, I should ask you what else you needed and do that too."

"I don't need anything from you," River said.

"She said you'd say that."

Startled, she met his gaze, which was calm and steady, not matching his words at all. Neither did his tone. In fact, he seemed . . . amused?

Which made no sense. "Shouldn't you be feeling bad about getting in trouble with the boss instead of laughing at me?" she asked.

"I'm laughing because you're as stubborn as she said you'd be."

"Maybe I just don't want to deal with a troublemaker." Or in other words, anyone of the male persuasion.

He shrugged. "That's probably a smart plan," he said.

Unable to help herself, she asked, "What did you do to make Cora mad?"

"Fell off a wild horse and got a concussion."

She gasped. "And that was your fault?"

"One hundred percent. There're wild horses grazing the land and we're supposed to protect them, not touch them. And we're certainly not supposed to ride them. They can be dangerous." He gave a wry smile and tapped a finger to his temple.

"I see," she said, though she didn't see at all. "I appreciate that she offered your assistance, but really I'm fine."

"She was pretty sure you'd say that too," he said and turned to look out the window. "The rusted blue Camry, right?" Without waiting for a response, he moved to the door.

"Wait!" she cried and struggled to stand up. It took her a

second and once she was up, his eyes widened at the sight of her belly and he held up a hand.

"Oh Christ," he said, his calm definitely shaken now. "Sit back down!"

"I'm pregnant, not helpless." But damn, she was dizzy from getting up too fast.

He came around and got ahold of her. "Whoa," he said. "Are you okay?"

"I'm fine."

"Low blood sugar? Do you need food?"

Yes and yes, not that she was going to say so. "I said I was fine," she snapped and pulled free. "My diet's fine. My baby's fine. And as it's my stuff out there, I'm going with you."

He looked her over, scrubbing a hand over his scruffy jaw, probably trying to determine just how serious she was.

She was as serious as a heart attack.

"Fine," he finally said and she gave him a point in his favor for accurately reading her level of determination. "You can point out the stuff you want moved. But you're not to touch *anything*, you understand me?"

"The way you didn't touch the wild horses?"

He slid her a look and gave a tiny hint of a smile. "Kitten's got claws," he said, sounding pleased.

"I do, and for your information, I'm not going to *not* touch my own stuff."

He nodded as if he'd expected that answer and took off his baseball cap with one hand, shoving his other through his military-short dark hair so that it stood up on end. The guy had clearly been working hard, probably all day, and was gleaming with sweat. "Cora's gonna kill me," he muttered and jammed his hat back on his head and strode out the door.

She assumed she was to follow, so she did. At her car, he stopped and looked in.

"Is this all of it?" he asked.

When she didn't answer right away, he turned toward her in question. Whatever he saw in her face softened the hard lines of his and he came toward her.

She backed up a step.

He stopped on a dime and went hands up. "You're looking a little flushed is all," he said quietly. "I just want you to back up a few more feet and sit on that bench, okay? You can boss me around from there just as well if that's your plan."

She sank with gratitude to the bench. "I'm not bossy."

He laughed a little, which confused her.

"You're doing all this for me," she said, baffled. "And I don't even know your name."

"Holden." Without asking her name in return, he opened the car door and grabbed the suitcase she'd been living out of. She had her purse on her, which left just a small backpack with a few essentials. He grabbed that as well and then went to pop the trunk.

"There's nothing else," she said.

He nodded. "I'll take this stuff to your cottage and then you can give me your address and I'll go get whatever else—"

"No, there's nothing else," she repeated softly. "As in . . . nothing else."

He paused, and she told herself if he looked at her with so much as even a single ounce of pity, she'd have to smack him with her purse, which was heavy as shit.

But he simply nodded. "Pretty *and* she packs light," he said. "I like it."

She had no idea how to respond to that, but the butterflies

in her belly did, taking flight. Holden showed her to her cabin, pointing out some landmarks on the way, such as the actual winery, the not-wild horses the family kept, the wide-open fields that to River were just about the most beautiful scenery she'd ever laid eyes on.

At her door, Holden pulled a key from his pocket, unlocked the place, and then handed the key to her. Then he shouldered his way in, strode to the small loveseat against the far wall, and set her things down. He looked around. "Never been in this one. It's nice, yeah?"

She took in the very small place with a kitchenette and a full-sized bed with bedding that looked soft and inviting and felt a weight lift off her chest that she hadn't even realized was there. "It's the most beautiful place I've ever seen."

The minute the words left her mouth, she felt embarrassed, but he simply nodded his agreement.

"I know exactly what you mean," he said, and then paused at the door.

She braced herself for him to do something stupid like every man she'd ever met, but all he said was, "If you need anything else, I'm three cottages down on the right. Cottage number two."

She ignored the flutter in her belly at that, telling herself it was just the baby. "Thanks," she said, and then with a gruff nod, he was gone.

That night, River lay in her comfy bed in her adorable cottage and shook her head. Guilt was her bedmate, but even she had to add, it was a hell of a lot better than being cold and hungry.

The baby kicked and she rubbed a hand over her belly. "I know," she murmured. "I can't believe it either. But there will be a price for this. There always is."

Chapter 5

It's rude to interrupt my anxiety with your positive thoughts.

By the time Mark finally dragged his sorry ass home from work several days later, it was six in the morning and he was dead on his feet after a disastrous, tragic pileup on Highway 5 that had left fifteen dead. He walked in the front door of the huge Capriotti family home and went straight to the kitchen.

He needed food, sleep, and some mind-numbing sex. Since only the first had any chance of actually happening, he opened the fridge and hit the mother lode.

The one bonus about coming back here to live so his girls would have family around during his crazy work schedule was that his mom and sisters loved to cook. And since they also seemed to think that the way to show love was through food, even more so since his dad had died a few years back after a shockingly short battle with cancer, there was always, *always* more food in the fridge than an army could consume.

He started pulling out containers, shifting mental gears from work to the state of affairs of his life. Being back here had never been part of his plan. He'd been career military, thriving on the danger and adrenaline. He'd been away from home for long stretches of time, but he knew that it'd been exactly that that kept his family intact.

His absence.

But that'd actually been just an illusion, one that had come crumbling down around him.

So here he was. Back in Wildstone. There wasn't a lot of action going on around here—unless you counted the occasional bar fight at the Whiskey River Bar and Grill, or the even more occasional ghost sighting at the B&B up the road.

The ghost actually made sense. Wildstone had been through several reincarnations in the past century and a half. In the 1890s, there'd been clapboard sidewalks and local silver mines, which had brought in a row of saloons and whorehouses. By the mid-1900s, the town had attempted to legitimize itself and had done away with most of the whorehouses, though the saloons had stubbornly remained. Then the county had discovered winemaking and ranching, and the hills had become dotted with ranches and wineries, including his family's.

When the economy had taken a dive, the town had played up its infamous past, marketing the place as a Wild West ghost town, using the historical downtown buildings to draw in tourists. The stunning rolling hills and hidden beaches helped some, but being three and a half hours south of San Francisco and four hours north of Los Angeles put a damper on the place hitting it big.

In other words, Wildstone was still a sleepy town, emphasis on *sleepy*. And if he was very lucky and played his cards right and kissed all the right asses as deputy sheriff, maybe, *maybe*, he could become sheriff of Wildstone. Someday.

Be still, his beating heart. He shook his head at the disparity of being sheriff compared to what he'd hoped for and kept digging in the fridge. Maybe nothing about the way his life had turned out was what he'd planned, not even close, but his girls needed him here. He wouldn't, couldn't, stay his course and let them be parentless. Which meant he'd deal with it. This was his life now. Being Dad.

Alyssa came into the kitchen, a diaper bag slung over one shoulder, Elsa's baby carrier balancing her on the other side, and her two boys, Chase and Tanner, bringing up the rear. The boys flashed Mark a fast grin and ran off to play. Alyssa set the baby on the kitchen table and turned to him. "There's an interesting rumor about you and Lanie."

Quiet but not shy, pretty in a girl-next-door sort of way, smart, *and* talented Lanie. "Is there?"

"That you're . . . interested."

He kept his mouth shut.

"So is it true?" Alyssa asked.

Growing up in this family, he'd long ago learned to curb his emotional responses. Denials or admissions, it didn't matter, his family would think what they wanted. So he didn't even blink, just paused in his food mission to bend over Elsa and give her a kiss on the top of her soft, downy head.

The baby spit out her pacifier and gave him a drool-filled smile that caused one of his own—smiles, that is. Not drool. And then he went back to pulling out leftovers from whoever had cooked dinner last night. It could've been any of them—they all cooked like five-star chefs. It was a point of Capriotti pride.

But though Mark could cook too, he much preferred to eat.

Gracie, hearing the fridge, came running, expression hopeful.

"You deaf?" Alyssa asked when Mark grabbed a fork from

a drawer and began to eat standing up, leaning against the counter.

"Nope," he said, flipping a bite to Gracie, who caught it in midair with an easy snap of her jaws. The overgrown puppy couldn't turn a corner without running into a wall, but if food was involved, she had the grace and skill of an Olympic athlete.

"The vet said she's getting fat," Alyssa said.

"She's just right," Mark said.

Gracie gave him a look of pure adoration.

Alyssa looked on in disgust as Mark continued to inhale the cold food. "Dude, there's a microwave just behind you."

He shrugged. He was way too hungry to wait two minutes for the food to get heated.

Alyssa sighed, grabbed another plate, loaded it up, stuffed it into the microwave, and when it dinged, she took his plate, exchanging it for the hot one.

"Thanks," he said.

"Ulterior motive," she said and grabbed a fork and proceeded to share the goods.

"You okay?" he asked when the hunger had slowed down some and no longer threatened to eat him whole.

"I'm great," she said. "Now you."

"I'm fine."

She slid him a look. "You know Mom taught us to think before we act, so know that when I slap the shit out of you for lying to me that I thoroughly thought about it first." Setting down her fork, she drew in a deep breath. "Now I'm going to ask you again. *Are you okay?*"

He closed his eyes against the worry and concern in hers. "Working on it."

She sighed and set her head on his shoulder. "What can I do?"

"Nothing. You're already doing it."

"If I could kill Brittney, I would."

"Lyssa—"

"I would," she said fiercely. "For what she did to you. To your adorable babies."

"Stop," he said gently. "We're okay."

"You're not. You won't get serious again."

"And that's not a bad thing," he said. "It's about the girls now. Not me."

"So you're going to abstain from love until what, they turn eighteen?"

At the yes she saw on his face, she made a soft sound of distress and her eyes filled.

"Lyssa," he said again, pained.

"Ignore me," she whispered. "It's mostly baby hormones. I'm driving Owen insane."

"Just Owen?"

She made a half-hearted attempt to slug him, but since he'd been the one to teach her how to hit, it still hurt. "Owen's never going to stop loving you," he said. The guy had loved her since they'd met in second grade, although every time Alyssa had a baby, her emotions went haywire for months afterward, driving them all a little insane.

Suddenly came the sound of either elephants storming the house or his own two heathens up and looking for him. They tore into the kitchen, hair rioting around their heads, eyes still sleepy, wearing matching-footed Supergirl PJs.

His babies loved superheroes.

They had their mother's unruly curls in a softer version of the dark brown of his own hair. For the most part they also had their mother's temperament, which meant that their every thought and emotion showed all over their faces. "Hey," he said, his smile fading because as they leapt at him, climbing into his arms, he could see worry and fear and tears in their eyes. "What's wrong?"

"You're home!" Samantha said, voice muffled against his shoulder. "You're finally home. We waited all night for you."

He craned his neck and met his sister's gaze. She was just as confused as he. "What do you mean?" he asked. "You didn't sleep?"

Samantha shook her head, all her dark hair flying around her head like an explosion in a mattress warehouse. "We kept sneaking out of bed to check your room," she said. "Grandma almost caught us twice."

Sierra tapped her sister on the arm. Samantha met her gaze and they did that thing they did, the silent communication that only they could understand, before Sam turned back to Mark. "Sierra even fake-snored. She's better at it than me."

Sierra, her face once again buried in Mark's other shoulder, nodded and he tightened his grip on the only anchors in his always-spinning-too-fast world. From the corner of his eye he saw Alyssa pick up Elsa and leave the kitchen to give them privacy.

"Why didn't you call me?" he asked.

"Because you were mad at us for staying up past our bedtime the other night. And this was *very* past our bedtime," Sam said. "And maybe you were busy catching bad guys."

The dead organ in his chest rolled over and exposed its underbelly. "Listen to me, okay? If you're worried, you call me. If you need me, you call me. I don't care if I'm working, if I'm sleeping, or if you think I'm angry at you—if you need me, I'm there for you, do you understand?"

Samantha lifted her head and stared at him, her eyes just a little too old for her age. "Because that's your job as our daddy?"

"Because I love you," he said firmly.

AT MARK'S LOW, fiercely uttered words, Lanie stopped short in the doorway to the Capriottis' personal kitchen. She'd come to meet Cora by request. She hadn't expected to see Mark leaning back against the counter, looking hollow and exhausted to the bone, a daughter in each arm, eyes closed, his jaw pressed to the top of one of their little bedheads, explaining to them how much he loved them.

It was an intimate moment, private and . . . the most moving thing she'd ever seen.

"Daddy?" Samantha whispered. "Are you sorry you're not still The Force?"

Mark cupped her head and made her look at him. "What?"

"You had to leave *Star Wars* and come home to take care of us. You had to give up the fight."

Mark looked confused at first, and then he laughed softly and pressed his forehead to Samantha's. "Sweetness, *Star Wars* is a story. It's made-up. When you overheard whatever you overheard—which we'll circle back to in a minute and go over the eavesdropping rules for six-year-olds—it wasn't about *Star Wars*."

"It wasn't?"

"No. I was in the *Air* Force, which is one of the branches of our government's military. It means I was in the fight to keep America safe and whole. On *this* planet."

Sierra giggled and Mark was still smiling until Sam said, "But you gave up the Air Force for us. And it was a big, important job, Grandma said so. You had big, important things to do."

"Yes," he said. "But not as important as you two." He paused as if considering his words carefully. "I *wanted* to come home. I want you both to know that."

"You mean when Mommy left?" Sam asked. "And when Sierra stopped talking?"

"Yes," he said, his voice a little strained now. "When Mommy left you both in Arizona. The minute I found out, I came home to get you." He cupped Sierra's head, still pressed tightly to the crook of his neck. "I gave up that job for a better one—taking care of you two. You're the most important things in my life."

At that, Sierra lifted her head and stared into Mark's eyes and he stared back, like he was willing her to believe.

Lanie was literally glued to the hallway. She couldn't move. She knew she had absolutely no business standing there, but her feet had disconnected from her brain's control. And so had her heart, because it was thumping hard and fast. Her eyes were burning too. She'd let him think she'd misjudged him and that was as bad as actually doing it. It also made her feel uncomfortably like her mom, who was very quick to judge and even quicker to cut someone out of her life.

"More important than the vines?" Samantha was asking her dad. "Because Great-Grandpa says *nothing* is more important than the vines."

"Baby, you're *way* more important than the vines."

"More important than Grandma?"

"Yes," Mark said. "But don't tell her."

"More important than—"

"Anything," Mark broke in to say. "Anything, Samantha. You and Sierra are my life. You get me?"

The twins nodded and he kissed each of their foreheads and set them down. "We good?" he asked.

"We good," Samantha said and fist-bumped him.

Sierra did the same. Mark caught Sierra's hand and reeled her in once more, rubbing his nose to hers in an Eskimo kiss that made her giggle. "You know, don't you, sweetness, that you can talk to me. Right?"

Sierra bobbed her head.

"Okay, then." He let her go and she went running off after Samantha. He waited until she'd vanished out the side door before turning and landing his gaze right on Lanie.

"I'm sorry," she said.

"For eavesdropping again?"

Feeling like a jerk, she shook her head. "No, although I'm sorry about that too." She paused. "I've been rude, I think."

"You think, or you know?"

His tone said he was teasing, but she still blew out a sigh. "I know." She was too nervous for this. Cora had asked her to meet for breakfast to go over some of the preliminary sample designs she'd come up with before presenting them to the rest of the family. The pressure of creating effective graphic design and branding for the wide variety of products the winery provided was starting to keep Lanie awake at night. She needed both eye-catching and inspirational designs to encourage customers to bring the product home. She hoped she'd done that. She wasn't sure.

In either case, Cora had dangled the carrot of a homemade breakfast.

Since Lanie's usual choice of breakfast was a Pop-Tart and maybe an apple, she'd been suitably lured, hoping for bacon, feeling more excited about the prospect of that than anything in recent memory. "I really am sorry," she said softly.

Mark stared at her for a long beat and then, though she had

no idea why—maybe it was because she knew she looked so miserable at her mistake—he shrugged. "It doesn't matter."

"It does, I—"

"Forget it," he said and began rifling through some open food containers on the counter.

"Why is there enough tension in here to give me a headache?" Cora asked, coming in behind Lanie.

Lanie jumped and opened her mouth to explain, before realizing her boss was talking to her son.

Mark snorted and grabbed a box of Frosted Flakes cereal before striding out of the room without calling Lanie out for being the rude one.

Cora watched him go, pensive. "Sometimes I forget he's still adjusting to civilian life." She turned to face Lanie. "I'm not going to apologize for him because he's been through hell and back. Several times. I know his heart is in the right place so instead, I'm going to ask you for understanding and compassion to see past his alpha asshole-ness."

"You don't have to ask me for anything of the sort," Lanie said. "It wasn't what you think."

Cora wasn't ready to let it go. "He did three tours of duty. He's only thirty-two, but can you imagine the things he's seen and done?" She took a deep, shuddery breath and her eyes went suspiciously shiny. "It's awful what we as a country ask of our men and women who serve. But we do ask, and they answer. Mark was good at what he did, very good. He'd just been promoted when his wife of four years took off." Her lips tightened. "Just up and vanished on her babies. That was nearly a year ago now. He took the deputy sheriff position because he is who he is, but it's not the same as what he was doing, and it's certainly not what he wanted."

Lanie's heart hurt for them. After all, she knew a little bit about being betrayed. "That's awful."

"Turned out, Brittney thought being a mom was too hard. She's living in some ashram in Australia finding herself these days, letting the universe fill her cup." She shook her head. "He won't thank me for telling you any of this, but I wanted you to understand."

"I do."

Cora gave her a small smile. "I know what we look like, from the outside looking in. Busybodies, noisy, stubborn, the entire lot of us. But we're more too."

Lanie nodded. "I know."

"Do you?"

"Yes."

Cora smiled. "Is your family big and intruding too?"

"Actually, no."

"So they're not crazy."

"Well, I didn't say that," Lanie said. Her amusement faded. "It's just my parents, and we're . . . estranged." Except it wasn't anything as concrete as that, really. Her parents were . . . remote, too focused on themselves and their careers and always had been. A child hadn't changed that—in fact, according to her mom, it'd only made things worse. Not a surprise, given the circumstances. "So, big and intruding and nosy or whatever you want to call yourselves," she said, "at least you're all connected by blood and stay close and that's . . . amazing to me." She paused. "And maybe also baffling. And a little scary to boot."

Cora's smile reached her eyes and warmed them as she took Lanie's hand. "There's one more thing you should know."

"What's that?"

"It's not blood that connects us. Which means you're a part of us now." And then, leaving Lanie speechless, she proceeded to make the most wonderful crepes she'd ever had in less than fifteen minutes—and bacon!—after which they worked at the kitchen table for hours, poring over what Lanie had so far.

Work and family. Family and work. It was all the same here, and that was just beginning to sink in.

Chapter 6

The human body is 90 percent water, so basically we're all just cucumbers with anxiety.

Over the next week, Lanie learned something about herself that she'd not paid any attention to in the past. She liked her work, a lot. But something odd was happening to her resolve of remaining emotionally distant.

She found herself sucked into the daily life of this beautiful place. And not just with the twins either, although they spent a lot of time underfoot. Literally. They loved Lanie's shoes—one of her vices—so they were constantly coming in after school to see which pair she was wearing that day, waiting to try them on. Lanie had actually brought in two spare sets to her desk today so the twins could each wear a pair at the same time, although she'd had to chase Gracie away from stealing them—twice. She'd finally gone back to her cottage for a pair of her old sneakers and given them to the dog.

Emotionally distant, her ass . . .

The offices were ramping up for the upcoming tourist and wedding season, and everyone was working hard. Uncle Jack's very spoiled teenage twin grandkids were working as office assistants and Mia had them running ragged, as she was overworked herself. When they complained that she was being mean, Mia brought Holden into the office.

He was a good-looking guy in his early twenties and in his prime, though at the moment he appeared to be done in. He wore jeans, a white T-shirt covered in various stains, was sunburned, and looked like he needed a nap and a burger and not in any particular order. "What can I do for you?" he asked Mia in a polite voice.

Mia looked at her cousins while jabbing a finger at Holden. "There," she said. "Did you hear that?"

"Yes," one of them said. "He's got a southern accent. It's cute. He's cute. Twice this week we've seen him trying to make friends with River, but she's mean to him. We wanted to be . . . *not* mean to him. But Grandpa told us if we tried to date him he'd take away our phones."

Holden grimaced but didn't say anything, just looked at Mia, brows raised. Waiting.

Mia shook her head at her cousins in disbelief. "So you're disrespectful on top of spoiled." She sighed. "Just like me. But unlike me, you're not going to take another decade to get things right. Holden is one of our best employees."

Holden looked a little surprised at this.

"He works his ass off," Mia said. "He's been at it since four thirty this morning and he should be off work now, but you know what? I called and he came in to ask me how he could help. That's pride of workmanship and dedication, and it's rewarded here. But those rewards have to be earned. Go tell Owen that I sent you out there to scrub barrels."

They both opened their mouths in protest, but Mia lifted a hand and said, "File your complaints with someone who cares. I'm done with you in these offices today. Come back when you understand hard work." She waited until they were gone. "I'd pray for strength and patience," she said to Lanie. "But then I'd need to pray for bail money too." Then she turned to Holden. "How's that new truck?"

For the first time he dropped his deadpan expression and grinned, and Lanie saw a glimpse of his personality.

"Fuckin' rocks," he said. "I can't believe your mom and Grandpa got it for me."

"Our horse wrangler needs a truck for his image." Mia tossed him a soda from the fridge, and he thanked her and left. When he was gone, Mia said, "He's a great kid."

"He's not a kid, he's your age," Lanie said.

"I know. And I've had a crush on him since he first showed up here at age fifteen, beaten half to death and on his own." She lifted a shoulder. "You know my mom, she collects lost souls. So she took him in and he's been family ever since. Just about broke her heart when he went into the army two years ago, but he said he had to find his own way. He's on leave for another month-ish."

"So you no longer have a crush on him?"

"Oh, I do," Mia said. "But Mom long ago told me that if I ever slept with him, she'd take away my phone."

Lanie laughed. "So you really do get your cousins."

"Yep."

Lanie shook her head. "But I'm pretty sure no one tells you what to do."

"There's that . . ." Mia looked at the door where Holden had vanished and sighed. "But he's done being wild and I'm just getting going. I don't want to be reined in."

Cora poked her head in. "Scrubbing barrels?" she asked.

Mia sighed. "Those little tattletales. I suppose you want me to go easier on them."

"On the contrary," Cora said. "Holden caught them smoking weed in the storage shed yesterday so I vote for doubling whatever workload you've got for them. My favorite punishment is making them work in the barn with their hands tied together so they learn teamwork." Then she winked at them both and left.

Lanie went to bed early, tired but . . . feeling pretty good. She was actually starting to enjoy herself here. Yeah, the winery was like a small town, complete with the gossip mill, and lunch continued to be a daily telenovela, but at least she was no longer the New Girl. River had fallen into that role. Oddly enough, Lanie was pretty sure River was avoiding her at all costs, but that didn't bother Lanie any. The girl was young, apparently very alone, and the Capriottis had gathered her to their collective bosom.

Not a surprise, given who Cora was. "She's a baby having a baby," she'd told Lanie quietly that first day. "She was living out of her car and I think she's running away from something. Or someone."

Say what you wanted about the Capriottis, but they were a protective, loyal bunch and they rallied around their own.

Unlike Lanie, River took to the attention, easily embracing the family. Lanie had to admire the spirit, but she was still happy at the farthest corner of the farthest table. She'd gone back to eating her bagged lunches. She'd had to, for the sake of her clothes. Nobody liked it and they teased her about it, but . . . they let her be.

And that was the thing she was just starting to understand.

As busybody and in everyone's business as they were, they understood individuality.

As often as he could manage, Mark showed up, blowing in like a wild force of nature, looking badass in his uniform as he accepted a huge plate of food from one of his sisters or his mom, shoved his lunch in his mouth, loved up on his girls, and blew back out again.

Which was a relief. For whatever reason, he just wasn't as easy to ignore as the rest of the Capriottis, especially as he was cool and distant now, not giving her that flirty smile as he had at first.

She deserved that. She'd earned that. And it was exactly how she wanted things. At least she believed it during the days, but the long, lonely nights . . . they told her something else entirely.

Which she steadfastly ignored.

One afternoon at the end of her third week, she was deep in computer mode, working on the different specs required for the variety of media she was creating, from billboards to boxes to sell sheets to stationery, when she realized her neck was burning like maybe she was being watched. Lifting her head, she found four eyes on her.

Sam and Sierra were leaning against the far corner of her desk. "You two need to wear bells," she said.

Samantha smiled. "Grandma says that too!"

Sierra nodded and Lanie felt her own smile curve her mouth. Sierra had gone from never making eye contact to actually smiling at her. She still hadn't spoken, but then again, there probably was no real need when Samantha spoke at one hundred miles per hour for all of them. "You two aren't my Secret Santa, are you?" she asked. She nudged her chin toward a mug of coffee that had appeared on her desk when she'd gone on break. And it hadn't been the first time either. She owed someone a most heartfelt thank-you. "Someone keeps leaving me a new coffee with three sugars in it, just the way I like it."

"We're not allowed to touch the coffeemaker," Sam said. "Not since the time we put peanut butter and chocolate chips in it to try and make a peanut butter hot chocolate. It sorta exploded."

"Okay," Lanie said. "Good to know."

"That's what I told Grandma, but she still got mad. We've got a question."

"I don't know how to make peanut butter hot chocolate," Lanie said.

"No," Sam said. "We want to know where babies come from."

Lanie choked on the coffee her Secret Santa had left her, spilling it down the front of herself.

Sierra patted her sweetly on the back and silently offered her a napkin.

Samantha just waited patiently for her answer.

"You know," Lanie finally said, swiping her chin. "Maybe this is a question for your dad."

"Oh, we're going to ask him too, but Tommy at school just told us a gross story about how his dog pooped out her puppies and that it was really, really icky. Do you think that human babies get pooped out too?"

God help her. "Uh . . ."

Luckily she didn't have to figure out an end to that sentence because Mark himself appeared in the doorway. He took one look at his girls crawling all over her desk and looked pained. "What have I told you about leaving Miss Lanie alone?"

"*Daddy, Daddy, Daddy!*" Samantha shouted in glee. "Miss

Lanie was just about to tell us where human babies come from!"

Mark's brows arched so high they vanished into his hairline and he too took a stance leaning against her desk, all long and leanly muscled, armed to the teeth, his expression mockingly expectant. "Was she now?"

Lanie narrowed her eyes, but all he did was smirk, the ass.

"'Cuz, Daddy! Tommy said his dog pooped out her babies! But we're not borned like that, right? Where did we come from?"

Mark's expression softened as he picked her up and swung her around to hang off his back piggy-back style. Then he reached his arms out for Sierra, who took a flying leap for him. "You both came straight from heaven," he said.

This invoked peals of giggles, and then Sam had one more question. "Daddy, will I have kids from heaven too?"

"Someday," he said. Then he paused. "Just promise me you'll ignore boys who text you after eleven o'clock at night."

"Well, duh," she said. "I'm sleeping then."

Mark smiled and he turned to the door to leave, but paused, looking back at Lanie.

"Sorry for the intrusion," he said.

"They're never an intrusion," she said and was shocked to realize she meant it.

He registered her words with a single nod of his head. Then he walked out with the girls, one upside down and one right side up, both beaming from ear to ear and absolutely not tugging at her cold, hard heart.

But only a little tug, she told herself. She needed to remember why she was here. To reset her life after Kyle had detonated it. With his $100,000 life-insurance policy payout in her bank account, she'd had the luxury of making this temporary change to recover. *Not* to get involved in these people's lives.

Period.

It was near the end of the day when Lanie walked by the front reception room and found River looking more green than the grass out front. River was still keeping her distance, so Lanie's first instinct was to keep walking, but she couldn't do it. "Hey, you okay?"

River held up a finger, closed her eyes, and did some deep breathing while rubbing her belly.

"Do you need a doctor?"

"No!" River drew in a careful breath. "I can't afford one right now, but I'm okay and so's the baby. I just still get morning sickness all day sometimes—" She broke off and moaned a little, and if possible went even greener. When the desk phone beside her rang, she moaned again and grabbed the trash can.

Oh shit, Lanie thought, wanting to take a big step backward. And maybe two weeks ago she'd have done just that, but one thing working here had taught her, they were a team.

Dammit.

So she leaned past River hunched miserably over her trash can and grabbed the phone. "Capriotti Winery."

"You're supposed to say how can I help you?" River managed to whisper.

"How can I help you?" Lanie added into the phone.

"Yeah, hi," came a nasally female voice. "I'd like to book a wedding for this coming Saturday for me and my husband. Well, husband-to-be. Okay, so he doesn't know he's my husband-to-be—he hasn't asked me yet, but he's going to.

Tonight, if he knows what's good for him. But in any case, I want to book our wedding for Saturday."

Lanie didn't know much about running the front desk, but she knew this much. "We're booked out the next six months of Saturdays."

"Okay, fine, we'll take Sunday. Or Friday, but I'd expect a deep discount to get married on Friday, so—"

"No," Lanie said. "All days are booked out six months."

"Are you shittin' me?"

Lanie looked over at River, who'd gotten her color back somewhat. Or at least she'd gone from green to a sort of opal. River shook her head and Lanie said into the phone, "Nope, I'm not 'shittin' you,' we're booked solid."

River let out a horrified laugh and shook her head *no* a little frantically.

"Well, that's just crap!" the bride-to-be said in Lanie's ear. "I'm going to stop drinking your wines immediately!"

Click.

Lanie shrugged and set the phone down. "Her loss. We make some damn fine wine. Do you deal with this stuff all day long?"

"Well, not exactly like that," River said. "You're supposed to be nicer."

"She hung up on me."

"I take it you've never been in a customer service job, like waitressing."

Lanie shook her head.

"You're supposed to make the customers happy."

"Well, I'm pretty sure she was a lost cause." Lanie pulled her blueberry-vanilla snack bar from her pocket and handed it over to River.

"What's this?" River asked.

"It'll give you a little energy boost and maybe soothe your tummy while it's at it."

River shook her head. "I can't take your snack."

"Sure you can, as I took it from the basket in the staff room. You need to keep a little something in your stomach."

River stared at her. "Why are you helping me?"

Lanie didn't quite understand the question. "Because I really wanted the chocolate chip bar anyway, so now I can just go back and—"

"You answered the phone for me. You gave me your snack."

"Yeah," Lanie said slowly. "That's what they do here, help each other."

"It's just . . . not what I'm used to," River said very quietly.

And Lanie, who kept promising herself not to get attached to anyone except the twins—and kept failing spectacularly, by the way—sighed because she felt her heart squeezing yet again. "Honestly? Me either," she admitted. "But this is a good place. And good people. You're safe here—you know that, right?"

River broke the eye contact just as the mail carrier came in with a huge stack of mail. He smiled at River and tossed her a package. "Looks like you got another one," he said and winked.

"Another what?" Lanie asked.

"Someone keeps sending me baby stuff from different online stores. And books too." She hugged the package to her chest.

Alyssa arrived with steam coming out of her ears. "You know what's sucky?" she asked the room. "When your husband asks if you're mad at him and you say no and he *believes you*!"

River and Lanie looked at each other in confusion.

"Let me spell it out for you," Alyssa said. "I'm never speaking to my husband again." And then she proceeded to go lock herself in the employee room.

Which wouldn't have been a problem except for the fact that both the refrigerator and the copy machine were in that room. Lanie, needing both her snack and some copies made, was the first to discover Alyssa's shut-in.

"Go away," Alyssa called through the door. "Especially if your name is Owen."

"It's not," Lanie said. Her stomach growled. "Maybe you could just hand me a—"

"Not until you tell Owen that he's never going to get laid again."

"He's not here."

"Then text him."

Lanie blew out a breath. "Alyssa—"

"Text him!" And then she rattled off his phone number.

River came up next to Lanie. "I need to make copies," she said.

"No one's making copies!" Alyssa yelled through the door.

River looked at Lanie.

Lanie sighed and pulled out her phone and texted Owen: *Your wife has gone over the edge.*

The return text was immediate: *Baby hormones are a bitch.*

"Well?" Alyssa demanded. "What did he say? Did you tell him he was never getting laid again? *Ever?*"

Lanie didn't answer because she was busy texting Owen back: *If you value your future sex life, you might want to come down here.*

This time she got no answer.

"Well?" Alyssa demanded. "What did he say?"

"I'm waiting to hear."

"Husbands are dumb," Alyssa said. "Men are dumb."

"Not all of them," Lanie said. "Some are good."

"Which was your husband? Good or dumb?"

River seemed to be hanging on whatever answer Lanie had, but she wasn't going to touch that one, not when the truth was she'd married a man who'd appeared too good to be true and she should've realized she was buying a really great act. But he'd taken out the trash and he'd made her laugh, and she'd settled for a lot less than she'd meant to. "I thought he was a good guy, but it turns out I was wrong," she admitted. "Very wrong. But Alyssa, I've seen Owen with you. He really is one of the good ones."

"Yeah." Alyssa sighed. "I know. Did he respond?"

No. So Lanie decided to wing it. "He said he loves you very much and that the two of you can work this out in private, somewhere other than the employee room," she said, grimacing at River, who was still standing there, now wide-eyed and slack-jawed, presumably impressed by her lying skills.

"Oh." Alyssa sounded somewhat mollified. "Did he say anything else?"

"Uh . . ." She looked at River, who bit her lower lip and gave her a *say more* gesture. Lanie closed her eyes and thought about what she might want to hear from the love of her life. But here was the problem: she'd never had a *real* love of her life.

Oh, Kyle had played the part. He'd romanced her—hard too. And he'd been good at it. But the thing was, love wasn't in the bouquet of flowers or the romantic, candle-lit dinners. It was in the everyday stuff, like knowing when your person was tired and needed help, understanding what made them tick, what to do to soothe and comfort.

How to be at their back when their back was up against a wall.

She knew from what she'd seen of Alyssa and Owen that they had that kind of love. So she made it all up. "He wants to take you out, just the two of you, somewhere special where he can tell you how attractive and gorgeous and amazing you are."

"We don't have a babysitter."

Okay, so she shouldn't have, but she couldn't seem to help herself. "Your brother said he'd babysit."

An almost inaudible snort had her turning around. Mark stood next to River in full uniform, arms crossed, dark sunglasses on, looking intimidating as hell. At just the sight of him, River let out a little squeak of surprise and/or terror and took a step toward Lanie. Lanie slipped her hand in hers and squeezed lightly.

"Do I need to haul you in for lying your cute ass off?" Mark asked Lanie, his tone sardonic and maybe slightly amused.

She simply pointed to the still-closed door. "This is on you."

"Me?" He removed his sunglasses and gave a look of disbelief. "How do you figure?"

"You've got a penis, don't you?"

River let out a horrified, choked laugh and covered her mouth.

Mark didn't take his eyes off Lanie. "I do in fact have a penis."

River pulled free of Lanie's hand. "I've gotta go back to my desk." And then she vanished faster than an almost seven months' pregnant woman should be able to move.

"I'm out too," Lanie said. "You people are exhausting!" With that, she stalked through the place, heading toward the office, where she worked for a few hours without pause. Finally her stomach told her it was going to riot if she didn't put something in it. She looked up and realized everyone was gone for the day. Telling herself to just grab another snack so she could finish up the last of her stuff for the day, she ran to the employee room and took another bar. When she got back to her desk, Uncle Jack was there. Baby Elsa was in her baby seat on top of Lanie's desk, her eyes screwed shut, her mouth wide open as she wailed at top decibel, her tiny fists waving in the air as she let anyone and everyone within a twenty-mile radius know that she was one seriously pissed-off baby.

"Sorry," Jack said, standing, saying something that couldn't be heard over the sheer volume of the baby's cries.

"What?" Lanie yelled.

"I took on babysitting but I can't get her to be quiet. I've tried everything!" he yelled back.

"I thought Mark was in charge!"

"I told him I wanted to do it! I was clearly temporarily insane!"

Just then Mark appeared and did what he did best—took charge. He leaned in and scooped up the baby. "What's the fuss, cute stuff?" the big, bad, tough sheriff crooned softly, his fingers tracing the outlines of Elsa's cheeks, wiping away her tears.

She immediately stopped with the screaming to stare up at Mark in that total absorption babies have when they've encountered something new and exciting.

He laid her against his broad-as-a-mountain shoulder and patted her back.

Elsa burped once and beamed a drooly smile at Mark that could've melted the polar ice caps. She then went on to babble and coo at him, all while pumping and waving her arms and legs like a very happy camper.

He smiled at her and kissed her forehead.

This caused a long string of "goo-goo-ba-ba" before Elsa stuck her thumb in her mouth.

Both Lanie and Uncle Jack stared at Mark, probably with the exact same absorption Elsa had. "How?" Jack asked.

Mark shrugged as the baby's tiny hand gripped one of his fingers in a baby death grip, like she was never letting him go.

Lanie couldn't blame her. She probably wouldn't want to let go either. Also, she was stunned. Was no female on earth immune to the Capriotti charm?

As if he could read her thoughts, he gave her a steady gaze that did funny things to her insides she couldn't have explained to save her life.

"You've got the touch," Uncle Jack said.

No kidding, Lanie thought.

"It's like you're Batman, Superman, and Prince Charming all wrapped up in one," Uncle Jack said.

And Lanie couldn't help it, she snorted.

Mark grimaced and handed the baby back to Uncle Jack. He then took Lanie by the hand. "We've got a thing."

Chapter 7

Things that give me anxiety:
—everything
—people without anxiety

Lanie shook her head. She and Mark most definitely did not have a thing. At all. But he had her hand in his one hand and her purse in his other. He walked them through the offices, not looking even remotely silly with her purse swinging from his fingers.

"What are you doing?" she asked, ineffectively trying to free herself. "I'm working."

"It's nearly six thirty and you've been at your desk since early this morning. Twelve hours."

"How do you even know that?"

He shrugged a broad shoulder, not slowing down. "I had a really early shift, saw you frowning and swearing at your computer."

"I didn't see you."

"I know."

She gaped at his back. "You're the one who keeps leaving me coffee."

He didn't answer.

"How did you even know I like three sugars?"

"Because I pay attention," he said. "And by the way, that stuff'll kill you."

"Says the guy who inhales three pieces of lasagna and cheesy bread almost daily for lunch."

"See, you pay attention to me too."

"Whatever," she said. "And it's hard *not* to notice because you eat whatever you want and you still get to look like you do."

He smiled. "So you *do* like the way I look while you're pretending to hate me."

She sighed. "I don't hate you."

When he stopped walking, she nearly plowed into him, having to plant her other hand on his back, which was how she discovered that the promise of a great body he gave in clothes most *definitely* was true because beneath his shirt, he was solid, lean muscle.

When he gave a soft laugh, she realized they were standing in front of her cottage and she was still staring at his body, so she closed her eyes. "What are we doing, Mark?"

"You're going to go inside and get your bathing suit. We're going somewhere."

"Somewhere where?"

He let out a long breath and stared at his shoes for a beat, either trying to hold himself back from strangling her or trying not to laugh. "Are you always this difficult?"

"Yes," she said immediately. "And I'm not getting my bathing suit."

Because she didn't have one here—not that he needed to know this . . .

"Fine." Once more they were on the move. Two minutes later, they were out front and he was helping her into the passenger side of his big truck.

"I'm not going swimming, or whatever you have in mind—" she started.

He shut the door on her, rounded the front of the truck, and ambled in behind the wheel.

"Wow," she said.

He slid her a look. "I know enough about women to know that even when she says 'Wow' I should be shaking in my boots."

"So why aren't you?"

"Maybe I am."

She snorted. "Right. Like you're afraid of anything."

He shrugged. "You'd be surprised."

"Try me."

"I'm afraid of something happening to the people I care about," he said and slid her a look. "Including you."

"What else?" she asked, trying to ignore the flutter at the "including you" thing.

"Dating apps. And a woman saying 'Wow.'"

She laughed. "This is kidnapping, you know. You're an officer of the law and you're breaking that law."

He just flashed her a grin that, damn, was potent as hell. "You want to call 9-1-1?" He tossed her his phone. "Go for it."

"I have my own phone." But she looked down at his and swiped her thumb across the screen. "Passcode required."

They were on the highway now. "It's Sam and Sea," he said.

She had to try three times to get the code right. It was

SamNSea. "Sweet," she murmured, not liking that she thought so. Because now that she knew a little bit about him—things like the fact that he was a pretty amazing dad—something was happening to her inner decree not to like him.

Emotionally detach, she ordered herself, *no matter that he smells good and has a body you want to lick like an ice cream cone.* But instead of calling 9-1-1, she accessed his photos. Hey, he'd been stupid enough to let her into his phone . . . There weren't many pics. A few of a group of military guys, of which he was one. It wasn't odd to see him in uniform, armed to the teeth. But it *was* odd to see him in *military* uniform, face blank of emotion, standing tall and stoic.

Then there were pictures of the twins. More of those than his military life.

And . . . little else.

She went to his texts next. He had a few ongoing conversations. A group text with Samantha and Sierra, and another with some guys named Boomer and Mick, something about an upcoming fishing trip, and one with his mom.

"Looking for anything in particular?" he asked in a lazy, casual voice that told her he was amused, curious about her curiosity, and . . . had nothing to hide.

"No," she said, almost annoyed she couldn't find anything to fault.

He pulled into a Taco Bell and turned to her. "What's your poison?"

"You live at a winery that has the best food on the planet and you're choosing *this* for dinner?"

He shrugged. "I'm hungry. You want something or not?"

She sighed and leaned in over him to read the menu, ignoring the urge to press her nose to his throat and inhale the yummy scent that was one Mark Capriotti. "Three Taco Supremes, nachos, and an order of Cinnabons," she said. She sank back into her seat and sneaked a peek at his face.

He was fighting a smile.

"You have a problem with my order?" she asked.

"Hell, no." He turned to the window. "Double that order, please, and add a few chalupas."

Gaze still locked on his because she couldn't seem to tear it away, she did her best to shrug casually. "Decent choice in food," she gave him.

He laughed.

"This is still kidnapping, you know," she informed him after he'd paid and taken them back on the road.

"Noted," he said, and ten minutes later pulled into a deserted parking lot.

"Uh-oh." She looked around. Green rolling hills, all wild grass, gorgeous sprawling oak trees reaching to the sky. No one for as far as the eye could see. "You're going to let me eat before you murder me, right?"

"Absolutely."

She snorted and he gave her a look that, well . . . made her damp in places that had no business going damp. Then he grabbed the food and got out of the truck.

"Hey," she said.

He shut the door. She watched him walk off and said "Hey" again, not that he could hear her. "You're not going to follow him," she said out loud. "No way." She really wasn't. But . . . she was hungry.

Dammit.

Rolling her eyes at herself, she got out of the truck and looked around. Ahead of her was nothing but a set of bluffs as far as the eye could see and . . . a set of long, steep stairs that led straight down to a beach.

The sun was close to setting, which meant that the entire horizon was on fire in glorious golds and reds, making everything look soft and beautiful.

Mark had walked over to a rocky cliff overhang and sat, his feet dangling over the ledge. He reached into the bag and grabbed a taco and a hot sauce packet, which he poured liberally over the taco. Then he did a wash-and-repeat with a second sauce.

"Hope you're saving some of those for me," she said.

"There's two kinds of people out here. The quick and the hungry. Learned that early at home."

Not wanting to be one of the hungry ones, she moved toward him. He gestured with a jerk of his chin for her to sit.

Which she did, keeping a healthy eye to the edge, where she most definitely did not hang her feet like he did. He handed her the bag, letting her choose what she wanted from it. "I'm trying to picture the insulted expression on your mom's face over our dinner choice," she said.

He snorted. "Don't let her fool you. I caught her last week at McDonald's inhaling a Big Mac and large fries. It was a long-standing joke date between her and my dad; they'd sneak out once a week for Mickey D's and sit on the beach and eat alone together. They did that for three decades until he died a few years ago." He said this with clear affection and something inside her melted a little bit.

"I'm sorry about your dad."

"Thanks. Me too." He caught her look and cocked his head. "So is your mom as batshit crazy as mine?"

"Yes, but not the nice kind of crazy. More like . . ." She mimed shooting herself in the head with one hand, using the other to simulate her brains flying out of her head.

He went brows up.

"It's a long story," she said.

"I like stories."

She grabbed a taco and two hot sauce packets and saw his mouth twitch. For that she took a third sauce. "Thirty years ago my mom and dad were having a bunch of problems. So she boinked the mail carrier and got knocked up. With me, in case that wasn't clear. Mr. Mail Carrier moved across the country without a forwarding address."

"What the hell."

She shrugged it off, or at least pretended to. "It is what it is."

"What it is, is fucked up."

"Yeah, well, my mom had that sort of effect on men," she said dryly. "And somehow she convinced my dad—the one she was married to, not the biological one—to stay. I think her inheritance from her grandma helped a lot. But there wasn't enough money to make them forget how I came to be."

She felt the weight of his stare but didn't look at him, instead carefully adding that third sauce to one of her tacos like she was Picasso.

"How young were you when you learned all this?" he asked.

"Five."

"Jesus, Lanie."

She'd wanted to hear him use that gentle voice on her, but *not* because he felt sorry for her.

"Don't take this the wrong way," he said. "But your parents sound like dicks."

She laughed, surprised to find it was genuine. "It wasn't just them, it was me too. I don't really trust love, and so people don't tend to go all in with me."

He opened his mouth, his expression a fierce intent that made her throat tighten uncomfortably. Not ready to hear whatever it was he had to say, she pushed the bag of food toward him. "If you don't think I can eat all of these Cinnabons myself, you're mistaken."

Getting the message, he humored her and let the subject drop. He was on his last Cinnabon when he eyed hers. She hugged them to her chest and he laughed. And his laugh caused her to laugh as well, which reminded her she still had no idea what was going on. "What are we doing here, Mark?"

He swallowed his last bite and looked off into the water. "When I was young, I'd ride my bike out here whenever my family pissed me off. Which was just about all the time."

"Your family is . . ." She stopped, searching for the right word.

His mouth curved sardonically. "Interfering? Nosy? Obstinate?"

"Wonderful," she said quietly.

He let out a long exhale and removed his sunglasses, tossing them aside before turning to her. "I know. And after what I went through in my marriage, I've never been so grateful for them as I am these days."

"Your wife ran off."

He nodded. "I made a stupid choice. She was young and spoiled, which didn't matter to me because she was beautiful and fun and a good time. Then I was sent overseas and she was alone and pregnant with twins. And then she was still alone and dealing with two babies. I was no help at all—"

"You were overseas," she said, unable to stop from defending him. "Working for our country."

"I was."

"So what did she expect you to do? Quit? You don't just quit."

"I reupped when I was with her," he said. "That was a choice I made, thinking she preferred it when I was gone, but as it turns out it was a bad choice. She bailed and I ended up having to come back."

"You didn't have to," she said. "You chose to. And it sounds like she's the one who chose to quit and leave you and her own children. Who does that?"

He laughed roughly and shook his head. "Who doesn't see it coming?"

She stared at him. "You think you're at fault."

"I am," he said. "At least for part of it. I thought I knew her."

"Yeah, well, people can hide in plain sight," she said grimly. "You think you know someone, you think it's safe to love them, and . . ." She clamped her mouth shut.

He met her gaze, his own dark one warm and curious. "Personal experience?"

"Maybe. Just a little." She shook her head and turned to look out over the water. "So this is your happy place?"

"Yeah."

"Are you happy?"

He didn't answer for a long time. Instead, he searched the bag, found one last chalupa, and took his time eating it, so she thought maybe the conversation was over.

"That would've been better with another sauce on it," he said. "But someone bogarted them all."

She lifted a shoulder. "Be quick or be hungry."

He laughed again and she realized she could get addicted to that sound very fast.

"I *wasn't* happy here," he said after a minute, surprising her. "Not for a long time after I came back. I was career military. I was good at what I did and I craved the adrenaline rush and the sense of accomplishment. I was angry and bitter and pissed off."

"What changed?" she asked.

"Not much on the inside." He gave her a wry grimace. "But Samantha and Sierra . . . they're the opposite of angry and bitter."

"I've noticed," she said with a low laugh.

"They lost their mom. The last thing they needed was an angry asshole for a dad."

"You fake it pretty good."

He toasted her with his soda in thanks. "You were married too," he said.

She nodded.

"You're divorced?"

"No. I'm a widow."

Mark didn't show a lot of emotion; he was good at hiding himself. Real good. But there was a flash of shock. "I'm sorry. I didn't know."

"But you did know I take three sugars."

He didn't smile or let her joke this away. "How long ago?" he asked.

She shook her head. "It doesn't matter. If he hadn't died when he did, I'd have killed him myself." There. She said it out loud. And it only hurt a little. A dull pain really, sort of like a boulder barreling into her. "Probably shouldn't admit that to a cop, right?" she teased at his silence.

"I'm not a cop right now. And I wouldn't judge a murderous urge."

"Because you've had one or two?"

"Or a hundred trillion million," he said.

She choked out a laugh. He challenged her like no one else, and he was also fairly effortlessly dragging her past out of her. At least part of it. But there was no way she'd tell him what Kyle had done to her. That humiliation was all her own, thank you very much. "I'm not actually kidding, you know, about the murderous urge."

"Neither am I."

She nodded. Anger, she understood. Anger was a wall she'd built to protect herself. She knew that because she could feel the weight of the bricks she'd built around her heart. What she didn't know was how to tear it down.

When the food was gone, Mark gathered the trash, stood up, and tossed it into his truck. Then he moved to the back of the truck and pulled out two . . .

"Boogie boards?" she asked in surprise. "I haven't seen one of these since I was in high school."

"Found them in the storage unit at the winery," he said. "You wouldn't believe the amount of shit my mom's saved over the years."

"I'm not sure what your plan is," she said. "But I think I'll wait right here."

"And miss out on all the fun?"

"I didn't know you were into fun," she said.

"I have my moments."

She watched him start down the stairs to the beach, jogging easily on the balls of his feet, not looking back to see if she followed.

"You're not giving in to that unspoken dare," she told the evening.

The evening didn't have a comment.

He was halfway down the stairs now. She looked out at the water. The surf was a good three feet, and something about it lulled and drew her in. She didn't have a lot of happy childhood memories, but being in the ocean was one of them.

"Dammit," she said, and headed down the stairs. They were steep, the bluffs on either side wet from all the rains they'd had. It'd been a wet year, and it looked good on California. By the time her shoes hit the sand, the sun had set into the water, leaving the landscape cast in long black and blue shadows.

Mark still hadn't looked back. Near the water's edge, he kicked off his shoes and tossed the boards aside. His shirt came off next and as his hands went to his belt, she sucked in a breath.

At the sound, he looked over his shoulder, brows up in question.

"What are you doing?" she asked.

"Swimming."

"But . . ." She sputtered because he unzipped and kicked off his pants.

His pants!

He'd left his weapons and utility belt locked in his truck. Now the only thing the man wore was a pair of black knit boxers slung low enough on his hips to give her a heart-stopping view of his sleek, smooth back, marred with two scars, one of which looked like a bullet wound. Along the waistband of the boxers was a strip of paler skin, then a set of dimples and what she already knew was the best male ass she'd ever seen.

She felt rooted to the spot, torn between wanting him to

pull his pants back on and hoping he stripped out of the undies too.

He did neither, instead bending for one of the boards.

"*You're* not in a bathing suit," she managed.

He flashed her a badass grin that she felt from her hair to her toes and in every single good spot in between. "Since you didn't grab one, I didn't either. Didn't want you to feel lonely." And then he walked straight into the water, dove into a wave, and vanished.

She gasped and found her feet taking her to the water's edge, watching as he reemerged only to swim out even farther and then, when she could barely see him, he caught a wave. She could see flashes of him as he rode the boogie board like he'd been born to it, losing sight of him in between the swells.

Her heart was pounding in tune to the surf, which felt like it was flowing through her veins as she continued to watch him take his pleasure in the water. Before she knew what she was doing, she'd kicked off her shoes. She was in a stretchy knit tee and a lightweight gauzy skirt—her work clothes—trying to remember what undies she'd put on that morning. *God, please don't let them be laundry-day undies*. She took a peek down her own top. White sports bra. Okay, she could work with that as long as she didn't get cold. In other words, good luck. Her panties were cheeky cut and DayGlo bright pink. Welp, she wasn't going to get lost, that was for sure. And hey, she'd be more covered than she would have been in her bikini, right? Right.

Taking a deep breath, she stripped out of her top and skirt. When she looked up, she found Mark suddenly at the water's edge, the water lapping at his calves. His eyes were dark, very dark, and she pointed at him. "Don't take this the wrong way."

"Is there a wrong way to take it when a beautiful woman strips out of her clothes?" he asked without a smile, although it was in his voice. "I'm taking it that you're planning a swim."

"Actually, I'm planning on kicking your ass at boogie boarding," she said. "And that is *all*."

His mouth quirked. "Duly noted."

"Your pants are ringing," she murmured as his phone went off.

He came all the way out of the waves, water sluicing off his extremely fit body. A few drops clung stubbornly to all those lean muscles and she had to admit, she'd have done the same thing if she were one of those drops of water.

He bent to his pants to fish out his phone. "Yes," he said into it. "I can hear you."

Even in only the moonlight, his eyes seemed to gleam as he stared at Lanie in a way that suddenly made her want to forget boogie boarding in lieu of something else entirely.

Not going to fall for him, she reminded herself sternly, no matter how grounded and real and charismatic he seemed. It would only bring heartache.

"I haven't forgotten the family meeting," he said into the phone. He listened to whoever was on the other end of the phone for a few long minutes and then, eyes still on Lanie as she bent to pick up the second board, he said, "Start without me, I'm going to be late." He paused as Lanie strode past him into the water and added "Very late" before tossing his phone back onto his pants. "Winner picks dessert," he said.

Sounded fair. Especially since she was going to win.

SHE *BARELY* BEAT him, a fact Mark attributed to several things. One, he was beyond exhausted from all the extra shifts he'd been taking on in the name of saving for the house he wanted to build for himself and the girls. And two, the bright moonlight cast the air around them a pale blue, not black, which meant he could see everything, and what he could see at every turn was Lanie.

Wet.

Laughing.

And swimming like she'd been born in the water. She took his breath away, and that was when the water was up to her chin. When she jumped high and dove with a wild abandon into oncoming waves he caught glimpses of that long, curvy, glorious body that had nearly done him in when she'd been standing on the shore.

Good Christ, he was a dead man.

"That's five to five," she informed him loftily, gliding up beside him, lifting her hands to push her hair from her face. They were counting strikes by whoever fell first. "Tiebreaker?" she asked.

"Hell yeah," he said and they both turned to face the waves.

She flashed him a mischievous grin and dove into the water. Her undies had ridden up, and her bra had gone completely sheer. She looked like some sort of ocean goddess and he found himself just staring after her before remembering that this was the tiebreaker. He made a quick, sloppy attempt to catch her, his gaze held and locked by the smooth way she held on to her board, her body moving in sync with the water and . . .

He took a wave right in the face, which pummeled him, sending him somersaulting across the water.

When he righted himself and shook his head to clear it, she was standing there, water lapping at her feet, grinning.

"Claiming my spoils," she said. "I pick cookies."

Chapter 8

The struggle between wanting to be invited but not wanting to actually go . . .

Mark drove Lanie to the grocery store because by the time they dried off and got into the truck, it was nearly midnight and the bakery was long closed. He'd wanted to get her home and in a hot shower to warm up first, but she'd accused him of reneging on a bet, so here they were, cookie shopping.

He watched as she stood there considering her choices very seriously. She'd pulled her clothes back on and then a jacket of his that he'd given her from his backseat. Her hair had been twisted and piled wet on top of her head, held there by some mysterious woman magic.

Her teeth were chattering.

And damn if he didn't want to warm her in the one way that would heat them both up. But he had a rule. He'd picked badly with his wife and was in no hurry to love again. He meant what he'd told Alyssa—he wouldn't even consider trying until the girls were grown.

But lust was different. And there *was* lust with Lanie, lots of it.

She shivered again and he shook his head. "Just pick one."

This had her looking up at him incredulously. All of her makeup had washed off in the ocean and she could've passed for a teenager, which made him feel like a complete perv, since all he could think about was how she'd looked in her sheer bra and those eye-popping DayGlo pink undies that had done some amazing things for her first-class ass.

"I can't just pick one," she said. "Picking out the right cookies takes a minute. Dessert doesn't go to the stomach, dessert goes to the heart."

He was baffled. "You're freezing, and cookies are cookies."

"I beg your pardon, but you are dead wrong. There're things to consider here. For instance, do I want double fudge, chocolate chip, or maybe lemon—"

He reached past her and grabbed one of each, adding several other boxes as well. Five in total, all different, and dumped them into the cart.

"Seriously?" she asked.

"Just covering all the bases. Let's go."

A stoner standing in front of the chips display shook his head at Mark. "Dude. It takes balls of steel to get between a woman and her cookies."

Lanie went hands on hips. "Why does having 'balls' equate to toughness?"

The stoner blinked. "Uh . . ."

"And in the same vein," she said, "why does the word 'pussy' equate to weakness, when even the slightest flick to a guy's 'balls of steel' sends him to his knees—but vaginas can push out an entire human being?"

Both men just stared at her. Stoner Dude covered his crotch with his hands. "Man, you're harsh. You're harshing my buzz."

Mark took Lanie by the hand, pushing the cart with the

other. Since her fingers were ice, he tucked them into his pocket. "You're frozen."

"But at least I have cookies," she said happily, and he had to laugh.

At the cash register, he paid and once they were in his truck, he cranked the heater on high, aiming all the vents at her.

"You ever going to tell me what tonight's about?" she asked after they'd been driving a few minutes. "I mean, I wasn't even sure we liked each other."

"I like you," he said. He liked how quietly smart she was, how creative too. She'd come from what sounded like a hell of a beginning and she'd made something of herself.

On her own.

He admired that. He also really liked watching her with Sam and Sierra. She didn't treat them like babies. She didn't patronize and she didn't try to be something she wasn't. She spoke to them like they were people. She was a whole lot nicer and kinder to them than anyone had asked her to be, but she wasn't putting on an act. When she was with them, he could see her real self, and he knew it was because she felt safe enough with them to let her guard down.

He couldn't help but want to see more of *that* Lanie, but she didn't like him as much as she did the twins, although he thought maybe that was changing a little bit. It was probably a good thing she was a temp. Two months total with three weeks already down. He didn't see her sticking around after the job was done, and that meant they had an expiration date.

A comfort zone in which to explore their chemistry within their own boundaries.

He drove past the turnoff for the winery, up a narrow, windy road, and parked at the end of it.

Lanie stared through the windshield at the woods in front of them. "I'm finally dry and warm and *now* you're going to murder me?"

"Not before cookies," he said.

She snorted and got out, slipping her hand in his as they took the trail. Not, he was sure, out of affection, but because the trail was dark and he supposed also a little intimidating if she didn't know where she was going. Whatever the reason, the connection was nice. And there *was* a connection. It was in the zing of awareness that vibrated up his arm and spread throughout his chest.

"Where are we going?" she asked.

"Favorite escape place number two. I grew up exploring these hills. With two sisters and way too many other family members, all with eyes in the back of their heads, I disappeared a lot up here too. Had a tree fort when I was young."

"Is that where we're going? To a tree fort?"

"Better," he said.

They got through the trees and came to a clearing on a bluff. In the center of the clearing sat an RV trailer. He led her toward it but instead of opening the door, he gestured to the ladder leaning against it.

She gave him a raised brow.

"You have a heights problem?" he asked.

"Nope," she said and shimmied up the ladder. He did his best not to peek under her skirt. Besides, he didn't have to. Those DayGlo pink panties were burned into his brain and were sure to be the highlight of his fantasies for weeks to come.

He met her at the top, where she was staring at the two beach chairs on a pad of synthetic turf grass. In daylight, one could see rolling hills and beyond them, the Pacific Ocean. In the middle of the night, like now, it was nothing but a blanket of black against a midnight sky littered with brilliantly shining stars. The only sounds were the winds whistling through the trees behind them and the faintest roar of the sea.

She sat in one of the chairs and leaned back, closing her eyes. "I can smell the ocean."

"That's us," he said and sat next to her, handing her the very full bag from the store.

She rifled through it and pulled out a bag of chocolate chip cookies and the bottle of Jack he'd added at the checkout with a grin. "You're right," she said. "This is better." She paused. "Do you do this a lot?"

"Kidnap a woman? Almost never."

Laughing, she leaned back and closed her eyes, looking very relaxed. "Never have you ever, huh?"

"And you?" he asked. "What have you 'never have I ever'?"

"That's not how the game goes," she said. "You have to ask a specific question."

"Okay," he said, willing to play in order to learn more about her. "Never have I ever . . . boogie boarded in my underwear before tonight."

She drank, which meant she'd boogie boarded in her undies before, making him laugh. "Didn't know you were a such a wild thing," he said.

"Let's just say I used to be an attention-seeker. Never have I ever . . ." She paused and then smiled. "Been tempted to kiss someone who wears a uniform—before tonight."

He reached for the bottle.

"Realllllly," she murmured.

"Had a one-night fling with a fellow officer," he said. "Her idea."

"Didn't go back for seconds?"

"No, I don't do seconds." He met her gaze, hoping she understood.

She nodded. "Me either, at least not anymore."

Their gazes continued to hold for a long beat and then by mutual silent agreement, they went light and silly for a while with the game. Things like never have I ever . . . cried/flirted their way out of a ticket (her), and never have I ever made out with a stranger (him), and never have I ever repurposed a household item as a sex toy (her).

"One time!" she said, blushing when he nearly bust a gut laughing. "I got a neck massager at an office Christmas party and it didn't look like a neck massager and it'd been a long dry spell . . ." She rolled her eyes when he only laughed harder.

When he got ahold of himself, her arms were crossed in mock annoyance, and he straightened. "Never have I ever," he said, ". . . brought someone here before."

She looked pointedly at the trailer beneath them. "Is this the man cave?"

She was wearing a soft smile and a flush, clearly warmed up and possibly a little drunk, though she'd only taken a couple shots before switching to cookies. Seemed tyrant Lanie was a lightweight.

"Am not," she said, making him realize he'd spoken out loud. "And I'm only a tyrant on the *outside*."

This, he knew.

"So . . ." she said. "Tell me. Is this where you bring your women and have your way with them?"

He laughed.

She stared at his mouth for a beat and then smiled. "I hope

you at least bring them inside the trailer to do the deed so no one gets mosquito bites in their secret places."

"Secret places?"

She blushed and it was cute. "No," he said. "This isn't my sex den. I bought this land, which butts up against the winery. I'm saving to build a house out here for me and the girls."

"Oh," she breathed and then nodded. And then shook her head. "I'm . . . conflicted."

"On the cookies? Open another pack. You've got four more."

She snorted. "Not on the cookies." She paused. "I wanted you to be an asshole, you know. A selfish dick who dumped his girls on his family so he didn't have to be a dad." She took another swig of the Jack and he gently took it from her.

"There were a few years that felt like that," he admitted, "when I was overseas."

"But when they needed you, you came back." She pointed at him, misjudging the distance and nearly taking out one of his eyes. "You gave up a career. You gave up everything and had to start over. All for them."

"It's what dads do."

"No." She shook her head. "I don't know if your alpha-ness can register this, but it's not true. Not all dads would do that. Mine wouldn't." She stared at him for a beat, let her gaze slide to his mouth, and then stood up abruptly.

He stood with her, righting her when she would've toppled.

"I'm not a very good drinker," she whispered. "When I forget that, I tend to do things I shouldn't." She licked her lips. "The last time I drank too much, I went to Vegas with my boyfriend of six months and got married."

He stilled. He could hold his liquor. Hell, he could drink his

entire unit under the table, but this made his head spin. "You got married on a drunken whim?"

"Are you judging me?"

"Hell, no," he said. "I married a woman who could walk away from her own kids."

"And you," she reminded him. "She walked away from you too."

He shook his head. "I'm an adult, I can take it. But the girls . . ."

Her eyes softened. "Your girls are amazing. You're enough for them, Mark."

He wasn't so sure about that, but the way Lanie was looking at him drained his tension. "Thanks," he said quietly, unable to help being moved by her. "I'm sorry your husband was a dick too."

She shook her head. "That's the thing. After five years of being married and only the first two of them being good, I knew we weren't right for each other. But I didn't know Kyle was a dick until after he died. I can't trust love to be good for me." She hiccupped. "Sorry. I'm *really* not good at the Jack."

Maybe Mark was the dick because he shouldn't have let her have three shots. She never would've talked to him like this if he hadn't. But there was no fucking way he was taking her home until he made her understand something. "Love can and should be good for you, Lanie. You just need to find the right person to trust, that's all."

"Shh." Reaching up, she set a finger over his lips. "My inability to get love right is a secret about me. Don't tell anyone, 'k?"

His heart ached and he opened his mouth to say something more, but she beat him to it.

"Never have I ever," she said softly. "Wanted to kiss someone that I didn't *want* to want to kiss."

He groaned and slid his arms around her. "Lanie—"

"No falling," she said. "And no going back for seconds. I know." She added a nod and a sassy salute.

He met her gaze and saw her wounds just beneath the surface. He hated that and slowly slid a hand up her arm, her throat, then around to the back of her neck, his fingers burying themselves in her hair. With his other hand, he cupped her face, his thumb softly caressing the skin beneath her ear and over her jaw.

She shivered, and her hands came up to his wrists, her eyes fluttering closed as he brushed his lips over hers in a questing kiss before pulling back.

"More," she breathed, eyes still shut, lips parted.

With a low groan, he covered her mouth with his and immediately lost himself in her. She wrapped her arms around him tight, pressing even closer, urging him on. He gave her what she wanted, what he wanted, kissing her slow and deliberate, teasing them both until she tore away and opened her eyes to stare up at him.

"Oh. Wow."

Yeah.

She licked her lips like she needed that last taste of him. "I didn't expect that," she said.

No. He hadn't expected it either. Not the explosive hunger between them and not the strength of the urge he had to take even more. Not trusting himself, he took her home after that and walked her to her cottage.

At the door, she hesitated, pressing her forehead to the wood. "Just go inside, Lanie," she said out loud. And then didn't move.

With a soft laugh, he reached past her to open the door for her. She turned and gripped his shirt in two fists, yanking him down to her. Then she planted her mouth on his and kissed every single thought right out of his head, and while he was trying to remember his name and why exactly she was such a bad idea, she pulled back and let out a breath. "Damn," she whispered. "Still wow."

He laughed again. Because yeah. Still wow.

She went inside without another word after that, shutting and locking the door behind her, and he walked away. Probably the smartest thing he'd done all night, but at the moment, it sure didn't feel like it.

Chapter 9

I don't have a nervous system, I am a nervous system . . .

The next morning, Lanie staggered into the office. Or tried to. She pushed a pull door and literally walked face-first into it.

Holden, who happened to be walking past, stopped. "You have to pull."

"That was my next plan," she said and sighed when he opened it for her.

She went straight to the fridge and whimpered when the light hurt her eyes. Hangover level: she needed sunglasses to look into the fridge. Since she didn't have any sunglasses, she did an about-face and headed for the coffee pot instead. Someone came in the office behind her, and since her happy parts quivered, she knew it was Mark. Slowly she turned around.

His lips quirked. The same delicious lips she'd kissed last night. Damn bottle of Jack . . . She'd kissed her boss's son.

And she'd liked it.

"Rough morning?" he murmured in a husky morning voice, looking annoyingly awake and chipper.

"Not at all," she lied.

With a soft laugh, he moved toward her just as Samantha and Sierra came flying into the room.

"*Daddy, Daddy, Daddy!* We found our hairbrush!" Sam brandished it around, nearly taking out one of his eyes. "Sierra has the hair ties!"

"Inside voice, baby." But he took the brush and the hair ties and set them on the counter. Then he scooped up Sierra and plunked her down on the counter as well, after which he proceeded to brush and then braid her hair with a practiced ease. He then executed a wash-and-repeat for Samantha, gave them both hugs and kisses that elicited happy squeals, and sent them on their way.

Lanie's dad had been distant at best. Kyle had never wanted kids. So watching the big, strong, alpha Mark Capriotti not only be the opposite of distant but also be a true, hands-on dad was almost unbearably attractive.

When he caught her staring, he smiled. "Need your hair braided too?"

Yes, her mouth nearly said, *oh please, yes, put your fingers through my hair* . . . "I'm good, thanks."

He poured coffee into a travel mug that said TIRED OF WAKING UP AND NOT BEING ON AN ISLAND, saluted her with it, and then walked out.

Which was just how she wanted things between them. Totally and completely. So why she let out a disappointed breath was beyond her.

At lunch that day, Uncle Jack walked by her. "Hey, what kind of bees make milk?" he asked.

"No idea."

"Jack!" Cora called out warningly from the far end of the other table.

"Boo-bees," he whispered, and with a very pleased-with-himself grin, he looked down at her salad-only plate. "That's just sad."

"I like salad." Well, she liked salad more than, say, liver and onions, but she actually much preferred lasagna. She was doing her best not to look at it.

Jack shook his head. "There's no accounting for taste. It's not your fault, though—you're not Italian."

"*Jack*." Cora again.

"Damn," he muttered. "That woman's got eyes in the back of her head."

"Heard that too!"

Jack sighed and looked over at Mia, who was in black boots, black yoga pants, and a long black sweater, hood up. "Whose funeral is it?"

Mia looked up from her phone and peered around at the crowd. "Haven't decided yet."

Jack nodded at her phone. "Texting wasn't always easy, you know. In my day, you had to work for it. You had to want it. You need an *X*? You'd better hit that seven button four times."

Lanie laughed, and he slid her a sly smile. "Did I tell you the one about the brothel? What does a sign on an out-of-business brothel say?" He beamed. "Beat it, we're closed."

"Jack, so help me God," Cora yelled, and with a wink, Jack stole a cupcake and vanished.

Lanie moved to a bucket filled with ice and drinks near the patio door and grabbed a bottle of water.

River stood nearby, apparently frozen. "Not again," she whispered.

Lanie realized she was nearly green. "Hey, are you—"

River slapped a hand to her mouth, whirled, and ran.

Nope. She wasn't okay. Lanie looked around to see if anyone else had seen River, say, maybe Cora, who was good at this whole taking-care-of-people thing.

But no one had noticed. Dammit. With a sigh, she found River getting sick in the employee bathroom.

This poor bathroom saw a *lot*.

"Go away," River gasped, hanging her head over the toilet.

Yeah, if only she could. With another sigh, Lanie moved forward and took over holding River's hair back. And then she closed her eyes while River wretched and gagged, and tried to picture herself on a warm, deserted island with puppies. And A/C.

Finally River got herself together and Lanie went to the sink. She wet some paper towels and brought them back to River.

"Thanks," she murmured, clearly mortified.

"You're still so sick. I thought pregnant women only threw up in the first trimester."

River shrugged. "Just lucky, I guess."

Lanie felt for her. She'd been here two weeks and hadn't had anyone come visit. River was every bit as alone in the world as Lanie felt, or so it seemed. "How often does this happen?"

River hesitated. "Every day."

"Are you sure you don't need to see a doctor?" Lanie asked. "Or talk to Cora about cutting back your hours?"

"No!" she said, looking panicked. "I'm fine, really. You can't tell anyone, okay? Cora might ask me to quit and I need this job."

"But—"

"*Please*," she said and turned beseeching eyes on Lanie, looking wan and anxious. "I can handle this job, I promise, I just . . . I just need a minute alone."

"I know you can handle the job," Lanie said. "I've seen you

do it. You do a good job, and I'm glad you're here. But I can't just leave you alone."

"Why not? It's easy, lots of people have done it. You just walk out the door."

Lanie dropped her head to her chest and took a deep breath. She didn't want this. She didn't want to get sucked in, dammit. But at every turn, it was happening anyway. First the twins. Uncle Jack. Mia and Alyssa. And now River.

But no one else, she assured herself. Absolutely no one else, including Mark, no matter how sexy and talented his mouth was.

River shuddered and Lanie held on to her, the only person she knew who might actually be standing on a bigger proverbial cliff than herself. It wasn't often she met someone just as screwed up as she, maybe even more so. It was a nice change, she had to admit.

And there was something else. She liked this girl. And she didn't take that lightly—it had never been in her nature to be open enough to draw people in. But there was something about River that made her feel protective, as if they were close friends. "I can't walk away, River. You're pregnant, you're sick, and I know, *believe me,* I know how much you probably want to stand on your own right now, but you can't. You need a minute, you need someone at your back, and like it or not, that's going to be me."

River looked stunned at this. But she didn't argue, she just nodded. "You said you're glad I'm here. Why?"

Lanie sighed. "Because I hate pitching in at the front desk. It's torture for me. I'm not good with people like you are. Everyone has questions, so many questions, and I never know the answers. You just effortlessly figure it all out."

Again River looked surprised. "Everything you do seems effortless."

"It's an act. Trust me, I'm a fish out of water here."

"Me too," River breathed softly. "So we have stuff in common."

"Seems like it."

"The front desk isn't that bad," River said. "It's all nice people that come through here, super nice. No one yells that their French fries didn't get cooked right or that I brought the wrong kind of beer. Instead of saying 'Touch my ass again and you'll be walking funny tomorrow,' now I just say 'Nice to talk to you and have a good day!' I like it."

Lanie laughed at that.

River smiled, but shook her head. "Seriously, you have *no* idea how amazing this place is. How lucky I feel."

Something else they had in common. "Waitressing when pregnant sounds awful. And hard. How did you end up in that job?"

"Started when I was fifteen."

Lanie gaped at her, trying to imagine that. "Fifteen!"

River shrugged. "I was on my own and it was the only thing I could do after school in the afternoons and night without hooking. I didn't want to drop out."

Lanie was stunned. Here she was going on about her life with a decent-sized chip on her shoulder for how she'd grown up. But at least her parents had waited until she was eighteen and off to college before giving her the boot. "Sounds like you had it rough."

"We've all had it rough one way or another."

Lanie nodded. "That's very true. But some people more than others."

Their gazes met and River whispered, "You've had it rough too."

A statement, not a question, but Lanie nodded, wanting her to know she wasn't alone.

"I'm not feeling sick anymore," River said. "I think I can get back to work."

Lanie looked at her doubtfully.

"No, really."

Lanie took stock. She could see the color was back in River's cheeks and she was breathing easier, and nodded. "Okay. But take it easy."

River grabbed her hand and met her gaze. "Thanks."

For most of Lanie's life, the fast, easy friendships most women seemed to find so readily among themselves had been something that had eluded her. But this felt different. She just squeezed River's hand and pointed to her water bottle. "Drink. Rehydrate."

And then she walked out of the restroom. Cora just happened to be walking by and gave Lanie a quick smile.

"Just who I was looking for," she said.

Oh shit. Someone had heard what'd happened between her and Mark last night. She steered Cora away from the bathroom and down the hallway, wanting to make sure River fully recovered before Cora caught sight of her. "I'm so sorry," she said. "It was a complete fluke. I'd had a few shots, and he's way too good-looking for his own good—" She grimaced. "Which you don't want to hear about your own son, I know, but—"

Cora arched one single, perfect eyebrow. "Are you talking about Marcus?"

Lanie froze. "Um, aren't you?"

"No," her boss said with some amusement. "But now I think you should go first."

Oh boy. "I'd really rather not," she said with a wince.

Cora looked at her for a long beat and then apparently decided to take mercy. "I was wondering how you'd feel about adding Owen's bottling company to your list of things you're designing for."

"Owen needs a whole new design?"

Cora nodded. "And he wants it from you. There's some other things we're looking at doing as well, all of which could add as much as another month to your contract if that appeals to you."

She couldn't deny that it was nice, *very* nice after Kyle, to be wanted and valued, but this was dangerous territory, staying another month—especially in light of her accidental kissing-Mark reveal.

Alyssa came around the corner. "Did you ask her yet?"

"Just did," Cora said.

"Yay!" Alyssa smiled at Lanie. "So . . . you down? Because it'd be so great for Owen, obviously. And us. But most especially it'd be great for Sam and Sierra, right, Mom?"

"Absolutely," Cora said. "They already love you so much."

Lanie felt herself go still inside. She wasn't sure she could commit to anything right now, especially this place with all these people, wonderful as they were. Her own axis was still too shaky.

"Why don't you just think about it, honey," Cora said. "No pressure."

Right. No pressure to get over her sham of a marriage. No pressure to get her life together. No pressure to decide whether to stay here at the first job she'd ever loved when it wasn't her work skills they coveted. No pressure on anything at all . . .

Chapter 10

Anxiety is having 99 problems and 86 of them are made-up scenarios that might never happen, but you stress about them anyway.

When River finally made it out of the bathroom, she leaned against the wall for a moment. Gracie was there, sprawled in the hallway. She clambered to all fours and licked River's hand in greeting.

"Thanks," River whispered and gave the big fluffball a hug before heading back to her desk. Needing calm, she put in the earbuds she'd found in her top desk drawer on her first day, left over from someone else's time in this position, and brought up her calm app. She opted for beach sounds, her favorite. Waves gently lapped at a shore, a breeze blew through some palm trees . . .

"Here," someone said with a southern accent that made his voice sound like melted butter. "Sip this."

River startled because she knew that voice. She'd been avoiding both it and the guy it belonged to, and she'd been good at it too.

Holden. He stood there in a cowboy hat, jeans, and boots, looking like every cowboy fantasy personified, Gracie at his side. Gracie adored him. Reluctantly, River pulled out one earbud, deathly afraid of being accidentally nice to him and being deserted and left alone and pregnant.

Oh, wait. That'd already happened.

"Easy," he said and she looked up into his blue gaze as he held out a cup. "Peppermint tea."

"Been pregnant a lot, have you?" she asked as Gracie lay down at her feet with a huge groan, making Holden smile.

And not that she wanted to admit it, but he had a nice smile.

"Drink," he said.

"Not thirsty."

He gave a barely there shake of his head. "Do you ever accept help?"

"No."

"Why the hell not?"

"Because then you might expect something from me in return," she said.

His gaze held hers for a long beat. "Fine. Consider it a favor to me, then, that you take a damn sip," he said. "That way, in your crazy logic, *I* owe *you*."

She sighed and took a sip under his watchful gaze. The tea was delicious.

"Better, right?" he asked.

Not wanting to encourage him in any way, she shrugged noncommittally.

"Wow," he said. "Which is heavier, the baby or the chip on your shoulder?"

"Here's a tip," she said. "When someone removes only one earbud to talk to you, then they probably don't want a lengthy conversation." She tried to hand him back the cup, but he refused to take it.

"How's the baby doing? You eating okay?"

"Sure. I had eggs for breakfast."

"So did I," he said. "But mine were Reese's Peanut Butter eggs."

She laughed, shocking the both of them. "I miss those," she said wistfully. "Bad."

"I guess chocolate's not good for the baby," he said.

"Or the mama," she said on a sigh, forgetting for a moment to keep him at arm's length. "And how do you know about chocolate not being good for the baby?"

He lifted a shoulder and made to go. "Whenever you sit at your desk, make sure to put your feet up. Your ankles are swelling."

"Yeah, well, I haven't seen my ankles in about a month, so . . ." She broke off when he removed his hat to push his hair back from his face, revealing a nasty cut along the underside of his arm. "What did you do?"

"This?" He looked at his arm and shrugged. "Mending fences this morning. It's nothing."

"It's going to get infected. You need to clean it out and cover it."

"Worried about me?"

Not that she'd admit it. "I think you're a big boy," she said. "You can take care of yourself."

This caused a slow smile to cross his face. "You're right about that. But if it makes you feel better, tonight when I shower the grime off, I'll handle it."

"You can't wait until tonight. For God's sake." She pulled her purse from her bottom drawer and grabbed the small first aid kit she had in it.

She tried to push him into her chair, but he made her sit in it instead and then he crouched at her side and laid his arm across her thighs. She bent over him to work, having to dig into the cut a little bit to get rid of some stubborn dirt. He didn't even flinch, and she looked up into his face, which was startlingly close.

His gaze locked on hers and held, and something inside her quivered, and she recognized it for what it was.

A connection, unwanted or not.

Ignore it, she told herself, as she'd been doing for two weeks now. *It'll go away.*

"Tell me you feel that," he said.

"Indigestion? Yes."

He smiled a little grimly. "Not indigestion. You feel that thing between us, I know it."

"Yes, it's a baby, and it's doing somersaults today."

He let out a breath and shook his head at her as he lifted his big hands toward her belly. "May I?"

People never asked her if they could touch. They just did it, like a baby bump was fair game. She hated that. But he'd asked and she nodded.

Then those big, work-callused hands settled on her swollen stomach so gently it nearly brought tears to her eyes. The baby kicked and the tough cowboy in front of her jumped, making her laugh for the second time in as many minutes. "It's not going to bite."

His startled eyes jerked up to hers and he smiled. "You have a pretty laugh. You should use it more."

He was still on his knees at her chair, his hands on her belly, their faces close enough to share air. Or kiss. It felt incredibly . . . intimate. Terrifyingly so, and she scooted back her chair so fast she almost tipped it over. She certainly would have if he hadn't caught the armrests and kept her upright.

"Careful," he said.

"Yes. I . . . need to remember to be careful," she said and busied herself with putting her things back in her first aid kit.

He rose to his feet. "You're good at this," he said quietly, stretching his arm as if testing it for pain, making her realize that he'd most certainly felt the cut—he'd just been able to ignore it.

"I was going to be a nurse," she said.

"Was?"

"I took a semester of early-morning classes before my waitressing shift, but had to quit."

They both looked down at the baby bump.

"Being an LVN wasn't realistic anyway," she said.

"Why not? You can do anything you want to do."

"Says a guy who probably has never found himself knocked up."

"Got me there," he said. "I've never been pregnant."

"Or devastated by life."

He slid her a look. "You think you've got a lock on that, do you?"

She looked into his deep blue gaze, saw the pain he hid, and closed her eyes. "I'm sorry. It was rude of me to make any assumptions."

"If you have a question you want to ask me, ask."

"I think maybe you have that backward," she said.

"Okay, I'll bite. Is it me, or all men?"

"All men," she said without hesitation.

He looked at her and nodded. "Okay, that I can work with."

"It wasn't a challenge, Holden. I'm not in a place to be interested in anyone, especially not . . ."

"Especially not what?"

"Someone I want to be interested in."

"Maybe that will change."

She was already shaking her head before he finished the sentence. He was stoic, rugged, had nerves of steel, and therefore was steady as a rock. All very attractive traits to her and maybe if she wasn't so . . . damaged, not to mention a huge fraud, she'd be tempted. "Don't count on it," she whispered, pulling free. "Or me. I'm not worth it."

"We're going to have to agree to disagree there," he said.

Cora came through. "Oh, Holden honey, I'm so glad to see you here. I was just going to text you. River's going to need some help and both Mia and Alyssa are busy."

"I don't need help," River said.

"Not yet, but I've got a group of fifteen coming through."

"I've got it," Holden said. "No problem."

River shook her head. "*I've* got it."

"You've both got it," Cora said. "It's Wildstone's city council. I've lured them up here for lunch, some wine tasting, and to visit our horses and spread, all in the hope of getting them to host some of their annual events here to up our coverage. So I need River's amazing hostess skills turned up to a ten and I need my horse wrangler to be the strong, silent cowboy type to put the fear of God and/or Cora into anyone who attempts something stupid to show off." She shook her head. "I went to school with five of those men, and trust me when I say stupid is likely to happen." She blew them a kiss and vanished.

Five minutes later, fifteen city council men and women

arrived. River was extremely aware of Holden at her side as she walked everyone through the place, and when they got to the stables, he effortlessly took over, introducing the group to the horses, showing them around, pointing out the wild horses in the far pasture.

"You're young to know so much about horses," one of the women said to Holden.

"I've been here since I was fifteen," he said.

"You're not a Capriotti."

"No," he said. "But they took me in as if I was."

"Oh," she said with a soft smile. "You're the young man she always brags about. She took you in off the streets."

"Yes, ma'am, she did."

"And you went into the army to make something of yourself. She's so proud of you."

"And I'm grateful to her," he said. "To all of the Capriottis. If you bring your business out here, they'll take care of you, I can promise you that."

River had turned to look at him, but he didn't meet her gaze, just went about handling the large group with what looked like effortless ease. Later, when everyone had gone and they stood in the reception area once again, she stared at him. "You must think I'm a self-centered, spoiled bitch."

"I don't think that at all."

"What do you think?" she whispered.

"That I'm grateful our thoughts don't appear in bubbles over our heads."

She laughed a little, but considered the look in his eyes. It was something different. She wasn't one hundred percent sure of what this look was, but it made her heart beat a little too fast and sent a rush of happy straight through her body. She was still staring at him when his cell phone buzzed. Without taking his gaze off her, he reached back and silenced it.

"What if it's work?" she asked, feeling panicked that he'd risk getting in trouble for her. "Holden, please. Get it."

And the moment he did, reluctantly, she scooped up her stack of things that needed copying and beat it to the employee staff room.

When she got back to her desk five minutes later, Holden was gone and she breathed a sigh of relief.

Or so she told herself.

She'd been so spoiled these past few weeks here, forgetting what it was like to worry about her next meal or if she'd have enough gas to run the heater when she got cold at night. Forgetting also that she wasn't the only one with a shitty past. But she didn't deserve Holden, or even to get to know his past. She didn't deserve any of this. Cora and the Capriottis had her worries easing away, and knowing it—and the real reason she'd come here—had guilt eating her insides away.

TWO DAYS LATER Lanie came by to get her for lunch, as she did every day now.

Like they were more than coworkers. Like they were friends. Lanie treated her like she meant something to her.

It both warmed River in ways she hadn't realized she needed warming and also only served to increase the weight of that ball of guilt seated heavily in her chest.

The tables were already filling up as everyone came outside. She and Lanie took the very end of the far table because Lanie preferred the quietest corner and liked to lay low.

Fine with River, since she felt like an imposter.

That's because you are, a little voice in her head whispered nastily.

Lanie looked over at her and gave a small smile, and a little bit more of River's happy bubble burst. Every time Lanie was nice to her, every single time, it was a visceral reminder that she shouldn't still be here. "You don't have to do this, you know."

"Do what?" Lanie asked.

"Be nice to me."

"Yes, but they taught us in kindergarten, so . . ."

River choked out a laugh, but it rang hollow because it wasn't funny. Not in the slightest.

"You feeling better?" Lanie asked.

"Yes," she fibbed. "Much."

"And you don't have to do that," Lanie said.

"What?"

"Lie."

River met Lanie's knowing gaze. "I'm a pro at it, you know," Lanie said casually. "Pretending to be good. Really good at it. I'm maybe even the queen, but you're close."

"So I'm what, the princess of being full of shit?"

Lanie laughed. "Yeah. You can be the princess."

Which made them family. She could see Lanie take in the same thought as well and she gave River a little smile that she absolutely did not deserve. Not one little bit. Because as much as she wanted it to be true, as much as she wished she'd never started this stupid deceit, that she could indeed be family with Lanie, she couldn't. She'd screwed that up and there was no taking it back.

Except, of course, to tell the truth . . .

Which she absolutely couldn't do.

"Something's bothering you," Lanie said quietly. "And before you deny it," she added when River opened her mouth to do just that, "remember I'm the queen."

River shrugged. "Do you ever feel like you're just a kid playing dress-up? But that no one knows it but you?"

"You mean you don't think you really fit into this world," Lanie said.

"I know I don't."

Lanie gave a wry smile. "I don't think the Capriottis worry about that sort of thing. They don't seem to mind that we're from different worlds."

River was surprised. "You fit in."

"No," Lanie said quietly. "I'm playing dress-up, just like you."

That couldn't be true. Lanie was refined and smart and sophisticated and . . . just about everything River wasn't. But Lanie didn't say things she didn't mean—River knew that much about her already—and for a beat they just looked at each other before River shook her head, trying to come up with something to say.

Thankfully Mia came over, muttering about not giving a "flying fuck" about something.

"You still mad about the girls not doing their fair share?" Alyssa asked from across the table.

"No," Mia said. "As I mentioned just now, I don't give a flying fuck."

"Well, you *should* give a fuck," Alyssa said. "You really should—but only about things that set your soul on fire. Save your fucks for the magical shit."

River thought that was the smartest piece of wisdom she'd ever heard. From now on, she was saving all her flying fucks for magical shit that set her soul on fire.

Mia took a sip of water and eyed her sister. "I heard Owen ate your last two cookies yesterday and you needed an exorcism. But by the look on your face now, you've made up."

"Last night," Alyssa said, "I came home to a note on the door that said: 'Hey, baby, welcome home—I'm hiding in the house with one of our two Nerf guns and here's the other. Loser cooks dinner tonight. May the odds be ever in your favor. Love you!'" She grinned. "He lost. He cooked. Both in the kitchen *and* the bedroom, if you know what I'm saying."

Mia rolled her eyes. "I only wish I didn't know what you were saying."

"Your problem is that you're going for the wrong guy," Alyssa said. "You know what's sexier than your usual bad boy? A grown-ass man with his shit together. Maybe try finding a guy *not* on a dating site."

Mia nodded. "I'm one step ahead of you. I've moved on to pizza delivery guys because at least I know they have a job, a car, *and* pizza."

"Do you see yourself finding a husband on a dating app?" Alyssa asked.

"No, because I don't want a husband. Fifty percent of marriages end in divorce. One hundred percent of pizza deliveries end in happiness."

Everyone smiled but River. Because she'd purposely dated up last time, going for the classy guy. And look where that had gotten her. And with that thought, the very last of her happiness drained and she palmed her baby bump.

Catching the motion, Lanie looked at her. "You sure you're okay?"

"Of course," she said, her automatic response. Because people always asked her how she was feeling, but she'd learned they didn't expect the truth.

Although here at the winery, it was actually the complete opposite. People asked because they cared, they *really* cared, and yet her rote response was still the same because what was her alternative? Tell the truth, be forced to give up the job, and go back to living in her car, feeling sick from fast food or worse, no food at all?

Cora came through with a tray of brownies for dessert and the entire crowd moaned in mutual delight. They were double fudge and one bite brought back memories of being in a warm kitchen, licking the spatula. "I used to make these with my mom," River heard herself say softly.

Everyone turned and stared at her, making her remember something else—that she'd managed to dodge almost every single personal question she'd been asked since starting here.

"Where's your mom now?" Cora asked kindly. She always spoke kindly, River had discovered, even when she was pissed off. Yesterday she'd spoken kindly to the mailman even when threatening to rip his favorite body part off and feed it to him if he didn't stop throwing their packages from the driveway to her front door just to avoid Gracie, who wouldn't hurt a fly.

Yep, her boss was the most gentle, most terrifying woman she'd ever met and River wanted to be her when she grew up. "My mom passed away a long time ago," she said into the curious silence. She went back to her brownie, but everyone seemed to be waiting for more, so she said, "I was fifteen."

"So young," Cora murmured in sympathy. "What happened, honey?"

"Cancer." By the time her mom had passed, River had been

taking care of her for three years, through treatment after treatment. That's when she'd realized she wanted to become a nurse, because it'd been the first thing she'd ever been good at.

"Who raised you after that?" Cora asked.

"I went into the foster system for a few years," River said. Until she'd turned eighteen, and she'd been on her own ever since.

There was a beat of silence.

"When *I* was fifteen," Mia said quietly, none of her usual sarcasm in her voice, "my mom and I were at each other's throats. One time I got so mad that I told her I was going to call child protective services to get taken away, and she handed me the phone and told me the number was one-eight-hundred-I-Don't-Give-a-Shit. Which was her doing me a favor because I didn't want to get taken away. I loved her, I was just a shithead."

Cora smiled at her daughter. "You did behave for a while after that. And your heart is always in the right place."

Mia blew her a kiss and Cora smiled fondly in her direction before taking River's hand in her own. "You've had a rough road."

River shook her head. "Not that much rougher than a lot of people." And she'd done okay for herself. Mostly. She'd tried to live good and honest like her mom had taught her, but now here she was, pregnant and sick and still at the place she'd come to steal from. Letting out a shaky breath, she rubbed her stomach.

"Have you been to a doctor recently for a wellness check?" Cora asked.

"Uh . . . not recently." Or at all in the past three months. She'd run out of money for that.

"My best friend runs the local ob-gyn's office in town," Cora said. "I'll get you an appointment. You shouldn't go alone, though. Do you have anyone to ask to go with you—say, the father of your baby maybe?"

"I'm okay to go alone," River said.

"Well, of course you are, but why should you have to? I'll take you." She smiled. "Who better than someone who had way too many babies herself?"

"Hey," two of her babies—Mia and Alyssa—said at the same time.

River was aware that Cora was fishing, but she was doing it in such a nice way that she couldn't take offense. She knew they all thought she was in over her head, that maybe she was running from something, and that she was scared.

They certainly had two out of three right.

Chapter 11

Overanalyze all the things!

At the end of the week, Lanie walked into the employee room for a snack and right into a family "discussion," aka a fight. Apparently, there was some sort of cork emergency that had set the entire family schedule board in chaos, the biggest problem being that Cora could no longer pick up the girls from dance class.

The thought of getting involved in the family matter gave Lanie a mini panic attack, but so did picturing Sam and Sierra standing alone in front of an emptied-out dance studio with no one there to pick them up. So she grabbed a dry-erase pen and wrote her name in the empty box.

This silenced the room. Breathe in for four, out for four. Repeat. Foods she'd eaten today: toast with strawberry jelly, antipasto salad, and dammit, a piece of lasagna because she was weak. Another deep breath, then she turned around and found everyone staring at her. "What?"

"Nothing," Cora said, hugging her. "Except *thank you.*"

Which was how several hours later, Lanie found herself driving through heavy end-of-the-week traffic to pick up the girls at dance class.

They were thrilled to see her.

"Do you ever take dance classes?" Samantha asked.

Lanie smiled. "My favorite exercise is a cross between a lunge and a crunch. I call it lunch."

The girls giggled and went on to chatter all the way home about their new ballet shoes, how Sierra had nailed an arabesque, and that Sam had really *really* wanted the headband that some girl named Camille was wearing but her dad wouldn't buy it for her because she'd already spent her allowance on candy.

"So save next week's allowance and buy it yourself," Lanie suggested, glancing into the rearview mirror at Sam.

The girl's brow furrowed, like she hadn't thought of this. "But what if I want more candy?"

"Well, then," Lanie said. "I guess you've got to decide which you want more, the candy or the headband."

Sierra nodded sagely.

Samantha sighed. "I want both."

"Real-world problems," Lanie said.

The girls cocked their heads in confusion.

"That's sarcasm," she explained. "See, having to choose between candy and a headband, that's a problem that a lot of people might *wish* to have. Instead they've got to choose between keeping a roof over their head and food on the table for their kids, and . . . I don't know, paying the heating bill, that kind of thing. Do you see what I mean?"

"Real-world problems," Sam repeated slowly, thoughtfully.

Real-world problems, Sierra mouthed to herself.

"Momma used to yell about the bills," Sam said, staring out the window. "All the time. She said we cost too much."

Sierra closed her eyes.

"Guess she solved her real-world problems," Sam said quietly.

Lanie grimaced. How to stand up for the girls without hurting any good memories of their mom they might have? "Some people aren't as good at . . . managing their problems," she said. "It doesn't mean they don't love you."

Sam didn't say anything to this.

Lanie ached for them and knew any of the Capriottis would've known what to say. So of course they got stuck in traffic getting home. She finally pulled off the freeway and into a drive-through and got them all burgers and fries, which greatly improved morale. As did the toys that came in the kids' meals.

It took them an hour to get back to the winery, and buoyed by the food, the girls used the time to barrage Lanie with questions such as "Why do socks come off in the middle of the night?" and "Why do daddies sometimes send you to your room for singing the alphabet song over and over?" and "Why do boys get to have a penis and we don't?"

By the time they got back, Lanie needed aspirin. And possibly alcohol.

Mark drove up just as they did. He got out of his truck, hugged and kissed the girls, and sent them inside. He looked at Lanie, his eyes hidden behind his dark aviator glasses. "How in the world did you get stuck with the dreaded Friday afternoon dance-class duty?"

"I volunteered."

"Thank you. I'll pay you for your time—"

"No, it's fine. Really," she said. "It wasn't a problem."

"Then how about dinner? Or a movie? Whatever you want."

Whatever she wanted sounded like a very dangerous proposition since the first thing that came to mind was more of his mouth on hers. The second thing that came to mind gave her a serious hot flash. "There's no repayment necessary," she said. "I wanted to do it and I did it, period. Just . . . don't take it for something it's not."

"Okay." One corner of his mouth quirked. "So I scare you that much, huh?"

She opened her mouth and then closed it because yes. He scared her that much. He held her gaze for one long moment before giving her a nod. Then, no longer smiling, he followed the girls inside, which was a good thing. She'd just put some badly needed distance between them, *emotional* distance. Shaking her head at herself, she leaned against her car, wanting a few minutes alone.

Which was when she saw the nail in her tire. Perfect. When she finally went inside, she ran into Cora.

"Just the person I wanted to see," her boss said.

"I'm not ready to decide on the contract extension," Lanie said.

Cora looked startled and then unhappy, but she just nodded. "I understand. But I was just going to thank you for getting my grandbabies."

Crap. Note number three to self: *Always let Cora speak first!*

"We will of course pay you for your time," Cora said.

"Not necessary, but say I was looking for a place to have my car looked at, where would you recommend?"

"You don't need a place. Both Holden and Marcus are excellent mechanics. What's wrong with your car?"

Just what she didn't need, more face time with Mark. "Nothing," Lanie said. "No worries."

The next morning she got up early with the intention of

driving her car to the closest gas station to see about getting the tire fixed.

But it already was.

She headed into the employee kitchen and found Mark leaning against the counter, mainlining coffee and thumbing through his phone.

"Was it you?" she asked.

He didn't stop scrolling or look up. "You'll have to be more specific."

She sighed. "You didn't have to fix my tire."

"I know."

"So why did you?"

Now he looked up, his eyes holding hers prisoner. "Because it needed to be done."

She was tired of circling around him. Tired of not knowing what to think or how to take him. It was exhausting. *He* was exhausting. "Fine. Thank you. What do I owe you?"

He didn't answer, just stood there, still leaning back against the counter, as calm as he pleased, wearing that uniform like he'd been born to authority.

"Well?" she asked.

"Are you really going to piss me off this early in the morning?"

She tossed up her hands. "It's a simple question. How much do I owe you?"

He sighed and set his coffee aside. "There's no repayment necessary. I wanted to do it and I did it. Period."

Look at him, throwing her own words back at her with absolutely zero inflection, which was more than she'd managed. And he'd left off the part about not taking it for something it wasn't, which made her feel even more petty and mean. "I'd rather pay than owe you a favor."

"What part aren't you getting here, Lanie?" He blew out a breath. "There is no price for what we give each other."

As she had absolutely zero idea how to take that, she was still standing there, mouth open, when his phone buzzed and he walked out of the room to take the call.

River walked in, looking wary. "Sorry, I wasn't trying to eavesdrop. I just wanted food."

Lanie sighed. "It's okay. We were done anyway."

"You don't like to accept favors," River said. "I get it. You don't want to owe people. They take advantage of you when you owe them favors."

"Yes." *Everything* with Kyle had been a deal. Which actually had been fun and exciting for a while. If she'd wanted something, she'd have to trade favors for what *he* wanted. He'd take her out on a date if she'd promise to have car sex after. He'd go to the grocery store if she cooked his favorite dinner, and so on.

It sounded so mercenary now, but it hadn't felt that way at the time. He'd been fun-loving and affectionate and passionate.

But in hindsight, he'd also been elusive, holding a part of himself back—much like her parents. And he'd made elaborate plans that he hadn't always followed through with.

Mark appeared to be his exact opposite in that way, but she'd been preprogrammed to not trust anyone who held something over her.

River refilled Lanie's cup. "You look like you need this caffeine more than I need a nap."

"Sometimes I feel like I landed on Mars here."

"Right?" River said with a little laugh, pressing her hand against her probably aching lower back. "It's like the Nice

Planet, but I keep waiting for the lights to come up and expose it for hell or something."

"Your back hurts," Lanie said. "Sit down."

"No, I've got to refill the pot."

"I've got it. Sit the hell down. And that's not me doing you a favor here on Nice Planet," she said before River could protest. "It's me not wanting you to go into labor because delivering a baby isn't on my bucket list."

"You're funny." River's smile faded. "And you know what else? You do belong here. On Nice Planet. I know you don't think you do, but you totally do."

"Right back at you."

River shook her head. "No," she said very softly. "I definitely do not."

Chapter 12

I'm not necessarily always anxious. I'm just extremely well educated about all the things that can and will go catastrophically wrong.

Sleep that night was not Lanie's friend. She kept seeing Mark's face when she'd asked how much she owed him for the tire fix. He'd been frustrated with her, and maybe hurt. Thinking about the ways she might make it up to him had led to a series of fantasies that had her giving up on finding any zzz's. Hot and bothered, she slipped out of bed.

It was a warm, moonless night, and restless, she slipped a pair of baggy sweats over her PJs and stepped outside. She walked to the end of the row of the cottages and around to the back of the big house where the real view of the valley was. Hoping to stay out of sight and just be alone to think, she slipped onto one of the plush lounge chairs at the very far edge of the patio.

There, she stretched out and tipped her head back to stare at the sky. She hadn't missed much about Wildstone, but she had missed this night sky. It didn't disappoint tonight, looking like a blanket of black velvet strewn with diamonds.

She heard the sound of water and followed it past the house, down the trail that led to the small, hidden lake. Someone was swimming, someone long and leanly muscled who, though she didn't want to admit it, was already in possession of a small corner of her heart.

Mark finished a lap and met her gaze, his dark eyes and dark smile promising to take her places.

She sat on the towel he'd clearly left for himself and returned his long look.

Rising effortlessly out of the water, he came toward her. At her feet, he shook his head and sent water drops spiraling all over her, making her shiver. Water ran off his body in rivulets.

He took her breath away.

He stood over her for a moment before sprawling that big body of his out at her side for her viewing pleasure.

And it was a pleasure. She'd seen it all the night they'd gone boogie boarding, but she still looked her fill. Anyone with warm blood in their veins would've done the same thing—

"So just what kind of an asshole was your husband?" he asked.

She froze. Not exactly what she wanted to talk about. She looked away from his all-seeing gaze and went back to stargazing. Discussing Kyle and what he'd done to her life—not to mention her confidence—was the last thing she wanted to do. "Why does it matter?" she asked warily. "He's dead. It's not relevant."

He waited for her to look at him again, and when she did, he simply raised a brow, making her sigh. "Okay, fine, it's relevant, but to be fair, it's not just you. I've got a chip on my shoulder for *everyone*. I'm an equal-opportunity chip-holder."

His mouth curved slightly. "Good to know."

She closed her eyes. "Have you ever wanted to believe in something so badly that you make it happen, except you're the only one in it?"

He was quiet for a long moment. Then his big hand reached for hers. "Yes."

She leaned into him, getting wet and not caring because he felt so good.

"It hurts like hell," he said, twisting to face her. "It's why I'm not looking for love."

"Ever?" she asked before she could stop herself. He'd already told her this.

Mark was quiet for a moment as his fingers ran along her temple at her hairline. "You're definitely the exception on making me want more," he said quietly. "But I'm not ready for love again, Lanie. My kids, they have to come first right now. I'm sorry."

This didn't surprise her. Nor did it stop her from wanting him. "What are you willing to give?"

"Everything but my heart. I've dated here and there, but I can't be pushed to go where I don't want to go."

She nodded. She got it. She did. He'd been hurt too and he had his girls to consider, but she couldn't help but feel the very tiniest bit of disappointment. But it didn't change anything for her. She wanted him. And the truth was, she wasn't ready for love either. Not even close.

"Is that enough for you?" he asked.

Yeah. It was, and she gave a slow nod.

He stood and pulled her up with him, giving her a chance to move away if she wanted. But apparently her body wasn't at all as conflicted as her brain because she leaned into him. Then those big, warm hands of his were on her hips, pulling her in closer. He lowered his head so that his jaw rubbed against her cheek, like a big, wild cat approaching a possible mate.

When she sighed in pleasure, he closed the nearly nonexistent gap between them and kissed her long and hard, lifting her up against him. She wound her arms around his neck and held him to her as they both dove in. When he pulled back, his eyes were dark, his voice so low as to be nearly inaudible. “Last chance,” he said quietly. “Go back to bed alone or stay here with me.”

She didn’t go back. Instead she leaned in and licked a drop of water off his neck. When he stilled and closed his eyes, she took a nibble out of the same spot, sucking a patch of his skin into her mouth, smiling against him when he groaned. And then she tugged him down to the towel.

He kneeled over her, his hands running up her spine, taking her sweatshirt with him. When he’d pulled it off, he took in her baby-blue camisole PJ top and said her name hoarsely.

A few low clouds had slid over the moon, making the night even darker, causing a sense of isolation and intimacy. The water lapped softly near their feet, the only other sound being the pounding of her heart and the sound of her whispering his name on the wind.

He buried his fingers in her hair, tugging lightly, exposing her neck. She could feel him, hot and hard against her, and her eyes fluttered closed as he played her like a fiddle. “Here, Lanie?” he murmured, voice husky and thick.

She looked up and found herself staring into twin pools of dark desire. He wanted her, and she wanted him even if he had stupid rules about love, even if it was only for the moment. “Yes,” she whispered against his mouth, “here,” and he slid the camisole straps down her arms, nudging the thin material southbound until it caught on the very tips of her breasts. She sucked in a breath at the sensation and then he gave another nudge and she was bared to him.

With a groan, he lowered his head, his mouth taking over for his fingers. And then he headed south, divesting her of all her armor as he went. Around them, the water continued to hit the rocky beach, a dissonant symphony of sound that mixed with her soft, desperate moans as he took her to head-spinning and heart-stopping heights. She came shockingly fast, and she might've been embarrassed about that if he hadn't lifted his head and looked at her with eyes so hot she felt scorched. Wanting to give him some of what he'd just given her, she reached for him, but his fingers lightly circled her wrists, stopping her progress.

She looked up at him and saw him smile in the darkness. He then rose to his feet and took a small step back as he untied his still-damp board shorts and pushed them off his lean hips. In the dim recesses of her mind she registered the wet thud as the shorts hit the ground behind him. Dropping to his knees between her legs, he braced himself over her, dipping his head to lick the skin of her collarbone, making her arch up off the towel. Reaching for him, she tried to tug him down to her, needing this. She expected him to be cool from the water, but he radiated heat and power and strength, and she craved more. "Please," she breathed.

With a groan, he dropped his head to her shoulder and squeezed his eyes shut tight. Then he rolled them so that she had the top all to herself. His hands went to her hips and rocked her against a most impressive erection and she started to lift up to take him inside her when he stopped her.

"I don't have a condom with me," he said, voice strained.

"Oh. *Oh . . .*" she murmured as understanding finally dawned. Looking down into his heated, hungry eyes, she realized that though she'd nearly forgotten to protect herself, *he* hadn't, and some of the cold deep inside her warmed. "It's okay," she whispered and bent low to kiss his chest, stopping to lave first one nipple and then his other like he'd done to her.

He groaned and tightened his grip on her, but she wriggled free to kiss his ridged ab muscles one by one as she too headed south.

"Lanie, you don't have to—"

She drew him into her mouth and he stopped talking, switching to muttered oaths and groans and fractured gasped phrases that made her feel like the sexiest woman alive as she took him to the same place he'd taken her . . .

THE NEXT MORNING, Lanie lay in her bed for a few extra moments, trying to decipher through her emotions to see how she felt about the incredible, erotically charged events of the night before.

She smiled a little smugly and decided she felt good. Very good.

An hour later she was at work, absolutely not reliving it all in her mind, like when he'd had his mouth on her—

"Good morning," Cora said and put a cup of coffee and a muffin on Lanie's desk. "You busy? You look like you're thinking very hard."

She felt herself blush and went with a distraction. "You're bearing bribes. What's wrong?"

"Nothing."

Just the day before she'd sent Cora the draft design for the new wine labels she'd been working on, and now she felt the anxiety grip her. Mark's mouth forgotten—mostly—she stood up. "You hate them."

"What?" Cora looked baffled and then horrified. "No, oh

my God, Lanie. I love the designs. I buried my lede, I'm sorry. I've passed all of it on to Owen and the others to see what they think, but you're onto something, they're gorgeous." Then she hesitated. "But I guess I am trying to bribe you in some way."

"How?" she asked warily.

"It's been a week and I'm wondering if you've given any thought to staying longer and extending your contract."

Lanie inhaled a deep breath. "I don't think I can."

"Are you . . . unhappy here?"

"Actually, I love it here." That also escaped before she could think. Dammit. She shut her mouth and drew in a careful, deep breath. "I mean, thank you. It's incredibly kind that you'd offer me more work, but I need to get back eventually."

"To Santa Barbara."

"Yes," Lanie said. "To Santa Barbara." Where her life was. Well, her old life. The one she needed to work on.

"You know what?" Cora said. "Let's pretend this conversation didn't happen, okay? So don't say no now. You can keep thinking about it."

Lanie nodded, grateful. Because she did need to think. Santa Barbara was her home, it was where her life was, her friends. The friends she'd made with Kyle, which meant in the end they'd been no friends at all, disappearing almost as fast as everything else had. It was as if her life had been a fresh painting and then it'd rained, smearing that old life away to nothing but a soggy canvas.

A soggy *blank* canvas.

Cora left and Lanie returned to work. But several hours later, Cora was back.

"Ready?" she asked Lanie.

How was it noon already? But if she'd learned one thing at

Capriotti Winery, it was that everyone, from the winemaker down to the last ranch hand in the fields, took lunch incredibly seriously. "I've got a lot I'm working on—"

"I know. I also know by how you're holding yourself that your neck and shoulders are sore, and I'd bet you my very last cork that you haven't budged since you first sat down at your desk this morning."

Lanie sighed. "No, but—"

"Come on. I'm not going to have you die of starvation on my watch. Besides, today's Anna's birthday and there will be extra family members to introduce you to."

Lanie had no idea who Anna was. For all she knew, Anna was the housekeeper. It didn't matter. To Cora, everyone was family, and that word held a whole different definition here than it ever had to Lanie. She thought about resistance but knew it was futile. Cora, she'd learned, was soft and sweet on the outside, but tough as nails on the inside. She was a mom, a grandma, and a CEO of a multimillion-dollar corporation, and she had the spine and spark to prove it.

Lanie stood up from her desk and stretched her aching bones. Cora was right—she'd been hyper-focused and hadn't budged.

Cora's cell phone buzzed on her hip. She took the call and Lanie watched the good mood vanish from her face. "No can do," she said. "But we can offer something else in Marcus's place—" She listened politely, her eyes ice. "No, I realize that he's quite the prize, believe me. I made him. He's the king of all prizes and I'll not see him auctioned off like a prime piece of USDA Choice. I will come up with something else and you won't be disappointed." She disconnected.

"Problem?" Lanie asked.

"That was the Wildstone Summer Festival chairwoman. It's an annual event that raises money for the local women's shelter, and we hold it out here on our property, donating the space, the wine, and the serving staff."

"That's generous."

Cora shrugged. "It's a good cause and it's good publicity. It's also on your list of things to do. We need logos for that as well. The problem is the auction. It raises a lot of money every year and I usually donate a few prizes. Last year I auctioned off a weekend working here at the winery." She smiled. "Made a mint and got some extra labor for the weekend."

"Nice. And not seeing the problem," Lanie said.

"This year they want me to put Marcus up on the auction block, said he'd make another mint."

Lanie had a flash of Mark towering over her, his mouth at her ear whispering all the wickedly naughty things he planned to do to her. He'd kept his word too. Hell yeah, he'd bring in a mint.

"You don't agree?" asked a deep, unbearably familiar voice.

She turned and yep, Mark stood in the doorway, propping up the jamb with a broad shoulder. He was smiling and her gaze went straight to his mouth, remembering exactly what it could do, and she felt heat rush to her face.

And her good parts.

His smile said he knew what she was thinking about, which didn't help.

"It doesn't matter," Cora said. "Because you're not doing it. I won't have it. We don't abuse our own here."

"And yet you have your grandnieces working in the barn with their hands tied together."

Cora didn't smile. "That's different. You . . ."

"What?" he asked.

Lanie tried to slip out of the room, but Mark didn't budge from the doorway.

"You're still adjusting to civilian life," Cora said, softer now. "When you didn't even want to be here."

Mark let out a breath. "Mom, you've got to stop saying that. If the girls hear you and—"

"They're playing outside."

Lanie tried to become invisible, but her superpowers failed her. She moved to the far side of her L-shaped desk and looked around for something to do with herself.

"I think you're holding back," Cora told Mark. "Another reason I wasn't about to let you be a part of this auction. That's not how I want to push you back to the land of the living, though I do want you to be free to date."

"Not happening," Mark said firmly.

Lanie tried really hard not to let that bother her. She didn't want to date either, so she had no idea what was wrong with her.

"You can't just shut off that part of your life," Cora said. "You need companionship. Eventually you're going to want to be in a relationship—"

Lanie couldn't quite catch Mark's response to that, but whatever he muttered had Cora's temper igniting.

"I know you're not about to tell me that you have no intention of falling in love again, because I raised you to be more sensible than that," she said.

He didn't sigh, but he looked like he wanted to. "I'm going to do this on my own time, Mom. And not even you can rush me."

"But you are going to eventually do it?"

His gaze flicked to Lanie. "We're done with this conversation."

Cora threw up her hands. "Fine. Go. They need help setting the lunch tables. I'll be right there."

Given the fact that she'd just ordered around the biggest alpha male Lanie had ever met, she was thinking it was pretty optimistic of Cora to expect Mark to actually go. Which was why she was surprised at the indulgent crinkle at the corners of his eyes and found herself actually floored when he turned and did as he was told.

Cora was amused when Lanie just gaped at her. "How did you do that?" she asked. "That was like magic!"

"No, honey, not magic. A man'll do almost anything for a woman he loves, but it's not the big gestures that mean the most. It's the small ones, if you see what I'm saying."

"Like setting the table."

She smiled bright as the sun. "Yes, like the setting the table." She took Lanie's hand and squeezed it. "Don't give up on him just yet."

"Oh. Um, I think you're mistaken because Mark and I aren't—"

"You sure about that?"

Lanie grimaced and zipped her mouth.

Cora smiled and patted her on the arm. "You don't owe me any explanations, honey. You're both grown-ups."

"Then what was that about wanting him to feel free to date . . . ?"

A smug light came into Cora's gaze.

"Oh," Lanie breathed. "You just wanted confirmation that he and I . . ."

Cora smiled.

"You're brilliant," Lanie marveled. "And a little scary."

"I know," Cora said.

Lanie moved to the door and then stopped and turned back. “But really, there isn’t anything going on between us, at least nothing permanent.”

“I understand. And it’s none of my business.”

No, but Lanie wanted to make sure there was no mistake. “Neither of us are in a place for it. I’m only telling you this because I don’t want to get your hopes up. In my experience, hope is the first step toward disappointment.”

“I understand,” Cora repeated gently, but she wasn’t looking discouraged in the slightest.

Lanie left, hoping that Cora was human and not some sort of a secret guardian angel who granted wishes that were made in the deep dark of the night.

Chapter 13

When someone says "Don't be anxious" and I'm miraculously cured. Not.

Halfway through the next work week, Mark was in the middle of acting as a referee at a domestic disturbance call when he felt his personal cell phone vibrate in his pocket. Since his family knew to contact him during business hours only with an emergency, he itched to reach for it, but had to ignore it because of the trouble brewing in front of him.

The wife had made the call on her husband, saying that she'd married an abusive asshole and needed help extracting him from her house. The husband had called immediately after, claiming that his soon-to-be ex-wife was threatening his manhood and life.

Mark had gotten on the scene to find the man had locked himself in the bathroom and the wife was pounding on the door with one hand, her other holding a lethal-looking spike stiletto heel.

He'd taken the "weapon" from her and made her sit on the couch in the living room in plain sight while he turned to the still-locked bathroom. Before he could say a word, the wife got in plenty.

"Come out of there, you no-good, pussy-addicted, lint-licking, soul-sucking piece of shit!" she yelled from her perch on the couch. "I'm going to stab you in the nads with your ho's shoe! Get out here and take it like a man!"

"I called the cops on you, you crazy bitch!" the husband yelled through the door. "I'm not coming out until I've got an armed protector."

The wife shook her head at Mark as if to say, *Do you see what I'm dealing with?* "The cop is *here*, you idiot," she snapped. "I let him in."

The bathroom door cracked open. A bleary, red-rimmed eye peeked out and focused in on Mark, taking in his uniform. "You armed?"

"Yes," Mark said.

"Thank God." The husband opened the door the rest of the way and pointed at his wife. "She's completely gonzo. I want her hauled off to jail and locked away."

The wife crossed her arms. "You're the one who cheated, you dipshit. And there's only one chick I know who owns these ridiculous knock-offs and that's our crack-ho of a neighbor with the store-bought knockers. I'm going to kill you both."

Mark grimaced. "If you don't want to be arrested, you're going to have to stop threatening him."

"Well, then he's going to have to stop being stupid, and I don't see either of those things happening."

In the end, Mark had the husband leave the home, which belonged to the wife's family. The guy left for a friend's house, his parting shot to his wife that he'd see her in court.

Fine by Mark. Better in court than in the morgue.

When he was back in his patrol Blazer, he pulled out his phone. The call he'd received earlier had come from the girls' school. Specifically from the principal. This wasn't a complete shock. Samantha didn't like her teacher, and when Samantha didn't like someone, the whole world paid the price. Twice he'd been called in when she'd gone missing—aka hidden in a tree on the playground after recess had ended—simply because she hadn't wanted to go back to her classroom.

He hit the number for the school and got the principal's assistant.

"She's gone missing again," she said immediately, not as calm as he'd have liked. "Just like the other times, but—"

"How long has she been gone?"

"Thirty minutes."

Fuck. "And Sierra?"

"Sitting right here in the office with me eating a Popsicle." She lowered her voice. "I thought it would entice her into talking because it's clear she's not stressed in the least, which in the past has been the signal that her sister is perfectly safe."

Not good enough for Mark. "Check the tree in the yard. I'm on my way." He disconnected and inhaled a deep breath, feeling the overwhelming sensation of being a single parent and not the best one at that. He had no idea what two little girls needed, none, though he gave it his all. Still, he knew damn well he fell fucking short.

The principal's assistant called back five minutes later. "Found her. She was in the tree."

"My ETA is twenty."

He made it in ten. When he pulled up, he realized it was a half day for some sort of teacher thing and the bell had just rung. He called the office and told them he was in the parent pickup line and to not put the girls on their usual bus.

Her mother's temperament was making an appearance in

every line of her body as Sam trudged angrily down the sidewalk toward him, dragging her backpack behind her, scuffing a path through a blanket of leaves that had fallen in the day's wind gusts. When the disobedient backpack declined to keep up, she jerked it angrily along with her, huffing and mumbling, sending leaves flying in her wake.

Mark watched them both approach with a mixture of deep relief and bad self-directed temper that completely destroyed his equilibrium. What was he doing wrong that one daughter couldn't handle school and the other hadn't spoken in a year?

He exited his vehicle. The girls had been walking single file, Sierra in front happily skipping, Samantha behind her, head down, torturing her backpack. Sierra was as put together as she had been when they'd left for school. Samantha was without her sweatshirt, her T-shirt was dirty, and her jeans were torn in one knee, revealing a bloody scratch.

Sierra beamed at the sight of him. He scooped her up for a hug and she put her hands to his cheeks, patting lightly. An unspoken signal for "go easy on her." He brushed a kiss to her forehead and deposited her into the backseat before turning back for Samantha.

"Sam," he said and she jerked her head up, her bad temper gone in a blink, replaced by sheer joy. "*Daddy!*" She leapt at him and he caught her, holding her tightly to him. She smelled like oak tree and maple syrup and a little bit like him, and he held on tight, thankful when she squeezed him right back. She laid her icy cheek against his and he turned them, shielding her from the wind.

"Daddy," she murmured again.

Her moods were pure and mercurial, but she loved with a fierceness that pushed everything else aside. And like always in these uncomfortable, unfamiliar moments with the girls that were his entire life, he was forcibly reminded that he was indeed grateful to Brittney for something after all.

"You're cold," he said. "When you take off like that, you need to plan ahead."

She looked away, avoiding eye contact. Another throwback from her mother, which meant she was thinking and thinking hard about how to get away with not telling him something he needed to know. "Talk to me, Sam."

At this, she leveled her big, dark, soulful eyes on him and gave him the full pitch. "I gave my sweatshirt to Julio. He doesn't have a sweatshirt and he's always cold. Don't tell Grandma."

"Grandma would be proud of you," he said.

"Maybe for the sweatshirt, but Sierra and I also gave him half our lunches. We always do."

"Baby."

Her eyes swiveled his way, her outrage clear. "He's *hungry*, Daddy. And he was the only one who made Trevor stop being mean to us on the playground."

Sometimes Mark was certain his heart no longer worked, and then at other times, like right now, the organ swelled so that it felt too big for his rib cage. "We'll double the size of your lunches."

She beamed at him and he felt a burst of pride that he'd been able to soothe some of the always-just-at-bay guilt that gnawed at him for not being the best parent at times. He'd never intended to raise sweet yet savvy little hellions, but somewhere along the way they'd adapted to his life and become his Mini-Mes. "Now tell me about this Trevor," he said.

"He teased Sierra about not talking and he told me I'm a

loser who chased off my mommy. But I didn't chase Mommy off, she left all on her own."

Jesus. He wasn't going to survive parenthood. He pulled her a little closer and brushed a kiss to her temple, wondering just how much jail time he'd do for killing a juvenile punkass kid. "I'm sorry he said those things to you," he managed evenly. "But I'm glad you know that nothing of what happened with your mom was your fault."

"I know, Daddy."

But God, could she really? Praying that his sins weren't going to come back to haunt his girls, he dumped her into the backseat, making her giggle. She crawled over Sierra and he leaned in to make sure they were buckled properly, tickling Sierra until she laughed out loud. He stroked a thumb lightly below the scrape on Samantha's knee. "From your tree-climbing expedition?"

"Yes. Don't tell Grandma that either, okay? She says climbing trees isn't becoming."

He snorted and got behind the wheel. Five minutes later, he pulled up to the winery. He helped the girls out and watched them run up the path, waving wildly at everyone just sitting down to lunch on the other side of the fence.

Everyone waved back and the twins vanished inside, appearing in the yard two seconds later. He strode up the path, smelling the food even from this distance. He felt some of the tension he had been holding off since getting the call about Samantha ease away.

Lanie was there. Both tables were completely full, and as he could've predicted, she was sitting on the very end, looking inside a brown bag.

She'd brought her own lunch again, even as she looked at

the growing food spread with longing. She still tended to hold herself back even after all these weeks, but she did smile easier at whoever approached her.

Pretty much the story of his life with her as well. She held back, but when he approached and pushed just a little to get past her barriers, she welcomed him in with that devastating smile.

And that one memorable night under the stars last week, she'd also welcomed him in with open arms.

"She's special," Mia said.

Mia had come up at his side. His baby sister smiled at him. "But you already know that, don't you?"

He pleaded the fifth.

"I know, I know," she said. "Mom's on a mission to mend your broken heart and you're on a mission that's counterproductive to that, to never be happy again—"

"Mia, don't."

She lifted her hands. "Hey, I'm not judging. I'm the one who wants to find someone."

"You find too many someones."

"I'm working on being more selective. Now I'm looking for The One. He needs to have intelligence, charm, and a sense of humor that is insanely fucking naughty."

He grimaced. "Don't need to hear this."

"No worries because I'm pretty sure that he doesn't exist."

He looked at her, really looked at her, and saw misery in her gaze. "Okay, who do I have to kill?"

"No one." She let out a low laugh. "And don't think I don't know that you made a visit to Sean last month."

"Who?"

She rolled her eyes. "My ex-boyfriend."

"Hey, I didn't kill him."

"True, you just threatened him with . . . what was it? Something about taking his favorite body part and shoving it up his own ass?"

Mark had no regrets. "He was a dick to you."

"True. But I let him be, so that's on me. I'm completely over him, though."

"Then what's wrong?"

"Nothing."

If only that was true. "Is this one of those 'nothings' where later on you'll send me a ten-page essay via text?" he asked.

"It's not about me," she said.

Mark looked at his watch.

Mia sighed. "Why do I try to help you?"

"Me?" Color him confused. "I don't need help with anything."

"Spoken like a clueless man." She jerked her head toward the table. And Lanie.

With a shake of his head, he started to walk away but she caught him. "Listen," she said. "You know how Mom collects people? Holden. Lanie. River—who she's already going to birthing classes with. Anyway, you're a collector too."

Mark watched as Lanie broke one of her cookies in two and gave a half to each of his girls. Okay, so maybe he *was* a collector, but so was Lanie. She just didn't seem to know it yet. "Do you have a point?" he asked.

"Yes, if you'd let me make it. I get that you're still off love, but it makes me worry for Lanie. Not that I think you'll hurt her on purpose, but . . ."

Mark let out a slow exhale. "I hear you."

"I hope so, because even as hurt as she's clearly been and

as careful as she is, she's let your girls into her heart. And she's well on her way to letting your family in too because, well, we're fucking irresistible. But up until now, the women you've let into your life don't go all the way in. They dig you 'cuz you're the sexy, badass military hero or because you carry a gun and know how to use it, but you're more than that. They've been takers, not givers. And Lanie . . . she's a giver. You need to protect her, Mark, even if it's from you."

It was excellent advice. It really was. And he needed to heed it, he thought, watching Sierra climb into Lanie's lap and press in close.

Lanie didn't hesitate to wrap her arms around his little girl and squeeze. She murmured something into Sierra's ear that had her giggling and wriggling with pure joy.

Sierra hadn't spoken a word since the day her mom had walked out on her, but she was still the best people reader Mark knew. That she was comfortable with Lanie spoke volumes.

Lanie smiled too and Mark wondered if she even realized she was letting down her guard for them. He doubted it.

The girls were safe for her, which made him smile because the girls terrified most people. In fact, the Capriottis terrified most everyone.

But not Lanie, and even thinking it had something tightening in his chest. Because if he wasn't careful, it was going to be *him* who got hurt at the end of this.

Good thing he was very careful.

THE WINERY ALWAYS settled down after the end of the workday. It was one of Lanie's favorite times to walk the property. It was quiet, majestic. Beautiful. But tonight as she walked the path to the end of the cottages, past the big house to the barn where the two boogie boards had been leaning against since she and Mark had used them and saw only one, she hesitated.

Don't do it.

But she did. She grabbed the board. And five minutes later she'd changed and was on her way.

She'd spent the past ten years in Santa Barbara, but before that, she'd grown up in Morro Bay, only fifteen miles from here, where her parents had a home. She'd always felt most comfortable on the beach, any beach, with wet sand between her toes.

The sun was just setting when she slid out of her car and ditched the sweatshirt and shorts she'd pulled on over her bathing suit. She searched the swells and found him, a silhouette of a male body surfing the waves as the sun sank below the horizon.

Mesmerized by the sight, she dove into the water and joined him. Long before she got out to him, he turned his head and found her. Between the swells, their gazes met and held.

She waited, holding her breath. When he smiled and gave her a *hurry up* gesture with one jerk of his chin, she smiled back.

They spent the next hour racing for the biggest swells, trying to best each other and, barring that, knocking each other off. They exchanged no words, nothing but long looks and the occasional laugh when successfully unseating the other. But there was plenty of touching, grabbing, patting, wrestling . . .

It was the most fun she'd ever had.

Eventually they came out of the water and collapsed to their knees onto his towel, panting from the exertion. She'd never felt more alive and it was doing things to her, revving her up. She wondered if he had condoms tonight . . .

"You shouldn't surf by yourself," he said.

"You do," she said. "And besides, I wasn't by myself."

He shook his head and gently pushed her wet hair from her face. "I just don't like the thought of you out here on your own."

"I'm good at being on my own." She brought her hand up to his, holding it to her face, belying her words.

Water drops clung stubbornly to his face and shoulders, some running down his chest and abs. "But that's my point," he said quietly. "You don't have to be, not here. You've got a lot of people at your back. Mia, Alyssa, River, my mom . . . everyone. They like you, Lanie. They care about you."

He hadn't included himself in that assessment. Not that it mattered, because she knew he liked her. He liked her a lot. But since he wasn't going to let it go anywhere, it didn't matter.

It was a reminder of something she didn't want to think about, because she couldn't control her emotions like he could and had to look away. But he took her face in his hands and ran his thumb lightly across her lower lip. She leaned in a little closer and could feel his abs tighten against her. She felt him take a deep, slow breath and watched as his eyes darkened.

She put a hand to his chest to feel the reassuring rhythm of his heart. God, she was so stupid happy to be with him. It was way too easy to fall right back into the only place that seemed to work for them.

Mouths locked.

Mark wasn't big on words but he was most excellent at using actions to reveal his thoughts. She tried to do the same now, letting him know with her kiss how much his presence here tonight meant to her.

Remember, not falling for him . . .

His hands slid up her back, sending shivers cascading

through her. She started to say something but was silenced by his hot mouth covering hers again. And again. Since that was nice, very nice, she pressed up against him for more and he angled his head and gave it to her, taking the kiss even deeper, and she felt herself wobble.

His arms tightened, pulling her hard against him in a silent *I've got you* and she let herself go, grinding into him, suddenly desperate to feel as much of him as she could.

Not falling for him . . .

A fact made much easier when he pulled free and met her gaze with reluctance. "This isn't a good idea."

"Did you decide that before or after the night at the lake?" she asked.

He winced and closed his eyes for a beat.

Pulling her hands from his delicious body, she tried not to notice that they were wound up against each other, only an inch—or more accurately eight to nine inches—away from having a very happy ending to the night.

"I was serious about this not becoming serious," he said.

"And I heard you."

He opened his eyes, his gaze unwavering on hers. "I just wanted to make sure there wasn't any misunderstanding."

It was like diving into the cold ocean without any of the feel-good euphoria to go with it. Or the boogie board. Or the ability to swim. He'd literally just jumped into her personal nightmare and found the one thing that could paralyze her. Her deepest, darkest fear.

That she didn't, couldn't, trust her own love meter in picking the right guy because she had no idea what a normal relationship was even like.

Which was ridiculous because she didn't even *want* that. So she nodded, like it all made perfect sense when actually, nothing made any sense at all; not the way her body still wanted his, not the stabbing, sharp pain where her heart sat in her chest, and not the way she wanted to beg him to change his mind.

But she no longer begged for affections.

She no longer needed *anyone's* affections at all and she blamed him for making her forget that even for a second. "Look at the time," she said, not wearing a watch or checking her phone. She rose to her feet and backed away. "I've gotta get going."

And then she ran to her car, where she paused to smack her forehead on the steering wheel a few times to knock some sense into herself before driving off into the night.

Chapter 14

When your anxiety goes away and having no anxiety gives you anxiety.

Lanie was on the road back to the winery when she took a call from Alyssa. There'd been some sort of electrical outage and the cottages were all out of power until morning.

Perfect.

"We've shifted people around in the big house," Alyssa said. "Everyone has a bedroom for tonight, so no worries."

Oh hell no. "Thanks, but I can get a hotel."

"Not in Wildstone, you can't," Alyssa said. "No hotels. There's a B&B, but why spend money? Plus, it's haunted. We've got a room for you here in the big house—it's all arranged. Second floor, right wing, last bedroom on the left."

After the call, Lanie let out a breath and decided she needed a little time out, and that time out needed to come with a drink. Wildstone was incredibly picturesque and quaint but it wasn't exactly hopping. She pulled into Whiskey River, the lone local bar and grill.

In the parking lot she quickly French-braided her still-damp hair and added lip gloss, her one point of pride being that she look as great as possible while feeling as low as possible. It made no sense to her, it really didn't. She'd gone into this thing with Mark with no expectations. Absolutely none. There was nothing to take; nothing offered except a good time.

It'd all sounded good at the time. So why, then, back at the beach with Mark hadn't she just expressed her understanding of the situation—because she *did* understand, more than he could know—and jump his bones?

Instead, she'd protected herself and walked away, hurt and surprised. Because while Mark wasn't planning on giving anything, *she* already had. More than one piece of her heart already belonged to his children, his family.

And, if she was being honest, him as well.

Wow. She was really throwing herself a pity party here. Wanting to be over it, she entered Whiskey River and then stopped short at the sight of River sitting at a table by herself, a huge platter of wings in front of her.

River looked embarrassed. "I'd like to say that I'm here with a party of eight, but it's just me and baby. You going to sit?"

Was she? She liked River, just another person she hadn't intended to like at all. But even after all these weeks, River still held back with her. Not anyone else, just Lanie. It was one of those things, she knew. She'd never really made friends very easily. But now she was actually trying, though she had no idea why.

Because you're tired of being a lone wolf . . .

So she sat. "I once ate an entire box of pizza rolls," she said, aiming to make River feel better. "That's thirty-six, in case you didn't know, and the box said it served eight."

River laughed and rubbed her tummy.

"You having pains?"

"No, the baby's just active. She thinks kicking my bladder is fun."

"She?" Lanie asked.

"Yes. Last week Cora changed my status to permanent employee so I could get benefits. She set me up with her friend in town, an ob-gyn. I had an ultrasound today. I'm glad she's a girl. I like girls far better than males right about now."

"So . . . you're staying here in Wildstone?"

River hesitated and then nodded. "It's nice not to have to worry about a job. And they're so wonderful here." She shook her head. "Earlier today Holden and Mark brought me a bassinet. They made it themselves, using the wood from old wine barrels. It's beautiful and . . . amazing." She hesitated. "I still feel like I landed on that Nice Planet."

"You deserve for good things to happen to you, like anyone else," Lanie said.

River met her gaze, hers suddenly hooded. "I'm not used to good things happening to me."

Lanie didn't want to be moved, but she was. "You heard about the electricity being out at the cottages?"

"And that we're in the big house tonight? Yeah." River didn't look put out or anxious about that at all. "It's going to be like a dream, sleeping in that big, huge place."

Lanie, not wanting to burst her bubble, forced a smile. "Yeah, like a dream."

Alyssa walked in with baby Elsa in a wrap against her chest. She started to go to the bar but saw River and Lanie, and headed their way instead. "Hey," she said. "I'm picking up some food for Owen and I. How you two doing?"

Before either could answer, a scuffle broke out at the bar. Two guys had started an argument, getting off their barstools to do it, shoving each other with one hand, their other hands both still occupied with their beers, which sloshed over with every subsequent shove.

The bartender leapt over the bar and got between them, arms outstretched to hold them apart. "I've told you both you're not allowed to be in here at the same time. I also told you that the next time it happened, I was calling the cops."

"Call 'em," one of them growled.

"Already did, dumbass," the bartender said.

"Hey, *he* followed me here," the other guy said, jabbing his beer in the direction of the first idiot.

"Because you told me you were going to ask my girl out!"

"Which I didn't have to do since *she* asked *me* out!"

They tried to jump at each other again but the bartender grabbed for them and the three went down in a tangle.

The front doors opened and Mark strode in, hair still wet, in a sweatshirt and those board shorts, and put himself right into the fray.

"Oh my God," River gasped.

"It's okay," Alyssa said. "This isn't his first bar fight."

Still, Lanie stood up in alarm, but in the next breath the fight was completely over. Mark had grabbed each of the idiots by the backs of their shirts and given them a shake. He then pulled them in closer and said something that had them both going still. He held on to them for an extra beat, holding their gazes with his quiet, badass, steely one before finally letting them go.

The two men slunk to the door, heads down.

"Oh my God," River whispered again.

Yeah, and . . . holy cow, Lanie thought. The man was sexy as hell, which was something she already knew, but seeing him in action was . . . yowza. She looked over at River to make sure the level of hotness hadn't put her into labor and realized River wasn't impressed—she was horrified. And maybe a little scared. "Hey, are you okay?"

"Yeah." She shook her head. "It's the uniform. I mean, he's not wearing it right now, but it doesn't matter because he's still all badass don't-mess-with-me cop, you know? Makes you nervous as hell, doesn't it? Like, he could decide to arrest you at any moment and lock away the key." She paused and then grimaced at Alyssa's and Lanie's brows-up expressions. "Just me?"

"Cops make you nervous," Lanie said carefully, not wanting to scare River off from talking about herself, but the truth was they were all insanely curious about her, as she'd said next to nothing about her background.

Not that Lanie was any better . . .

"Very nervous," River said.

"My brother would never do anything to scare or hurt you," Alyssa said, bouncing up and down a little as she talked, trying to soothe a now-irritated Elsa. "Well, unless you ate the last of Mom's brownies. He really likes those." She was obviously teasing and just as obviously trying to put River at ease.

But River didn't look quite there yet.

Since Elsa was still fussing, Alyssa pulled her free of the wrap. "Here," she said to Lanie. "Hold this a sec." And then she thrust the annoyed little wiggleworm at Lanie.

Lanie automatically took her and then tried not to panic. "Um, I don't know what to do with a baby."

Alyssa looked amused. "Well, you pull her in closer to you, for one thing. She's not a stink bomb."

Right. Lanie did just that, settling the baby against her chest and shoulder like she'd seen Mark do.

Elsa stared up at her, not sure if she was pleased or pissed.

Alyssa grabbed a wing. "You've had bad experiences with cops?" she asked River.

River reached over and patted Elsa's back with a soft smile for the baby. "Where I grew up, a cop sniffing in your business was nothing but trouble."

"Was it just you and your mom growing up?"

"Yeah."

"I can't imagine how tough that was when she passed away," Lanie said quietly.

"It wasn't all bad. I waitressed at the truck stop and the other waitresses were really nice to me. I had all the food I could want and they let me couch surf when I needed."

"And when you didn't couch surf?"

She looked away and Lanie's heart sank for the girl River had been. "You don't have to tell us."

River gave her a small smile. "It's funny how easy it is to remove those memories from my mind right now with a great job and a roof over my head, you know?"

Lanie had never suffered for money like River had. Things had been tight after leaving home. She'd had to get loans for college and there'd been months and months where she'd lived paycheck to paycheck. But even so, she'd never worried about not having a bed or food.

"Things are really good right now," River said softly, her hands on her baby bump.

Lanie had to smile at that. The girl—and she really was just a girl—was pregnant, with apparently no one at her back, and she thought things were good. Optimism. Something she herself was missing. She looked down at a now sleeping Elsa and felt a totally unfamiliar ache in the region of her ovaries.

Kyle hadn't wanted kids. She'd told herself she'd been okay with that and maybe she'd believed it at the time, but right now, at age thirty, her ovaries were definitely starting to say otherwise.

Mark had turned to the bartender, offering him a hand, pulling him up off the floor, clapping him on the back. They spoke for a moment and then Mark eyed the crowd. His sharp gaze found them, and with one last word to the bartender, he headed right for their table.

His gaze was on Lanie and Elsa, eyes soft. "You look like a natural."

Oh boy. That look combined with the warmth of the sleepy baby against her chest was probably potent enough to make her pregnant. Because she couldn't help herself, she pressed her nose to Elsa's neck and inhaled that unique sweet baby scent.

And there went her ovaries again.

"She's cute, right?" Alyssa asked. "It's not just me?"

Mark laughed. "Are you kidding me? They have big, suck-you-in eyes and they smell good. It's a scam." He set himself to the task of untangling the sleeping Elsa's fist from Lanie's hair, then gave the baby a quick hug. Talk about being a natural. He rubbed gentle circles on the baby's back and then handed her off to Alyssa.

He then pulled Lanie upright—in a much nicer fashion than he had the fighting idiots. He slid one arm around her waist, buried his other hand in her hair, and kissed her hard and with quite a bit more tongue than she would've expected in public before he pulled back.

"I'm an ass," he said quietly, pressing his forehead to hers. "I don't always think to pretty up my words before I speak."

She felt like she had whiplash. She'd just seen him as the

tough, impenetrable, stoic cop, and now she was back to dealing with the sexy, alpha man who'd kissed her on the beach before reminding her he wasn't going to ever fall in love again. "I don't want you to pretty up your words for me," she said.

"I appreciate that, but I'd still like to try. After I deal with the dicks outside. Will you wait?"

She hesitated and then for some reason nodded.

He gave her a small smile. "Later?"

"Later," she whispered and watched as he strode outside to make his perps regret their most recent life choices. Then she sank shakily back to her chair.

"That was the hottest thing I've ever seen," River said. "If I didn't hate men so much, I'd start dating again just to get kissed like that."

"It was a pretty great kiss," Lanie managed.

They turned their attention back to the platter of wings, splitting a pitcher of iced tea in deference to the baby. Not what Lanie had come for, but it worked.

Holden showed up with a couple of other guys, but broke from the pack when he saw them. Well, not them, exactly, because he didn't seem to notice Lanie or Alyssa at all.

Just River.

He'd changed from his work gear. Clean jeans, cleaner boots, and an untucked button-down shoved up on his forearms. His cowboy hat had been traded in for a baseball cap, which he took off. "Ladies," he said. "Looking good."

River rolled her eyes. "I'm big as a house."

He shrugged. "I stand by my statement."

River didn't seem to know how to take that so Lanie kicked out a chair for him. "Want to join us?" she asked, purposely not looking at River shaking her head *no-no-no* behind his back.

"Thanks." Holden sat and looked at River. "Wanted to know if you'd have dinner with me."

"I already ate."

"I meant another night. Any other night."

River flushed. "Are you asking me out in front of Alyssa and Lanie?"

"Trying." He slid them an apologetic look. "I've been trying to catch her alone to ask her, but she's surprisingly sly and fast on her feet given how pregnant she is."

Lanie smiled because River was beet red now.

"She'd love to go out with you," Alyssa said.

Holden gave a rare smile, reminding Lanie just how good-looking a kid he was. "Great. I'll pick her up tomorrow after work." He rose, winked at Lanie, and stroked his fingers once over the back of River's hand before walking away.

River gaped at them. "I can't go on a date!"

"Why not?" Alyssa asked. "You're single, right?"

"Yes, but look at me! I weigh as much as a two-ton cow. And I'm pregnant. And I don't even know him!"

"You're not even close to two tons," Lanie piped in. "I'd be shocked if you were much over a hundred pounds. And being pregnant doesn't mean you're dead. As for not knowing him, that's easily fixed by going on a date."

River stared at her. "Why do you care?"

Lanie shrugged. "Maybe I want to see you happier than I am."

"I don't need a man to be happy."

"Well, ain't that the truth," Alyssa said. "Look, you work hard, but you seem a little lonely. Holden's a good guy with a good job and it's clear he's interested in you. What could be the harm in that?"

River shook her head and opened her mouth, but then closed it again. Lanie wondered what she'd been about to say, but it was really none of her business. And an hour later, when Mark still hadn't returned, she drove herself back to the winery. Turned out that the bedroom they'd procured for her on the second floor at the end of the hall was . . .

Mark's.

He would apparently be taking the twins' room, who were having a sleepover in Aunt Mia's room. Lanie stood in the middle of his bedroom looking around at the dark, masculine furniture and lush bedding and tried not to picture him lying in that bed wearing nothing but luxurious sheets.

Shaking off the image, she stole one of the T-shirts from his dresser for PJs and used the toothbrush someone had thoughtfully left for her on the bathroom counter. When a knock came, she debated whether to chicken out by turning off the lights and hiding under the covers—or running for the hills.

"I can hear you breathing," came Mark's low, amused voice. "Open up."

Said the Big Bad Wolf . . .

Chapter 15

Why limit yourself to panicking in a crowd? Panic everywhere. Follow your wildest, most anxious dreams.

Lanie rolled her eyes at both herself and Mark and cracked open the door. "Yes?"

He hadn't changed his clothes and his hair had dried a little crazy, as if he'd shoved his fingers through it a lot. "Try out my bed yet?"

Oh boy, she thought. Her body liked the low velvet in his voice way too much. "No. How did you know the bar needed a cop tonight?"

"The bartender's an old friend. Boomer called me instead of 9-1-1."

"That seems like a huge risk. What if you couldn't get there in time to stop the trouble?"

"He knew I'd get there."

So matter-of-fact. So confident. Not cocky, just very sure of his abilities. She wondered what that utter lack of self-doubt was like. She'd sure like to know. "So . . . did you want something?"

"Yes. It's later. Sorry it took me so long at the station." He leaned on the doorjamb looking like sin personified. "You going to invite me in?"

"You're a bad idea. *We're* a bad idea, remember?"

He laughed low in his throat. "How could I forget when I've told myself the same thing a hundred times?"

So he'd been thinking about them too. There was comfort in that. "I don't think this is the time or place."

"I know." His dark gaze swept over her from head to toe, slowing at some strategic spots that quivered in response. "But you're standing there wearing my favorite T-shirt from when I was a teenager and near as I can tell, nothing else."

She tightened her grip on the door because she didn't trust herself not to give in at his first touch. "It's your childhood bedroom," she said. "We can't do it in here."

He just smiled.

She gaped at him. "How many girls have you had in this room?" She narrowed her eyes. "And if you tell me you lost your virginity here in this very bed, I'll—"

"Zero," he said. "I've had zero women in that bed. Hello, you've met my nosy-ass family, right?"

"So . . . you *didn't* lose your virginity in here?" she asked.

He smiled. "Your fascination with my virginity is cute, but no, the main event happened in my dad's pickup truck when I was fifteen."

"By yourself?"

He laughed, the sound dissolving the rest of her resolve. "Trust me, there was plenty of that too, but no, I actually talked my chemistry partner into an experiment of . . . animal magnetism." He flashed a grin and leaned in to speak softly into her ear. "We did some okay work that night, but I've learned a lot since then." He nipped her earlobe. "Let me in, Lanie."

He'd most definitely learned plenty, she thought wryly as her nipples tightened and her thighs clenched. "I don't think so."

Undeterred, he nuzzled her throat, brushing light kisses along her skin, setting her on fire from the inside out. "You in that shirt," he murmured. "You're a fantasy come to life, Lanie."

She was trying to come up with a brilliant retort for that when he stepped into her and slid his magic hands to her hips. "I really am sorry about tonight."

She looked into his eyes and saw that actually he wasn't his usual confident self. He wasn't sure what she was thinking or what she was going to do, and there was some unexpected power in that. Stepping back, she gave him room to pass. He held her gaze as he came in, his own revealing his surprise. He hadn't expected her to let him in. Reaching past him, she quietly shut the door and then . . .

Pushed him up against it.

He raised a brow. "Feeling aggressive?"

"Apparently. You have a problem with that?"

"Are you kidding me? You're every walking, talking fantasy I've ever had." His hands went to her waist and squeezed gently before gliding up her body to cup her face. "Tell me what you want tonight."

She didn't miss the distinction but neither did she hesitate. "Your body on mine."

His eyes both darkened and softened. "Lanie—"

She put a finger on his lips. "I know the rules. No need to complicate anything," she whispered and went up on tiptoe to kiss him.

His groan rumbled from his chest through hers as his hand slipped beneath the hem of the shirt to palm her still-panty-covered ass, and she decided his clothes needed to come off and fast. He let her be in control for all of a second and a half as she tugged at his sweatshirt before he reversed their positions and had her up against the door, arms pinned over her head, kissing her until she couldn't remember her name or why she'd ever thought to resist.

The shirt she wore hit the floor, exposing her bare breasts. The touch of his mouth working its way down her throat made her gasp in pleasure and arch into him as she reached for the string on his board shorts and tugged. "Tell me you have a condom."

"I've got an entire box," he said and covered her mouth with his.

She was nearly blind with need when someone knocked on the other side of the door right next to her head.

"Lanie?"

Oh dear God, that was Cora.

"I was just walking by and heard a thunk up against the door," her boss said. "Are you okay?"

Mark lifted his head, his half-lidded sexy eyes both heated and amused.

Not Lanie. She stared up at him in horror. "I'm fine," she called out. Or at least tried. Her voice was completely gone. She cleared her throat and tried again, but it wasn't easy with one of Mark's hands on her bare breast, the other fisted in her hair, a thick muscled thigh between hers.

And she was no better. She had her hands in his shorts!

"Honey?" Cora called. "I have a master key. Do you need help?"

"No!" she said. Maybe yelled. She grimaced and, eyes locked on Mark's in sheer horror and panic, she said, "I'm fine! Totally fine! One hundred percent fine! Never been finer!" She winced. "Good night!"

Cora's voice sounded suspiciously amused. "'Night, honey."

"I think I've mentioned," Mark said in her ear, "my family's insane."

"None of you have any concept of personal space boundaries!" she hissed. "Not a single one of you!"

He took a nip out of her ear. "Ironic, considering where your hands are."

She snorted and tugged her hands free and gave him a push.

He laughed, low and soft and annoyingly sexy in his throat and . . . opened the door.

She stilled, shocked. First of all, his board shorts were opened and dangerously, illicitly low on his hips, revealing more than concealing anything. And second of all, he was leaving? He'd put her in this state and he was going to walk away and leave her to it? She'd self-combust!

Mark took a careful peek out the door.

"What are you doing?"

"Making sure the coast's clear," he said and looked down. "Not tonight, Gracie."

The dog was in the hallway, giving him the sad eyes. With a huff, she ambled off to find another sucker. Mark shut the door and took in Lanie's panic with a hint of a smile. The slow scan of his eyes made her very aware that she was wearing only a pair of bikini panties. The look also made her very hot in all the places he'd touched. And in the places she still needed him to touch. "Well?" she demanded. "*Is* the coast clear besides Gracie?"

His mouth twitched. "Out there? Yeah. How about in here?"

"What does that mean?"

He smiled. "You want me bad."

God help her, but she did. "Not as bad as you want me," she said with a pointed look at his still-pretty-impressive erection.

"Hard for a man to hide it," he agreed.

"Will she be back?"

"Gracie? Yes. My mom? Probably not, but I stopped trying to figure out any members of my family a long time ago." He flicked the lock on the door and turned back to her. "That'll hold them all off for long enough."

"Long enough for what?"

He smiled and she nearly orgasmed on the spot. But a part of her was also coming to her senses. "There's a baby in the house. And impressionable children, *your* children, so—"

"Lanie, they're all asleep."

She bit her lower lip. "What if I make noise?"

His smile was both soft and wicked. *"If?"*

"What? It's not my fault, I can't help it!"

"I know. And I love it." He snaked an arm around her waist, snagged her in close, and lifted her up so that she could wrap her legs around him, and then he turned to the bed.

"But—"

He tossed her to the mattress and followed her down, pressing his body to hers until every inch touched.

And there were some pretty damn great inches.

He kissed her deep and raw and shatteringly intense, the kind of kiss that stopped hearts and melted brain cells as he slid her panties down and made himself at home between her legs. When he pulled back to meet her gaze, she was panting, squirming for more, and pinned to the bed, spread for his viewing pleasure.

"We're not going to hurry," he said. "But we are going to be very quiet. Can you be very quiet, Lanie?"

Was he kidding? She'd do anything as long as he didn't stop touching her. Arching up into him, she sought more contact even though they were already practically suctioned together.

"Lanie." He caught her roaming hands. "I asked you a question."

"Yes," she gasped. "I'll be quiet."

He was kissing his way down her body, her breasts, her belly, a hip . . . "I love the way you look in my bed," he whispered huskily against her skin.

A low, breathless laugh escaped her, which turned into a gasp when he found her very favorite kissable spot.

"Shh," he reminded her, tightening his grip on her hips to hold her still for his special brand of delicious torture.

And when she couldn't be still or quiet, he climbed up her body and kissed her again, probably to shut her up. She shifted as much as she could with a goal-oriented, sexually deprived male on top of her, wrapping her legs around him so he could rub himself against her with deadly precision.

She opened her eyes and he let out a very badass smile as he pulled out a condom and tore it open with his teeth. When he slid home, they moaned into each other's mouths and as he moved over her in that sexy way of his, she lost herself completely in him. And in perhaps the most amazing part of the night . . . she knew he did the same in her.

Chapter 16

Me: It's going to be a great day.
Anxiety: Let me show you how wrong you are . . .

When Mark woke, it wasn't to the warm, sensuous glide of Lanie's limbs around his body, but to her trying to shove him out of his own bed.

"You've got to go," she whispered.

He cracked open one eye. It was two in the morning. "Hmmm," he murmured into her hair and pulled her into him, smiling at the feel of bare skin. He cupped her sweet ass and started to roll her beneath him, but she shoved at him again.

"Mark! Wake up!"

"I'm up," he said and flopped to his back.

"Yes," she said, eyeing the part of him that was most definitely *up*. "But that's not what I meant!"

He snorted and sat up. "You're panicking."

"Yes! Join me, won't you?" She yanked on his T-shirt and slid out of the bed. The cotton fell over her curves and made him sigh. Apparently round two wasn't on the calendar.

She pulled him off the bed, tossed his clothes at him, and pushed him to the door.

"Shouldn't I actually put these on first?" he asked wryly.

She stood there, arms crossed, toe tapping while he pulled on his board shorts. "Where's the fire?" he asked.

"We can't sleep in the same bed in your family house."

"Actually, there hasn't been all that much sleeping involved," he said. "There was some nice begging, though, especially when I—"

"Oh my God." She put a hand over his mouth, but she was laughing now. "I absolutely did *not* beg."

He chuckled because she had *so* begged. Sweetly. Sexily. And now that he was thinking of it, he wanted to hear her do it again. And again . . .

"Look," she said. "We agreed it's okay to do . . . what we did. But sleeping together is different. It's more. It's . . . intimate."

He felt his smile fade and he pulled her in for a hug, resting his jaw on the top of her head. "You need your space."

She paused, and then pulled back and stared at his chest. "Yes. I need space."

He lifted her chin and what he saw in her eyes made his heart constrict. "Us not getting involved emotionally is on me, Lanie," he said. "Not you. Never you."

She nodded, but he knew she didn't understand and he felt like such an asshole. "Please tell me you believe me."

"I—"

They both froze at the knock on the door, though Mark didn't need a peephole to know who it was. At night his children tended to turn into dehydrated philosophers who needed lots of hugs. And yep, right on cue came . . .

"Daddy?" came Samantha's little voice. "Me and Sierra are thirsty."

He'd been a soldier. He was a cop. Both required catlike reflexes and instincts that had saved his life more than a few times. He was quick on his feet and he slept with one eye open. And yet in that moment, he was frozen. Not because his kids had found him in a questionable situation, but because for whatever reason, Lanie honest-to-God believed she couldn't trust love, and he'd just cemented that in her head for her.

The girls knocked again. Lanie jabbed a finger at the closet and added yet another push that was far more like a shove so that she could go greet his adorable little heathens and protect him.

Not happening. It was time someone protected her for a change. So he gently nudged *her* into the closet and put a finger to his lips. Then he opened the bedroom door and looked down at his favorite heathens plus one oversized dog, all looking hopeful.

They were the cutest little night owls he'd ever seen, who didn't seem to need any sleep no matter what time he decreed bedtime was. Sometimes even after he'd put them to bed, they'd come looking for an excuse to get into *his* bed, claiming to need water, a story, whatever they could come up with, and it was his own fault that he'd let them. But after all they'd gone through, he'd spoiled them some. They deserved it.

"Wait a minute," he said. "I can't possibly really be looking at my two favorite short people because they're in bed, long asleep, dreaming about ponies and kittens and rainbows."

They giggled and tried to push their way in, Gracie leading the way, but he held firm. "Not tonight, sweet things. It's *way* past your bedtimes—"

"But Daddy," Samantha said. "My sock fell off and we're thirsty."

"There's two water bottles by your beds. Where's your aunt Mia?"

"She fell asleep. We wanna story."

Sierra nodded eagerly, smiling at him so adorably that he felt his chest pinch. She was finally getting her two front teeth in and she was clutching the teddy bear he'd given her last month, looking at him in overt adoration that he still wasn't sure he deserved. Bending, he scooped them both up and started down the hall toward their bedroom, Gracie on his heels.

"But Daddy—"

"Shh," he whispered, hugging Samantha in tighter. "Don't wake up the house, baby."

"But—"

"Samantha, if you wake up Grandma, I'll tell her it was you who ate her last cupcake."

Sierra giggled at this empty threat because they all knew it'd been *him* who had eaten the last cupcake. But Samantha stopped talking and set her head on his shoulder.

He quickly glanced back. No sight of Lanie. Three minutes later he had the girls tucked into bed. "When you're teenagers," he said, "I'm going to wake you guys up in the middle of the night to tell you my socks came off."

They laughed and cuddled in. He kissed them each, told Gracie to "guard the babies," and went back to his room and directly to his closet.

It was empty.

He let out a slow breath. Yeah, he deserved that. He padded out of the room and down the hall. It was a cold night and he was barefoot and shirtless but he had to make sure Lanie was okay. He got to the row of cottages just in time to see her step inside her dark one.

Fair enough. Mad at himself for hurting her, he went back to the big house.

He'd honestly believed that he could keep his heart safe. But that had been before Lanie slid in beneath his barriers. Now the only thing he was sure of was the one thing he didn't want to admit to himself.

She was going to have him breaking his every rule for her.

HIS ALARM WENT off three hours later. He had an early shift, which turned out to be long and busy. It was late that night before he got away, and after checking on the girls, he went to the cottages—power had been restored—and knocked on Lanie's door.

She answered in the shirt she'd stolen from him.

He met her gaze. "Thought maybe we needed to have a conversation."

"Not even a little bit," she said politely.

"Lanie—"

"I don't want to talk, but there is something else I do want to do."

"Anything," he said.

She pulled him inside and to her bed.

OVER THE NEXT week, Mark worked ridiculously long hours thanks to a flu running through his staff, visited his girls as often as he could, even if it was just watching them sleep, and then ended up in Lanie's bed.

Where they hadn't done much talking, although there'd

been a lot of murmured "Oh, please" and "Do that again" and "Don't stop."

One day things finally slowed down enough at work that Mark was able to take his lunch break at the winery. He tried to do this the same day a week that coincided with the twins' half day at school, offsetting all the nights where he didn't get home before their bedtime. His job wasn't ideal that way, but it was a hell of a lot better than being overseas and not present at all.

Still, the dichotomy between the insanity of his work life—which most days meant slugging through the worst of what humanity had to offer—and then coming home and having to empty the dishwasher and braid the girls' hair like a normal person, when he felt anything but normal, was harder than he'd imagined.

But it was what he'd been dealt.

Today, on his way into lunch, his mom waylaid him before he made it out to the patio.

"I asked Lanie to extend her contract," she told him.

"You did? When?"

"Two weeks ago."

"You didn't think to mention it?"

"Why would I?" she asked, cocking her head to watch him carefully. "You've denied the fact that there's something going on with you two, and I run the winery, which makes her my responsibility, not yours."

True enough. "And she said . . . ?"

"That she'd think about it." His mom looked worried. "You do realize she's been here six weeks already and only has a few weeks left, right?"

Mark blew out a breath and stepped out onto the patio.

Everyone was there. Everyone was *always* there at two very full tables. Lanie, as usual, sat all the way at the far end. River was with her. River looked up and met his gaze, her own quickly skittering away, also as usual.

She'd been here five weeks now, and everyone loved and adored her, and . . . she'd not said one word directly to him. When he talked to her, everything about her stilled, and she looked anywhere else, as if she was desperate for him to go away. He had no idea if it was because he was male, or because he was a cop.

Lanie didn't look at him at all. About six hours ago, he'd had his mouth on every inch of her body—and vice versa—and yet apparently they were only nighttime bed buddies now.

Because you told her this was all you had to offer.

Yeah, this was all on him. He tried to catch her eye and flash her a reassuring smile, but she didn't notice him.

Or pretended not to.

He grabbed a plate and went to her end of the table. Samantha and Sierra saw him and went nuts, climbing all over him. He went through their routine of hanging them upside down off his shoulders and tossing them around for a minute before setting them back at their seats, both grinning happily from ear to ear. Nice to have someone always happy to see him.

"They light up when you come home," his mom said, handing him an iced tea.

It was funny to him that he'd come from this big, crazy family where he'd spent most of his growing up years just wishing for a space of his own where his sisters couldn't hound him or steal his shit. He'd never imagined a family of his own, but Sam and Sierra had come along and he wouldn't change that for anything.

He felt his chest tighten at the thought of ever walking away from these two little crazy pods of life that were more important than anything. He knew he'd step in front of a bullet for them, he'd do whatever it took to give them the life they deserved.

He glanced at Lanie, who was still doing a bang-up job of ignoring him, and felt another tug on his heart. She was becoming important too.

"Daddy?" Samantha was standing in her chair because she always stood when she could sit, just as she always ran when she could walk. "You going to sleep in your room tonight or in Lanie's again?"

Everyone froze, and he did mean everyone, some with utensils halfway to their mouths, which were all gaping wide open in collective shock.

"'Cuz we're not allowed to have sleepovers on school nights, remember?" Sam asked. "Makes people tired." She caught Mark's expression. "And grumpy."

Lanie had frozen with everyone else. River reached for her hand.

Shockingly, it was Mark's pesky little sister who came to his rescue. Mia smiled at Samantha. "You mean when we had the power outage and Lanie borrowed your dad's bedroom. But that was only for that one night, pumpkin. Hey, did everyone try my lemon bars? Because honestly, I'm thinking of marrying them and having their babies. I mean, I've already given up on men anyway, so—"

"No, I mean *all* the nights," Samantha said. She smiled at Mark. "You and Lanie have sleepovers. Right, Daddy?"

"Seems like a certain two little someones are night-wandering again," Cora said, her smile a little forced as she stood up and gathered some dishes to clear. "And since you've been naughty and not following the rules on top of telling fibs, you can make it up to us grown-ups by helping me clear the table."

"It's not a fib, Grandma," Samantha said. "Daddy, tell her."

He loved this child. He did. He loved her to the moon and back, but at the moment he wouldn't have minded having two mute twins. He met her warm chocolate gaze and had to sigh. He wouldn't lie to her, but even if he could, he'd never do that to Lanie, because he had the feeling that denying what was going on would hurt her far worse than just admitting it. "You've been snooping," he said. "Which is a big no-no. But you're not lying."

Sam had the good grace to look slightly ashamed. "Sometimes I get thirsty."

Uh-huh. He stood. Everyone was still staring at him.

And at Lanie.

He hated that for her. "Listen," he said to the entire bunch. "This has been . . . well, a whole lot of fun today . . ." He walked over to Lanie and pulled her out of her seat. "But we're out."

"Where are you taking her?" his mom wanted to know.

"You know, Mom, much as I enjoy a good inquisition, I've got to go back to work and I'm not about to leave Lanie out here with the wolves."

"Don't be ridiculous," his mom said, affronted. "We don't blame her for this nonsense."

"Nope, we blame *you*," Mia said. "Men are dicks, all of them."

He looked at Alyssa, and she shook her head. "Don't look at me to save you. My silence doesn't mean I'm on your side. It means your level of stupidity at getting caught by this gang has rendered me speechless."

Mark blew out a breath and bent a little to see into Lanie's eyes. "Hey, you okay?"

"Well, of course she is," his mom said. "What the hell's wrong with you?"

He jabbed a finger at everyone. "This subject is being dropped right now. Everyone get me? No one brings it up when I'm gone, no one even thinks about it, *capisce?*"

"Daddy, Daddy, *Daddy*," Sam said, jumping up and down, clapping her hands. "Kiss Lanie good-bye like you do in the mornings!"

Could one actually feel an aneurism coming? He crouched low and gave each of the twins a kiss. "Okay, peanuts, time to give the adults a minute, please."

They skipped out.

Cora raised a brow. "Reminds me of the time you got caught with a girl in the school locker room," she said and shook her head. "Straight A's, in the National Honor Society, and yet in trouble every single day. The principal had me on speed dial."

Lanie snorted and he slid her a look.

"Having a hard time picturing you as a nerd," she said.

"Because I wasn't. I cut classes and smoked weed in the school locker room."

His mom gasped in horror. "Marcus Antony Edward Capriotti! You smoked marijuana?" She sucked in a breath, her eyes narrowed. "Did you smoke in this house?"

Jesus. How had they gotten here? "Do you really want the answer to that question?"

"So much for being the one who can do no wrong," Alyssa said with glee. "Can't wait to tell Bae."

Mia rolled her eyes when Alyssa took out her cell phone. *"Bae?"*

"It's my new nickname for Owen. If you have pet names for each other, it keeps the love alive, you know."

"What I know," Mia said, "is that the word *Bae* is the Danish word for *poop*. You're not doing another of those silly cleanses, are you? 'Cuz they're killing your brain cells."

"I find them helpful," Alyssa said. "You should try one with me."

"Drinking Bloody Marys is as close to a cleanse as I'll ever get."

Suddenly came the sound of a car starting up in the parking lot. Mark looked around.

Lanie was gone.

"Nice going," he said. "You've all chased her off." He started to go after her, but his mom grabbed his hand.

"She's just going to town to pick something up at the print shop. She'll be back. Leave her be for a moment to think."

"You're sleeping with that wonderful girl," his grandma said, her hand to her chest. "My heart's happy. When's the wedding?"

There was a collective choked sound. Some, wiser than others, dug back into their food, but only a few, because the Capriottis loved nothing more than drama.

"Mom," Cora said without taking her gaze off Mark. "Not now."

"But—"

"Mom, love you," Cora said. "But this is *my* child, so I get to be point on this. I know my son. He's an unmovable tree unless he *wants* to be moved."

Mark raised a brow, but she cocked her head, daring him to say otherwise.

"You're so certain she'll be back?" he asked.

"Of course. I don't hire quitters. I might have an idiot for a son, but that woman's at the top of her game, and I'm paying her to be. She'll be back in spite of you. Once she's had some time alone, she might even forgive you for being an idiot."

Someone began a slow clap. Uncle Jack. The others joined in, laughing.

"You're all a bunch of lunatics," Mark said in disgust.

His mom hugged him. "We're Team Marcus, that's all," she said. "We want to see you happy."

"I woke up plenty happy. You all sucked it right out of me."

Mia laughed and opened her mouth, but Alyssa wrapped an arm around her neck and covered her little sister's mouth. "That's not what we're trying to do," Alyssa said. "We just want you to know it's okay to be happy. It's *not* okay to close yourself off because you made one stupid choice about one stupid woman."

"We know what you gave up to be here," his mom said quietly. "You gave up everything."

"Not everything," he said. "There are men who'd kill for what I have right here."

His mom squeezed his hand and smiled, but her eyes were still worried. "I agree with you. So why on earth wouldn't you drop your silly rule and let someone into your life?"

Mark turned his head and gave Alyssa a death glare. "It was a secret for a reason," he said. "You're all on me to let a woman into my life. But we're not talking about an anonymous woman here, we're talking about one of the winery's employees." He shook his head. "And in case you've forgotten, there are two little girls inside the house who already had one parent desert them. I'm not going to do the same."

"If you think that by loving a woman you'd be deserting

your children," his mom said, "I've taught you nothing at all." She stepped a little closer and got right up in his face. Which she had to crane her neck to do, but somehow she managed to make it feel like she was two feet taller than him. "And sidenote," she said. "This wouldn't be coming up at all if you yourself weren't clearly feeling something for Lanie."

"Mom." He shook his head. "There's a difference between sex and love, and the reason I know this is because the day I turned sixteen, you sat me down and threw a box of condoms at me and told me that until I knew my heart as good as I knew my other body parts, it was just sex."

"The condoms were because you'd gotten caught and nearly arrested in the backseat of some girl's car. You were back there with her *and* her best friend, and everyone's parents wanted me to castrate you."

Alyssa snorted but shut up when both Mark and Cora gave her a level glare. She lifted her hands in surrender. "Hey, don't look at me. What do I know about such manners? I'm an angel with a great husband. I'm also Mom's favorite."

Cora ignored her. "Listen to me, Marcus. That woman challenges you, and we've all been amazed at how she is with the girls. She treats them like adults and they eat it up. She loves them and they love her. So why can't you just drop your stupid rule and let yourself be happy with her?"

"Because the last time I dropped my 'stupid rule,' I ended up being a single parent to twins, of whom one still isn't speaking."

"Mark," his mom said softly, looking behind him.

He turned around and shit, there stood Sierra, silent, staring up at him with those soulful eyes. Fuck. "Hey, munchkin—"

She whirled and ran off into the house.

Fan-fucking-tastic. Lanie was gone and now so was Sierra, two of the most important females in his life, hurting because of him.

He pulled out his phone as he strode into the house, calling Lanie.

Not only didn't she answer his call, she ignored it. "Call me back," he said to her voice mail. "We need to talk."

Someone "tsked" and he turned to face his grandpa. *"What?"*

"Nothing."

"Look, Grandpa, I've got a lot on my plate, so either get it off your chest or keep it to yourself."

"Women don't like to be told what to do."

No shit. "I didn't tell her what to do."

"You told her that you two needed to talk. You can't go in like that, barrels blazing. They'll circle around to your six and stab you dead."

Mark's eye started to twitch. Good. He was going to stroke out. It would save him a lot of trouble.

"All I'm saying," his grandpa said, "is that you have to nicely ask if she has time to have a chat. And then you let her come to you. Otherwise, you're a sitting duck."

Shaking his head, he went upstairs and found Samantha in her room playing a game on the kid tablet Mia had bought for her.

In the meantime, his phone remained ominously silent. "Hey, baby. Where's Sierra?"

Samantha, without taking her gaze off the screen, shrugged.

Mark sighed and then crouched before her, having to put his face between hers and the screen to get her attention. "Hi."

"Hi, Daddy."

"Do you remember the other night when we were talking about the difference between adults and children?"

"Yes. You told me I couldn't stay up all night like you get to."

"And why is that?"

"Because adults are old and have experiences. They get to do what they want. And when I'm old I'll get to do what I want, but I'm not old yet."

Close enough. "Good. Remember that the next time you leave your bed in the middle of the night. Where's Sierra?"

She hesitated. "I don't know."

"You always know."

Samantha's gaze skittered to the shut closet door and then back to Mark's.

Nearly outsmarted by a pair of six-year-olds.

He moved to the closet and opened the door. Sierra was lounging in her hamper of dirty clothes, playing on her tablet. She didn't look up. Like Sam, she had unruly curls—although they were a slightly softer version in the same dark brown color of his own hair—but her unique, quiet, old-soul temperament was all her own. "Hey, you."

She was engrossed in her game. Or pretending to be. Mark lifted her out of the hamper and then sat in her place with her in his lap. The hamper strained under his weight and they didn't quite fit, but he made it work, leaning back against the closet wall with various pieces of clothing hanging in their faces.

Sierra giggled and, in spite of himself and his worries, he smiled at the sound. "Baby, you need to know that I love you with all my heart."

"Hey," Sam said from the bed.

"I love *both* of you with all my heart," he called out and then looked at Sierra. "I don't care if you don't want to talk. That's okay. But I do care if you choose to never talk again because I miss your voice very much."

Sierra stared at him, eyes luminous.

"So I need to know," he said softly. "Are you ever going to talk again?"

She paused, thinking about it before giving him a slow, single nod.

"Good," he whispered, jaw pressed against the top of her head.

Sam came into the closet and climbed into his lap too, and then his heart felt too big for his chest as he hugged them both tight.

Chapter 17

Anxiety: Beware.
Me: Can you be more specific?
Anxiety: . . .

After a run to the print shop and a quick side field trip through the ice cream shop, where she got a triple scoop of chocolate chip cookie dough, Lanie shut herself in at her desk.

After a few minutes, she heard someone coming her way and braced herself for it to be Mark. She would absolutely not be moved by whatever he had to say.

Probably.

"Hey," Mia said. "How's things?"

Lanie sighed. "You don't have to pretend that I didn't completely mortify myself in front of every one of you Capriottis at lunch."

"Oh, that?" Mia shook her head and laughed. "That was nothing. When I got dumped by Sean, I stood up on one of the tables and sobbed. You've been here, what, a month and a half? A few weeks before you started, Alyssa and Owen had a huge fight and food was their weapon of choice."

"They had an actual food fight?" Lanie asked. "Seriously?"

"Serious as a heart attack. Someone joined in and put a pie in Mom's face."

"Someone?"

"Okay, me," Mia said and winced. "Not my most shining hour. But my point is that what happened today was nothing. No one ended up standing on a table sobbing or with pie in their face."

Lanie just stared at her. "You guys are so . . ."

"Awesome. I think the word you're looking for is *awesome*."

Lanie laughed softly and turned back to her desk.

"Listen," Mia said. "About my brother."

Lanie closed her eyes. "I don't want to talk about it."

"No, I get that. And normally my relationship with my siblings is somewhere between 'I'll help you hide the body' and 'don't even breathe in my direction,' but in this case, I'm with you. And you should know Mark would've gone after you today, but Sierra ran off."

"What? Is she okay?"

"Yeah, he found her." Mia perched a hip on Lanie's desk. "He's a great dad."

Lanie pretended to be very busy on her computer, grateful it was turned away from Mia because she was literally just watching an apple bounce slowly across the screen. "Yes, he is."

"I know my mom asked you to extend your contract that ends in two weeks and stay longer."

Two weeks . . . Was that all she had left? Her gaze locked on the bouncing apple. "She did."

"And I know you haven't said yes yet."

"Mia—"

"Look, you fit in here. I think you know that."

Lanie didn't want them to, but the words . . . warmed her.

Growing up, she'd been extremely aware of being different from her parents. And different hadn't been good. Never fitting in with her own people had scarred her, she knew this. Hearing that she fit in here was both amazing and terrifying.

"We want you to stay," Mia said. "All of us want that."

"Yes," Lanie said, still staring at her computer. "For the sake of the girls."

"Well, of course. They've been through hell and we're still trying to heal them from that, but this is more than just about them. It's about the rest of us. And you. We all like you, Lanie. Very much. You feel like one of us."

Lanie didn't know how to react to this. She wasn't good with emotions outside of her anxieties, and she sure as hell had no idea how to deal with them. She'd promised herself not to get involved. A promise she'd broken because she *had* gotten involved, and she had no idea what to do about that. "I'm thinking on it," she finally said.

Mia smiled. "So not a quick no, then. Good."

When she was alone again, Lanie went to the employee room for tea. Sipping it, she stood in front of the humongous whiteboard calendar on the wall. It had everyone's schedule there, but the most important one to everyone was the twins'. There was a blank spot for tomorrow's dance class. She grabbed the pen and wrote her name in the spot.

"I'm going to owe you for that too," a low, sexy voice said quietly behind her.

She stilled as Mark pressed up against her back. Or her body stilled.

Her mind did not.

Mark turned her to face him. "I'm sorry about my family."

"I'm not mad at your family."

He studied her for a moment. "When I was a kid," he finally said, "I used to wish for a superpower. I wanted to be able to fly, but if I could have a superpower right now, I'd want to be able to read your mind."

"No, you wouldn't."

He let out a low, mirthless laugh. "You're mad at me."

"Look at that," she murmured. "No superpower required."

Cupping her face, he ran a thumb over her jaw, his fingers sinking into her hair. "You're mad because . . . I went after the twins first?"

"No." She shook her head. "I'll never be mad at you for putting your girls first."

His eyes never left hers as he clearly wracked his brain, and she decided to help him. "You told me we needed to talk."

"Yes. Because we do."

"You told. You didn't ask, you told." He blinked and then closed his eyes and dropped his head to her shoulder, muttering something about his grandpa being right and an impending stroke.

She gripped his arms. "Your grandpa's having a stroke?"

"No, I am." He lifted his face. "I'm sorry. I'm bossy and demanding."

"Because of the military?"

"Because of all the females in my life."

"The females in your life are the best thing about you," she said with a small smile she couldn't seem to hold back.

"If you think that," he murmured with a small smile of his own, "I need to get you back in bed."

She laughed softly, but her amusement faded fast.

"Look," he said, "let me revise my earlier statement. Can we please talk at your earliest convenience?"

"Wow. Did that hurt?"

He laughed, and dammit, he melted away the rest of her mad. "I wanted to thank you," he said quietly.

"For the orgasms?"

His eyes darkened. "Most definitely, but that's not what I was going to say. I wanted to thank you for putting up with us Capriottis. I know you think you're out of your comfort zone here—"

"I don't think, I know."

"—but you're a natural. You fit in, you care—"

"It's a job."

"You care," he repeated softly, running a finger along her temple, tucking a stray strand of hair behind her ear. "You care deeply."

"You're thanking me for caring deeply?"

"Yes."

She didn't know how to take this. No one had ever accused her of such a thing before. And since her MO had been to not care at all, she was at a loss as to when exactly everyone had sneaked in under her radar and made themselves comfy and at home in her heart. She shook her head. "I don't want your thanks."

"So you don't want my thanks, and you won't let me pay you for your extra time that you spend with the girls. What *can* I do for you?"

"There's no price," she said. "Remember?"

"But say that I *wanted* there to be a price," he said. "What would it be? Name it," he whispered, his voice now filled with all sorts of naughty conjecture.

She barely caught her moan as he brushed his rough jaw to hers, taking her earlobe between his teeth and giving her a shiver. "We're in the office," she whispered. "Isn't this what got us in trouble only a few hours ago?"

"We're in contract negotiations," he said. "Name your stipulations."

She considered him. He was teasing and she liked that. A lot. And since she did, and because this really wasn't the place or the time, she teased back. "Would I have to call you *sir*?"

The look that came into his eyes made her heart rate skyrocket and other parts of her body start to override her brain.

"You can call me *sir* anytime you want," he said, his lips traveling up the curve of her jaw, his stubble prickling against her skin as he pressed a kiss to her ear. "But you won't get any work done if you do."

With a laugh, she pushed him away. "Speaking of work . . ."

"Okay, but later then," he murmured, more of a promise than a statement.

"Later," she agreed softly.

And then counted the minutes until she was done for the day. She made her way to her cottage, her mind skipping ahead. Her life had been a train in a dark tunnel for a very long time. But it was like she'd somehow changed course and now she could see a little bit of light.

She was smiling, she realized in surprise. Happy. It was such a shock, this unusual feeling coursing through her veins, that it didn't register that someone was already inside her cottage.

She knew she'd locked it when she left that morning—force of habit—and the lights were off, but there was someone with a penlight going through her closet. She froze in the open doorway, then smacked the light switch so that she could see.

River was on her knees going through Lanie's things.

Lanie was frozen to the spot in shock. "What are you doing?"

"It's not what you think," River said quickly, struggling to get to her feet.

"You sure? Because what I think is that you're stealing from me."

River closed her eyes.

Lanie stayed right where she was, a lead weight in her chest where her heart had been only a moment before. She actually felt glued to the floor. She couldn't have moved toward River to save her own life. "What the hell's going on?"

"Please," River said, breathing like she'd just run a mile, bending over to catch her breath. "I'm not stealing."

Lanie looked at what River held—the one and only thing she had of her grandma's, a small gold diamond necklace. "Your hands seem to disagree with you."

Chapter 18

It's almost time to switch from my everyday anxiety to my fancy holiday anxiety.

River felt the panic clutch her so thoroughly that the baby in her belly rolled a slow somersault, leaving her winded enough that she had to put a hand on the wall for balance.

Lanie was patting herself down, clearly looking for her phone.

"No!" River cried. "Please don't call the police. I can't go to jail. I can't have her born in jail."

"I wasn't going to call the police," Lanie said. "I was going to call Cora—you look like you're going into damn labor and more than you don't want to have this baby in jail, I don't want to *deliver* this baby."

"I'm not in labor."

Lanie sighed and came close enough to take River's hand and guide her to the bed. "Sit."

As soon as River sat, Lanie dropped her hand and stepped back, like she couldn't stand to even look at her. The gesture made River's heart hurt even worse because this was all her own fault.

Stupid. She was so stupid.

"Why were you stealing from me?" Lanie asked, arms crossed.

River opened her mouth, but then shut it again because what could she say? Nothing. She couldn't tell the truth. No one would believe the truth. Hell, she hardly believed it herself.

"Hello," Lanie said.

River looked into Lanie's eyes. Behind the anger was pain. Pain River had caused. She had no real choice here, she realized, or at least not a choice that she wanted to face. *Maybe* if she'd opened up on her very first day and told Cora the truth about how she'd landed on their doorstep.

But she hadn't.

And now she had to live with her lie. She'd taken the job because she'd seen an easy way in, only the joke was on her because she'd fallen for this place and everyone in it. She'd had it so good here that she'd become . . . happy.

And that had been the slippery slope. She'd gotten comfortable in this life where there wasn't a daily worry about a roof over her head and food to eat, no stress over how she'd be able to take care of her baby. She'd forgotten how far from this world she belonged.

And in the end it didn't matter since she'd just sabotaged it all. "I'm sorry," she whispered.

Lanie let out a sound that very clearly said *not good enough*. "What were you looking for?"

One last lie, as it was easier than the truth. "Something I could pawn for quick cash."

Lanie looked around her cottage and shook her head. "No. You're lying. I left my purse on the counter—it's right there in plain sight, and yet it's still zipped. You didn't even look in there for cash. You're in my closet searching through what's mostly an empty suitcase. Like you're looking for something specific."

With that rather shockingly accurate assessment, River managed to get back to her feet. She started to hold out the necklace, but Lanie came close and snatched it from her hands, hugging it close to her chest. It was an unguarded reaction that made River deeply ashamed. Her heart was pumping in her throat now with the need to somehow fix this. "Lanie—"

"Please just go."

"Are you going to call the cops?"

"Just get the hell out!"

But River couldn't leave, not like this, and she dug her feet in. "Not yet. Please, Lanie, please let me—"

"What the hell's going on in here?" Cora asked from the still-open front door.

River startled in shock and would've gone down if Lanie hadn't grabbed her. She waited until River had found her feet before once again jerking her hands away as if she'd been burned, taking a big step backward, carefully not looking at River again.

And just like that, the warmth that had been with her ever since she'd first come to Wildstone five weeks ago evaporated out of River's chest, leaving her cold and chilled at the loss.

She'd done this.

"Someone answer me," Cora said, using her scary CEO voice with River for the first time ever, which made her want to cry.

But it was Lanie who drew a deep breath and spoke first. "When I got back here after work, I found River searching through my stuff. She had my grandma's necklace in her hands." She didn't mention River's lie of needing something to hock for cash.

Cora's mouth fell open in shock and surprise, and her gaze whipped to River.

But River couldn't have spoken to save her life. Not with her heart in her throat.

"Oh, River," Cora whispered.

"Is there a problem in here?" another voice asked, this one male.

Mark.

In uniform.

Oh God, River thought, beginning to shake like a leaf. This was bad. So bad. The shame that had filled her veins pumped even hotter and even more destructively through her body.

"Yes, there's a problem," Cora said. "Lanie came home to find River with her grandma's necklace." She looked at River with such worried, kind eyes that River felt herself start to break. She stole a quick glance at Mark, who was standing there looking stern, but clearly willing to hear what she had to say for herself. She opened her mouth and . . .

Burst into tears.

And not the pretty kind of tears either. Nope, this was the humiliatingly loud, can't-catch-her-breath sobs as she let the entire sordid tale fall out of her, unable to keep it to herself any longer. "I wasn't trying to steal anything of hers, I swear! I was trying to find something that's mine. He stole it from me. He'd told me I was his moon and his stars, but that turned out to be a lie too, just like everything else he told me!"

She felt Lanie jerk in surprise but she couldn't look. She couldn't do anything but shake and cry. She was getting close to hyperventilating as the sobs wracked her frame, but she couldn't stop talking now, not until she made them understand. "I thought I was m-m-married, but it turned out I w-w-wasn't. It wasn't ever r-r-real. Kyle f-f-fooled me and d-d-destroyed my life and left me alone and p-p-pregnant. And it was all my f-f-fault for trusting him." She had to stop for a second and suck in air, which gave her the hiccups. "H-h-he told me we'd be a family and that I w-w-wouldn't be alone ever again and then v-v-vanished on me. Turned out he'd d-d-died and I wasn't his only w-w-wife."

At that, she ran out of air and covered her face and let the sobs take her.

Cora hadn't said anything more and she knew Mark was still standing there. She couldn't see him, but she could feel his presence, along with that ever-present sense of rock-solid, stoic authority. "I'm s-s-so sorry," she tried to say, but she wasn't sure the words were even understandable. She was horrified, humiliated.

And terrified.

"River."

This was a new voice. Holden's voice. And her heart about stopped now because she couldn't let him know what she'd done. Then they'd *all* hate her. "No—"

Two arms came around her. Strong, warm arms attached to a solid body that smelled like the mountains and the sea. "Shh," Holden said in her ear. "Slow deep breaths now, River. Do it with me. In . . ." He demonstrated by inhaling deep. "And then out, slow . . ." He exhaled against her jaw and she clutched at him, the only lifeline on her sinking ship.

"You've got this," he said.

They breathed in and out for a few minutes, during which

she shuddered with the last of her tear storm, doing her best to pretend she was anywhere but where she was, with a silent audience, waiting her out.

"That's it. More." Holden ran a big hand up and down her back in a soothing, comforting gesture that melted her into his embrace—until she realized he might hear things about her that she didn't want him to hear because then he too would stop looking at her with all that warmth and affection in his gaze. "What are you doing here?" she managed to ask.

"I heard the yelling. Keep breathing, River."

"You've got to go." Panic had her shoving him now. "Please. Just go."

Holden looked around the room, his gaze landing on Mark first, then Cora and Lanie standing there, all very serious, before his gaze came back to her. "If you're worried about me hearing what's going on, you're too late. And I think that more than you need me to go, you need a friend on your side. So I'm staying."

She swallowed hard and looked away, unable to meet his eyes. But she wasn't strong enough to let go of his hand, which she gripped tightly.

Cora came to sit on the other side of her and stroked her damp hair from her face. "Water," she said and snapped her fingers.

Mark was way ahead of her, having already helped himself to Lanie's kitchenette, where he grabbed a bottle of water from the small fridge. He opened it and handed it to River, who took it with shaking hands.

"I'm sorry," she whispered.

"I know you are," Cora said.

But River had been talking to Lanie.

Who still wasn't looking at her.

She sipped at the water, awaiting her fate, shaking in her boots because she'd really managed to do it now, hadn't she, sabotaging the greatest thing that had ever happened to her. Not only with Cora and her family, but with Lanie, who'd been the best friend—no, the best sister—she'd never had.

But instead of sending her away, Cora just sat next to her, hand on her shoulder. Anytime someone tried to speak—Mark tried twice, Lanie once—Cora stopped them with a look.

She was clearly waiting until River got ahold of herself and stopped hiccupping for breath like a scared five-year-old, but she couldn't because she felt so ashamed. She somehow forced herself to look at Mark. "I'm ready."

"For what?"

"For you to arrest me."

Silence.

Mark slid a look at Lanie, who wasn't looking at any of them. She'd moved to the window and stood with her back to them all, hugging herself tightly. Unreachable.

Mark headed toward her but Lanie held up a hand and gave a single head-shake. This didn't stop him. He still moved to her side, but he didn't touch her, just stood next to her, silent, supportive. A presence of security that River was both painfully jealous of and also wistful for.

"Lanie?" Mark said.

From the window, Lanie didn't move except to sigh as she answered a question River didn't realize had been asked. "No. I don't want to press charges."

All of the tension seemed to drain out of Cora at that. "Extremely generous," she said quietly to Lanie and gave River a small smile.

"Thank you," River whispered to Lanie's stiff back.

"I'm not doing it for you."

River nodded even though Lanie still wasn't looking at her. She stared down at her tightly clasped fingers in Holden's big hand.

"Talk to us, River," Cora said softly.

It was the last thing she wanted to do. The *very* last thing, right behind having a root canal without drugs. But she'd been braced for Mark to cuff her and drag her off and he hadn't done that. She owed them all, but she especially owed Lanie.

"You thought you were married," Cora prompted.

"Yes," River said.

"But you weren't?"

"No, because Kyle was already married." She wanted, desperately, for Lanie to turn around so she could see River's regret, but Lanie still didn't budge. "To Lanie."

The sudden silence was so absolute that River wasn't sure any of them were breathing. Then in unison, they each turned to look at Lanie.

Who was still doing an impression of a statue.

"Since my marriage wasn't real," River said, "I got nothing when he died. Not that I wanted a thing from that rat-fink bastard. I don't want anything from anyone that I haven't earned, but . . ."

"You ran out of money?" Cora asked.

"Yes," she whispered. "Kyle told me he'd paid my rent up to a year, but that wasn't true. I lost my apartment and when I couldn't hide the pregnancy anymore, I lost my job as well."

"And you had to stop going to school," Cora said, but she was looking at Mark as she said it.

"Yes." No use thinking about her dream job of being a nurse, helping others the way she'd watched nurses help her mom.

"What did you want from Lanie?" Mark asked. Calmly. Quietly. But with an unmistakable tone of unbendable steel.

She wasn't out of the woods with him, not yet.

"I was desperate," she said, equally desperate for them to understand. "You have to understand, it took me forever to figure out what even happened to Kyle. At first I thought he'd just vanished on me. Two months went by and I got kicked out of our apartment—"

Lanie made a soft sound of . . . pain? Hard to tell. Everyone looked at her but she never took her gaze off the window.

"Go on," Cora said quietly to River.

She swallowed hard. "I needed a new place, but didn't have enough money, so I went to hock the ring Kyle had bought me."

Cora nodded encouragingly. "But . . . ?"

"But it was fake." He'd given her a *fake* diamond. The humiliation of her stupidity burned deep. "*I'd* bought *him* a real ring." With her entire nest egg. "And I want it back. I need it back so I can sell it and get a place for me and the baby. But when I tracked down Kyle's family to ask about it, they told me his wife had his belongings." The words were bitter in her mouth. "That's when I found out I wasn't married to him at all. That he had another wife."

Lanie finally turned to face her, her expression so carefully blank it broke River's already broken heart all over again. "You tracked me down and came here to make pretend friends with me, to feel things out and see if you could somehow get to Kyle's belongings through me."

River winced at the harsh truth. "Yes."

Lanie nodded and turned back to the window.

River stared down at her hands, feeling the same helplessness as she had when her mom had died. She was going to be kicked out, maybe arrested, and once again she'd be on her own.

Stupid.

She was so stupid.

"Everyone, follow me to the big house, please," Cora said, eyes on Lanie's back. "This is Lanie's private space; we will finish this without further intrusion on her."

More guilt slashed through River, but Cora wanted them to move, so they all moved. Even Lanie.

Cora kept a close eye on them all as they walked to the big house, waiting until everyone settled in the living room, even Holden. Lanie tried to keep to herself, but Gracie wasn't having it, leaning all her considerable doggy weight against Lanie until she was pretty much forced by cuteness overload to pet the dog.

"River," Cora said, "look at me."

She forced her gaze up to Cora's.

"I understand why you did what you did," she said and River stilled.

"You do?"

"Yes. You were alone, terrified, and pregnant. We'd have to be monsters not to understand."

Mark cleared his throat. "Mom—"

"She's a kid having a kid, Marcus. She needs us."

Mark just looked at his mom.

"We're all about second chances," Cora told him. "And she didn't actually steal anything."

"Yet," Mark said.

"You heard her, she's only looking for what's hers."

There was another long look between mother and son.

"She was taken advantage of," Cora said and took River's hand. "It's going to be okay."

"So . . . you don't want me to leave?"

"No," Cora said. "I most definitely don't want you to leave."

A tiny flame of hope flickered. "I can keep my job?"

"You're keeping your job. We've got you, River," she said.

No one had ever had her, not since her mom died. She couldn't help it, her eyes filled again. "Are you sure?"

Cora turned to Mark, who just gave her a single nod. Cora looked at Lanie next.

She didn't react.

"Lanie," Cora asked softly. "Are you okay with that?"

And River held her breath, waiting for the only answer that mattered.

Chapter 19

A haiku about getting out of bed:
No no no no no.
No no no no no no no.
No no no no no.

Lanie felt trapped. In a nightmare of her own making, no less. A pleaser at heart, she liked when people liked her. Especially the two Capriottis in this very room.

But her heart felt cold and shrunken in on itself and at the moment, she couldn't access any of the happy she'd had only an hour ago.

You're my moon and my stars. Kyle had told her that on numerous occasions. She'd loved those words; she'd thought them sweet and had felt special when he'd said them.

But apparently it'd been his signature line, and that made her angry all over again, so angry she couldn't even speak.

Had she really thought her past was behind her?

Had she really believed that she could let it all go and live in the present? Because her past had just shown up without an evite. So was she okay with River doing what she'd done and getting to stay? Hell no. But there was no way she could say so. "It's fine."

"Lanie," River whispered softly, entreatingly, her tear-ravaged face looking even younger than her twenty-one years. "I'm sorry."

She tried to feel nothing at that, nothing at all. And normally she was really good at it. But it seemed everything was failing her today, even her own emotions. The thing was, she actually did believe River was sorry. She was sorry she'd been caught, and Lanie got to deal with the consequences—that being that now her secret humiliation had become public. Everyone knew she was every bit as pathetic as River, that she'd been cruelly fooled by a man, by her own husband.

"I really am," River said. "So very sorry."

Extremely aware of Mark's and Cora's gazes on her, watching her reaction, Lanie turned to her. "Sorry for what?" she asked, really wanting to know. "For faking our friendship? For invading my privacy? Or for telling everyone a past that I didn't want to share?"

"Lanie," Cora started but stopped when Mark shook his head at his mom.

"All of it," River whispered. "I'm sorry for all of it."

Cora looked at Lanie. "Honey, what do you want to do?"

Lanie wanted River shown to the door, but that was the selfish, hurt, pissed-off child inside her.

Kyle had married River.

Kyle had . . . oh good God, she thought with sudden shocking clarity . . . River's baby was Kyle's. He'd refused *her* a child, but he'd given one to River.

It all washed over her, the shocking betrayal and now having it aired out in front of everyone. Clearly Cora had no problem forgiving River, and more than that, she wanted to continue to help her because River was the victim here.

Lanie's wounds were all on the inside, shoved purposefully deep where no one could see them. She'd made damn sure of that. She was a stone.

But not River. She stood there with her pregnancy glow, face still wet from her tears, looking like a lost soul in desperate need of help.

Cora would never turn away from that. Neither would she understand anyone who could. And much as she didn't want to, Lanie cared what Cora thought of her. So she shook her head. "Nothing. I don't want to do anything."

When everyone looked at her in varying degrees of doubt, she added a smile. "No, really. No harm, no foul." She jerked a thumb to the door. "But I've got to go. I've got an appointment."

"Wait," River whispered.

Holding back her sigh, Lanie turned to look right at her for the first time, hardening herself to the fear and regret and those lingering tears in River's eyes.

"The ring," River whispered. "Was my ring in his personal effects? I wouldn't ask, especially after what I just did and how I didn't tell you the truth from the beginning, but I . . . I really need the ring back."

The irony was that she didn't have the ring. She didn't have *any* of Kyle's belongings with her here. The one box of his stuff that had been sent to her, she'd left in her leased town house garage in Santa Barbara, two and a half hours south of here. Life had once again bent her over a barrel and all she wanted to do was crawl into a dark hole and disappear. Maybe eat a full-pound bag of chili-flavored Fritos. Nap. Marathon a season of any CW show.

Forget her life existed.

But she couldn't do that. She needed to suck it up and make the motions and at least pretend to be as understanding and forgiving as everyone else was being when the truth was she hated Kyle to the very depths of her soul.

And now she hated River for bringing it all back to life inside of her again. "I don't have his things with me, but I got his life-insurance policy payout. I can give you the money you need. Would five thousand work?"

River blinked. "But my ring's only worth about twelve hundred," she said faintly.

Lanie shrugged, over it, all of it, but especially this conversation. "I received a hundred-thousand-dollar payout from his life insurance." The money was still sitting in her account. Ever since she'd started being contacted by the other "wives" who'd come out of the woodwork, the money had felt dirty to her. Just because she'd been the first woman Kyle had fooled didn't make it right. She was going to have to divide up the money. "Consider it your due for what Kyle put you through. Put us all through."

"You'd do that for me?" River asked. "Why?"

So that we never have to discuss this again . . . "Because it's the right thing to do," she admitted, willing to go that far and no further.

"That's incredibly generous of you," Cora said and hugged her tight. "I knew I picked right when I found you," she said softly. "You're truly amazing, Lanie."

Lanie did her best not to stiffen, instead patting her boss

awkwardly on the arm. When Cora pulled back, still looking unbearably touched, Lanie smiled a smile that she hoped reached her eyes.

"It *is* incredibly generous," River said, looking floored. "But I can't take it. I can't take a penny from you."

"Then think of it as coming from Kyle."

River was still shaking her head, her eyes lit with pride and a sheen of tears. "You're a good person," she said. "But it's more than I deserve. You were his first wife, Lanie. You're entitled to the money. I'm not."

"Don't be ridiculous—"

River's chin came up. "I'm a lot of things," she said. "Pregnant. Too trusting. Maybe not as smart as I should be. But one thing I'm not is ridiculous."

Lanie nodded and then shrugged. "Suit yourself." She headed to the door.

Mark caught her. His hands came up to her arms and he cocked his head to see into her eyes.

She'd been an actress exactly once. In her freshman year of high school she'd played the part of Rizzo in *Grease*. Her entire repertoire was fake smiling. She'd sucked balls in that play, but she'd gone for Oscar gold anyway.

And she did so now too, doing the fake smile, including teeth and everything.

Mark studied her for a beat and she knew by the look in his eyes that her acting was still bad, that he could tell she was full of crap, not forgiveness, that she wasn't being nice at all, but self-serving. And he was going to have to be okay with that because this is all she had to work with. "Excuse me," she whispered and hightailed it out of there.

MARK STARTED TO follow Lanie out, but his mom stopped him. When he looked at her, he knew he wasn't going to like what she had to say.

"I'm worried about Lanie," she said softly when she'd pulled him aside so neither River nor Holden could hear her. "I had no idea. No idea what she'd been through."

That made two of them. Mark had known her marriage had been rough but he hadn't known how rough.

"I'm afraid tonight will be the excuse Lanie needs to seal the deal on her *not* taking the contract extension." His mom shook her head. "I figured I had time to persuade her, but now . . ."

Lanie was a lot of things—caring, loyal, sweet, kind, smart as hell, and *amazing*.

And also incredibly private.

She'd hate that they all knew what she most likely considered to be her deepest, most humiliating secret. He just hoped she wasn't packing her bags even as he thought it. "I'm going to go talk to her. You got this?" he asked, meaning River.

His mom nodded. "Of course."

In the hallway, Mark came across his favorite heathens and scooped them up. "What are you two doing? Thought you were with your great-grandma baking."

Which they clearly had been, given the twin smears of chocolate across both of their mouths.

"Daddy! Great-Grandma made chocolate chip banana muffins," Samantha said. "They're for tomorrow."

"So why are you wearing them tonight?"

They laughed and Sam explained. "See, Sierra here hadn't ever tasted chocolate chip banana muffins and she wanted to know what they tasted like."

Mark looked at Sierra, who shook her head.

"Okay," Samantha said. "So *I* wanted to know."

Sierra nodded her head.

"So we sneaked back into the kitchen for a taste, even though they were still cooling off. But it was a good thing," Sam said. "Because Lanie has a sad. She needed a muffin too."

"You saw her?"

"Yep. We just gave her a muffin. It'll make her feel better."

Sierra nodded.

"Did she tell you why she was sad?" Mark asked.

"No, she said she just needed hugs from her two favorite little girls in the *whole* wide world," Samantha said. "So we gave her lots of hugs."

Sierra tugged on Samantha's hand.

"And kisses too," Samantha added for Sierra.

Another nod from Sierra.

Mark brought the girls to their room and supervised a round of face-washing and teeth-brushing, trying not to get impatient, but the only thing slower than these two would've been a herd of elephants wading through peanut butter. When they were finally cleaned of all signs of chocolate, he set them up coloring in their favorite coloring books.

"Are you going to go give Lanie hugs and kisses too?" Sam asked. "'Cuz I think she needs 'em."

Sierra nodded.

He stared down at the two sweetest, most loving beings in his life and wondered how the hell he'd gotten so lucky as to have them. "I was on my way to see her when I found two munchkins wandering the hallway."

This caused some giggling, but then Samantha got serious. "She said she was fine, but Daddy, I think it was a fib. You know, the kind that you tell Nana sometimes when she wants to know if you're okay and you're not but you say you are anyway?"

"Samantha," he said on a soft exhale. "Anyone ever tell you that you're too smart for your own good?"

"You, Daddy. You tell me that all the time."

He went to leave, but stopped when he saw a pink sparkly keychain on the nightstand. "What's this?"

"It's Lanie's extra key."

"I know that," he said. "What I don't know is why you have it."

"She gave it to us a few days ago. Said as long as we weren't running from doing something we were supposed to do, and as long as someone knew where we were, we could come in anytime."

Mark's chest tightened. Lanie's protective layer was thick, but it was no match for his girls, who were like windows into her soul. It was through their eyes that he was slowly discovering just how deep he'd fallen for her. "Why?"

"Because everyone needs a place to hide sometimes, Daddy. And sometimes, Lanie says, it's not a place you run to, but a person. She said that she knew we had you and Nana and everyone else, but that she's also our person. If we ever need her."

He nodded, and speechless, he kissed them both on the forehead and left, pocketing Lanie's key.

Everyone needed a place to hide sometimes. Lanie knew that better than anyone. Only . . . where did she go to hide when she needed to?

And who did she talk to?

He wanted to be *that* person. He hadn't seen it coming—he hadn't seen *her* coming—but that didn't mean he couldn't recognize a good thing when he saw it. A great thing. They were amazing together, and instead of complicating his life, she'd added to it. Improved it.

Already he couldn't imagine what it was going to be like when she left.

The night was noisy. A light wind rustling the trees. Insects buzzed. Something howling in the distance. But luckily he ran into no other Capriottis between the big house and the cottages.

Lanie's lights were off and the shade drawn, but that didn't deter him. He knocked and when she didn't answer, he let himself in. The bathroom light was on and the shower was running. He stood there a moment, taking in the pulse of the place, and knew without a single doubt in his heart that she was in trouble.

He shut and locked the door behind him and moved to the bathroom door, where he again knocked.

Nothing.

"Lanie." He put a palm on the wood. "You okay?"

More nothing.

Shit. "I'm coming in." He opened the door to a room shrouded in steam. He found Lanie in a ball in her shower, sobbing as if her heart had been broken all over again.

The dam had burst.

He stepped into the shower fully dressed and picked her up. "I've got you," he said gruffly, feeling her sorrow to the depths of his soul as he wrapped her in his arms. He sat on the tub's edge with her, rocking gently, running a hand up and down her back, waiting the storm out.

"I didn't want you to know how pathetic I was, that my husband needed more wives than just me."

Anger burned through him for her as he tightened his grip into a hug. "Lanie, I'm so sorry."

"I didn't even know until they started showing up after he died."

His heart broke for her. "Are you sure he's dead? 'Cuz I could kill him for you."

She choked out a soggy laugh. "I feel like an idiot."

"You're not. You're one of the smartest, most amazing women I know."

She lifted her head to meet his gaze and a few strands of her wet hair stuck to the stubble on his jaw, but neither of them moved. They sat there like that until the water started to chill. He reached forward and turned it off, then stood up with her still in his arms. Stepping out, he wrapped her in a towel the best he could without letting go of her.

"You're wearing clothes," she said.

"Yes."

"You're all wet."

"Yes."

She sighed and set her head back on his shoulder. "That was dumb."

Yeah. He'd done a few dumb things as it pertained to her. He squeezed her tight and pressed a kiss to the top of her head. She sniffled against him, clearly trying to stanch the flood of emotion.

When she had it together, he leaned back slightly. "Better?"

"I don't know." She leaned her head back against his shoulder. "I wasn't planning on dealing with this until I ate the chocolate chip banana muffin the girls gave me."

He let out a low laugh. "Proud of you," he said softly and she looked up at him, her clear surprise causing a rush of affection to flow through him. "And I'll steal you all the muffins you want."

"Be still, my beating heart," she said.

He set her on the bed and then stripped and dried himself off before coming back to her and drying her too. Then he tugged down the bedding and nudged her in.

"You going home in your birthday suit?" she asked.

He looked down at himself. "It is a dilemma."

Their gazes met and held, and then she lifted the covers, silently inviting him in. She didn't have to ask twice. He got in and pulled her chilled body into his. With a sigh, she cuddled close, pressing her face into his throat.

"Mark?"

"Yeah?"

"You once said you couldn't be pushed where you didn't want to go. But can you be seduced?"

She appeared to hold her breath on his answer, and that just about killed him. She'd had a shitty night, but more than that she'd had a shitty time of it in general, being with a dick of a husband who hadn't appreciated what he'd had, and worse, he'd taught her to doubt herself.

"Don't say I should be alone tonight," she warned. "Because I thought that too at first, but . . ." She shook her head, her voice raw from crying, her eyes hollow and hurt. "From the moment you stepped into my shower like you did, I realized I didn't want to be alone at all."

"What do you want?"

"Honestly?"

"Always."

"Oblivion," she said without hesitation. "I want to be taken out of my own damn head. I want to be reminded that though

I might not be the sort of woman anyone wants to keep long-term, I'm still desirable."

"Lanie, you're the most desirable woman I've ever met," he said, never meaning anything more. "I—"

She put a finger to his lips and leaned over him, brushing her bare breasts across his chest, her hair floating around them as her mouth ran up his jaw, teasing the spot beneath his ear that got him every time.

Then she kissed him.

He let out a rough groan and fisted his hands in her hair. "I'm seduced by you when you're not even trying," he said huskily. "But tonight, Lanie, it's all on me." And with that, he kissed her hot and deep before gently sinking his teeth into her lower lip to tug lightly.

She moaned and clutched at him and heat and desire seemed to flame them both. Wrapping his hands around her wrists, he slid her arms up over her head and then slowly made his way down her body, using his mouth and tongue to make her forget the past few hours.

When she was limp and boneless, he sat back on his heels and looked over the long, curvy body that he'd just worshipped every inch of. Glowing. Sated. Just how he wanted her. When he thrust into her, she cried out his name and wrapped herself around him.

He moved inside of her, his need for her consuming him as she arched her hips to meet each thrust, her body straining against him, taking everything he could give her. She was hot and tight, so tight he lost it, burying his face into the sweat-slicked crook of her neck as he let go, so lost in her he couldn't remember his own name. Only hers . . .

Chapter 20

Just need a pinch of anxiety for flavor.

After Lanie had walked out, River wanted to go after her, but Cora had stopped her.

"Not now, honey."

"But—"

Cora squeezed her hand. "She needs some time." She turned to Holden. "Give us a moment?"

Holden nodded, but instead of leaving he looked at River. "I'll wait right outside for you," he said. "I'll walk you back to your cottage."

River, humiliated at all he'd heard, shook her head, but Holden held firm.

"You haven't scared me off yet," he said quietly.

Not willing to have this conversation in front of her boss—at least she hoped to God that Cora had meant what she said and that River still had a job here—River didn't argue. She couldn't. She was plum out of fight.

When they were alone, Cora took her hand. "You okay?"

River let out a mirthless laugh.

"Let's start with physically. Anything wrong physically?"

River took stock. The baby was for once quiet and settled. "No. We're okay."

"Good." She cupped River's face. "It's been quite a day, I know. I also know when I say I don't want you to fret too much about this, that you still will—but the important thing is you came clean. The worst is over now."

"No," she said. "I still have to talk to Lanie and make her understand that I didn't mean to hurt her. I wasn't faking our friendship."

"And you *will* talk to her," Cora said. "But for now, she needs to think. She's a thinker, our Lanie. You need to give her some time. Time and patience."

"I'm not very good at either of those things." River closed her eyes. "And I meant what I said. I won't take a penny from her. I wouldn't. I couldn't."

"Then maybe you'll apply for a scholarship from the winery and go to school on that."

River's eyes flew open. "What?"

"We give away three scholarships every year. If you were awarded one, you could go for your RN. It'd be a ticket out for you."

River had to choke down the lump in her throat. "I can't—I can't think about that right now."

"I understand," Cora said in that voice she used when she intended to get her way and was willing to wait patiently for her moment to strike. "We'll need to leave in thirty minutes to make it to the doctor for a quick check before our prenatal class."

"What prenatal class?"

"The one I signed us up for at your last doctor appointment," Cora said calmly. "Unless there's someone else you'd rather have at your side when you're in labor?"

River stared at her. "I . . . haven't let myself think that far ahead. I've got to have someone with me?"

"No, you can do it alone if you'd rather."

River's gut sank to her toes. She hadn't felt alone in the five weeks she'd been here. The thought of going into the hospital to have this baby on her own was paralyzing. "You'd really do this with me?"

"In a heartbeat. Come now." Cora led her out of the house. Holden was indeed waiting for her, leaning against the porch, his long denim-clad legs crossed. Cora gave him a long look and then moved off, giving them a moment.

Holden pushed off the railing. "You okay?"

River nodded yes, then thought about what she'd done and the look on Lanie's face, and shook her head.

Holden took a step toward her but she held up a hand. "Here's the thing," she said slowly. "I've spent a lot of my life not being okay, letting other people rescue me. It's not done me any favors. And I was rescued yet again. I need you to walk away from me, Holden. I need to learn how to upgrade from Kyle before I even think about moving on."

He didn't look happy. "River—"

"No, it's time that I learn how to stand on my own two feet," she said. "I have to, if I'm ever going to believe in a future for myself and this baby." She met his deep blue eyes. "Can you understand that?"

"More than you know," he said a little grimly.

She took a longer look at him, into his warm gaze, and knew there was a lot more to him than pretty eyes and broad shoulders. "How did you learn to do it?"

"The hard way."

She nodded, then drew a deep breath and took the step between them, closing the distance. “Will you tell me?”

He held her gaze. “You know I was a homeless teen and that Cora took me in. What you don’t know is that it took her two years to convince me I was good enough.”

She closed her eyes. He did get it.

“And here’s something I shouldn’t tell you, as it doesn’t work in my favor,” he said and tipped her face up to his, waiting until she opened her eyes again. “You don’t always have to find someone else in order to upgrade from your ex. Sometimes just letting their ass go is a fuckin’ upgrade.” And then he did as she’d asked—he walked away.

She didn’t let herself think about that, or the loss of something that was really only the promise of what could be. She didn’t believe in promises, she reminded herself.

Cora took her to the doctor after a quick side trip to Target, where she bought her some baby things like onesies and diapers. River tried to talk her out of it, but Cora insisted.

“It helps if you pick up a few things every time you’re out,” Cora said. “Then your list of must-haves after the baby comes won’t be so overwhelming.”

Yes, but every time she’d left her desk over the past month, she’d come back to an anonymous present for the baby. Sometimes it was wrapped, sometimes not, sometimes it was diapers, sometimes it was clothing or a piece of equipment, such as a car seat.

She’d tried to figure out who the gifter was, but she was starting to suspect it was everyone. Just the thought had gotten her through some dark nights.

On the drive to the doctor’s office, she clutched the bag like it was a pot of gold. “Thank you,” she said softly.

"Oh, honey, you're so welcome. Shopping for babies is a true joy."

"I meant thank you for everything," she said.

"You're welcome for everything."

River shook her head. "I don't think you get it. What you all mean to me. Until you took me in, I didn't even have a bed. Mostly I was trying not to think about the future because . . . well, to be honest, I'm not sure I'm going to be any good at being a mom."

Cora gave her a soft smile. "You had a wonderful mom. She taught you how to depend on yourself and be a good person. You're going to be a great mom."

River nodded, but she wasn't sure she believed, even though a small part of her wanted to.

Dr. Rodriguez was a tiny little dynamo with dark skin, dark eyes, and a happy smile for River. "How we doing?"

"Fine."

"Let's see." The doctor checked River's stats. "You have some signs of hypertension."

River froze. "What's that?"

"High blood pressure. But no worries. Rest and relaxation and good nutrition should get you through. But I'm serious about the rest part. It needs to include lots of off-your-feet time."

"But I have a job," River said.

"Do you stand for this job?"

"No."

"Then you should be okay if you cut back to a few hours a day, tops."

River stared at her in horror. "I can't make a living on a few hours a day."

"Yes, but it won't be for long," Dr. Rodriguez announced happily.

"But I'm just over seven months. I still have two months to go."

"One," Dr. Rodriguez said.

River stared at her.

Dr. Rodriguez's smile faded. "We talked about your due date last time, didn't we? It's why your appointments will now be weekly."

River shook her head. "I was so nervous last time that all I heard was everything looked good." River put her hands on her hot cheeks as a hot flash overcame her. "Oh my God."

"Okay, just take some deep breaths," Dr. Rodriguez said, coming close, stroking her back. "Listen to me," she said softly. "Lots of moms have a panic attack this close to giving birth. It's totally understandable."

Oh, was it? Gee, how comforting . . .

"Would you like me to bring Cora in?"

"No," River gasped.

"Are you sure, sweetheart? A woman in your condition really needs her support team to rally around her."

"No, you don't understand—I'm trying to learn to be on my own."

"Now's not exactly the best time for that. Who's your birth coach?"

"I think Cora is."

"Then we should fill her in, don't you think?"

River hesitated and then nodded. "Okay."

When Cora was brought into the room, River had to admit, she felt relief.

"Update," Dr. Rodriguez told Cora, chipper again. "Baby's all good, but coming sooner than expected. Mama here needs some rest and relaxation and must stay strong with her nutrition. If she keeps her blood pressure down, all those nasty, annoying symptoms of breathlessness and shakiness will go away. She's young, she'll bounce right back with help from her team."

And that was that. Cora was her team.

They then went to the prenatal class, where River learned how to breathe through pain, which to be honest, she was pretty skeptical about.

She went to bed that night after having knocked on Lanie's door.

Lanie hadn't answered.

Telling herself she deserved no less, River had let herself have one last cry. "Our very last pity party," she told the baby, alone in the dark.

THE NEXT DAY, Lanie got up and headed to work with more than a little trepidation. Everyone now knew her torrid secret—that she hadn't been enough for her husband; he'd had to get himself some other wives.

The night before Mark had tried to comfort her, but she'd made it clear that the only comforting would be done naked and would not involve any more words on the matter.

He'd complied. Her body felt very comforted this morning.

Her mind, not so much.

She found Alyssa in the employee room shoving down a doughnut. "Started to go to the gym," she said. "You know, to work off some of the baby fat. Only I couldn't find my membership card and a new one was ten bucks. And since a doughnut and coffee was only three bucks, guess who saved seven bucks this morning?"

"I like the way you think," Lanie said.

They toasted with their coffee cups and then came an awkward silence.

"So . . . how are you doing?" Alyssa asked.

"You know damn well how I'm doing. I'm tired, grumpy, and need ice cream, preferably delivered by puppies."

Alyssa squeezed her hand in sympathy and took a call.

Lanie was grateful to have gotten out of the conversation she didn't want to have. Because she actually didn't know how she felt. She knew she needed to process on her own time schedule, although she was a slow processor. But she could feel things boiling just beneath her surface. Way too many things . . .

Mia walked in yawning and headed directly toward the coffeepot.

"Where's everyone?" Lanie asked.

"If by everyone you mean River, she's out in the field today. Come to me, my precious," she said to her cup of coffee.

Lanie's biggest hope for the day had been to avoid River and her relief was instant, like a huge weight lifted off her chest. "The field?" she asked.

Mia shrugged. "She's working from the big house today, doing some online research for Mom. I think it was more for you than anything else. It'll be easier for you to avoid her and pretend you're not mad when we all know you are."

Lanie froze for a beat. "I'm not—"

"Oh, please." Mia met Lanie's gaze, her own surprisingly kind. "Listen, you've got a right to be, at the very least, bitchy as hell. And I've been there."

"Really?" Lanie asked. "You've been married to a man you thought you knew only to have him die and then find out he collected wives like some men collect change in their pockets?"

"Well, maybe not exactly that," Mia said. "But the important thing here is to remember to practice self-care in times of stress. Take a walk, paint a picture, murder someone, burn the body, and clean up the crime scene."

Lanie laughed. She hadn't thought she'd had a laugh in her, but she'd been wrong. "Thanks."

"Anytime."

"I'm going out with some friends tonight," Mia said. "And I know Mark's working. Come join us."

"Can't," Lanie said, more than a little bummed that Mark wouldn't be able to further distract her with more orgasms later. But it was just as well because she knew he expected her to talk eventually. He was just waiting her out. But he didn't know the lengths she was prepared to go in order to *never* talk about it. "I have too much stuff to do."

And that night she got to the "stuff," which involved spending hours taking Buzzfeed quizzes to see what kind of pizza she was and which Harry Potter character she resembled.

And so went the next week, during which she managed to continue to avoid River so easily that she knew River was avoiding her too.

Chapter 21

"What state do you live in?"
Constant anxiety.

By the end of the week, Lanie still hadn't made peace with what had happened. Cora—or maybe just fate—had been kind enough to keep River in the front building and out of the offices.

Lanie was grateful for the time to think. Or *not* think, as the case might be. She dug into work as an excuse to busy herself and to not have to see or talk to anyone—though they'd tried.

All of them.

The only one who'd gotten through had been Mark, and that was only because he had the key to her cottage and knew how to get past her defenses by not using words.

Nope. He used his body instead.

And he'd used it well. The things he'd done to her in the deep dark of night were the only highlights in an otherwise spectacularly shitty week. Granted, it was probably only a matter of time before he tried to get her to talk, but for now he let her be.

And for that alone, she fell for him just a little bit harder.

Then one afternoon Alyssa texted her with an "employee-room emergency." Lanie raced over there to find no Alyssa in sight.

Just River, looking very young, very pregnant, and very nervous.

Lanie froze in the doorway. "Where's Alyssa? She texted me."

"I asked her to," River said.

Lanie turned to the door to go.

"Lanie, please. I want to apologize. I want to talk to you and explain—"

Lanie sighed and faced her. "You've already apologized and there's nothing to talk about."

River's expression was one of devastation and Lanie hardened herself to it. *It's like the glass partition at the zoo between the dangerous animals and the patrons*, she told herself. *You're looking at this situation from behind a huge window. Nothing can get to you. You're safe.*

And best yet, not even emotions could get through the glass. It was how her mom and dad had dealt with her. They did what they'd had to in order to be parents, but there'd been no emotion, no feeling.

The glass was a good thing.

"If there's nothing to talk about," River said, "then we can get past this, right? We can go back to being friends?"

That was just it. Lanie had believed them to be friends, but it'd been a ruse from the get-go. She turned to pour herself a cup of coffee and saw that Alyssa and Cora had come into the room, so she managed a smile. "Sure," she said through her imaginary glass wall. "Of course."

Cora looked relieved. Alyssa seemed to buy it as well.

But River's eyes said she knew the truth. That Lanie was being nice only to keep the peace.

"Thanks," River said quietly. "I'd like that."

Lanie nodded.

River, clearly trying to hide her disappointment behind her smile, walked out.

Cora gave Lanie a quick squeeze, a gentle sweet hug before reaching for an empty mug. "So how are you doing? You're hanging in there?"

Her boss had been gently probing all week. Lanie had been avoiding her the best she could because she really did care about Cora. She cared about Sierra and Sam. She cared about Mia and Alyssa. She cared about all of them.

Including Mark.

Especially Mark.

Nothing had changed about any of that, but caring about these people gave them great power over her. They could manipulate her. They could hurt her.

Cora—who had a way with timing, or hell, maybe she could read minds—grabbed an apple from a basket on the counter. "I'm going into a bunch of meetings," she said, "one of which is in regards to the bottling business." She looked at Lanie expectantly. She'd said she wouldn't push Lanie about extending her contract. This was Cora, not pushing.

But Lanie couldn't hold off this discussion any longer. Her decision was made. Maybe there'd been a few weeks where she'd actually considered staying, but she knew she couldn't now. "I'm sorry, but I'm not going to take the extension," she said, managing to meet her unwavering gaze. "I'm grateful for the generous offer, but I'm going to leave at the end of my contract."

Cora's phone rang, which she ignored. "I promised you that I'd accept whatever decision you made. But I just want to make sure this wasn't a hasty decision made in a moment of high emotion. In other words, don't make it personal."

Hell, yes, Lanie had made this decision emotionally. And it *was* personal. And here was the other thing—the deep, dark, humiliating, terrible thing she'd finally figured out. Lanie wasn't just upset at River. She was upset at the Capriottis. They'd brought her into the fold, shown her love and easy affection. They'd made her one of them.

And then they'd done the same for River.

The irony here was that Lanie hadn't even *wanted* them to love her in the first place, so why she was so inexplicably, ridiculously . . . *jealous*, she couldn't even say.

But the truth was, she wanted the Capriottis to feel the same anger and hatred and resentment that Lanie herself had felt about what had happened to her. And she wanted them to feel it against River.

Instead it'd brought the pregnant woman even tighter into the fold. And Lanie couldn't seem to get out of her own way about that. It made her feel like an awful person, but no matter how unreasonable, the feelings were real and wouldn't go away.

"You know, Lanie," Alyssa said quietly, "if you ever want to talk about it—"

"I don't."

Alyssa looked at her for a beat. "What happened wasn't your fault, you know that, right?"

Lanie had taken on a lot of guilt about a lot of things, but that Kyle had turned out to be addicted to women wasn't one of them. "I know."

"Good. Because River doesn't blame you."

Lanie stilled. "What?"

"River doesn't blame you for being the other woman, for being the woman who made her marriage illegitimate, for being the one to get his entire life-insurance policy payout, leaving her with absolutely nothing."

Lanie blinked slowly, willing her brain to catch up with the ball of emotions bouncing inside her. "That's nice of her," she managed. She gestured to the door. "I've got a busy day ahead, so . . ." She then walked out it, shutting it behind her.

She got all the way to her car before she realized she'd been followed. "Still not talking about it," she said, turning to face Mark, assuming Cora had just told him she wasn't going to stay.

He stepped in closer and cupped her jaw, the rough pad of his thumb swiping away a tear she hadn't meant to shed. "Hey. Hey, come here," he murmured, pulling her in. "I know it's been a rough week—"

"I'm not that pathetic that I need you to 'there, there' me again. And I know you've just talked to your mom, and man, she works fast, but—"

"Actually," he said, "I haven't seen her today."

Okay, so he didn't know. Yet.

"And I think you're a lot of things like impressive and hot, but pathetic isn't one of them."

He was very close, his scent intoxicating, the intensity of his stare dizzying. "I know you don't want to hear this, but you've handled a really shitty situation with serious class and grace. What can I do to help?"

"I'm fine." She was fumbling through her purse for her damn sunglasses, which she could never seem to find when she needed them—

Mark pulled them off the top of her head and held them out to her.

Shit. She snatched them from his fingers. "Thanks. Gotta go."

"I used to wonder what your wall was about," he said quietly, stopping her in her tracks. "All I knew was that it was thick and well built."

She met his gaze. "You really want to go there? Because I'm not the only one with walls, you know."

"My walls are to protect my daughters. Your walls are to protect yourself, your heart. Not a healthy way to live."

"You don't know, you don't understand."

"I'd like to."

"No." She gave him a push away even though he wasn't touching her. Just his close proximity, with that easy, confident stance and those broad shoulders that could handle the weight of her world made her want to move in close *way* too much. "Look," she said. "We share orgasms when it suits us, but we're not sharing emotions, remember? *You* decreed that." And then, without waiting for his response, she slid into her car and sped off, literally leaving him in her dust.

Five minutes later she was on the highway, roof window open, windows down and inhaling the ocean air in big gulps, trying to figure out where her important place to be was.

Fifteen minutes later, she turned into a narrow, windy driveway on a hill a quarter mile from Morro Bay, because apparently her place to be was her family home. She parked and sat there, pissed off at the world.

Her mom opened the front door and from twenty feet, they studied each other, each giving nothing away. After about fifteen seconds of the stare down, her mom nudged her chin in the barest of movements.

The only invite Lanie was going to get.

Proving it, her mom vanished inside, but Lanie took heart—and also a good amount of annoyance—in the fact that she'd at least left the door open.

She found her mom in the big, huge country kitchen, which had been updated and renovated to the latest and greatest. Her mom, tall, elegant, and coolly beautiful, resembling a model playing a real person—a person who juiced most of her meals—actually baked like a boss.

The evidence was all along the counters in the form of cookies, cakes, and pies, and Lanie's mouth immediately watered. Nothing helped stroke-level stress like a sugar overload. "Looks like a heart attack walking in here." The first words they'd spoken face-to-face in years.

Her mom shrugged. "Bake sale for the adult literacy program tomorrow."

"Of course," Lanie said. "Because heaven forbid we not have our causes. Never mind the children as long as the world thinks you're a giving, loving philanthropist."

Her mom sighed. "Still with the dramatics. You're hardly a child, Lanie."

"I was."

"Which I well know, as I pushed all seven and a half pounds of you out of my vagina. I did what I could, but as I've told you, I'm bad with babies."

"And children."

"And children."

"And teenagers."

Her mom rolled her eyes and went to the bottle of wine on the counter between a strawberry pie and a cheesecake. "To be fair, you were a horrid teenager. But I'm good at adults. Which I'm assuming you've finally become." She handed Lanie a glass and gently knocked their two together in a toast. "To the both of us being adults at the same time."

Lanie tossed back her wine and reached for the bottle.

"That's a very expensive Napa Valley cabernet," she said. "You don't want to drink it too fast."

"Yes, I do."

"Well, then, darling, next time warn me that you're having a moment and I'll drop by the store for a boxed wine."

Lanie took her second glass in hand and reminded herself she'd come here to see about actually getting along for a change. After Lanie had moved out at eighteen and gone off to college, things had gotten better between her and her parents. They all checked in with each other via a phone call once a month. Very civilized. When Lanie had gotten married just before her twenty-fifth birthday, her parents had come to Santa Barbara for the festivities. Since then, they'd met for some of the holidays but not all. More civility.

But instead of appeasing Lanie and making her feel good, it left her yearning for more.

So here she was. Looking for that more. Only she had no idea how to get it. She perused the counter and picked up the cheesecake. She grabbed a fork from the utensil drawer and headed to the table.

"What are you doing?"

"Having a moment, apparently." Lanie sat and dug in. "Oh my God," she moaned around a huge bite. "This is amazing."

"Did you just compliment something I did?"

Lanie paused, the fork halfway to her mouth as she licked some of the cheesy goodness off her lips, considering something she'd never considered before.

Was she equally at fault for this strained relationship? On the one hand, she couldn't be blamed for her mom not wanting to be a mom during Lanie's growing-up years. But now that she *was* grown up, had she perpetuated the crappy communication out of resentment and festering emotional wounds?

One hundred percent.

She took another bite and swallowed before answering.

"Yes," she said. "I just complimented you. And here's another one. Thanks for letting me in to eat and drink you out of house and home."

Her mother looked surprised but recovered quickly. "You're welcome. And I'd say anytime, but I think I'll wait until the end of this visit to make sure."

Lanie choked out a laugh, but remembering her shitty day, it turned into a sob so she carefully pushed away the cheesecake and set her forehead to the table.

Silence from her mom.

After a moment, the bottle of wine appeared in front of her face and the cheesecake was nudged close again.

A peace offering.

Lanie felt her eyes sting, but she ruthlessly beat back the tears. "I'm not falling apart or anything."

"Well, that's good, as one, us Jacobses don't do falling apart, and two, I've got a meeting in fifteen minutes."

This got another choked laugh out of Lanie. She lifted her head and grabbed the wine bottle and drank right from it.

"I'm going to assume someone's dying," her mom said, sounding more than a little pained. "Because otherwise certainly you would be civilized enough to use the glass."

"No one's dying." Lanie took another long pull of wine. Finally, it was starting to warm her up from the inside out. About time. "He's already dead. Though there are days when I wish I could kill him all over again."

"If you'll recall, I told you not to marry him."

Lanie shook her head with a mirthless laugh. "Aw, there it is. The 'I told you so.'"

"Well, I did tell you so. What happened?"

Lanie hesitated. She'd spoken to her mom quite a few times

on the phone since they'd seen each other at Kyle's funeral, but Lanie hadn't told her about the wife addiction. Maybe opening up and trying for a real relationship had to start with her, she thought, and drew in a deep breath. "A bunch of his other wives keep knocking."

Her mom stared at her for a full beat. "Are you drunk?"

"Yes." Lanie sighed. "And he was cheating on me. He married at least four other women. One of them says he had a ring of hers and she wants it back."

"Tell her to take a fucking hike."

Lanie choked on the unfortunate sip of wine she'd just taken. "Did you just say *fuck*?"

"Yes."

"You never say *fuck*."

"No?" her mother asked. "Well, I think it a lot. For instance, fuck using a glass. This situation calls for drastic measures." Taking the bottle of wine back from Lanie, she lifted it to her lips for a long pull. "Don't give in to this woman."

"Her name's River, and she's like, twelve."

Her mom looked horrified. "He was a pedophile too?"

"I mean she *looks* twelve. She's legal, barely. She just turned twenty-one." Lanie sighed. "She also looks like an angel, one that's about to pop."

Her mom sat straight up like a hot poker had been rammed up her spine. "She's pregnant?"

"Yes."

Her mom stared at her for a long beat and then closed her eyes. "Well, damn."

"What?"

"I'm going to say two words to you that I've never said before and don't intend to ever say again. I'm sorry."

Lanie nearly fell off her chair. "Why are *you* sorry?"

"Because I have to revise my statement. She's young, alone, pregnant, and came to you for help. You, when you're most likely the very last person on the earth she wanted to need anything from. My God." Her mom rubbed her forehead like her head hurt. "Do you have any idea how desperate and terrifying that is?"

Lanie stared at her. "Why do I get the feeling we're not talking about River anymore?"

Her mom finished off the bottle of wine and swiped her mouth with her arm, the most undignified thing Lanie had ever seen her do in her life. If she'd burped the alphabet, Lanie couldn't have been more surprised.

"We need more wine," her mom said.

"Actually, I don't think that's what we need at all," Lanie said carefully, because yes, her mind was a little muddled, but not so muddled as to not realize they'd just acknowledged the elephant in the room.

The big, fat, huge pink elephant, who might be a little drunk to boot. "I feel like I'm missing a piece of my own puzzle here," Lanie said. "A big piece too, like one of the corners or something."

"I was nineteen when I got married," her mom said. "And I thought I knew everything there was to know about love. I didn't, by the way, and neither did your father. I caught him boffing my best friend up against my refrigerator and immediately retaliated with my own torrid affair with the mailman. I was the only one stupid enough to get pregnant."

Lanie stared at her, shocked to finally learn the truth of this story. Her story. "But . . . Dad cheated first."

"Two wrongs don't make a right, Lanie."

"No kidding, but it seems to me you're the one who paid the most." Lanie shook her head. "And you stayed married."

"We worked through it. Bottom line, we'd both been young and stupid, but after about a year of hating each other, we realized we still also loved each other."

"Why didn't you ever tell me?" Lanie asked.

"Oh, come on," she said with a rough laugh. "That kind of baggage doesn't fit into the overhead, you know what I mean?"

"Not even a little bit," Lanie said.

"I didn't want your pity!"

"Oh, Mom." Lanie went for more cheesecake. "We're a pair."

"Well, you know what they say. A pair beats . . ." She shook her head. "What does a pair beat?"

Lanie knew this one because she'd been married to an asshole who'd loved poker. "Depends on how good of a bluffer you are," she said, setting the plate on the table between them.

"Well, then, we're in fine shape."

Lanie actually laughed a little at that.

"Do you realize we just spent an entire hour together and didn't yell or hurl insults at each other?"

Lanie looked up at her mom and caught a glimpse of wistfulness on her face before she schooled her expression back to her usual implacable, unruffled calm. "Yeah," Lanie said slowly. "You're right. Should we go at it just for old times' sake?"

Her mom shrugged. "Why feel emotions when we don't have to?"

Yeah. That made perfect sense, but at the same time it squeezed Lanie's heart a little, making it hurt. Because for once, for damn once in her life, it'd have been really nice to have someone *want* to feel emotions when it came to her.

Chapter 22

Is it the anxiety or the two double espressos?

Fifteen minutes later Lanie ordered a Lyft and stood on the sidewalk, waiting. She'd chosen to wait outside instead of pushing her luck and the relatively decent visit karma.

Fifteen minutes later, her Lyft pulled up and she slid into the back of . . .

Uncle Jack's car.

He grinned at her via the rearview mirror. "Hey, cutie."

She gaped at him. "What are you doing here?"

"You requested a Lyft. I'm a Lyft driver." He looked very proud of this. "It's great side money. Plus I get to talk to people. Something wrong with your car?"

"No, I'm sort of toasted."

"Ah," he said, and with absolutely zero judgment drove her toward the address she'd requested—the Whiskey River—driving like a complete madman.

"Um . . . there's no rush," Lanie said, holding on to the "oh shit" bar above the window as they took a turn on two wheels.

"I'm not in a rush," Uncle Jack said and pulled into the lot, where he was honked at—loudly and repeatedly—by the car behind him.

Uncle Jack's response was to flip the guy off.

"Maybe if you used your blinker to signal you're turning," Lanie suggested.

"Hey, it's no one's business but mine where I'm going," he said and then handed her a card with his phone number on it. "Call me direct when you're ready for a ride back."

"Why would you do that for me?"

His smile went a little sad. "Because not every human who has a dick *is* a dick. Have one on me, cutie."

She thought about that as she headed inside and straight to the bar.

Boomer the bartender recognized her and smiled. "Your usual?"

"I've only been here once before."

"I remember all the pretty faces."

"Do you flirt with all of them?" she asked.

"Nasty habit." He leaned on the bar, his smile harmless. "But it's not going anywhere. I'm taken."

"Good, because that's the only kind of man I can handle right now," she said. "Vodka and lemonade, please. Heavy on the vodka, light on the lemonade. Ice cubes optional."

He served her drink just how she liked it and kept them coming. Apparently she'd been deep in denial, because it'd taken her a whole week to lose her shit. But it was official now. Her shit was lost. She was mad. And hurt.

Not a pretty combo for her.

Boomer made another drive-by and with a sympathetic smile, left her the bottle. "Been a rough week, I hear."

With a sigh, she reached for the bottle. She didn't even particularly like vodka but she hated that people knew how screwed up her life was. When her vision was pleasantly blurry and she could no longer feel pain in the region where her heart usually sat, she stood up.

And only weaved very slightly.

Proud of herself, she made her way outside. In the very front parking spot was her silver Honda. Even though she still wouldn't drive, it'd been sweet of Uncle Jack to somehow get her car to her. Incredibly sweet. Maybe she'd reduce her Capriotti ban for him.

But only him.

She located her key pod in the bottom of her purse and beeped her car unlocked. Only it wouldn't unlock. No matter how many times she pushed the button, nothing happened. So she carefully set it on the ground and used one of her heels to stomp on it.

Still nothing.

Rude.

She kicked off her high-heeled boot, picked it up, and hit the driver's side door with it. "I hate you," she said. The car was the one thing Kyle had bought for her with his own money. She'd forgotten that until right this very minute, but suddenly she couldn't stand the sight of the car, as it was the very manifestation of everything wrong in her life.

So she hit it with her boot again.

And again.

And on the fourth hit, the window smashed in. It was incredibly satisfying and she stopped hitting the car and stared at the broken window. "Ha!" She pointed at it. "That's on you."

The whoop of a siren, accompanied by a flash of red and blue lights, had her holding up a hand in front of her eyes.

"Ma'am, I'm going to need you to step away from the car and put down your weapon."

"Me?" she squeaked.

"Put the weapon down, ma'am."

"I don't have a weapon."

In the next beat, her boot was wrenched from her hand and she was turned and pushed up against her car.

And cuffed.

Which is when, cheek down on the hood of the Honda, she realized something.

It wasn't her car.

Well, crap. "Uh-oh," she said. "I think I made a mistake—"

"Ma'am, we need you to answer a few questions."

"No, you don't understand. I thought this was my car, the one my dickwad of a dead husband gave me—"

"Dead?"

"Hey, it's not like *I* killed him. I mean, I really wish I had, I really, really, *really* wish that, but it wasn't my bad."

Which was when she took a ride in the back of a squad car to the station.

Chapter 23

Brain: I see you're trying to sleep. Can I offer a selection of your worst memories from the last ten years of your life?

Mark sat at the desk on the other side of the locked cell, his gaze on the woman asleep on the narrow bench. She was missing a boot, smelled like a bottle of vodka, and half of her hair had escaped its twist, giving her the overall appearance of a fallen Hollywood starlet.

He sipped at the soda he'd gotten from the vending machine. The rest of his cash had gone to the three Snickers bars in front of him, one of which was nothing but wrapper since he'd consumed it and called it a late dinner.

Late, *late* dinner.

It was midnight, and he stayed where he was as in the cell Lanie stirred, moaned, and sat up holding her head like it was in danger of rolling off her shoulders.

"Ouch," she said.

Then she focused with what looked like difficulty and leveled bloodshot eyes on him. "*You*," she said, looking pissed off.

"How you feeling?" he asked.

"I don't know. Why is the sun so loud?" She blinked. "Wait—" She looked around her. "What the hell?"

Standing up, he went to the cell. "What's the last thing you remember?"

"Not wanting to see *you*," she said and looked around. "Seriously. *What. The. Hell?*"

He waited while she ran things through her addled brain and saw the exact second it all clicked together.

"I was arrested!" she gasped.

"No. You were brought here to sleep it off, and for questioning in the matter of destruction of property."

"I thought it was my car," she said and put her hands over her eyes. "Oh my God. I beat up the wrong car."

"Did a good job of it too."

She dropped her hands and narrowed her eyes at him. "I haven't been given my phone call."

"Because after you got here, you went right to sleep."

She was still glaring at him like this was somehow his fault. "You weren't there," she said. "So why are you here?"

"Boomer called me after your parking lot show."

"So you came here to what, save me?"

"Are you still in a cell?"

"Yes."

"Then I haven't saved you," he said.

"Good." She crossed her arms. "Because I don't need saving."

"No shit."

She narrowed her eyes. "What does that mean?"

"Nothing."

"It means something."

"Fine. It means you're the most stubborn, most frustrating woman I've ever met."

"Yeah, well, you're . . ." She grimaced and went back to holding her head. "Lots of annoying stuff too."

"I didn't say you were annoying." He moved closer. "Look, I know this week's sucked for you and that you feel all alone in what you're going through, but when are you going to get it? You're *not* alone. There're people here who care very much for you and want to help."

"You?"

"Yes, me," he said.

"You have no idea what I'm going through."

"Because you won't talk to me. Or, for that matter, River."

She crossed her arms. "If I'm not arrested, let me out of here."

"Sure," he said. "Soon as you're sober."

"I'm stone-cold sober." A statement she ruined by nearly falling over.

The bench caught her.

"Okay," she said with a sigh. "So I'm not all the way sober. And you know what? I'm glad. No one should be sober for this. Also, I'm hungry."

He tossed her a Snickers.

"My favorite." She eyed him. "It might be cute if I wasn't so mad at you. How did you know?"

"I know a lot of things about you," he said.

"Such as?"

"Such as your eyes change color to suit your mood," he said. "They darken when you're aroused and spark like fire when you're pissed off."

"Are they sparking like fire now?"

"No." He smiled. "Because I just fed you your favorite candy bar. And you can't be pissed off at me, I'm 'cute.'"

"*Cute* was one hundred percent the wrong word," she said and took a big bite of the Snickers before rattling the bars. "Let me out of here."

"You're done playing destructo?"

"It was a *mistake*," she said.

"Trying to get into a car that looks like yours is a mistake," he said. "Breaking and entering a car that looks like yours is destruction of property."

"I didn't enter."

She was standing there, hands on hips, hair more than a little crazy, makeup smudged, looking fierce. She was not a woman to back down when up against a wall, and damn if that wasn't attractive as hell.

"Look," she said. "I'm sorry about the car." The thought of staying in jail had the air backing up in her lungs. Breathe in for four, out for four. Repeat. Today's foods . . . she struggled to think back that far. A breakfast bar. Some pasta. Chicken wings. And a Snickers. "I'll pay for the damages, of course. No need to arrest me."

"You're right," he said. "There's no reason to arrest you because the owner of the car you beat up isn't going to press charges."

She dropped some of her bad 'tude. "They're not?"

"It's Boomer's car. Let's just say he understands mistakes."

She dropped her hands from her hips, looking hugely relieved. "Wow. Thanks."

Twenty minutes later they were in Mark's truck. He found a drive-through for Lanie and stole glances at her as she ate, making tiny sounds of pleasure that were his undoing. "Lanie?"

She licked ketchup off her thumb with a loud sucking sound that made him hard. "Yeah?"

"On a scale of one to Britney Spears shaving her head, how drunk are you?"

"Not even close to shaving my head."

He wasn't sure he believed her with that flippant tone, but he let it alone. She was doing her damnedest to hold it together and he knew from his experience with all the women in his house that it was most likely a front, but hell if he'd call her out on it. She'd had a rough night.

He took her to the bluffs, backing in to park. He pulled a blanket from his truck and sat with her on the tailgate, the blanket wrapped around her shoulders as the sky slowly began to shift from midnight black to a kaleidoscope of purples and blues as dawn hit. The reds, oranges, and yellows came out next as the sun came up, casting impressive beams of sunlight across the water.

"Wow," Lanie murmured softly, and with a sigh she snuggled into the crook of his arm, pressing her face to his throat. "Mark?"

The way she said his name never failed to get him and he tightened his grip on her, an utterly reflexive move. No matter what his brain tried to tell him, his body wanted hers close, as close as he could get her. "Yeah?"

She let out a shuddery sigh, her limbs going heavy as the last of the tension seemed to leave her. "Thanks," she said softly.

"For . . . ?"

"Everything." After a pause, she sighed again. "This is nice."

He looked down at the top of her head and smiled. "You're not even watching the water."

"Maybe I'm not talking about the water." She was quiet a moment. "I've never stayed up all night and seen the sunrise."

"And you still haven't," he said. "Your face is planted in my throat."

She gave a shuddery sigh, her breath warming his skin. "I'm still hungry," she said apropos of nothing.

"Okay," he said. "We'll get more food. What do you want?"

"I don't know. Everything."

"I'll make you breakfast."

"You'd do that?" she murmured.

"Yes." He was surprised by the realization that he'd do just about anything for her.

"Maybe . . . pancakes?" she asked hopefully.

"Sure."

He felt her sigh against him and then, not two minutes later, her body got heavy.

She was out cold.

He held her close while she slept through a pretty fucking great sunrise. He'd always known she harbored some deep wounds, but he was just starting to get how deep. She was strong and independent and tough as nails, and a little prickly to boot.

That was one of his favorite things about her.

But she was vulnerable now, right this minute, tucked up against him. Vulnerable and oddly trusting him in a way she hadn't allowed before, which had a surge of protectiveness going through him. Until River had come clean, he hadn't known Lanie's story. What had happened to River sucked. But it'd happened to Lanie too. She'd been with a man, her husband, thinking that she was the one and only woman in his life, but there'd been more. And she hadn't known.

Her takeaway from that had been to close herself off.

The same lesson she'd learned at home growing up.

And now he had her in his arms, this amazing, prickly, suspicious, hardheaded woman that he was falling for in spite of himself because she was also sweet and kind and had the biggest heart of anyone he'd ever met.

Falling hard.

It was going to take a lot to convince her that he was a good idea, although he was pretty sure her body might've already made its decision.

He had no idea what it would take to persuade the rest of her.

LANIE WOKE UP to a little man hammering at her eyeballs from inside her head. "Ouch," she said on a moan.

Someone giggled, but then it was muffled, and Lanie froze. "I know that giggle," she whispered, because talking in a normal voice hurt.

This caused another giggle.

Lanie groaned and sat up. A big mistake because she had to put her hands on her head to hold it on her shoulders.

There was a man in her kitchenette. He was in his uniform and he was—be still, her heart—flipping pancakes like he'd been born to the task.

Sam and Sierra were sitting cross-legged on her counter eating what appeared to be pancakes rolled up so they could do it without utensils.

"Lanie! You missed the first round!" Sam yelled.

Lanie moaned and took a hand off her head to point at the girl. "I'm going to need your inside voice."

Samantha grinned her toothless grin. "You're funny."

"I'm actually not funny. I'm just really mean and people always think I'm joking." Lanie managed to sit up and stagger out of bed, realizing at the last minute that she didn't remember getting into bed so she looked down to make sure she was dressed.

She was in a very large T-shirt that fell to her thighs. The same T-shirt that Mark had been wearing when he'd rescued her from jail. Still had on her panties. That was good news, since the twins were watching her every move. She whimpered her way to the table where she'd left her sunglasses and put them on.

Better.

The girls giggled again and Lanie pointed at them again, which only made them giggle some more.

"You gotta go to bed earlier," Samantha said in all her six-year-old wisdom. "That's what Grandma says when we wake up grumpy."

"Your grandma is very wise." She met Mark's amused gaze. "Blanks," she said. "Fill them in."

"We got back an hour ago," he said. "You needed a nap."

He said this with an utterly straight face. She sighed and slid onto a stool at the counter. She looked over at the girls and realized their pancakes were rolled with peanut butter in the middle.

"Daddy doesn't let us have syrup in the morning," Samantha said. "It makes our teachers not like us."

"Your daddy is also wise." She turned to Mark. "But I don't have a teacher, so I'm hoping for syrup."

"It'll cost you," he said.

She met his gaze and got a hot flash. Two seconds later he slid a plate in front of her. Then he held up a bottle of syrup in one hand and a jar of peanut butter in the other.

She pointed to the syrup.

He went brows up, smiled, and handed her the syrup. She'd pay later.

In private . . . and she'd have no regrets.

Chapter 24

I put the "I" in anxiety.

River knew she couldn't ambush Lanie and force her to go back to being . . . whatever they'd been. Almost close friends? Yes, River was sure of it, and she missed her, wishing . . . well, wishing for a lot of things.

She'd never in a million years have imagined that coming here to Wildstone would lead to the most amazing time of her life, to the most amazing people she'd ever met, Lanie being the most amazing of them all.

Not that Lanie felt the same way at the moment. And River couldn't relax until she'd made things right.

But she had no idea how to do that.

For days now she'd tried to catch Lanie when she was on the move in the hallway between the offices, employee room, or bathroom. But it was as if the woman was wearing her own invisibility cloak.

Finally, Mia gave River a long look when she paced the hallway for the thousandth time. "You okay?"

"Fine," River said. "Why?"

"Because you've walked ten miles in the past few days."

River managed a smile. "The baby's restless."

"Or . . . ?"

River blinked. "Or what?"

"Or you're waiting for Lanie so you can beg her to be your friend again."

River sagged. "How did you know?"

"Because you talk to yourself."

"I talk to the baby."

"Oh." Mia looked sympathetic. "Look, I like you. A lot. So I'm going to talk to the baby too, okay? And if you happen to listen, well, then, that's not really my fault, right?"

"Um . . . right," River said, surprised when Mia hooked a chair with her foot and dragged it close, then sat in it. Head lowered, she lightly knocked on River's belly. "Hello, anyone here?"

River laughed. "You know she can't answer yet, right?"

Mia lifted her head. "She?"

"That's what the sonogram says."

Mia smiled and then started talking to River's belly. "First of all, you should know you've got a great mommy. Maybe she's made a few mistakes, but she's trying real hard to fix them. Which is amazing because most people don't own up to their wrongs, much less try and right them. I hope you learn from her, 'cuz she's pretty great. But if you could do one thing for me . . . maybe tell your mommy she's not alone. She's never alone." Mia lifted her gaze to River's.

River tried not to cry. And failed. "Thank you," she whispered.

"For what?" Mia got to her feet. "Just saying hi to the baby so she recognizes me when she comes out. This one's going to have a lot of people who care about her."

River's throat was too tight to speak, so she just nodded as Mia headed out. "Mia," she managed.

Mia turned back.

"Do you think she'll ever forgive me?"

"I think Lanie's a very smart woman. When she gives it some time, she'll get it." Then Mia pulled a candy bar from her pocket and handed it to River. A Snickers.

Lanie's not-so-secret favorite.

"You think I can bribe her into being friends again?" River asked, amused in spite of herself. "Because I stalked her, got a job where she works, and got close to her, all without telling her that oh yeah, we shared a rat-fink bastard of a husband and I was here only to steal back my ring."

"Well, I didn't say it would be easy," Mia said. "But you do have one thing on your side that you haven't considered."

"What's that?"

"You aren't the only one who wants to put your past behind you. There's common ground there, and where there's common ground, you can usually find forgiveness right behind it."

"You and I are the same age," River said in marvel. "How do you know so much?"

Mia's smile was tinged with sadness. "The way we all learn stuff. Hard-core experience. I know we're supposed to be grateful for all the mistakes we make, but mostly I'm just grateful that thoughts don't appear in bubbles over our heads."

When Mia was gone, River headed back to the front building and by sheer luck nearly plowed into Lanie.

"Hey," River said breathlessly.

"Hey." Lanie tried to go around her, but River was wide as a house. Heavy as one too. She put herself right in the way and there was no going around her.

Lanie stopped and sighed.

"I don't know how to beat around the bush," River said.

"So I'm just going to come right out and ask—what are the chances you're going to forgive me before I have this baby?"

"River, please don't do this." Again, Lanie made a move to go around her, but River planted her feet wide.

"I've got a Snickers bar."

Lanie hesitated. "Just one?"

"Yes, but it's a family size." She pulled it from her pocket, sending a silent thanks to Mia.

Lanie opened it right then and there and took a big bite, sighing, closing her eyes to savor it.

River started to speak, but Lanie held up a finger. She took another bite and looked to be in heaven. "Yeah, it hits the spot every time." She opened her eyes, saw River still watching her, and sighed before breaking the Snickers in two to offer the other half to River.

"Chocolate's bad for the baby," she said. "But I miss it so much."

"Sorry." Lanie slid it back into her pocket. "Guess it's been a while for you."

"For a lot of things," River said.

Lanie looked at River's belly and blew out a breath. "We slept with the same man. I don't know what to do with that."

"Me either," River said quietly. "But I swear I didn't know about you."

Lanie nodded. "Me either."

They were quiet a moment but suddenly the quiet didn't feel quite as awkward.

"And honestly?" River said. "The last time I slept with Kyle I had a Snickers bar in my car and I couldn't stop thinking about it."

Lanie looked at her doubtfully.

"No, I mean it. He was trying to be sexy and kept asking

me what I wanted, but all I could think was that I wanted my damn Snickers."

Lanie actually let out a low laugh at that, startling River. Then she shook her head. "I've gotta get back to work. I know you know I've been avoiding you. I just . . . need time. I need to think. You okay with that?"

Did she have a choice? "Yes."

"Thank you." And then she was gone.

River went back to work. She felt lighter than she had before. She stayed off her feet as she'd promised Cora and Dr. Rodriguez, and at the end of the day, Holden showed up at her desk. "Ready?" he asked.

"For what? A nap? Because then yes, I'm ready."

Holden picked up her purse and slung it over his shoulder. A big guy wearing her purse should've looked ridiculous.

Ridiculously handsome. "What are you doing?" she asked in shock.

"Taking you on a date."

"But—"

"We're going out to dinner. There will be candles and wine and no drive-through." He grimaced and glanced at her belly. "Well, candles and fancy sparkling water," he corrected. "Not wine."

Ridiculous. Silly. And dammit, sweet. "Holden—"

"But first we're going somewhere that'll put a smile on your face."

"You can't know that," she said. "I've given up smiles right now."

"Trust me, you won't be able to resist this."

He took her to the local SPCA, where they sat together in a big playroom and had a playdate with a bunch of puppies.

Simple.

No strings.

He knew she didn't want someone to take care of her. He knew she wanted to stand on her own two feet. And he also knew that sometimes it was just nice to have company while you were adulting as hard as you could.

They had dinner, and after that he brought her home to her cottage full, content, and somehow feeling happier than she had all week.

She saw the look on his face though. He wanted to kiss her good night. He wanted that and more. "Thanks for tonight," she murmured. "It's been a long time since I spent a night doing something other than worrying about my future."

His gaze went serious. Well, it was always serious—except, it turned out, when he was cuddling puppies like he'd been born to do the job, letting them crawl all over his big, muscled self. But he was even more serious than usual at the moment. "Thought you understood by now that you're not alone, River."

"So people keep saying," she said lightly, belying the fact that her heart had leapt hard. There was just something about the stoic, quiet-but-not-shy guy standing in front of her, so close that she could see the dark blue rim around the lighter blue of his irises. He was tough, impenetrable. And *not* vulnerable. She wanted to soak that up. And okay, yes, maybe she also wanted the things she saw in Holden's eyes. But that would be selfish, and she no longer did selfish. "I thought you understood that I *need* to be alone right now."

"To figure your shit out," he said, quoting her with the smallest of lip quirks.

"You think it's dumb."

"No, I think you have to do what you have to do. But I also think there's no reason to be alone while you're doing it."

She drew in a shuddery breath. It'd be so easy to invite him in, to give in to that warm, welcoming heat in his gaze. In fact, her body overruled her brain and she reached behind her to open the door and . . . She caught sight of Lanie sitting on her loveseat, clearly waiting for her. River blinked, and felt something slide into her belly.

Hope.

"Holden?" she whispered, gaze locked on Lanie. "I'm going to need a rain check."

His gaze swept past her to the loveseat. He squeezed River's hand, his eyes coming back to her. "If you need anything, you know where to find me." Leaning in, he brushed a warm kiss to her temple.

And for the briefest of beats, she clung to his hand, needing to borrow his strength. He brought their joined hands to his chest and it was like he'd actually infused her with that strength she'd needed, because when he left, she was able to walk in calmly. "This is a surprise."

Lanie met her gaze. "Cora let me in. I didn't think we needed an audience of well-meaning, nosy Capriottis." She smiled wryly. "Turns out my need to hate you is overruled by my need to get answers. I really need some of those, River. I'm guessing we both do."

River nodded. "I'm ready," she said and hoped that was really true.

Chapter 25

Crippling anxiety is my cardio.

Lanie didn't know what to expect from this talk with River. But what she did know was that Mark had been right. She had questions and she was pretty sure River had at least some of the answers. She watched as River swallowed hard and came close, her expression painfully earnest.

"I'm so glad you're here. I thought you despised me."

Lanie grimaced. "Not despised. Despised is a little strong. It implies that I'd unplug your life support to charge my iPhone, so I save that word for things like chia seeds, infomercials, and slow walkers in the aisles of the grocery store."

River snorted. "Even when you're mad, you're funny. Can I go first?"

Lanie let out a breath and nodded.

River nodded too and came closer. "First, I just want to say that you don't have to forgive me. You just have to know how truly sorry I am for lying to you. For sneaking into your room and invading your privacy. For *all* of it."

The ironic thing was that if River had only told her the truth from the beginning, Lanie would've . . . *what? Been a bitch like you were anyway?*

River sat on the loveseat next to Lanie. She wriggled around in frustration until Lanie finally plumped a pillow behind her.

"Wow," Lanie said when River finally sat back against the pillow, huffing with exertion. "I didn't realize how tough it was for you to move around."

"This is nothing. You should see me try to go pee in the middle of the night by myself. It's a beached-whale situation." She grimaced. "And you didn't come here to hear any of that." She met Lanie's gaze. "I really didn't know about you until after Kyle was gone."

"I believe you." And with that, Lanie had to admit something else as well. "You aren't the first other wife to show up."

River stared at her, mouth open. "That fucker," she finally said. "That sexy, charming rat-fink motherfucker."

"Yeah." They sat in silence for a few minutes, both mired down by what they'd both fallen for.

Finally, River sighed. "You have questions for me. That's why you're here, right?"

She did have questions, but by asking them, by giving a voice to the doubts that came to her deep in the night, she was going to be revealing herself. Completely. She'd thought long and hard about it, but in the end her curiosity had won. "How did you meet him?" she asked. "*When* did you meet him?"

"I worked as a waitress at a truck stop on his route." River paused. "Wait—he really did drive a truck for a beverage distributor, right? He didn't lie about that too, did he?"

"No," Lanie said. "He delivered beverage orders to restaurants, bars, and truck stops the entire width of Southern California every other week. He was gone half the time, always. It's why I never caught on."

River nodded her agreement on that fact. "I knew him for

months before anything happened. He'd come in during the afternoons when I was run the most ragged and buy two iced teas and then make me drink one. He'd order an extra meal and get me to eat." She hesitated again. "He was so . . . warm. And funny. And . . ."

"Charismatic," Lanie finished softly. Deep down, she realized she'd been okay with Kyle being away all the time because she truly hadn't wanted or expected any sort of hugely deep relationship. In hindsight, that sucked for the person she'd been and she was starting to realize that maybe, someday, she'd be ready for a real relationship with a real partner. "I know. He really drew people in. But River, you're so young."

River lifted her chin. "I was nineteen when I met him. Twenty when I got pregnant. I turned twenty-one after he died."

"Yes, but Kyle was so much older than you. He should never have touched you."

River frowned. "Twenty-eight's not that much older than me."

Lanie sighed and then found herself defending this girl that she didn't want to care about. "River, he was thirty-eight. *And* married. He should be shot for what he did to you."

River gasped and shot up to her feet. Well, not shot, exactly. Lumbered was more like it. *"Are you kidding me?"* she shrieked. *"I slept with an old guy?"*

Lanie actually laughed. "Yes. I'm sorry."

River stared at her for a long moment before letting out a long breath. "Okay, so he definitely made mistakes. A whole lot of them." She put her hands on her belly. "But this baby, she's not one of them," she said fiercely. "And *she'll* never feel like she is, I won't allow it."

Seeing this girl so possessively claim a baby that had by all counts only made her life even more difficult than it already was . . . well, Lanie didn't even have the words. Her parents had never been penniless or on their own, but nor had they been willing to set aside their circumstances to jump into the joys of parenthood.

And here was River, loving her baby with such intense protectiveness, it nearly brought tears to Lanie's eyes. "Of course the baby's not a mistake."

River gave her a small smile. "Thanks. And not that I want to defend him, but Kyle didn't take advantage of me. When I was with him, he was nothing but kind and caring."

Lanie wasn't feeling so generous. She thought the man was a card-carrying douchebag. "River—"

"No, listen. After my mom died, I was . . . really alone." She lifted a shoulder. "It was hard. I missed her so much. She was . . . everything. And I didn't know how to go on without her. But she wanted me to become a nurse, said I was good at it. So that became my dream. Get through high school and then become a nurse." She gave a rough laugh. "It seemed so simple, but it's proven to be anything but. Until Kyle came along. He encouraged me to start taking classes, and when I didn't have the money he paid for my tuition." River met her gaze. "He was amazing to me, and so wonderful that I never thought . . ." She shook her head. "I never thought to doubt him or question him."

"He told you he was single?"

"Well . . ." River grimaced. "I've been going over that in my mind. Honestly?" She shook her head. "I'm not sure I ever even asked him. We were just friends for a long time, months really, and he was out of town a lot for his job. Whenever he'd come back through, he never said much about himself." She stopped talking. Swallowed hard. "That's been keeping me up at night. That he got me to let my guard down so thoroughly that I didn't even ask him. I'm sorry about that too."

Lanie didn't say anything for a minute. She didn't know what to say. Kyle's job had required him to travel. She'd never second-guessed him either, and that was on her. But in hindsight, it'd been easy for him to lead a double and triple and apparently quadruple life. He *had* been persuasive and charming and charismatic, and she'd been flattered by his attention. By his easy love. "I let my guard down too," she admitted.

River let out a shuddery breath, like she'd been holding it for too long, and Lanie realized that she really did care what Lanie thought of her.

It'd been easy to resent River from the moment her dead husband's name had left the younger woman's lips. But it was another thing to hold on to that resentment given the facts. Which was also making it hard to hold back the other emotions vying for space in her brain.

Self-pity. Sorrow. Regret.

Shame . . .

And suddenly she wanted River to have her damn ring back. If she could do that, locate it in the single box of Kyle's things she had in storage, then she could absolve herself of the entire situation. She could walk away knowing she'd done the right thing since Kyle couldn't. It'd be over, the entire nightmare. She was very close to the end of her contract and basically done with all the heavy lifting. All she was doing now was making sure everything was in place and running smoothly. She could do that from anywhere, including Santa Barbara.

She could get the hell out of Wildstone and never look back. "We're both off the day after tomorrow. You up for a road trip?"

"If there's food involved. Why?"

"We're going to get your ring back."

And maybe *then* she'd also get her life back.

LATE THAT NIGHT, Mark came to Lanie's cottage. He had her backed to the wall with his hands inside her clothing and his mouth on her throat when she stopped to sniff him.

He pulled back slightly. "What?"

"You smell like chocolate."

"Just made cupcakes with the girls for school tomorrow," he murmured and went back to kissing her neck.

Which felt great, but . . . "There're chocolate cupcakes to be eaten?" she asked.

He stilled and then pulled back again, a light of amusement in his eyes. "They're for school."

"But you smell like chocolate. It's making me hungry."

He dropped his forehead to her shoulder, then smoothed her clothes back into place and grabbed her hand, tugging her to the door.

"What are we doing?"

"I know better than to try and seduce a woman whose mind is on something else," he said and brought her to his truck.

"You have the cupcakes in your truck?" she asked.

He cupped her face and kissed her, and then belted her in. "No."

"But—"

He shut the door on her nose and then slid behind the wheel. This time they did things in reverse. Store first—because according to Mark they'd burned the first batch of cupcakes and had only the exact number they needed. Gratified with store-bought brownies, they boogie-boarded under a full moon, racing for the right swells, laughing and competing like they were teenagers, trying to knock each other off.

Well, she *tried* to knock Mark off, but he was solid as stone on his board and couldn't be budged. However, she was *not* solid as stone and he took her down and into his arms. He had her wrapped around him and was kissing her when a wave washed over them both.

They came up sputtering and laughing, and when they were too cold to keep going, they warmed each other up beneath a blanket of stars.

The next day she was buried with work, determined to make sure she finished her contract with her best work when River rushed past her to the bathroom for the hundredth time that day. "You okay?" she asked the blur that was a very pregnant River.

"I'm fine. It's my bladder and the baby's tap-dancing on it."

As soon as the bathroom door slammed, the main phone line rang. This always happened. Lanie looked around. She was the only one at her desk. Dammit. She grabbed the phone. "Capriotti Winery, how can I help you?"

"I need to talk to my daddy."

Lanie immediately recognized Sam's voice and she twisted to see the clock. Ten o'clock in the morning on a Tuesday. "Hey, Sam, it's Lanie. Your dad's at work. What's wrong?"

"I forgot to bring cupcakes and it's my turn for Make-New-Friends Day."

Once again Lanie looked around for someone more qualified to handle this problem. "Um . . ."

"Daddy helped us make them last night, but we forgot them this morning."

Lanie stilled and flushed as she remembered Mark showing

up smelling like warm chocolate and her trying to eat him alive before he'd taken her to the beach. They'd stayed up way too late. He'd probably been exhausted this morning and she felt at least partially responsible.

"We called Daddy's work, but they didn't like that," Sam said.

"You called his cell?"

"No, 'cuz this is an emergency. I called 9-1-1 and asked real nice and everything."

Lanie winced. "Okay, let's not bother them again. What time do you need the cupcakes?"

"Right after lunch. They're in the kitchen next to Great-Uncle Jack's special sippy cup that we're not allowed to use 'cuz it's got adult juice in it, the kind that makes him wobble when he drinks too much of it."

Lanie had to laugh. There were no secrets in this place. "Got it," she said. "I'll bring them to you."

"Thank you! Love you!" Samantha yelled in enthusiasm.

"Um . . ." While Lanie struggled with the ease of those words being flung at her and her own difficulty in saying them back, she realized with a short laugh that Samantha had already disconnected so it didn't matter that she was completely emotionally challenged.

Okay, then.

She went to the kitchen and found Mia fixing the big fancy Keurig with Uncle Jack hovering over her.

"Hurry up," he said. "You millennials, you take forever to mobilize. No one's ever lit a fire under any of your asses."

Mia stopped working on the Keurig and gave him a long look. "You know, it's okay if you're old so you hate all of us twentysomethings, but then next time you can't figure out how to fix your electronics, you don't get to ask a millennial for help!" And then she walked out past Lanie, muttering about how sometimes she just had to remind herself that it wasn't worth the jail time.

Uncle Jack went palms up. "She's so sensitive."

Lanie didn't care about any of that. What she did care about was the plastic container containing the cupcakes. It was opened and filled with . . . a few chocolate crumbs.

The cupcakes were gone.

"Were they yours?" Uncle Jack asked from behind her. He belched and patted his gut. "'Cuz they were amazing. All this time I thought you could only make PB&J sandwiches. You've been hiding a secret talent."

"Oh my God," she said, horrified. "You ate the girls' school cupcakes!"

His face fell. "Are you sure?"

She picked up the empty container and waved it around. "I'm pretty sure!"

"Shit. Fuck. Damn."

Uncle Jack had been listening to his George Carlin tapes again. "I thought Cora took away your cassette tape player."

"She did. I bought another on eBay."

"Forget that. You need to make more cupcakes," Lanie said urgently. "And fast."

"I can't."

"Why not?"

"Because I can't bake. I can cook, but the last time I baked something I nearly burned the house down and now I'm not allowed."

Well, this was just great. She pulled out her phone.

"What are you doing?" he asked.

"Calling Cora. She'll know what to do."

"Yeah. She'll know what to do. She'll kill me!" He shook his head. "You can't tell her."

Lanie wasn't one hundred percent sure where she stood on the whole divine issue, but she tilted her head up to the ceiling anyway. "Are you kidding me with this week?"

"If you're talking to God, he's busy saving the whales. And anyway, I don't think he'd care that I ate the cupcakes, because I *prayed* for those cupcakes."

Lanie narrowed her eyes at Jack, who cleared his throat and pulled out his wallet. "Look, here's . . ." He counted out some bills. All ones. "I've got . . . uh-oh. Four bucks."

"Forget it," Lanie said and grabbed her purse. "I'll handle it." It'd be faster to go buy something new and try to pass it off as homemade anyway. Or so she assumed, but she'd never had to pull off a stunt like this before. So she did the only thing she could think of, she improvised and drove like a bat out of hell to the supermarket.

There she stood in the bakery section. No cupcakes. "Excuse me," she called to the guy slicing bread behind the counter. "I don't see any cupcakes."

"They're just about done," he said and turned to the oven. He peered inside, nodded with satisfaction, and pulled out a huge tray of cupcakes perfectly browned.

"I'll take them," she said.

"Can't sell these," he said. "They're not frosted yet."

"Can't you just frost them real quick?"

"No. They have to cool first."

"Okay, then I'll buy them as is."

"Lady—"

"*Please*."

He looked pained. He was maybe twenty-two, twenty-three tops, and she knew just how to reach him. "Cash," she said.

He craned his neck, making sure they were alone. *"Cash,"* he said. "And this never happened."

"Deal."

Five minutes later she was in the car with the warm, naked cupcakes and several cans of frosting she'd picked up in the baking aisle. She was also the brand-new owner of a box of plastic knives—since they hadn't sold just one and there'd been no one in that aisle to bribe. She'd also picked up two baking sheets and a roll of aluminum foil.

Thirty bucks poorer, she drove to the elementary school and then sat in the parking lot, where she covered the baking sheets in aluminum foil, set the cupcakes on them, and got to frosting. A few minutes later, she realized she'd made a tactical error.

Okay, so more than one.

First, she'd forgotten napkins. And second, she might be a professional cupcake eater, but she was in no way even *close* to a professional cupcake froster.

By the time she carried the tray into the school, she was wearing frosting all over her. She signed in at the front desk and was escorted to the classroom by an aide who kept looking at Lanie's hair. Since that didn't make any sense, she shrugged it off because, hello, *bigger problems.*

Then suddenly she was in the classroom and the twins came running up all smiles, helping her set the cupcakes on a table.

Sierra pointed to Lanie's hair.

"Okay," Lanie said. "What's up with people staring at my hair?"

"You're wearing frosting in it," Mark said.

She turned and found him in uniform looking his usual badass self, a fact that the smile on his face only amplified.

"What are you doing here?" she asked, slapping his hand away when he tried to touch her hair.

He simply used his other hand and swiped his finger over her head, which came away smeared in chocolate frosting.

"Dammit," she said.

"That's a bad word," Sam said. "Our friend Alesia gets a spanking if she says a bad word or fibs."

Mark arched a brow at Lanie, and in a reaction that she did not approve of, her body disconnected from her brain and quivered. "No, but seriously, what are you doing here?"

"Dispatch got ahold of me," he said. "I stopped at the bakery in Paso Robles."

She eyeballed his perfect, bakery-made cupcakes. "Those aren't homemade. They're supposed to be homemade. You cheated."

"So . . . you made yours, then?"

"Yes." She paused. "Sort of."

He leaned in and with his mouth against her ear said softly, "You remember what happens to fibbers, right?"

She got a hot flash.

From the front of the room, the teacher clapped her hands twice, which was apparently the sign for class to start because people started to scatter.

"You guys gotta go now," Samantha said in a rush and both girls flung themselves at Lanie and Mark, giving hugs and wet kisses. "Thanks, Lanie," Sam said. "Thanks, Daddy. Don't go too hard on her, okay? Her heart's in the right place."

The words were Cora's. Lanie could hear her boss saying those exact words and knew that was where Samantha had gotten them. If she hadn't been so frazzled—and covered in chocolate—she'd have taken a beat to admire the wonderful qualities the woman was imparting to her family, and maybe even ache a little bit since she'd not gotten much of that from her own.

Mark was still chuckling as he and Lanie headed out of the school.

Lanie bit her tongue, refusing to ask him what the hell was so funny because—

She gasped when Mark pulled her around the corner and pressed her up against the wall of the building.

"What the—"

Before she could finish the sentence, his mouth came down on hers. He kissed her long and quite thoroughly before lifting his head and licking his lips. "Definitely store-bought frosting," he chided.

She gave him a shove and he took a step back, laughing outright now. "You are so spoiled rotten," she exclaimed. "You have no idea!"

His smile faded a little, as if maybe he suddenly remembered what had happened and all he'd learned about her, and just like that her humiliation renewed itself. She whirled around to leave, but he caught her hand and reeled her back in.

"Don't," she said, not sure what she was saying "don't" to exactly. To looking at her in that way he had that both made her bones melt and her heart go squishy? To kissing her again? Because if he did, they'd end up in bed—where, granted, they did their best work—and that thought scared the hell out of her. It was getting hard to keep her heart out of the mix.

Actually, scratch that. Not just hard, but outright impossible.

Mark used his free hand to stroke her hair back from her face. Then he looked at his finger—streaked with chocolate—and licked it.

She made a sound that was half laugh, half sob and his hands tightened on her.

"You're still avoiding talking to me," he said quietly, no longer amused.

"No."

"Lanie."

She sighed. "Okay, yeah. A little. I've been avoiding talking to you a little."

"Why?"

She stared up at him. "Have you not been paying attention?"

"I have. I'm paying *all* my attention." He leaned in close. "What are you so afraid of, I wonder?"

"Honestly?" she asked. "I'm putting all of my energy into not seeking the answer on that." She paused. "I'm going on a road trip tomorrow."

"With River. You're going to go through Kyle's things to see if you can't get her ring back."

She shook her head with a sound of annoyance. "Do you know everything?"

"I try to. For instance, I know that you're the most incredible, caring, warm, most amazing woman I've ever met."

She snorted and rolled her eyes. "You need to meet more women then."

His lips curved into a very small smile. "You coming back, Lanie?"

His eyes were like lasers, burning into hers, and she supposed it was somewhat of a relief that he could read her so well.

Saved a lot of time. "I'm not quite done with my contract," she said. "And I don't leave in the middle of my obligations."

His gaze held hers prisoner. "Is that all this is? An obligation?"

"No," she whispered.

"Good. And you know damn well you don't have to go at all; everyone here, including me, would love for you to stay."

She dropped her head to his chest again. Let herself soak up the innate and delicious guy scent of him, his strength, his goodness. Then she pushed off. "I've got to go."

He let her, and a minute later she was in her car. She drove to the winery on autopilot and parked. And then sat there, head down on the steering wheel.

What the hell was she doing?

She was still straddling that line of telling herself she couldn't possibly stay. Still telling herself there was nothing to keep her here, a vow that had become even more serious once River had revealed herself.

But now her commitment to her self-pity was wavering, along with her resolve to stay unattached to anyone here. Her roadblocks were falling away one by one and it was . . .

Well, terrifying.

All the more reason to go, she told herself firmly. *Stick by that. Own it. Finish your work and get out, walk away while you still can.*

A few minutes later her phone vibrated in her pocket, nearly giving her heart failure. It was Mark. "Hey," she said, annoyed at how breathless she sounded.

"Hey, yourself. I'm back at work, but according to Holden, you've been sitting in the parking lot talking to yourself for ten minutes. Am I worried?"

"No." She paused and closed her eyes. "Mark?"

"Yeah?"

"Thanks for caring."

There was a beat of silence. She'd surprised him, she realized. "I care a lot," he said very quietly, as if he didn't want to scare her off.

And when had *she* become that person? she wondered. The one of the two of them who was afraid of her feelings and emotions? Okay, so she'd always been that person.

The truth was, she'd hidden behind his no-relationship stance because she was afraid, afraid that her feelings for him left her feeling as if she were naked in school and vulnerable. And she didn't do vulnerable. "I know you do," she said and then let herself say it. "I, um . . . care a lot about you too." And then, because she was in uncharted waters without a navigation system, she ended the call.

By this time tomorrow she'd be on Lanie's and River's Most Terrifying Adventure.

Chapter 26

My anxieties have anxieties.

The next morning, River stood in front of her closet trying to figure out what to wear for this road trip when Holden knocked and came in looking like the cowboy he was in boots, jeans, and a cowboy hat, shoulders broad enough to carry any burden that came his way.

He smiled at her and moved to her side. "You about ready to go?"

"I would be—if any of my clothes fit."

"So you're really going to do this thing with Lanie?"

"Yes." And if she was being honest, she was excited about it too. It was a chance to get Lanie back in her life. She missed her, like she imagined she'd miss a sister if she had one.

Holden nodded. "Nice."

"That I'm going?"

"Your smile," he said and gave her one of his own rare ones. "But yeah, also that you're going."

She gave him another smile in return. "You know what I like about you?"

"My charm and sexy eyes?"

She laughed and God, that felt good. "That you don't try to tell me what to do."

"Why would I ever do that?" he asked. "And also, full disclosure, my eyes aren't even my best feature."

She rolled her eyes and went back to studying her closet, but she'd be lying if she said she didn't wonder what his best feature might be. "None of my sweaters fit me anymore."

"Here, take this." He shrugged out of his sweatshirt, which was indeed big enough to fit her. He wrapped it around her shoulders and didn't step back after, ensuring that his airspace intersected with hers.

She stilled, trying to decide what that odd sensation going through her was. Excitement or anxiety?

Both, she decided.

Holden caught a stray curl and tucked it behind her ear, his fingers lingering at her temple. And then he leaned in an inch. And then another. Going slow . . .

For her, she knew.

She kept her eyes open as he gave her the chance to pull away. But she didn't pull away, and he brushed his lips across hers.

A test kiss.

One that deepened in the best way when she relaxed into him. He checked himself before it went too far, nuzzling her cheek, smiling against her when she made a sound of protest that he'd stopped. "Don't want to rush you," he whispered.

"A little rushing wouldn't bother me."

He pulled back slightly and studied her, his eyes crinkling at the corners. "You want me."

"Well, I'm not dead, am I?" she asked. "But I refuse to tie

anyone down." She held her arms out and looked down at herself. "I'm a complete disaster, Holden."

"Hey, if you want to tie me down, I'm game. But turnabout is fair play."

She rolled her eyes, but there was no denying that quiver deep inside was all excitement now, no anxiety.

"And you're not a disaster," he said. "Not even close. You haven't let the right people in, that's all. But the right people are here, just waiting on you to decide."

She stared up at him. He was unlike anyone she'd ever met, a little rough-and-tumble around the edges. Smart. Stoic. *Real.*

"Your hair's smoking," he said. "What are you thinking about?"

"I'm thinking you might be too good to be true."

He did the oddest thing. He tipped his head back and laughed, and it was a beautiful sight. "I'm a lot of things," he finally said, still smiling. "But too good to be true isn't one of them."

She shook her head. "So what happens now?"

He pulled a key from his pocket and slid it into hers. "That's to my cottage. It's an open-ended invitation." He lifted her chin and kissed her again, soft and deep and hot enough to melt her bones. "Think about it," he said.

She wanted to. Oh God, she wanted to. But deep down in her gut she knew she couldn't. She couldn't do it to him, saddle him down with the likes of her and a baby that wasn't his. Heart in her throat, she shook her head. "I can't, Holden."

He looked at her for a long moment, nodded, and then walked away. Without taking his key back.

"Your key," she called after him.

But he rounded the corner and was gone.

FROM THE SHOTGUN position of Lanie's car, River shifted for the hundredth time. "Ungh."

Lanie glanced over with a look of complete exasperation. "Are you serious? Again? It's only been ten miles since the last pit stop."

"Hey," River said, feeling defensive, and uncomfortable as hell. They'd been on the road for two hours and it was two hours too long. Granted, the drive was beautiful. They were going south on 101 toward Santa Barbara. Green rolling hills after green rolling hills, dotted with oak trees that reached north to the stunning clear blue sky. Having never traveled anywhere except to Wildstone, she wanted to soak it in and enjoy it, but she couldn't. "You try surviving with two feet kicking your bladder like it's a drum set. You know what we need? A TV. I'm going to miss *Ellen* today."

"We're almost there. Can you make it?"

"Define almost."

Lanie sighed and found a gas station.

When they were on the road again, River needed something to take her mind off her inability to get comfortable. "So . . . you and Mark?"

Lanie didn't react except to grip the wheel tighter.

"Closed subject?" River asked.

"Unclear subject," Lanie corrected.

"What does that mean?"

Lanie sighed. "That other than enjoying each other and the fact that he makes me laugh, I don't know what we're doing. But I do know it's a dead end."

"My mom used to say that if you find someone who makes you laugh and your life flow easier, you should keep them because that's all you'll ever need."

Lanie glanced over. "Maybe you should take that advice."

"Are you kidding? Look at me." River gestured to her belly. "Until I got this job, I was homeless. I'm about to pop. What would a guy want with the likes of me?"

"Holden doesn't seem bothered by any of that."

River turned to look out the window. "Maybe I'm just not brave enough."

"Well, that makes two of us."

Twenty minutes later, Lanie pulled into a town house complex and parked in a driveway. They entered one of the town houses.

"This is your place?" River asked, looking around. It was small, neat, and utterly devoid of personal clutter.

"I leased it after Kyle . . ." Lanie showed her the bathroom with a straight face and no sarcastic comment, saying only "I'll be in the garage when you're ready."

River met her out there five minutes later and stared in surprise at the boxes stacked against one wall. "What's all this?"

"Stuff I didn't want to unpack when I moved."

"Why?"

Lanie shrugged. "Didn't feel like seeing any of it."

River nodded even though Lanie hadn't looked at her. Then she asked a question she hadn't thought to ask before now. "So how long were you with Kyle?"

Lanie was squatted low before one of the boxes, and oh how River admired that easy, nimble athleticism. She couldn't remember how long it'd been since she'd seen her own feet, much less been able to crouch low and tie her shoes.

"Dated six months, married for five years," Lanie finally said.

River sucked in a shocked breath. "Five years?"

"I know. Clearly, I was an idiot."

"Well, you weren't alone there," River said.

Lanie gave a rough laugh. "Not exactly a consolation. And I was a bigger idiot than you."

"No way."

"Yes way," Lanie said and hesitated. "I believed him when he said he didn't want to have kids, when clearly what he meant was that he didn't want to have kids with *me*." She didn't look up, just kept her head down, and River felt sucker-punched by Lanie's pain and humiliation. She opened her mouth to express her sorrow for Lanie, but at the tight, closed look on Lanie's face she didn't speak after all. And really, what could she say?

Lanie gestured to a box. "This is it—this is the only box I have of Kyle's; it came from his boss. I got rid of his clothes, and until I did that, I didn't even realize how few of his personal effects I had. In hindsight, that should've been a glaring sign." She shook her head. "I've not looked in here yet."

River still had to try. She needed the money. But damn, she had to pee again and plus she was hungry. And on top of that, her lower back was killing her, her feet were swollen—or so she assumed by how tight her sandals felt—and the stretchy waistband on her capris was cutting into her. She wanted to lie down and close her eyes and not open them again until she won the lottery or labor was over, preferably both. "I'd like to look through it anyway."

"Suit yourself."

LANIE MANHANDLED THE box open, very aware of the fact that River stood above her holding her breath. From inside Lanie's pocket her cell phone vibrated an incoming text. Probably

Mark. He'd texted her during the drive, checking in on them. Ignoring him for the moment, she peered into the box.

"What's in there?" River asked tightly.

"His cell phone." Lanie pushed it to the side. "His wallet . . . empty of cash, of course." She rifled through a file. "Work stuff." She pulled out his work badge and a watch. And then a stack of five journals, each with a different name on the front. Stacy, Kendra, Brigit . . . Lanie flipped through them and stilled.

"What?" River asked.

"Nothing." Heart pounding, she hurriedly tried to shove the journals back in the box, not wanting River to see.

"No, stop." Somehow River managed to drop to her knees and she had a death grip on Lanie's wrist. "*What* is it? Come on, Lanie, you're scaring me— Ohmygod," she gasped when she caught sight of the last two journals, one labeled Lanie, the other River. "He was keeping journals on each of us?" She gasped again. "Are there . . . pictures? Like nude photos?"

Lanie blinked. "You posed nude for him?"

River bit her lower lip, looking panicked. "Once," she whispered. "It was his birthday—"

"Stop." Lanie pressed her heels into her eyes. "I don't want to know things that are going to implode my brain."

River grimaced and closed her eyes. "I'm never falling for a man again. Do you think I could become a lesbian?"

"You can be anything you want, but to change teams, you'd have to give up Holden."

"He's not mine to give up."

"Because his leave is about over and he has to go back? Or because you're as screwed up as I am?"

River suddenly doubled over and Lanie reached for her. "What? What is it, the baby?"

"No. It's just a cramp in my back." She paused. "And maybe my heart. Dammit. His leave is up?"

"Yes. In a few days," Lanie said. "You didn't know?"

River closed her eyes as if pained. "I think he might've tried to tell me this morning, but I screwed up. I've wasted so much time and now he's leaving to go back to hell. I'm so confused."

"Welcome to the club."

River blew out a sigh and stared at the journal with her name on it. "Can you peek and tell me how bad it is?"

Lanie cautiously opened the journal and froze.

"Oh God, it *is* nude pics."

"No. No, it's okay," Lanie said and slid an arm around River because she was suddenly looking ill. "No, I mean really. It's not like that," she said.

"So what is it like?"

"Well . . ." She was having a hard time believing her own eyes. "He appears to have written about each of us, meticulously and . . . with love."

River stared at her and then grabbed the journal, opening it up to a random page dated about a year ago.

> *I've never met anyone as sweet and loving and caring as River. She'd give a perfect stranger the shirt off her back. Life hasn't been kind to her, but you wouldn't know it because she treats everyone who crosses her path with sweet generosity.*
>
> *Including me.*
>
> *The day I met her, I'd just screwed up at work and in life, big time. I was tired, frustrated, and scared. She served me lunch. I'd been sick and had just gotten off the phone with my doctor. My heart condition worsened and*

I didn't know what to do with that shit news other than keep it to myself. It would've destroyed the people in my life and I was weak, far too weak to be strong for them.

Selfish.

But River's the opposite of selfish. She sees me as funny and smart and on top of my world, none of which is true. But God, I love seeing myself through her eyes . . .

River looked up. "I don't understand. He was sick? Did you know?"

Lanie shook her head, stunned. "He never said a word." She was flipping through her book too. "It looks like he only says nice things about us all. Maybe . . . maybe he really did love us in his own sick way, the two-timing, polygamist asshat." She pulled something else from the box. A picture of a pretty young woman wearing an apron with a popular grocery store chain logo on it. Her little badge read: *Carrie, store clerk and world optimist.*

Lanie turned the photo over. On the back was Kyle's familiar scrawl: *My next wife!*

River stared at it. "Can you kill a dead man?" She looked into the now empty box.

No ring.

Lanie squeezed her hand. "I'm sorry. I'd hoped it'd be here."

Looking numb, River nodded and tried unsuccessfully to get to her feet. Lanie helped her. "You okay?"

"Yes," River said. Clearly a big, fat lie.

Five minutes and yet another quick pee stop later, they walked silently out to the car. Lanie could tell River was hurt and angry but she had no idea how to make it better. When they were on the highway, Lanie's place miles behind them, she tried in the only way she knew how. "I'm writing you a check."

River turned from where she'd been staring out the window. "What?"

Lanie inhaled a deep breath. "I'm serious. I'm writing you a check. I'm writing all of you a check. We're splitting the life insurance money."

"Stop the car."

Lanie glanced over. "What? Why?"

"Just stop the damn car!" River yelled.

Lanie jerked the car to the side of the road. "What's wrong, are you sick—"

River wrenched the door open and stumbled out. "Yes," she said. "I'm sick. And tired. I'm sick and tired of being a victim. I'm sick and tired of being sick and tired. And most of all, I'm sick and tired of pregnancy hormones that make me sick and tired and . . ."

"Crazy?" Lanie ventured, meaning only to tease her out of her mood.

"Yes!" River grabbed her ratty backpack and glared at Lanie with shimmering eyes. "You're not writing me a check. I'm not some charity case." She grimaced. "Okay, so maybe I am, but I don't want to be!" She slammed the door and turned and started walking down the road.

Actually, it was more of a waddle, one hand holding the backpack, the other cradling her belly.

"Oh, for God's sake!" Lanie drove forward to catch her, which took all of two seconds. An eight-and-a-half-months-pregnant woman moved at the pace of a sleepy snail. She rolled down the passenger window. "Get back in the car, River."

"No. I'm taking the train back to Wildstone."

"Are you kidding me? And what am I supposed to do?"

"Leave!"

"I can't just leave you out here!"

"Sure, you can," River said. "I'm absolving you from being responsible for me. You never asked for this headache and you certainly don't want to be my friend now that you know who I am and what I did. And I get it. Believe me, I'd hate me too."

"River—"

"I'm officially no longer your problem," she said and kept walking. Slash waddling.

Lanie checked traffic—none—and inched her car forward. "Seriously, River. I'm not leaving you here. I can't."

"Yes, you can. You just use the long, skinny pedal on the right. It's called the gas."

Lanie rolled her eyes, pulled the car over behind the stubborn pregnant chick, and parked. She started to get out of the car, but there was a very clear NO PARKING sign on the side of the road.

Terrific.

River left the road and walked along the edge of a parking lot toward a dive bar called Double Down Saloon. Lanie looked at the time. Four o'clock. The bar would be open. Dammit. She pulled in and parked just as River got to the door. Lanie turned off the engine and answered an incoming call from Mark.

"How's it going?" his deep baritone asked, just the sound of him providing a sense of comfort that she told herself she didn't need.

"Great," she said. "Really great. Fantastic. Awesome."

He paused. "I'm going to ask that again. How's it going?"

How did he do that? Read her from a hundred miles away?

"You wouldn't believe me if I told you," she said, eyes on River as the bar door shut behind her. "I've got to go."

"Just tell me you're okay."

"I'm okay." *Crazy for doing this, but okay.* "I'll see you later," she said.

"Promise?"

Her heart did a happy little wiggle that should've set alarm bells off in her brain, but apparently her brain was on overload. "Promise." She disconnected and went in after River.

RIVER CROUCHED IN the bar bathroom and threw up everything she'd eaten that day. Which had been an unfortunate lot. Her throat burned, her eyes watered, her back hurt like a bitch, and . . . she was exhausted. So fucking exhausted . . .

"Here." Someone came in behind her and pressed a wad of damp paper towels in her hand.

Lanie. Of course.

"Go away," she moaned miserably. "Please. I know you want to."

"Actually . . ." Lanie pulled River's loose, sweat-dampened hair back from her face and fastened it with something. "I'd like to. But I can't."

"Why not?"

"Because you're . . ."

River arched a brow, daring her to say crazy.

Lanie wisely said nothing and helped her up.

Together they stood at the sink and stared at their reflection. Lanie's hair was loose and a little wild. She'd clearly given River her own hair tie. River wasn't pale as a ghost. She was positively green.

But there was something else, something River had never noticed before. They actually looked a bit alike. In fact, they could've been sisters. At this thought, her eyes filled again because she'd had many daydreams that they *were* sisters. That they were a real family.

But that wasn't ever going to happen. She'd screwed that up, and even worse than that, she and the baby were an everyday reminder to Lanie of how badly Kyle had hurt her. Lanie had paid enough, and as for River's own problems, well, they were just that—her own problems. It was time, past time, to finally, once and for all, learn to stand on her own two feet.

"Think you can make it back to the car?" Lanie asked. "Or do you need a few minutes?"

She needed more than a few minutes. She needed about a year to hole up and process all of this, but she didn't have a year. Given the way her body felt, she had a day or two at most to prove to herself and everyone else she was a grown-up.

"River?"

God help her, but she was going to lie to Lanie one more time. "I need a few minutes," she said. "Alone."

Lanie stared at her for a beat and then nodded. "I'll be at the bar. You need a lemonade or a Coke, something with some sugar in it. I'll get each of us a drink to go and wait for you."

River nodded.

When Lanie left, River straightened and eyeballed herself in the mirror. "You're doing the right thing," she whispered.

And hoped it was true.

She sneaked out of the bathroom, but instead of going right down the hall to the bar, she went left and out the back door.

LANIE SAT AT the bar for ten minutes nursing her lemonade and watching the ice melt in River's. Something was wrong. She could feel it and went back to the bathroom.

The empty bathroom.

"Dammit!"

Five minutes later she was at the train station, standing next to the tracks watching the Amtrak take off.

She'd run inside to find out where the train was going and if anyone had sold a ticket to a pregnant woman in the last ten minutes. The train was heading north to San Francisco with many stops along the route, Wildstone being one of them.

And yes, a pregnant woman had boarded.

Lanie had missed River by a minute, tops. Pissed, she went back to her car and followed the damn train.

It turned out the train was a lot slower than a car. Lanie followed it to make sure that River didn't get off before Wildstone. The return trip took six hours instead of two and a half, and it was dark as sin and near midnight by the time Lanie got out of her car to watch the passengers unload at the Wildstone station.

There was only one.

Lanie blew out a relieved sigh and stepped forward.

Chapter 27

I can be spontaneous, but first I must carefully plan everything and imagine all that could go wrong.

At the sight of Lanie waiting for her, River sighed as she got off the train. She was exhausted, nauseous, starving, and still all kinds of crazy. "What are you doing here?"

"Are you kidding me?" Lanie asked. "You deserted me in a dive bar, sneaked onto a damn train when you're sick as a dog, and you want to know what I'm doing here? Trying to look after your ungrateful ass, that's what I'm doing here!"

River felt her eyes fill at that. "You think I'm ungrateful?"

Lanie tossed up her hands. "What else would you call making me climb out the bathroom window of that bar to follow your footsteps?"

River blinked. "You climbed out the bathroom window?"

Lanie dropped her arms and blinked. "You didn't?"

"Hell, no. Do I look like I'd fit out that window? I could barely fit onto the train. I went out the back exit."

Lanie stared at her for a beat and then let out a long breath. "Yeah. That would've been easier . . ." She sighed. "Why did you do it?"

"Because you deserve better than to be saddled with me," River said.

"I'm not saddled with you. I chose to go on this trip, remember? But I can't keep doing this, this see-saw thing we have going. I didn't want to like you and then I did. And then you weren't who you said you were and I didn't like you again. And now . . ."

"You're confused," River said softly.

"Yeah, and honestly it was a lot easier to just hate you."

"I get that," River said. "I'd hate me too."

"See?" Lanie asked. "But then you say stuff like that and I feel like Cruella de Vil kicking puppies."

"Who?"

"Hell," Lanie said with a grimace. "How is it that I'm only thirty and feel old?"

"Do I have to answer that?" River asked and then broke off with a startled groan as a pain ripped through her lower back.

"Maybe you should sit down," Lanie said.

She'd been in damn pain all day, and it'd made her cranky as hell. River shook her head. "Just stop being nice to me."

"Fine, then. Sit the fuck down before you fall down," Lanie snapped. "See? That's me being *not* nice, but bitchy as hell."

River felt the tears coming and sniffled. "Well, you're the nicest bitchy person I ever met," she said soggily, swiping her nose on her sleeve.

"Just get in the damn car, River. *Please*."

So River got in the car. Lanie had to help her. It was humiliating. Her body had become as cumbersome as navigating a wide load on a busy freeway, and she felt like she had an alien in her belly. But worse, far worse, was the silence between her and Lanie.

Lanie parked and turned off the engine. She turned to River in the dark interior of the car. "He didn't deserve either of us," she said quietly.

"No," River agreed. "What are you going to do with his things?"

"I don't want the box. It's yours. That's why I put it in the trunk."

"If you give it to me, I'll burn everything," River said grimly, shifting her weight in the seat, trying to get comfortable. Which was impossible. "I'll make a bonfire, toss his things in it, and then roast marshmallows over the remnants of his life. I'd go tap-dance on his grave if I didn't weigh as much as a house."

Lanie opened her door. "Come on."

The night was warm and balmy. Lanie brought River through the winery and out the back door to the deck there. There was a fire pit and chairs. Beyond that was a hidden lake that River hadn't ventured out to.

"Wait here," Lanie said.

So River waited in the night, trying to ignore her unbearable back pain.

Lanie returned five minutes later and River went on pretending that she was fine, even managing a small smile through the pain.

Lanie squatted before the fire pit and began to build a fire. When it was roaring, she vanished again, returning with Kyle's box.

River found a laugh on this shitty night, and together they tossed the contents of the box into the fire.

Lanie then pulled out the makings for s'mores—marshmallows, Nutella, and graham crackers—which she'd apparently confiscated from the winery. "With Nutella, 'cuz you can't eat chocolate when you're pregnant apparently, which, by the way, sucks golf balls."

She was one hundred percent River's hero. They still weren't speaking much, but the silence was no longer seething with bad tempers.

Progress.

The next pain came so suddenly it stole River's breath, and she bent over into herself. Vaguely she heard Lanie swear and run over, dropping to her knees at River's side.

"What is it, River? A cramp? Are you going to be sick again?"

She literally couldn't catch her breath enough to answer. The pain rolled over her, into her, through her, wrapping around her torso and squeezing like a vice. When it finally passed, she was shaken and sweating.

"Talk to me," Lanie said tightly.

River realized they were holding hands and she was gripping Lanie's hard enough to bruise. She forced herself to let go. "I'm fine."

"Uh, you're pretty far from fine."

"I think . . . I think I might be having contractions."

Lanie's eyes widened. "For how long?"

"All day," River admitted. "I think I'm in labor."

"*Now?*"

"No, last week! Jesus," she gasped, bending over to catch her breath. "Dr. Rodriguez and my birthing class didn't tell me it was going to feel like I was being slowly murdered."

Lanie leapt to her feet. "Okay. Okay, it's going to be okay." She turned in a circle and then stopped short. "You're early, right?"

"Two weeks."

"Maybe it's false labor."

River was gripped by another all-encompassing pain, and when she came out of it, Lanie looked upset.

"It's my fault," she said. "I shouldn't have dragged you on the road trip. That was dumb. I should've left you here and—"

"I wanted to go."

"But we fought. All that unhappiness made you go into labor."

"Or maybe the baby's just ready," River managed.

Lanie nodded, clearly hoping that was it. "We need to get you to the hospital." She gasped again, like it'd just occurred to her. "Oh my God, you're going to have a *baby*!"

Strange as it was, the more panicked Lanie looked—and she looked very, *very* panicked—the calmer River felt. "Not yet," she said. "The pains need to be closer together. I—"

The next contraction hit unexpectedly, insidiously squeezing her from the inside out so that she couldn't do anything but cry out. It felt like it took forever, but when she could breathe again, she sucked in air like she'd just run a mile. "How long was that?"

Lanie looked worse than River felt. Flushed and damp with sweat, eyes filled with fear. "Maybe a minute."

"No problem," River said with only the smallest of doubts. "And like ten minutes from the previous one, right?"

"Also only a minute," Lanie said. "This isn't false labor." She jumped back up and pointed at River. "Don't move. I'm going for help."

Lanie ran off into the night and River lay back with a short little laugh. *Don't move.* As if she could. She was stuck in this lounger until the cows came home—or someone came along that was strong enough to hoist her out. And they were going to need a crane.

Another pain began from deep inside and she placed her hands on her belly and tried to breathe through it the way she'd been taught in the classes Cora had brought her to. In the middle of it, the baby kicked hard and she managed a smile.

Today had been the day from hell all the way around, but tonight . . . "Tonight I'm going to meet you," she whispered, cradling her belly. "And that's going to make everything okay."

MARK CAME OUT of a dead sleep when someone slipped into his room with all the subtlety of a bull in a china shop. "Someone better be dead."

Lanie stepped in closer, stopping in front of his window where the moonlight slanted in, highlighting her in bold relief. With a low growl of sleepy pleasure, he wrapped his fingers around her wrist to reel her in.

"Good, you're up," she said in relief, moving toward him, practically falling on top of him, her silky hair brushing his face. Still half-asleep, he groaned at the feel of her body on his and went for it, rolling, tucking her beneath him.

"Yeah," he said against her mouth. "I'm . . . up." He punctuated this with a nudge of his hips.

She gave a half-hysterical laugh and pushed at his shoulders, waking him the rest of the way. "No, you don't understand," she said. "I need you."

"I need you too."

"River's in labor."

He stilled. "So . . . this isn't a booty call?"

"No!" She pulled him out of bed and then stared at him. "You're bare-ass naked."

"Yeah. See anything you like?"

She threw a pair of jeans at him. "Hurry!" She tossed him

a shirt, which hit him in the face. "I don't know what the hell I'm doing."

"And you think I do?"

"You always do," she said, and at the backward compliment that might not have been a compliment at all, he followed her running form out of the house and through the night.

River was in a lounge chair in front of the fire pit, clutching her belly, bent at the waist, gasping for air.

"Contraction," Lanie said and dropped at River's side. "I've brought Mark," she murmured, stroking back the younger woman's hair. "He knows what to do."

Mark liked the easy confidence she had in him, but in this case it was overrated. He'd been overseas when his girls had been born. And the two times a woman had gone into labor on one of his shifts, Emergency Services personnel had gotten to the scene before him.

He knew his mom had been taking River to labor classes and he pulled out his cell phone to call her when he remembered. "My mom's in San Francisco until tomorrow."

River lifted her face, fear etched into her features. "She's my labor coach."

"It's okay," he said. "We'll figure it out at the hospital."

He picked River up, ignoring her protests that she was too heavy, and carried her to his truck, while Lanie ran ahead and opened the door for him. They got River buckled in through another long and what looked like painful contraction, and then the three of them were off into the night.

He tossed Lanie his phone. "Text my mom. Tell her what's happening. First babies sometimes take a while; she might be able to get back in time. Text my sisters, let them know where we are and that they're on twin duty, and that someone needs to go out to the fire pit with the hose to extinguish the fire. Then call the hospital and let them know we're coming."

Lanie handled all of that while at the same time holding onto River's hand and talking her through each contraction that hit.

Mark drove, fascinated by this new Lanie. Whatever had happened on their road trip, whatever her personal feelings, she'd pushed through them enough to keep it together for River.

They arrived at the hospital and a nurse helped River into a wheelchair before turning to Mark and Lanie expectantly. "Who's her coach?"

Mark looked at Lanie, who was looking right back at him.

"One of you needs to come back with us," the nurse said impatiently. "To keep Mama here comfortable and calm."

River's gaze was glued to Lanie with fear and hope and expectation.

"I don't know what I'm doing," Lanie reminded her. "You'd be better off without me."

"No!" River clutched Lanie's hand tight enough that the skin went stark white.

Mark felt Lanie brace herself and nod. "Okay," she said. "Okay, I'll go with you." She walked off at River's side and just before she vanished behind the swinging double doors of the ER, she glanced back at him with a fearful expression.

He smiled with what he hoped was confidence. "I'll be right here waiting for you," he said, and he knew that he wasn't talking about just tonight. Whether she got that or not, he had no idea. But she nodded and vanished.

He headed to the front desk, thinking about how she'd come through for River in spite of how she really felt about her. In fact, she'd come through for all the people he cared about one way or another: his mom, his girls, his sisters, hell, his entire family. He could bury his head in the sand all he wanted, it wouldn't change the fact.

He wasn't just falling in love with her, he actually *already* loved her, every single stubborn, frustrating, gorgeous inch.

Chapter 28

Anxiety: Okay, but what if—

Me: Dude, we went over this a hundred times already.

Anxiety: I know, but hear me out. I've found twenty new reasons you should be worried.

Me: Go on.

Lanie stood at River's hospital bedside, watching her grimace through an internal exam.

"Four centimeters dilated and fifty percent effaced," the nurse said and gave River a sympathetic smile. "Still a ways to go yet, I'm afraid. We can't do an epidural until the anesthesiologist gets here."

Sweaty and flushed, River dropped her head back to her pillow and stared up at the ceiling. "I don't think I can do this. I'm too tired." She lifted her head again. "I want to go home. I'll come back tomorrow instead, okay?"

She asked this with such sweet desperation that Lanie actually felt her heart squeeze.

The nurse looked to Lanie for help.

Lanie screwed up her courage. "You can do this, River."

"No, I can't."

"You can. You're the strongest person I know."

The nurse smiled at Lanie and left the room. Some of her fear must have shown in her face because River let out a choked laugh and went back to staring up at the ceiling. "Look, I know how you feel about me but if you could just stay with me through this, I'll never ask another thing of you." A contraction hit hard and swift and River nearly broke Lanie's fingers.

"Whew," Lanie said, sinking to the chair, swiping her brow.

"Hard on you, is it?" River asked dryly.

"Hey, I don't know what I'm doing." Lanie looked at all the various things River was hooked up to. "I know nothing about having a baby."

"It's okay," River said. "I know. I just need to keep breathing through the contractions." As yet another contraction hit, River squeezed Lanie's hand and inhaled through her nose and exhaled through her mouth.

Lanie found herself doing the same right along with her, so that when another contraction hit, harder, faster, and stole River's breath, Lanie was able to guide her through the breathing and slow her down.

"Good job," River said weakly when the contraction had passed and she flopped back to her pillow.

Lanie had to laugh. "I should be saying that to you."

And she did. Many, many times over the next two hours as the contractions continued. Nurses came and went, but the only constant in the room was Lanie at River's side. And then suddenly there was a lot of talk about centimeters and dilation, all of it going over Lanie's head.

"I think I'm going into transition now," River translated, panting but somehow sounding shockingly calm.

"Transition?"

"It's the last, most intensive phase of labor. The baby's engaged in my pelvis and has dropped close to my cervix, making it soften and become thin."

"That sounds . . . painful," Lanie said, more than a little horrified at how barbaric all this seemed. "Where are the drugs?"

"Still waiting on the anesthesiologist," the nurse said with empathy. "But at this point, you're past the stage when an epidural would work anyway."

"I'm okay," River said, though she didn't look it. She was breathing heavily and looking pale. "But I really should be breathing much slower," she said through gritted teeth.

Lanie turned to the door. "This is inhumane. I'm going to go find you some drugs—"

"No, wait." River grabbed her wrist with shocking strength, digging in too. "I can't do this without you."

"But you already know what to do." And plus, the realization that there was really a baby coming was just hitting her. Kyle's baby. The man she'd loved and trusted, the man who'd denied her a child but had given River one. Suddenly she wasn't sure she was strong enough to be strong enough for River.

"I want you here," River said tightly, getting a grip on the front of Lanie's shirt with the strength of an Olympian champion. "I *need* you here, okay? So please, shut the fuck up, hold my hand, and breathe with me, and for Chrissake *don't leave me,* or so help me God, I'll kick your scrawny ass, and trust me, I could do it and hide your body where it will never be found."

The nurse patted Lanie's hand. "Don't worry about it, dear. She doesn't mean it, it's the pain talking."

Lanie was pretty sure River did mean it, every single word. So she didn't leave. And River was . . . unbelievable. It was really incredible. By the time she was fully effaced—a word Lanie didn't want described, thank you very much—the room was suddenly filled with nurses and a doctor.

Lanie was there through the whole thing and damn if it wasn't the most amazing thing she'd ever been a part of.

"What if she looks like Kyle?" River asked during a rare break from the pushing.

"She won't," Lanie promised, and hoped to God that was true.

The tiny infant girl who finally made her way into the world and was set on River's chest was covered in gunk and looked disgusting and . . . she was the most amazing thing Lanie had ever seen. So much so that she found herself frozen in place. The baby was here. Kyle's baby.

River was both crying and laughing. "Hi, sweetness," she whispered, stroking a finger along the baby's cheek. "You made it. We made it. And look at you, you're so beautiful."

The baby's eyes were wide open and locked on River, like she was listening and understanding every word. And it awakened an ache inside Lanie, a deep, unrelenting ache that she thought she'd gotten past. "A baby," she said quietly. "You actually had a baby in there. Like, you just pushed a human out of your hoo-ha."

River laughed softly. "Yeah, who knew? Delaney, meet Lanie," she said to the baby.

Lanie's heart caught. "What?"

"That's your full name, right? I want her to be named after you."

Lanie didn't have words; she was undone.

"Here." River tried to hand Lanie the baby, but she backed away, sticking her hands behind her back.

"What are you, five?" River asked. "Hold her. It'll take the mystery out of her."

No. The mystery was good. She didn't want to get close or attached because she needed another string on her heart like she needed a hole in her head. And it was more than that. This baby—Delaney!—was a vivid reminder of everything that had gone wrong in her life.

A nurse stuck her head in. "Mama and baby have a whole bunch of visitors named Capriotti, but we try to limit to two at a time, so—"

Lanie jumped up, eager for the reprieve. "I'll just . . ." She gestured to the door and then escaped through it like her life depended on it.

The nurse was right. There were a lot of Capriottis in the waiting room. *All* of them, it seemed, and some extras. Such as Holden. He met Lanie's gaze, clearly hoping River was okay. She nodded and he nodded back, and then the guy slipped back out the door.

Mia and Alyssa went in to see River first and Lanie looked out the windows and realized it was almost morning. She stood there, a little lost, a whole lot exhausted, feeling raw and hollow.

"Hey." A big, warm hand grasped hers and she looked up into Mark's face, etched with easy affection and worry. "You okay?" he asked.

"Sure."

"Uh-huh." He pulled her away from the crowd and sat her down. "Don't move."

"I don't like it when you're bossy unless we're in bed."

He flashed a grin. "Humor me."

He was back in two minutes with a hot cup of tea.

"You're a god among men," she murmured.

"I'm going to want that in writing." He sat next to her and let her be for a few minutes, their silence comfortable.

"So the baby's here," he finally said. "River named her after you."

Lanie felt her heart get all squishy. "I don't know why."

"Yes you do."

Lanie sighed and flashed to the squirming, squishy newborn being set on River's chest, how the infant had immediately settled down to stare so sweetly up at her mama. "Yeah."

"And . . . you're good?"

She closed her eyes and could see the nurse helping River put the sweet little bundle to her bare breast. "Yeah."

Mark slid an arm around her shoulder and pulled her close, brushing his lips across her temple in an incredibly comforting and also intimate gesture. It was tempting to sink into him. She was so tired she couldn't even hold her head up, but she didn't need him. Yes, he was strong and warm and dammit, he smelled amazing, but he wasn't hers. She was alone. Very alone. "I'm fine," she said.

"Yes, you're *very* fine. You're also upset."

"Of course I'm not. That would make me an asshole."

"It'd make you human," he said quietly. "You have every reason to resent River and the baby."

She felt her throat burn but she refused to cry. "You were there when River told us her story. No one else feels that way about her and I can't either."

He squeezed her gently. "It's not the same and you know that. You've pretended to be okay with it all, but we both know you're not. And Lanie, it's okay to not be okay. Hell, I've spent half my adult life not being okay."

She lifted her head and met his warm, compassionate gaze.

He had those faint lines fanning out from his amazing eyes. Laugh lines. And probably also worry lines. But somehow they only served to make him look . . . real. He was a man through and through, one who didn't shrink back from reality or truths, no matter how ugly.

From his hip, his cell phone buzzed and he swore softly.

"Work?" she asked.

"Yeah." He kissed her temple and held her another beat. "Go easy today."

"On River?"

"On you."

And then he was gone.

Lanie looked up and met Grandma Capriotti's gaze from across the waiting room. She was sitting there, calmly, quietly, serenely, knitting, her fingers moving at the speed of light.

"Do an old lady a favor," she said to Lanie. "And get me a hot tea."

It wasn't a request. Lanie rose and did as was bid, and then sat next to her.

"Marcus was right, you know," Grandma said.

"About?"

"Everything. He's got smarts." The old woman smiled. "He got them from me."

"Got his modesty from you too, I see."

She smiled a little. "You're upset about the baby."

Lanie blew out a breath and slumped. "Of course not, that would make me a jerk."

"I believe the term you used was *asshole*."

Lanie sunk down even more. "I wasn't looking for any of this."

Grandma Capriotti looked up from her knitting, though

her fingers didn't slow down at all. "You do realize why God brought you two together, right?"

"Because he has a sick sense of humor, putting two of Kyle's wives together?"

Grandma Capriotti's lips curved. "I actually meant you and my Marcus. And yet River is yours too. As is everyone else here. You're part of us now."

"I appreciate the sentiment, but I'm a temp contract worker, nothing more."

Grandma Capriotti just smiled serenely and tucked her needles away. "I'm tired. I'm going to nap now." She folded her hands together, closed her eyes, and did just that.

Lanie got up and moved back to the window. It was just before dawn, that magical in-between time where the sky turned an indescribable kaleidoscope of colors that never failed to steal her breath.

Or maybe that was Wildstone and the Capriottis. Closing her eyes, she pressed her forehead to the cool glass. "You are one screwed-up chick."

"The best ones are."

Lanie sighed at the sound of Cora's voice. She must've driven like a bat out of hell from San Francisco to get here so fast. "You Capriottis as a whole don't really get personal space boundaries much, do you?"

"Nope." Cora ran a hand down her back. "Why do I feel like you've done all the heavy lifting over the past twenty-four hours?"

"It's okay, I'm good at mental gymnastics."

Cora laughed softly. "Is my son driving you crazy?"

She opened her eyes and met Cora's deep brown, warm ones. "Actually, he's done nothing but be there supporting me in everything when he has no reason to care about me at all."

Cora smiled. "Sometimes the best thing in life is finding that one person who knows all your mistakes and weaknesses and *still* thinks you're completely amazing."

Lanie shook her head. "Nothing's that simple."

"Maybe. But maybe life will surprise you."

Chapter 29

Anxiety: Hey, let's get upset over nothing and push people away and be weird about stuff, okay?

Mark ignored his exhaustion at work. It certainly wasn't the first time he'd been gritty-eyed through an entire shift. Luckily the worst he had to deal with was a couple of belligerent hitchhikers on the highway and a drunk trying to break into a grocery store.

Not exactly an adrenaline-filled shift.

But thanks to zero sleep the night before, by the time he got home, he was ready for food and bed, in either order. But his life didn't lend itself to fulfilling his own needs very often and today was no different. He knew from the slew of texts he'd gotten all day that River and the baby were home and his entire family was abuzz with excitement. No one cared that River wasn't a Capriotti. When the Capriottis fell for someone, they gathered them in and treated them as their own.

And that's just what they'd done with Lanie and River, whether the two women liked it or not.

And Lanie didn't. Or at least she didn't trust it.

Or him.

He wanted to prove her wrong. Wanted to prove that she could, and had, fallen for this family, this place, *and* him—since he'd most definitely fallen for her no matter what he'd promised himself.

But he had no idea where she stood. For a guy who'd put his life on the line and trusted his instincts on the job, he actually wasn't sure of anything when it came to Lanie.

Inside the house, everyone was hovering and helping with the baby, and after being home for a couple of hours and taking in the goings-on, he realized something not all that surprising.

Lanie was doing everything in her power to *not* hold the baby.

After he'd gotten Sam and Sierra into the tub, Mia showed up with something called a bath bomb and took over, so he left them to it. He made his way into the huge living room where Alyssa, his mom, his grandma, and River were sitting on the couch, staring in loving marvel at the baby asleep in a little bassinet in front of them.

"I just want to eat her up," Cora said.

"Nibble on her fingers and toes," Grandma said.

"Me too," Alyssa said with a laugh as she cupped her hands protectively over her own baby swaddled to her chest. "She makes my ovaries ache."

Lanie was standing near the ceiling-to-floor windows, looking out into the night.

"How about you?" he asked, coming up next to her. "Your ovaries aching?"

She didn't take her eyes away from the window. "I think mine might be defective." She met his gaze in the glass, still not turning to face him. "Do you look at a baby and wish you had one?"

"I've already had two."

"I mean . . . do you ever want more?"

He could tell by her sudden stillness how very important his answer was to her. Reaching out, he ran a hand up her back, trying to soothe, even though he wasn't one hundred percent sure what was wrong. "My life feels full with what I have," he admitted. "And only a few months ago, I'd have said I've no need for anything more."

At this, she turned and faced him. "And now?"

He smiled into her worried eyes and gave her the utter truth. "Things have changed. I've learned that life is a crapshoot, and at any moment someone can walk into it and change it forever."

She closed her eyes. "Don't," she whispered.

He started to ask her *Don't what?* but from behind him the baby began to cry at the same moment the twins came into the room wearing nothing but wet towels from their bath.

"Hey," Mia said, coming in behind them. "I'm looking for two cutie-pie escape artists, has anyone seen them?"

The twins giggled and the baby wailed louder, scrunching up her eyes and waving angry fists.

"I'll get her," Alyssa said.

"Wait," River said, holding out a hand to stop Alyssa from getting up. She smiled over at Lanie. "You haven't had a turn to hold her at all. Don't you want—"

"I've got it," Lanie said.

Mark glanced over in surprise, as he knew damn well she hadn't so much as looked at the baby, much less touched her.

She moved away from the window and . . . went straight for his kids. She scooped up a giggling Sierra in one arm and then Samantha in the other arm. With the girls grinning from ear to ear, she swept them out of the room.

"One of these days," he could hear Lanie saying as they vanished down the hall, "I'd love to hear what your objection to bedtime is. Because that's my personal favorite time of the day."

River met his gaze, her own worried.

"Lanie's just amazing," Cora said. "So sweet and kind and helpful. Whatever's needed, we can always count on her."

Mark nodded. "She is amazing," he agreed, because she was.

An amazing actress too, as she was hiding in plain sight, doing to River and the baby exactly what her parents had done to her—freezing them out. And no one, least of all him, could blame her.

Chapter 30

If overthinking burned calories, I'd be dead.

Late that night, Lanie lay in bed trying to chase sleep. It should've come easy, as she was to-the-bone exhausted. Clearly, it was time to go. She hadn't been meant to stay here. She couldn't even warm up to the idea of a damn baby and as soon as everyone realized it, they'd know her truth.

She was a horrible person.

Every time she closed her eyes, she saw the look in Mark's gaze. He was on to her. He knew she couldn't hold or even look at the baby. Who couldn't love a baby? But she couldn't seem to help it; she felt like Delaney was the very manifestation of everything wrong in her life.

Not that it'd be easy to leave Wildstone. The entire Capriotti family had seriously wormed their way into her heart. Uncle Jack, who told the same dirty joke every day at lunch and still made her laugh. Mark's sisters, who'd become friends. *Real* friends. Cora, who'd taught her so much about acceptance and love.

But she was in way too deep.

A knock sounded at her door, a single knock that had her nipples going hard.

Mark.

She lay there another beat, toying with not getting up. It was the safest route for sure. Mental health–wise, anyway. But her body overruled her brain because her body, knowing she had one foot out the door, wanted every last minute in his arms that she could get.

Slipping out of bed, she looked down at herself. She was wearing a pilfered shirt from his own back. It was big and comfy, and best of all, it smelled like him.

He would read into that, she knew, but she opened the door a crack anyway.

His gaze slid over her and heated. "You going to let me in?"

The truth was, she already had. She'd let him into her bed, into her mind, into her body, and she was afraid, into her heart. She stepped back and in he came, shutting the door behind him.

He'd changed into running shorts and a T-shirt that hugged his lean, muscled bod in all the right places. It said: WORLD'S BEST DADDY.

He grimaced. "In hindsight, not exactly a seduction shirt, but . . ."

She found a smile. "It's cute."

"See, now, that's the thing," he said, voice all husky as he crowded her, tugging her into him. "I wasn't going for cute."

"What were you going for?"

"The best thing you've ever seen. Something you can't walk away from."

The words came so close to what she'd just been thinking about. The air backed up in her lungs and she met his gaze. "Mark."

His smile faded. "Come on, Lanie. Are we really going to

keep pretending that this is just a temporary job, a temporary relationship? That I'm just a one-stop for you?"

"We're not pretending," she said. "We started this thing with you saying you had no intention of being with someone until your girls were grown."

"Like I said, things change."

She stared up at him with no idea how to feel about that. "Relationships are complicated."

"They don't have to be," he said. "I take care of you and you take care of me. End of story."

She absorbed this for a moment, feeling the panic lick along her limbs like flames. But along with that, there was something else, something she didn't want to acknowledge.

The fact that every time he spoke about them, or alluded to a tie between them, a very tiny little spark warmed her from the inside out.

Hope, when she didn't believe in hope.

But Mark stood there, steady, calm. Patient. There was something new in his eyes, or maybe not new at all—something that had been growing over time since she'd been here.

Holding her gaze prisoner in his, he stroked his fingers along her jaw and the question that she wasn't sure she wanted the answer to escaped her lips. "What are you thinking when you look at me like that?"

He smiled and pulled her closer. She liked that because if she stood on tiptoe she could put her nose right at the hollow of his throat and get high on the heady scent that was his alone.

Then the world stopped spinning because he told her what he was thinking. He ran the pad of his thumb over her lower lip and said, "I love you, Lanie."

She stared up at him. He *loved* her. *He* loved her. He loved *her*.

And she had no idea what to do with that. In fact, she was pretty sure that other than the lying-his-ass-off Kyle, no one had *ever* said those three words to her. At least not while meaning them. "I bet you say that to all the girls," she said in what she hoped was a teasing tone.

"Don't," he said with a single shake of his head. "Don't make it a joke because you're scared."

"I'm not scared. I just don't think you've thought this through."

He cocked his head to the side and for the first time since she'd met him, she'd have sworn he looked at her with pity. "Have you ever known me to not think something through?"

"No, I . . ." She closed her mouth and shook her head.

"Do you not believe me?" he asked. "Are you *that* sure you can't stop being terrified of what we could have?"

Goddammit. Why was he putting this back on her? Her throat tightened and her eyes burned. "I think you should go."

"Not until we talk."

"Forget it. I'll go." She would've strode right out her door if he hadn't stopped her.

"Pants," he said quietly.

She looked down at herself and closed her eyes. A second later, her jeans were pressed into her hands. She opened her eyes and met his gaze and realized that for the first time since she'd known him, he was hiding himself from her. Blank eyes. Blank expression. "Thanks," she whispered but before she could put on her jeans, *he* was gone.

She nodded to herself. Okay, so that had been easy, chasing him away. And it was for the best. She didn't belong here. And with that in mind, she left her cottage. A storm was brewing and the wind battered at her as she walked the path, looking for Cora. She was surprised to find the woman in her office. "You're working at this hour?"

Cora smiled a happy smile and shut her laptop. "Well, we've set aside a lot of work in the past few days. Trying to catch up." Then she caught a glimpse of Lanie's expression and she stood up. "What is it? What's wrong?"

Was she that transparent? "I just wanted to let you know that the work you hired me for is basically done. I'll continue to monitor it for as long as you want to make sure it all runs smoothly, but I won't be staying in Wildstone. I . . . can't."

Cora opened her mouth, but clearly changed her mind because she shut it again. Looking sad and worried, she simply nodded. "Okay," she said softly. "I understand."

But she didn't, Lanie knew. She couldn't. She thought of Lanie as a fiercely brave woman who stood strong against the odds.

It simply wasn't true, not any of it. She was weak and alone, and terrified of getting hurt. "I'm sorry," she whispered, and left like her own ass was on fire.

The wind had picked up and it'd begun to rain. She ran through it straight to her cottage and to the small closet, where she'd shoved her suitcase two months earlier. She yanked it out and tossed it to the bed before going to the dresser and opening the top drawer. Grabbing everything in a handful, she dropped it into the suitcase.

Her door opened. She'd neglected to lock it. Mark stood there in the opened doorway, the rain slashing behind him. He met her gaze, his own dark and stormy, matching the night behind him. "Are you kidding me?" he asked. "I said 'I love you' and you didn't say anything. In fact, you had no reaction.

After the past two months we've shared, you let me walk away thinking that not only did I mean *nothing* to you, you didn't give a shit about my feelings."

Well, when he put it like that . . . "Look, I'm not good at this, okay? I told you that from the start."

"I call bullshit."

She went hands on hips. "You can't call bullshit on my feelings, Mark. And there's something else too. I'm not all that good of a person."

"You're a fucking *amazing* person," he said. "One who maybe hides behind her cool front because she's a chickenshit . . . . Which is entirely different from not being a good person. And if I say something you don't like, I expect you to tell me."

"Yeah, well, you don't always listen."

"I *always* listen. I just don't always agree. See," he said, "*that's* how this works. Give and take. Compromise. If what I said was too soon, you tell me. If what I said is the opposite of how you feel, you tell me. Whatever you feel, you tell me. And then we figure it out. Together. That's how a relationship works, Lanie."

She couldn't form words. She could feel the panic rising in her chest and she was clearly now holding her breath because she was also light-headed. She had to somehow defuse this and now, because though she was leaving, she didn't want to leave on bad terms, not with anyone, but *especially* not with him. "I didn't mean to hurt your feelings."

He stared at her for a beat and then came closer. "But . . . ? Because I sense a really big *but* coming here."

"But . . ." She paused. "I didn't expect you to say what you did either."

"You mean when I said I love you."

Her stomach tightened. "Yes." She swallowed hard. "That."

"Jesus." He shook his head, ran his hand over his face. "You can't even say the word in a sentence. How did I not see this coming?"

She tossed up her hands. "That's what I want to know! I told you I was messed up in the head!"

He sent her a fulminating look. "You're not, though. Messed up in the heart maybe, but not the head."

She wasn't amused. "I can't do this, Mark. I'm not ready. I'm not sure I'll *ever* be ready. I'm not programmed like all of you Capriottis are."

He took in the open suitcase on the bed. "So you're what, turning tail and running away?"

"The job is done."

"There's more here for you if you want it and you know that."

She inhaled a deep breath and faced him. "This isn't all my bad, you know. You told me in the beginning that you weren't going to ever fall for another woman again, at least not until the girls were grown up and out of the house. It was a rule, Mark, and you were very serious about it."

"I told you, things change."

Shaking her head, she started to back up, but he caught her hand. "Things change," he said again, softer now, no longer angry but something else, something just as wild and passionate as he slowly reeled her in. "You're scared," he said quietly. "I get that. You're scared because you love me too."

She pushed him away. "No." Yes. God, yes. She loved him so much it hurt, and she had no idea what to do with that, not a single one. She turned away, back to the dresser, where she opened the next drawer down and scooped up her things. "Which is why I have to go."

He stood there watching her, arms crossed. "So is it that I gave you a reason to go, or that you were just looking for one?"

Mark held his breath for Lanie's answer.

"This was your rule," she said.

"So you've already mentioned. But I've also already mentioned—things happen. Real feelings happen. You love me."

"No." She shook her head, her eyes locked in on his as she backed up a step. "I can't. I don't."

At the words, he stilled and actually rubbed his chest where it felt like he'd just been hit by an IED. It was all suddenly a terrible echo of what Brittney had said to him, the words bringing it all back like it was yesterday.

I don't love you and I never wanted children . . .

Had he learned nothing from his past? Apparently not, because at the first sign of trouble and hard times Lanie wanted out.

Just like his ex.

"Shit," he said, feeling stunned at the realization. "It's me. *I'm* the common denominator here. I'm the dumbass who did the same thing while expecting a different outcome."

Lanie frowned. "What do you mean?"

Unable to discuss this rationally, he whipped around to get the fuck out, just as a scream went through the walls, followed by a thud—like a body hitting the floor in the next cottage over.

"Oh my God," Lanie said. "That was River!"

Mark was already running out the door with Lanie right on his heels. "River!" she yelled, pounding on the door. "River, are you okay?"

No answer.

"I'll go get a key," Lanie said.

"Just back up," Mark said and kicked the door open.

They found River lying on the floor in a growing puddle of blood.

"Oh my God!" Lanie cried.

"Call 9-1-1," he said and dropped to his knees at River's side.

Chapter 31

I don't fall asleep, I overthink myself into a coma.

River was both hot and cold, shivering and sweating, and she knew what that meant. High fever. Something had been nagging at her all day, she'd felt off, but she had attributed it to having just given birth and a serious lack of sleep.

But as she lay on the floor in a puddle of her own blood, she knew she'd gravely underestimated her problem. She was delirious, unable to open her eyes beyond slits, unable to speak as she watched Lanie's pale face hover above hers. "Delaney," she tried to say, needing them to look after the baby.

She heard Mark's calm voice telling Lanie to call for an ambulance, felt him take her pulse.

"The baby," she tried again, but Lanie was shakily telling someone to come in a hurry because there was a lot of blood.

When River managed to open her eyes again it was because someone took her hand.

Lanie, who smiled down at her, but it was one of those smiles that was full of fear and terror. Damn. She must look really bad. Like, on-death-row bad. "Delaney," she said but Lanie just stroked the hair back from River's face.

"It's okay," she whispered. "It's going to be okay."

Was it, though? Because it didn't feel okay. She'd finally started to get her life together for herself and the baby, and now she was going to die right here on the floor and never see Delaney again.

Not that she was surprised. Karma always had been a bitch.

ONCE AGAIN LANIE found herself standing in the hospital waiting room, staring out the dark windows into the night, only this time it was so much, *much* worse.

The thing about Wildstone, there weren't any city lights. It was so different from Santa Barbara, where she'd lived for so many years she'd nearly forgotten the beauty of the simple rolling hills, the stillness of the night, the peace and quiet . . .

Not that the hospital was peaceful or quiet. Behind her she could feel a wave of grief and panic and fear. She had her own wave going on, and she was still covered in blood.

River's blood.

God, the vision of her bleeding out all over her cottage floor was going to haunt her until the end of time, as was the way she'd left things. Just thinking about it had her closing her eyes tight.

If River died, she'd never know the truth—that Lanie didn't hate her. That, in fact, Lanie admired and respected her so very much.

According to the doctor who'd come out to talk to them, River had suffered a late postpartum hemorrhage and had nearly bled out on the way to the hospital. If Lanie and Mark hadn't gotten to her when they had, she'd have surely died. They'd found placental tissue still in her uterus and the doctor said they were giving her transfusions and he was going in to do an emergency surgical procedure to remove the tissue and hopefully stop the bleeding.

The entire Capriotti family was here, but Lanie was only aware of one—Mark standing on the other side of the room; tall, silent, stoic.

Another person she cared deeply about whom she'd wronged. Her last words to him kept playing in her mind.

I don't love you . . .

Apparently when she decided to sabotage herself, she went big.

Cora came up to her side. "How you holding up?"

Since Mark hadn't approached her at all, not so much as to meet her gaze, on top of which they hadn't heard a single word on River from the doctors, other than she was still in surgery and it was a touch-and-go situation, she had no idea. Because touch and go? The ominous words struck terror in her heart.

"Lanie?"

She looked into Cora's concerned face. "I blew up my life," she whispered, unable to hold the words in. "Me. I did that, all by myself." She'd lost Mark. Now River might die.

"Mistakes happen."

"No, you don't understand. I'm talking *big* mistakes," Lanie said.

"I hear you. But sometimes you just have to have courage in your ability to right your wrongs and make things right."

Lanie looked at her. "What do you do when you're short on courage?"

Cora squeezed her hand. "Courage doesn't always roar, you know. Sometimes it's just a quiet voice at the end of the day, saying, 'You can try again tomorrow.'"

Lanie was still thinking about that when a nurse poked her head into the room.

They all froze, and Lanie felt herself stepping forward, heart in her throat. "River. Is she—"

"We normally wouldn't let anyone back, but she's conscious and asking for a . . ." She consulted her iPad. "Lanie."

Lanie froze. "Are you sure?"

The nurse gave her a small smile. "Yes."

Lanie turned to find Mark watching her.

"She trusts you," he said.

She waited for a sign that he also trusted her, but his face was blank, eyes hooded from her. If he'd trusted her at one time, she'd blown that up as well. Feeling like her feet were made of cement, she followed the nurse back.

RIVER CAME AWAKE in slow degrees, layers of sensations. Hearing came first, a dull, steady *beep, beep, beep*ing that bounced around in her head. Then the fogginess in said brain, which told her she'd been medicated, heavily, but even through that fog she could feel feathers of pain not completely masked.

Damn. She must've done something really stupid, but for a long beat it had escaped her what.

Then she'd remembered. Blood. So much blood. And then flashes of an ambulance ride.

And Lanie's terrified face, her hand in River's, her voice saying, "It's going to be okay, it's all going to be okay."

But it wasn't. She'd had surgery. She'd heard the doctor telling the nurse it was still touch and go, had seen the look in the nurse's eyes.

It wasn't going to be okay. It was why she'd asked for Lanie.

She opened her eyes again just as the nurse brought her in and River had never been so relieved to see anyone in her life. There was something she had to do, *now.* So for the second time that week she grabbed Lanie by the shirtfront and held tight because Lanie was always a flight risk. "You have to promise me something."

"What?" Lanie gasped, clearly caught by surprise.

"That you'll raise Delaney."

"River, *you're* going to raise her."

But she wasn't. She could see the crazy worry in Lanie's eyes, could tell she'd been crying.

Lanie never cried.

"You have to promise me," River said desperately. "If something happens, you'll—"

"River." Lanie closed her eyes. "I can't," she said quietly. "As in, I literally can't. I . . . I think I hate her," she whispered.

River only tightened her grip. "No, you hate Kyle because he denied you a baby. There's a difference, Lanie. And I know you don't believe me, that you think you really do hate Delaney, but you used to think you hated me too, remember?"

Lanie choked out a half sob, half laugh. "I *do* hate you."

River actually laughed. It was a weak, barely there expulsion of air, but it was genuine. "No, you don't." She softened her grasp on Lanie but still didn't let go. "My mom always said that love's in the actions, not the words. I've seen your actions, Lanie."

Lanie opened her mouth, but River simply tightened her grip again. "I'm not letting go until you hear me," she said.

"For a dying woman, you've got a hell of a grip," Lanie muttered.

"You pick up the girls from dance class on Fridays even

though you sit in traffic on the way back every time. You listen to all of Uncle Jack's stories and laugh at the same joke every time. You let me in when I gave you no reason to do so and became my best friend. Sisters, really. You're the sister I always wanted."

Lanie made a soft sound, half protest, half sob.

"You're the one I want to take in Delaney if something happens," River said fiercely. "You're the only one."

Lanie stared at her before her eyes filled. *"River."*

That was it, that was all she said, just her name, but in that moment River knew. Lanie would do it. Which meant that deep down, she liked her again. "Thank you," she whispered fiercely, reaching for her hand, clutching it tight. *"Thank you."*

Chapter 32

Fashionably late? More like anxiously early . . .

A few hours later, Mark was with the twins at home. They were lying on Samantha's bed, where he was reading them a story and doing his damnedest to ignore the fact that his heart had been torn in two.

I don't love you . . .

"Daddy." Samantha put her hand over the words on the page. "We've got another question."

Oh good, another question. He did his best not to groan. Ten minutes ago he'd had to answer a bunch of them on what had happened to River. How she'd almost died, and what would've happened if she had. Which had brought on the question of what would happen if *he* died . . .

Or went away, like their mom.

That was always a tough one because the fact was that Brittney could get on a plane and visit. She could call. Hell, she could text or e-mail, but she didn't. After that hard discussion, Sam's questions had gone in another direction, but no less easier to answer. She and Sierra wanted to know specifically *where* had Delaney come from if River hadn't pooped her out. He'd told her River's belly, which she'd accepted—but Mark knew he was on borrowed time.

He just hadn't realized *how* borrowed.

"So the baby came out of River's belly," Sam said slowly and paused, clearly giving him a minute to change his story. He didn't, so she went on. "But *how* exactly?"

Jesus. "Well," Mark said slowly, trying to bide time, because when the hell had his babies become old enough to worry about such things? "It's a really long story."

They both smiled and nodded. They loved long stories. *Shit.*

He looked around for another adult. An adultier adult than him, someone more qualified to deal with this, but unfortunately he was on his own. "There's a birthing canal. That's where the baby came from." He inwardly winced, afraid of the next question, but to his utter shock they both accepted this with a sage nod.

Mark thought he was home free, but unfortunately he wasn't that lucky. Sierra nudged Samantha, who said, "Oh, right! We have one more question."

Okay, one more. He could do this. "Shoot."

"Are you going to give us a baby sister with Lanie?"

He tried to curve his mouth into some semblance of a smile. "The two of you aren't enough?"

Proving that he was no actor, both girls' smiles faded and they looked at each other for a beat and then back at him. Sam pushed his hair off his forehead in a very tender gesture. "Daddy, are you sad?"

The breath backed up in his throat. "Little bit, pumpkin. But it's nothing for either of you to worry about."

Sam slipped her hand in his. "I like that you live with us all in the same place now."

At this, he found a real smile. "I like living with you."

"Are you sad 'cuz Lanie's leaving? I heard Grandma telling Auntie Alyssa."

He wasn't sure what to say to that. He wasn't just sad, he was decimated, when he hadn't realized he could even be decimated.

Sam crawled into his lap, followed by Sierra.

"We want to hug you," Sam whispered. "'Kay?"

He felt the sharp sting of emotion behind his eyes and in his throat. "Very okay."

They wrapped their little arms around his neck and squeezed the air out of him, and he was nearly undone as he pressed his face into their hair.

Just then, Delaney let loose with a wail that said she was starving or wet or both, and she was going to bring the house down if someone didn't get to her right away. He pulled the covers down and waited while Sam and Sierra slid beneath. Standing up, he kissed them each. "Good night," he said softly. "You've been to the bathroom, you've got water, you've had a story, so I don't expect the pitter-patter of little feet until morning. Got me?"

"Got you," Samantha said.

"Good. Love you," he said and headed for the door, stopping short when not the usual one voice but *two* little voices said "Love you, Daddy" in unison.

He whipped back around and stared at Sierra. "Did you just . . ."

She smiled shyly and he felt his heart squeeze tight and his eyes burn as he strode back to the bed, yanked her out from beneath the covers, and hugged her to him, pressing his face into her hair, hoping like hell he didn't start crying like Delaney. Then Samantha jumped at him as well and he squeezed the hell out of them both for as long as he could before they squirmed to be free. And since Delaney was still screaming, he shut the bedroom door. And if for a beat he leaned back on the wood, eyes closed, trying to compose himself, no one was the wiser.

He knew Lanie had left the hospital and River's bedside reluctantly, and only because River had *made* her go, to be with the baby. The baby she'd told Lanie was hers if anything happened to her.

Mark would like to say he didn't know how that felt, but he'd ended up raising his two girls without a mom, so he *did* know. He knew the fear, the panic, and the dead certainty that you were going to fuck it all up without a backup.

Except he did have backup. He had his family at his back, always.

Lanie didn't have that. Or rather, didn't want it, since she'd cut him and his entire family loose.

He could only hope that she wouldn't run from Delaney like she had from him.

He entered the small upstairs den, which his mom had turned into a temporary nursery. Delaney was pissed off, red in the face, and waving her fists. Scooping her up, he brought her in close to share his body heat. "Hey, munchkin," he murmured and just as his girls had always done, she stopped crying to hear him better.

"I'm guessing you're wet and hungry and pissed off at the world," he said. "Yeah?"

"Neither," his mom said softly, coming in behind him. "I changed and fed her a few minutes ago."

"Lanie?"

"Since she looked like death walking, I sent her to bed, told her I'd watch over the baby for a few hours."

So she hadn't left. At least not yet. The amount of relief that sent through him was ridiculous. "You look like death walking too," he said. "I've got her, Mom."

His mom kissed him on the cheek and left.

He carefully set Delaney back into her bassinet and sat in the rocking chair in the dark corner of the room, where he tipped his head back and closed his eyes. He was still there an hour later when soft footsteps coming into the room woke him.

Lanie.

Not seeing him in the corner, she went straight to the baby bassinet. "Hey," she said softly. "Look at you, you're awake and being so good."

The baby must have given her some reaction because she laughed softly, the sound tugging at Mark's heart. He began to stand to let her know he was there, but she dragged a chair close and sat, leaning in to put her hand inside the bassinet.

She was as exhausted as the rest of them, he knew, or she'd have certainly noticed him in the corner. "If you can't be with your mama right now," she said quietly, "you should know that you're in the best possible place. The Capriottis are . . . wonderful. I mean, don't get me wrong, they're nosy as hell and they're going to be all up in your business all the time, but they . . ." She shook her head. "They work hard and they love even harder. All of them. They've been good to me, all of them, but especially Mark."

The baby cooed at her.

"I know," Lanie said on what sounded like a soggy laugh. "He's smart and strong, inside and out. He's a cop and was a soldier, so he's also pretty badass— Wait, scratch that! That's a bad word and I'm going to try real hard not to teach any of those to you. " She sighed. "He's tough as nails on the outside; he's had to be. But on the inside . . ." She shook her head. "He's guarded. At first I thought we were alike there, but it turns out that he knows when to let down that guard and show what he's made of. He's steady, the calm in the storm . . . and he never lets a situation dictate his actions. He's taught me so much," she murmured. "And you probably think that this story is going one way, but it's not. See, I imploded my whole life, my relationship with him included. I was so stupid. But you're not going to be stupid, okay? You're going to listen to all my mistakes and do better than me, right?"

The baby cooed again and she laughed softly. "Is it wrong of me to admit that I'm relieved that you look like your mama? Not that I'm ever going to talk bad about your daddy to you, that wouldn't be right, but . . . I'm just glad you look like . . . well, you."

The baby made another soft sound, like she was listening intently and trying to talk.

"I envy you, you know," Lanie said. "Well, not that you still have to face middle and high school, but that you have a clean slate. You haven't screwed up your life. You've got it all out in front of you with a mama who's going to love and accept you, no matter what. Because that's how she rolls, Delaney. She's not going to spend your impressionable years resenting your presence. You'll grow up cherished and adored, and that's how it should be. And then someday you'll let the right people in because you'll know how. You'll have great friends and family, and maybe you'll even fall in love. And if you're lucky, which you will be, that person will fall in love with you too. Not that you'll need that love to complete your life. No, it'll be more like . . . icing on the cake."

The baby was staring up at Lanie with luminous blue eyes, clearly fascinated by her voice.

"That's where I've made most of my mistakes," Lanie said, gently touching the baby's cheek. "I let the wrong man in and that backfired in a big way. Then I let the right man sit outside my brick walls because I was afraid." She shook her head. "I'm *still* getting it wrong. I don't want you to do that, I don't want you to suffer and then have regrets. I'd like you to learn from my mistakes, but life doesn't work that way, so I'll just say this. Do what I haven't managed yet. Follow your heart. Trust it. I'll do my best to walk you through it. I won't fail you, Delaney. I promise."

The baby's eyes slowly drifted closed and Lanie smiled sadly. "And when the person you love more than you've ever loved anyone before tells you how they feel about you, don't be afraid to give them your feelings back, okay?" She gave a little sniff. "Because that's something I'm not sure a relationship can come back from."

The hell with staying quiet, Mark thought, and stood up. "Lanie."

She jerked around, trying to quickly swipe the tears from her face. "Mark," she gasped. "I . . . didn't see you."

He stepped out of the dark corner as she stared at him. "How much did you hear?"

"Everything."

She winced. "I'm sorry," she said. "About a lot of things, but mostly for fighting you and your family's easy acceptance and love." She met his gaze, letting him see her regrets, loneliness, sadness. "I'm not trying to give excuses, but it's taken me a while to believe I deserved—" She shook her head. "But then River believed in me so much too and . . ."

"Did you mean it, Lanie? What you told the baby?"

She closed her eyes for a beat and then opened them on his. "Yes. But I'm not like you, Mark. The depths of what I feel for you is nothing short of terrifying."

"And yet every day you show up," he said, catching her hand and slowly pulling her in, pressing her palm to his chest over his heart. "What do you think the definition of courage is?"

"You," she said, surprising him. "You were a soldier. You spent years overseas fighting for your country. And then you came home and faced being a single dad with the same ease."

He had to laugh. "*Ease* isn't exactly the word I'd use. For *any* of my life." He paused. "I've been scared plenty of times. What I've never been is fearless. If you can run into a battle unafraid, you're not courageous, you're just a dumbass. It's knowing the price you're going to pay and being willing to pay it anyway that makes you brave."

"See? You *are* the bravest man I know. And . . ." She swallowed hard. "I'm trying to learn from that. From you."

He'd spent a lot of years learning how to control his reactions, but there was no controlling his heart in that moment as it took a good heart leap. "What are you saying?"

"I'm saying . . ." She stepped in closer so that they were touching from chest to thighs. "I'm saying that I don't want to keep running. Not from you."

He stared at her. "Which means . . . ?"

"I love you," she said softly but without any hesitation, her voice firm and knowing, the words a balm over his wounded soul.

"What turned the tide in my favor?" He cupped her face. "My two little heathens that interrupt us night and day? My insane family that constantly sticks their noses into our business? Or maybe it's the impossible hours I work?"

She gave him a small smile. "Would you believe all of the above?" She slid her hands up his chest and wrapped her arms around his neck. "But it was also that you saw me at my worst. You saw me when I had one foot out the door and was ready to blindly run off and leave everything because I was scared, and you *still* looked at me like I was one of the most important people on earth to you."

"Because you are."

"Right back at you." She slid her fingers into his hair. "You know that, right?"

He smile was slow and warm and sexy. "I do now. We make a good team, Lanie. Say you know that."

"I know it. I love it. And I love you, Marcus Capriotti, so much."

WHEN RIVER WAS released from the hospital, Lanie picked her up. She'd somehow managed to talk the entire Capriotti family into letting her go alone, not wanting River to be overwhelmed, thinking that mama and baby might need a few minutes of quiet time before being inundated with the whole clan.

Once they were in the car, River buckled into the backseat, the baby safely in her car seat next to River, Lanie carefully pulled out of the hospital parking lot and onto the street.

"Hey, Granny," River said after a few minutes. "Did you know they can give you a ticket for going too slow?"

"I'm not going too slow."

"If you were going any slower, you'd be going backward."

Lanie didn't speed up.

At a red light, River spoke. She was twisted to face the baby, smiling at her like she was talking right to her. "So . . . when are you leaving?"

Lanie glanced at her in the rearview mirror.

"I heard you and Mark fighting," River said. "The night I almost . . ."

Bled out on her cottage floor.

The light turned green and Lanie put her eyes on the road as she pulled out into the intersection. "I'm not. Leaving."

"But you said you didn't want the extra work."

"I changed my mind," Lanie said. "I told Cora I'd stay for as long as she needed a graphic designer."

"How long is that going to be?"

Lanie slowed for the next intersection even though she had a green light.

River rolled her eyes.

"Cora offered me a permanent job," Lanie said.

River gasped in delight, reminding Lanie of Samantha. "So you got your head out of your ass?" she asked, clapping in glee. "You're staying? Are you going to marry Mark and live happily ever after?"

"Seriously, you've got to stop watching Hallmark and Lifetime."

River was smiling. "Come on, say it. Tell me."

"Yes. I'm staying."

"And . . ." River pressed.

"And . . . I'm going to make a go of this thing with Mark." She couldn't say it without grinning wide like an idiot. She clapped a hand over her mouth. "I don't know what that is," she said from behind her fingers. "I can't get rid of the smile. It's been there since last night."

"It's happiness about your happy ever after."

"You've got to stop saying that," Lanie said. "You're making me nervous. I don't want to jinx it. Let's call it a happy for *now*, okay?"

"A happy for now," River said, looking thrilled. "I like the sound of that. I could live with that."

Lanie met her gaze in the rearview mirror. "You'll get your chance."

River looked out the window and didn't comment, and Lanie got it. She knew River felt as if she'd blown things with Holden, who'd had to leave to go back to his post. He'd waited as long as he could, staying until they knew River was going to make it after her surgery.

"Hey," Lanie said softly. "I'm the queen of messing up a good thing, but mistakes happen and they can be forgiven. Cora told me that and she was right."

River looked at her pensively and slowly nodded.

Lanie pulled them up to the winery and helped River out of the car, turning back for the baby carrier. "I've got her," she told River. "You're not to lift anything more than a tissue for a week, remember?"

River bent over Delaney and kissed her little nose. "You're in good hands with Aunt Lanie, baby."

Aunt Lanie.

There were worse things . . . She found herself smiling with pride as they headed inside to find most of the family in the front reception room, where there were streamers and balloons and a huge banner that read WELCOME HOME, RIVER!

Cora, Mark, and the twins were there. No one else.

"I told everyone else to stay at work," Cora said. "I figured you needed a quiet homecoming." She walked up to River and hugged her tight. "Welcome home, honey."

River burrowed in and wrapped her arms around Cora. "Thank you," she whispered.

Lanie heard a sniffle and didn't know if it came from River or Cora, but she suspected both.

Mark took the baby carrier from Lanie and set baby Delaney on a tabletop. Then he reached for Lanie's hand. "Hey. You good?"

Lanie squeezed his hand and nodded.

"Lanie, Lanie, Lanie!" Sam yelled in greeting.

Lanie sank to one of the chairs so that Sierra could crawl into her lap. Lanie wrapped her arms around the girl and leaned over Mark to his other side where Samantha was sipping on red punch, complete with a red mustache. Lanie puckered up for a kiss and got a raspberry-flavored one. "Hi," she whispered to the three most important people in her world.

"Hi!" the twins said in unison, with matching grins.

Lanie's heart skipped a beat. She loved hearing Sierra talk.

Mark was only slightly more restrained than his girls. He wrapped an arm around her and gave her a slow, not-raspberry-flavored kiss that would have had her knees buckling if she hadn't been sitting down. "Love you," he said easily and then playfully tugged a wayward strand of hair.

"Love you back," she said with equally shocking ease.

His smile said he could see her surprise and was amused by it.

"Our dance recital's in two weeks," Samantha said excitedly. "You'll come?"

"Wouldn't miss it," Lanie said.

"Good, 'cuz on the calendar in the office it says you'll be gone. You won't be gone?"

Lanie needed to change the calendar pronto. "I won't be."

"You'll be here?" Samantha asked, apparently needing a two-step verification.

"There's no place I'd rather be."

"That's good, 'cuz Daddy's life doesn't work without you in it." Sierra smiled at her daddy. "Right, Daddy? That's what you said to Grandma this morning when she asked."

Mark, not looking embarrassed in the slightest, nodded as emphatically as Samantha had. "One hundred percent right, baby."

Lanie leaned in past the girls' faces. "Close your eyes," she told them both. "I'm going to kiss your daddy real quick." She did and then whispered against Mark's mouth, "My life doesn't work without you in it either."

"I know." He smiled that just-for-her smile, the one that never failed to warm her from the inside out. "But it's nice to hear," he said. "So . . . how do you feel about forever?"

Samantha bounced up and down in glee. "I love forever!"

Sierra nodded vigorously. She was back to talking, but clearly only when she felt it necessary.

Lanie stared at the three of them, her heart full to bursting. "I love forever too."

"Then welcome home."

Epilogue

One year later

It was lunchtime at the winery with all the usual pomp and circumstance. Lanie had Sam on one side and Sierra on the other, both of them digging into their cupcake dessert. Across from her sat River with Delaney in her lap, surrounded by Mia and Alyssa and the rest of the gang.

So much had changed in a year. For instance, it was Sierra who recounted the story of Great-Uncle Jack farting in the employee room and then yelling "Who stepped on a frog?"

Another change, Mia was texting someone who was making her smile softly. She was dating a woman who owned a horse ranch not too far from here, and while everyone was surprised at this change, no one had blinked an eye.

"You're doing it again," Lanie said.

Mia looked up, her eyes alight. "Grinning stupidly?"

"Well, maybe not stupidly . . ."

Mia shook her head and laughed. "I know. It's crazy, right? Me being ridiculously happy?"

"It's beautiful," Alyssa chimed in with. "We're all happy for you."

Someone came through the gate and River's head came up and froze in shock.

Lanie twisted around and saw it was Holden. Shorter hair, his body more leanly muscled than it'd been, but there was no mistaking the man who stepped onto the patio. He wore dark sunglasses, his face carefully blank, but Lanie knew his gaze went straight to River.

Cora, who'd been standing at the head of the table pouring wine, was the closest to him. She stepped in front of him, cupped his face, and said something softly, for his ears only. He nodded and she pulled him in for a warm hug.

Holden dropped his duffle bag and returned the hug. Then he pulled away and turned to River.

She'd dropped her fork onto her plate with a loud clatter at the first sight of him and stood up. She had a napping Delaney strapped to her chest as she just stared at the man in front of her.

He took a step and then hesitated, clearly unsure of his welcome.

But River didn't look unsure at all as she closed the distance between them and reached for him. She slid her hands up his chest and into his hair and pulled his head down for a kiss.

"That'll make things pretty clear to him," Mia said. "And if not, her tongue down his throat should do it."

"It's so romantic," Alyssa said. "I talked to him last week and he didn't mention he was coming home. I'm guessing by the tears streaming down River's face that she didn't know either."

"They've talked on the phone and via e-mail a lot this past year," Lanie said. "She knew he would be coming soon, but he kept it a surprise." Lanie watched, a little choked up as Holden and River stopped kissing long enough to laugh and talk at the same time, soft words no one could catch.

"Damn," Mia said. "The least they could do is speak up and let us in on it."

River took Holden's big hands in hers and set them on Delaney, clearly introducing them.

Holden lowered his head and brushed a kiss over Delaney's cheek. Then he met River's gaze again, his own serious until River smiled through shimmery eyes.

And then he pulled her in as close as he could with Delaney between them, pressing his jaw to the top of River's head, closing his eyes, his arms tight around her like she was the most precious cargo he'd ever held.

Lanie sighed, her heart happy. But not the rest of her. Nope, the rest of her was twitchy and sweaty. She shifted and fidgeted there at the table, fanning her overheated face, blowing out a long breath, which lifted some of the hair off her face—until it fell back into her eyes.

She was miserable and it was time to share some of that misery. Pulling out her phone, she texted Mark.

I'M HOT.

"Yeah, you are hot," said a sexy familiar voice right behind her.

"Oh my God," Mia complained. *"Overshare."*

Lanie craned her neck to find Mark standing right behind her. He wore his uniform stretched taut over his broad shoulders, his impossibly long legs bringing him up against her, and her entire body gave a hungry little quiver.

"*Daddy, Daddy, Daddy!*" the girls yelled in unison as Mark slid his arms around Lanie and rubbed his scruffy jaw to her face before claiming her mouth in a hungry kiss.

"Hey," Mia complained. "Enough's enough. I want to be the next person kissed!"

This didn't stop Mark. He crouched at Lanie's side and kissed her again, softly, languidly, his lips gentle against hers.

In the meantime, Sierra ran around the table and kissed her aunt Mia, who laughed and pulled Sierra onto her lap. "Thanks, munchkin, I can always count on you."

Mark's hands slid down Lanie's arms to cup her eight-months-pregnant belly. "How are all of my girls?"

"We're good, Daddy!" Sierra yelled.

Sam nodded.

Mark smiled and turned to Lanie. "And you two?"

"Baby's good. But me . . ." Lanie stretched into his hands. "I'm feeling like an overinflated balloon, like I'm under a lot of pressure right now."

He smiled. "Don't worry. You've done some of your best work under pressure."

Author's Note

I grew up in Los Angeles, but these days I live in the wild Sierra mountains near Lake Tahoe. Two entirely different worlds—one fast and one (sometimes) painfully slow. ☺ But no matter where I've lived, I've always spent a lot of time in San Luis Obispo, Morro Bay, and Avila Beach, all three nestled on the central coast of California. It's all wineries and ranches and gorgeous hidden beaches, and truly my favorite place to run away to for a break. As a family, we have a lot of memories tied up there.

I'm going to let you in on a little secret: My oldest daughter's name is Kelsey. So a few years ago, when we found a little family-run winery between San Luis Obispo and Avila Beach, we couldn't resist. When you pull up, a bunch of peacocks greet you, the males all aflutter with their huge spread of vibrant feathers. The land is lush, the winery quaint, the people who run it friendly. So friendly that we sat and talked with the owner and the winemaker as we sampled their wines. And then they gave me a private tour and I got a peek at the behind-the-scenes of how a family-run winery works.

And I fell in love. Not just with the family and the people, but their closeness, their joy of working the land together, their love of each other and their wines.

So it's not a surprise that I used Kelsey Winery as a backdrop for this book. *Rainy Day Friends* is set at a fictional winery in my equally fictional town of Wildstone ▸

Author's Note ***(continued)***

(same as my last book, *Lost and Found Sisters*, also based on the central-coast area I love so much), but in my heart, it's really Kelsey Winery, that small, quaint, wonderful place that has given us so many hours of joy.

Enter my characters. I've had Lanie in my heart for a long time—a woman who's been deeply and devastatingly betrayed by love on many levels. River, however, didn't come to me until she showed up on the page, chin up, heart broken, still a fighter and willing to take on the world for her unborn child.

Oh, the fun I had with this sisters-of-the-heart story between Lanie and River. But no Jill Shalvis novel is complete without a love story, and oh, how Mark Capriotti fulfilled both my heart and, eventually, Lanie's.

And once again, Wildstone claimed my heart. So stay tuned—more from the old Wild West town is coming soon. And thanks again for coming along for the ride!

Happy Reading!
Jill Shalvis

Reading Group Guide

1. What would you do if you found out the person you loved had been living a double life?
2. If Kyle hadn't died, would Lanie have stayed married to him? Would River?
3. Would you be able to be friends with your husband's mistress?
4. After such a big betrayal, would you be able to trust and love another person again?
5. Was Lanie right in running away from her home?
6. What do you think Holden's backstory is?
7. Do you think Lanie and River would want to meet the other women Kyle was "married" to?
8. Do you think Lanie and her mother could ever be close? They made amends somewhat, but could they ever be a real part of each other's lives?
9. If you were in Lanie's position, how would River being pregnant affect your feelings toward her? Would you be able to accept the baby and not be jealous when you had also wanted children?

Reading Group Guide

Coming Soon . . .

An excerpt from *Hot Winter Nights*

Keep reading for an exclusive sneak peek at Jill's next book in her *New York Times* bestselling Heartbreaker Bay series, *Hot Winter Nights*, on sale fall 2018.

IT TOOK LUCAS KNIGHT longer than it should have to realize he had a woman in his bed, but to be fair, he had a bitch of a hangover.

He took quick stock. One, last night was a complete blur. Two, other than the bundle of sweet, soft curves against him, his head was threatening to secede from the United States of Lucas, and his side hurt like . . . well, like he'd been shot.

It had been two weeks since he'd gotten caught in some crossfire on the job, and he hadn't yet been cleared for more than light duty—something he'd obviously managed to ignore last night, given that he was palming a nice, warm, feminine ass.

Think, man, he ordered himself. He did remember taking a pain med before going to O'Riley's Pub to meet up with some friends. A client had been there, someone he'd recently helped save from multimillion-dollar corporate espionage. The guy had ordered shots to toast Lucas and . . . shit. He'd hesitated, knowing better than to mix pain meds and alcohol, but everyone had been waiting on him, glasses in the air. Thinking one couldn't hurt, he'd knocked back the drink, which ▸

had clearly been enough to mess him up big time.

Something that he hadn't been in years, not since his brother had been killed. Shoving that thought away for another time—or never—Lucas cracked open one eye, but when his retina was stabbed by a streak of sunlight glaring in through the window, he immediately slammed it shut again. Taking a deep breath, he told himself to suck it up, and he opened both eyes this time.

Okay, so he was naked and completely uncovered. The woman snuggled at his side was rolled up in his comforter like a burrito.

What. The. Hell.

But some images from the night before began to filter into his brain. Kicking ass at the pool table and winning two hundred bucks from his boss, Archer, who ran Hunt Investigations, where Lucas worked as a security specialist. Dancing with a sexy brunette. And then making his way upstairs . . . but not alone. His head was pounding too hard to remember more, but clearly the brunette had come home with him. She was cuddled up close, but he couldn't see her face the way she had the entire blanket wrapped around herself. Just a mass of shiny brown waves peeking out the top.

So not good.

Holding his breath, he slowly pulled away until he could slide off his bed.

The brunette's hair never so much as quivered.

Letting out a relieved breath, he

shoved on the clothes he'd so thoughtfully left for himself on the floor—seriously, he was never taking another pain pill or drinking alcohol again—and headed for the door.

But unable to do it, unable to just leave her, he stopped, detouring to his kitchen to make her a coffee. Leaving her caffeine was a nice gesture, right? Right, and . . . he was out of coffee. Not surprising, since he usually grabbed his at work because Molly, who ran the office at Hunt Investigations, made great coffee. And since one of the benefits of living on the fourth floor and working on the second of the Pacific Pier Building meant convenience, he texted the coffee master.

Any chance you'd send up a cup of coffee via the dumbwaiter?

A few seconds later, he heard a cell phone buzz an unfamiliar tone from his bedroom and froze. If his plan was to leave before the awkward morning after—and that was *always* the plan—he was on borrowed time.

Since he hadn't heard back from Molly, he was moving on to Plan B and scrawled out a quick note: *Had to get to work.*

Then he hesitated. Did she even know his name? Having no idea, he added: *I'm leaving cash for an Uber or Lyft—Lucas.*

He dropped some money next to the note and grimaced at himself for being a complete asshole. He stared down at his phone.

Still nothing from Molly, which meant ▸

she wasn't going to save the day. She was smart, sharp, and amazing at her job, but for reasons unknown, she wasn't interested in pleasing anyone, *especially* him. Locking up behind himself, he left.

The Pacific Pier Building was more than a century old and sat in the center of the Cow Hollow district of San Francisco. Five stories of corbeled brick, exposed iron trusses, and big windows built around a legendary fountain. Retail stores and businesses took up the ground and second floors, with residential on the third and fourth. The fifth-floor penthouse belonged to his friend Spence Baldwin, who owned the building.

All of it, thanks to the building's manager, decorated for the holidays like it was about to star in a Hallmark movie.

Lucas jogged down two flights of stairs to Hunt Investigations, fully prepared to be blasted by Molly at the front desk. Not just for his text, but for his appearance at all. Off duty since the shooting, he wasn't supposed to be back at work until next week, and that was *if* his doctor cleared him.

But he couldn't stay home another day, a fact that didn't have anything to do with the stranger in his bed.

Or at least not *all* due to the stranger in his bed.

He scrubbed a hand over his unshaven jaw, feeling incredibly tense, which, for a guy who'd apparently gotten laid last night, didn't make much sense.

Nor did the fact that sitting on a bench outside Hunt Investigations' front door were two old ladies dressed up as elves. Knitting elves.

The one on the left looked to be making a Christmas stocking. The one on the right was working on something too small to see. They smiled at him in greeting, lips coated in bright red lipstick. Left Elf had a smudge of it on her teeth and her little elf cap seemed to quiver on top of her white hair. "Hello there, young man," she said. "We were hoping you were Molly. We've got a problem involving a bad Santa, and she said to meet her here."

Lucas blinked. "A bad Santa."

"Yes. We work for him at a small Christmas village in Soma. Obviously," she said, gesturing to herself.

Oh, good. So they didn't believe they were real elves.

"Santa promised us a certain cut of the profits," Right Elf said. "But we're not getting them. He says there aren't any profits, but that can't be true because he just bought himself a brand-new Cadillac. Molly's my neighbor, you see."

Lucas didn't see at all. He was good at certain things, such as his job of investigating and seeking out the asshats of the world and righting injustices. He was good at taking care of his close-knit family. He was good, when he wanted to be, in the kitchen. And—if he said so himself—also in bed.

But he was not good in social situations, such as those that required small talk, especially with old ladies dressed up as elves.

"Do you know when Molly might ▸

arrive?" Right Elf asked. She was looking at him even as her knitting needles continued to move at the speed of light.

Everything Lucas knew about crafting was stuff he'd learned from his mom and sister—you took something you were going to throw away and instead spent a bunch of money on it to make something else. "I don't know Molly's schedule."

And that was the truth. Hunt Investigations was run by the biggest badass he'd ever met, Archer Hunt, and he employed a team who was the best of the best. Lucas was honored to be a part of that team. All of them, himself included, would step in front of a bullet for each other, and had.

Literally, in his case.

The lone woman in their midst was Molly, equally fearless, though in other ways. She was the one to keep them all on their toes. No one would dare venture into her domain at her desk and put their hands on her stuff to check her schedule, but he could ask around. "I'll go check her ETA," he said, and headed inside.

"ETA?" he heard Left Elf ask. "What's an ETA?"

"I don't know," Right Elf said. "Maybe . . . Easy Tits and Ass?"

This caused them both to cackle and Lucas shuddered. He found Archer and Joe in the employee room inhaling donuts. Grabbing one for himself, he nodded to Archer and looked at Joe, one of Lucas's best friends and his work partner. "Where's your sister?"

Joe shrugged and went for another donut. “Not her keeper. Why?”

“There’re two elves outside waiting to talk to her.”

“Still?” Archer shook his head. “I told them this wasn’t a case for us.” He headed out front. Lucas followed.

“Ladies,” Archer said to the elves. “As I explained earlier, your case isn’t the kind of case we take on.”

“Oh, we heard you,” Left Elf said. “We’re just waiting for Molly. She promised to help us personally if you wouldn’t.”

Archer looked pained. “Molly doesn’t take on cases here. She’s office staff.”

The two elves tucked away their knitting. “Fine,” Left Elf said. “We’ll just go straight to her at home, then.”

Archer waited until they’d gotten on the elevator before shaking his head. He looked at Lucas. “Why are you here?”

“Gee, good to see you too.”

“Let me rephrase,” Archer said. “How’s your side? You know, where you have a GSW?”

“It’s no longer a gunshot wound—it’s practically just a scratch now. I’m good enough to get back to work.”

“I didn’t get a report from your doctor clearing you.”

Lucas squelched a grimace. His doctor had told him—repeatedly—he had to wait at least one more week. But he’d be dead of boredom after another week. “We’re having a minor difference in opinion.”

“Shit.” Archer swiped a hand down his ▸

face. "You know I can't put you back on the job until he clears you."

"If I stay home another day, I'll lose my shit."

"It's only been two weeks since you were shot and nearly bled out before we got you to the hospital," Archer said. "*Way* too close of a call."

"Practically ancient history."

Archer shook his head. "Not even close. I told you to abort. Instead, you sent the team out to safety and then you alone hauled ass deeper into that yacht, knowing it was on fire, thanks to our asshole perps trying to sink it for the insurance payout."

"I went deeper because there was still someone on board," Lucas said. "Our lead suspect's teenage kid. He was sleeping and would've died if I'd left him."

"And instead you almost did."

Lucas blew out a breath. They'd had this argument in the hospital. They'd had it twice since. He didn't want to have it again. Especially since he wasn't sorry he'd disobeyed a direct order. "We saved an innocent. You'd have done the same damn thing. So would any of us."

Archer looked over at Joe, who'd been silent through this entire exchange.

Joe lifted a shoulder, an admission that yeah, he might have done the same thing. And so would Archer, and Lucas damn well knew it.

"Shit," Archer said. "Fine. I'll unground you, but only for light duty until I hear from your doctor personally that you're one hundred percent.

Lucas didn't dare smile or pump a fist in triumph. "Deal."

Archer went from looking pissy to mildly amused. "You don't know what light duty I'm going to make you do yet."

"Anything would be better than staying at home," he said fervently.

"Glad to hear you say that." Archer jabbed a thumb at the door. "Molly's going to want to take the elves seriously. She's been asking to take on a case for months now, but our cases are too dangerous."

Lucas rubbed his side. Wasn't that the damn truth. "And?"

"And *your* 'light duty' job is to make sure she turns them down," Archer said. "She's not ready yet."

Joe nodded his agreement on that and Lucas let out a mirthless laugh. He got why Archer would tell Molly not to take on a case, but Joe should know better. "Hello, you've met her, right? No one tells Molly what to do. Not even her brother."

Again Joe grimaced, acknowledging the truth of that statement.

Archer apparently didn't care. "Improvise. And remember, you're still in hot water. Fail and let her take the case and you're done. Sleep with her and you're done. In fact, breathe wrong and you're done. Got me?"

"I'm seeing the pattern," Lucas said. And granted, he didn't tend to be all that discriminating when it came to the fairer sex, but this was Molly they were talking about. She wasn't the type to go for one-time hookups as he favored, plus she was the baby sister of his friend and ▸

coworker, all of which meant she was *not* on his radar.

Though the fact remained that she'd spent more than a few nights starring in his fantasies. His own deep, dark secret since he liked breathing.

Joe moved away toward his office but Archer stayed put, eyes still on Lucas. "Elle and I saw you at the pub last night," he said quietly. "Flirting with Molly. What the hell were you thinking? You were lucky Joe was late."

Wait. What? He'd flirted with Molly? Was he crazy? Okay, yes, there was an undercurrent of electricity between them, an unacknowledged awareness and attraction that neither of them ever admitted to. Him because he had zero interest in mixing business and pleasure, and even less interest in hurting Molly.

And he *would* eventually hurt her.

Not to mention what Joe would do to him after that. And if Joe failed in that new mission, Archer would happily finish him off. Lucas drew a deep breath and thought of the woman in his bed. "Trust me, nothing happened with Molly last night. Apparently, I was . . . preoccupied with someone else."

Archer went brows up. "The brunette at the bar?"

At Lucas's nod, Archer clapped him on the shoulder. "Glad to hear you're not going to have to die today."

Lucas let out a rough laugh. "When Molly finds out you've put me on babysitting duty, she's going to kill us both."

"That's why she's not going to find out."

Lucas stared at Archer, a very bad feeling coming over him. "I'm supposed to keep it from her?"

"Now you're getting it."

Lucas didn't know much about Molly's past other than something bad had happened to her a long time ago and she still had a limp from whatever it'd been. Joe kept a tight lid on his and Molly's rough childhood, but both brother and sister had some serious trust issues. "This is *worse* than monitor duty."

"Is it worse than dying?" Archer asked mildly.

Shit. Lucas went back upstairs. He needed a shower, fresh clothes, and a clear head before he went to seek out Molly. As well as a good story because he couldn't tell her the truth. He hoped to hell that a long hot shower would clear his brain enough to come up with something believable, because there was something else Molly was—sharp as they came. He stalked through his bedroom, hit the switch on the wall, and froze.

The brunette was still in his bed.

At the bright light flooding the room, she gasped and sat straight up, clutching the sheet to her chin, her hair a wild cloud around her face.

And not a stranger's face either. *Molly's* face.

Molly was in his bed and his first thought was *Oh shit*. His second thought tumbled right on the heels of that—he was going to die today after all, slowly and painfully.

Meet the friends of Heartbreaker Bay as they discover that falling in love can be as glorious and tempestuous as the beautiful San Francisco waters.

Meet Pru, Willa, Elle, Colbie and Kylie in

'If you're picking up a Jill Shalvis book, you're in for a treat'

Julie Cohen

HEADLINE
ETERNAL

Welcome to Cedar Ridge, Colorado, where the only thing more rugged than the glorious Rocky Mountains are the rough-and-tumble Kincaid brothers.

Meet Aidan, Hudson and Jacob in

'Humor, intrigue, and scintillating sex. Jill Shalvis is a total original'
Suzanne Forster

HEADLINE
ETERNAL